SECRETS OF CHRONOS ACADEMY

ORDER OF RAVENS

BY: D. EVANS AND T. EYSTATHIOY

Cover art/design: T. Eystathioy

A Little PhDs Book

Secrets of Chronos Academy

Book One: Order of Ravens

Library & Archives Canada Cataloging-in-Publication Data,
D. Evans, T. Eystathioy

Secrets of Chronos Academy: Order of Ravens
written by Dee-Ann Evans and Theophany Eystathioy

Cover art & design by T. Eystathioy
Editors: Lynn Slobogian, Merel Elsinga

ISBN 978-0-9952552-6-5 (pbk)

For our children

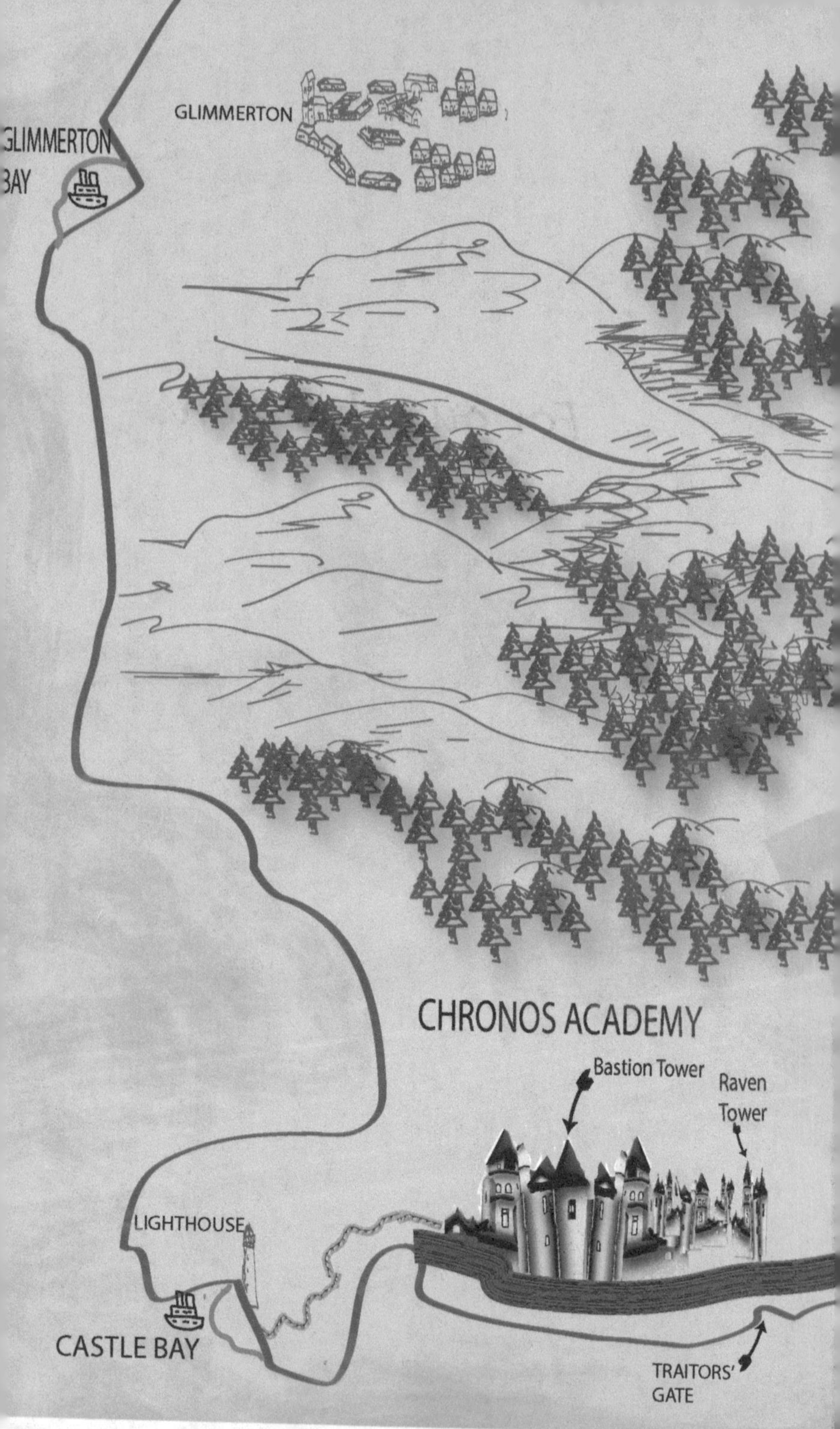

GLIMMERTON
GLIMMERTON BAY
GLIMMERTON
CHRONOS ACADEMY
Bastion Tower
Raven Tower
LIGHTHOUSE
CASTLE BAY
TRAITORS' GATE

CHRONOS ACADEMY & AREA
N
W
E
S
KINGSBURG FOREST
BLACKSMITH COTTAGE
FARADAY LANE
SPORTS COURTS
FRANKLIN LANE
ELDRITCH PITCH
AMPHITHEATRE

1

"Run!" Cleo yelled as a chunk of the cavern ceiling crashed down. It pushed the water out of the tranquil pond, creating a mini tidal wave.

"We have to get out of here!" Luke hollered, protecting his head from the falling rubble.

Water started to percolate upwards through the web of fissures in the cavern floor. As the cave shook in anger, the stream quickly transformed from a trickle to a roar, gushing in and creating an underground river.

Cleo and Luke collected Ollie, Nia, and Andy who were crouched under an outcropping. "Where's Ronan?" Andy asked.

"I'm right here," Ronan said, joining them. He had his hand on his forehead, covering a small cut and a goose egg.

"I told you these Stones are trouble!" Ollie screamed desperately as the cave shook again.

They were definitely in trouble, Cleo thought. Big trouble!

"Which way?" Luke yelled.

2

Luke

Nine months earlier

"Look at this place," Lorraine said, twisting her long brown straight hair and bunching it to the back of her head in a clip. "It's so pretty." She slid her sunglasses up her slender nose and gazed at the vast crystal blue water of the North Atlantic Ocean. Several fishing boats were docked along the branching pier that stretched into the ocean. In the distance near the moored boats at the east end, Luke saw a lone seal break the surface of the water only to resubmerge.

It was the beginning of September and the start of another school year. Only this wasn't a typical school year for Luke. He had dreaded this moment all summer long. Other than the occasional camping trip in the Nevis mountains, Luke had never been anywhere outside of Wicker, his landlocked hometown in the northern part of Pandia, and that had been fine by him. Now, against his wishes, he was in Glimmerton, headed to Chronos Academy.

Luke frowned, took in a puff of his inhaler for his asthma, and leaned against the rustic wooden sign on the pier that read

An occasional car hummed behind him on the narrow stretch of road that separated the pier from the rest of the town. On the south side of the road was the Keys Hotel, a square brick building that sat smack in the middle of Main Street. The summer holiday season was almost over, and Luke could only spot a few tourists with backpacks and maps in hand, strolling the paths and entering and exiting the village shops. Behind Main Street, tapering streets connected tall and narrow multicoloured houses that peacefully dotted the sloping hill.

The pier Luke was standing on was not peaceful. The students, excited to get to Chronos Academy, looked like a shoal of fish, twisting and turning in synchrony, shouting as they moved.

A large blue and white passenger ferry was docked at the pier, and its engine hummed as it waited for the noisy students to board. The ferry would travel down the coastline from Glimmerton to the southernmost tip of the island, home of Chronos Academy. The back of the ferry had three tiered open decks outlined by white railings. Luke saw several members of the crew in their crisp white collared shirts and black slacks moving around the decks. Others were standing on the dock close to the moored boat, talking and giving hand signals to their crewmates. The bottom deck of the ferry was draped with a banner that read

Happy Chronos Day!

Luke shook his head. He didn't think it was a happy day at all, no matter how festive the *Trillian* looked with orange and white flags strung from the top deck.

The large island of Pandia was known for its windy and cloudy coastline. Today the Atlantic Ocean was atypically calm, and already in the early morning it felt hot under the bright, cloudless sky. Luke tugged on his shirt where it stuck to his body. The day was humid and without a stitch of wind to cool him off.

The sudden sound of a tuba caught Luke's attention. He noticed a six-person band tuning their instruments at the other end of the dock. It didn't take long before they started to play, the loud music now competing with the noisy crowd. Small groups of people, here and there, stopped to listen. Frustrated, Luke let out a sharp huff of breath. He would've preferred being in Principal Abernathy's pink office at Nevis School back home rather than being here at this moment.

"I think Chronos Day is … okay, yep, here it is." Lorraine looked at a brochure in her hand and spoke loudly. "It's a party to celebrate the start of the school year." She clapped when the band finished their number and announced they would take a quick break. "And a live band, too. How fantastic!"

It was not fantastic, and the band was certainly not good. Luke dumped his duffle bag to the ground with a thump and stepped in his mom's line of sight to get her attention. When she looked at him, he spoke intensely. "I don't want to be here. I don't care that this school has lots of science and—" he made air quotes, "'encourages curiosity.' And I don't care that there's kids from all over the world. I want to go home."

Luke could see his reflection in his mom's sunglasses.

His thick brown mop of hair was dishevelled, flopping this way and that, because he'd refused to cut it before school. He could make out the larger-than-life pimple on his chin that would burst open at any moment. He looked right at his own reflection, felt miserable, and crossed his arms in persistent defiance.

Lorraine removed her sunglasses and slowly shook her head. Her blue eyes softened as she looked at him. "Here's the thing, sweetheart. If I take you home now, you'll wither away."

Tears burned his eyes remembering the day, several months ago, when his life changed forever. Watching a movie with his mom. Eating popcorn. The phone call.

Lorraine threw up her hands in exasperation. "Ooohhh, this is so hard!" Tears sprang into her eyes. "I know you're struggling, and I don't know what else to do."

Luke just stared ahead with a blank expression on his face. When their eyes met again, his mom said gently, "If you come back with me now, you will check the news online every day and wake up several times in the middle of the night to see if your dad is home. I know you will." She closed her eyes for a moment and then opened them again. "Because I'm guilty of it, too."

He winced. He didn't know his mom knew about his nightly vigil to check for his dad's return. "Is that why you're sending me away?" Luke asked as he kicked at his duffle bag, creating an impression of his shoe on its side.

"No! I love you, Luke, and I want to help you. The counselling sessions haven't helped. And everything I've tried has failed." Luke was surprised when his mom pulled him into a hug, and in that moment the chaos around him dissolved. When she stepped back, she gently held his shoulders. "You need to get away. Just for a little while. Try Chronos Academy. If you hate it, I'll come get you. But I want you to give it a chance. You're only twelve years old. I want you to be a kid and have that spark of curiosity again. This school will be the perfect place for that. Their motto is 'Let curiosity be your compass'!"

"Mom—" Luke began.

"Before I forget, I have something for you." Lorraine handed him a plastic-wrapped comic book. "That's what you wanted, right? Special edition number 5, of *Knights of Darkness*?"

Blocking the sunlight with his back, Luke examined the colourful 3D cover with his mouth gaping. "Where did you get this?" he asked. "It's been sold out for months everywhere!"

"A mom never tells her secrets," Lorraine said, grinning. Her eyes showed the tiniest hint of her old sparkle. "I have something else for you, too." She dug through her battered purse. "Your dad took this on all his adventures. He always said it gave him luck." She placed a box into Luke's hand. When he opened it, he was stunned for a second time.

"Is this Dad's pocket watch? But why is it—?"

"I had a leather strap added so you could wear it. Other than that, it's exactly the same," she said, and wiped her eyes under her sunglasses.

Luke gulped, not wanting to remove the treasured timepiece from the box. "Won't he need it when he gets back?"

"Luke, we've been through this. We don't know what happened." His mom's voice quivered as she spoke. She paused as a few students squeezed past them. "They looked for him twice and again this summer at my request. I've seen the reports. Dad's been gone for a long time. We need to be realistic."

"You don't know. No one knows." Luke swallowed hard and gazed upwards. He noticed a herring gull, white-headed with a light grey back, beak open and wings extended. It swooped down towards a young boy sitting on his dad's shoulders, holding a banana up high in his right hand. In a flash the herring gull snatched the banana with its beak and swallowed it whole. The kid started crying.

Luke felt like doing the same.

His mom hugged him again and spoke into his tousled mop of thick brown hair. "If I'm wrong …" She stepped back and wiped at her tears. "Then in the meantime, you need to keep his watch safe. Wear it every day and think of him." She added with a small hopeful smile, "And me."

Brushing the palms of his hands against his own stinging eyes, Luke wiped his hands against his shorts. Carefully, he removed the watch from the box and, after fumbling a bit, managed to place it on his left wrist.

"You look like your father more and more each day," his mother said, choking up as she looked at him. They stood together facing the crowd before them, both too emotional to speak.

A scrawny kid with red hair and wearing a white T-shirt over his long-sleeved blue shirt ran along the dock. "Outta my way!" he cried as he moved, forcing the crowd to part.

He was pursued by a much taller boy with short red hair who was dripping wet. As the taller boy squeezed water from the ends of his shorts and the sides of his shirt, he yelled,

"Andy, I'm gonna get you!"

Another boy, stout and wearing a pith safari sun hat that had fallen off and hung from his neck, followed the two red-haired boys. He had an interesting black and blond streaked haircut and thick white smears of sunscreen all over his nose, face, and legs. He shouted, "Andy, wait up!" as he went.

Luke couldn't even relate to the playful nature of it all. He just felt, well, numb. Suddenly he felt something bump hard against his legs and he jumped.

"Pardon me, comin' through, 'eavy crate," a man bellowed in a deep voice. He was wearing a long brown leather apron. His white handlebar moustache highlighted his red face as he strained to push the crate forward on a pallet jack.

As Luke and his mom stepped back, they noticed a procession of seven herring gulls following closely behind. The crate was labeled

Raven Food: May contain animal parts.

On top of it was a net full of fish that were still alive and flopping around. As the crowd separated, his mom chuckled. "Fresh fish, huh? I hope for your sake they have mac 'n' cheese."

Luke did not find her joke funny.

Now closer to the edge of the dock, Luke's attention was drawn to a man perched atop a unicycle. The man wore a white lab coat and a Chronos Day collared orange shirt, like all the other Chronos Academy staff. But his face was unique. His brown and grey hair formed a V-shaped hairline on his forehead, and his dark eyes were set close to his long nose, which put him on the verge of being cross-eyed. His brown beard, streaked with white, completely concealed his neck so when he turned his head it seemed to rotate on top of his polka-dot bowtie. He looked like an owl.

He was shouting instructions in clear hoot-like bursts to a tall, Black man with muscular arms. "You see, Adio? To keep your balance, pedal forward." The professor began pedalling the one-wheeled cycle right there on the dock. "And you may extend your arms like this." As the professor spread his arms, his lab coat splayed behind him. He looked like an owl taking flight. Professor Gregor then hopped off the unicycle, holding the seat with his hand.

"Gotcha, Professor Gregor. I'm ready for my turn now," Adio said, his voice rhythmic, smooth, and drawn out. A Jamaican accent, Luke guessed.

Shaking his dark hair, which was twisted into locs, over his shoulders, Adio swung his leg over the seat effortlessly. He was a lot taller and younger than Professor Gregor. His Chronos Day orange shirt fit tightly around his biceps.

Adio began to pedal faster and faster. Students and parents jumped out of the way, providing Luke with a clear line of sight. He was headed straight for the man pushing the crate of raven food. The six-piece brass band struck up "Flight of the Bumblebee."

Professor Gregor yelled as he ran after him, "Adio! You need to turn. Turn!" Somehow, with a flurry of arm motions, Adio managed to turn the cycle sharply away from the crate but was now careening towards the end of the dock! The tempo of the music increased to match Adio's wobbly warp speed.

"Adio! Come back! Safety first, Adio! Adio! I know you can hear me!" hooted Professor Gregor.

Adio and the unicycle went over the end of the dock with a big splash, followed by the sound of cymbals crashing together. The tuba sounded a final earthy note as the crowd swept Luke and his mom towards the action.

Leaning over the dock, Professor Gregor was in hysterics. "I specifically told you to be careful, Adio! Do not let that unicycle sink! Do you hear me?!" The unicycle bobbed gently next to Adio in the water, its one wheel breaking the surface. "Adio! Get that unicycle back onto this dock right now!"

Luke's mom chuckled with the cheering crowd as other orange T-shirt clad staff helped haul both Adio and the unicycle back up onto the dock. "Think of this as an adventure," she offered, smiling broadly.

Luke pulled on his mom's arm to move away from the action. He wanted to know what "giving it a chance" really meant. "Mom, how long—"

The loud ferry horn tooted twice and a commanding voice in the distance shouted, "All aboard!" The band started a song that Luke didn't know. A kid walked by them singing along, "We're all in the same boat …"

"Oh, honey," Lorraine sighed. She squeezed Luke hard. "I'll miss you! And I love, love, love you."

Before he could ask how long he'd have to stay at Chronos Academy, she gave him one last hug and helped heave his duffle bag onto his shoulder. The bag weighed a million pounds. Luke tried to speak up again, but the crowd separated him from his mother, pushing him past a giant poster advertising the Pandia Games—"Hosted by the Chronos Academy Vikings this spring"—and towards the boat ramp. Over his shoulder he caught a glimpse of his mother blowing him kisses.

Luke was swept into the line of students waiting to board the *Trillian*. He recognized the owly Professor Gregor taking attendance. "Joe! You are soaking wet!" the professor screeched, wiping the spray from his face as the tall boy shook his head like a wet dog.

"Sorry, Professor Gregor," Joe replied, then turned to the boy next to him. "I'm so going to get Andy for pushing me into the water. Me! His own brother!" He squeezed out some more water from his shirt and shorts. His sneakers sloshed on his feet, leaving soggy footprints in his wake as he boarded the ferry.

Adio, just as wet but wrapped in a Chronos Vikings towel, jumped the queue of kids. Professor Gregor turned his pointy nose and beady eyes toward him. "Are you quite done with all these water shenanigans?" the professor asked while marking something on the paper on his clipboard. "My poor unicycle, Adio! Look at it!" The unicycle was leaning against the dock post, dripping salt water. It appeared to be sprouting glistening strands of green seaweed. "It's going to need a full tune up!" Professor Gregor hooted and looked off, as he contemplated this serious conundrum.

Adio, on the other hand, had a playful look in his eyes as though debating what to say. In the end he nodded, gave a half smile, patted the older man's shoulder as an apology, and offered to take the clipboard for the rest of attendance duty. Professor Gregor twisted his head side to side disapprovingly and sharply flapped his hand, motioning Adio to board the boat. Adio's grin lit up his warm ebony complexion. He shrugged his lean muscular shoulders, and waddling like a duck, followed Joe aboard. Despite himself, Luke laughed a little.

"Okay, name?" the professor asked.

Serious once more, Luke answered, "Luke Alexander."

Shuffling aboard, Luke decided something right then and there. He would give Chronos Academy a chance. *A one-week chance.* And then he was going home.

3

Cleo

It was September 1st and Cleo and her grandma CeeCee had left CeeCee's holiday cottage early that morning. They'd been driving for hours. Their destination: Glimmerton. From there Cleo would take the ferry to Chronos Academy. A school focused on everything exciting, including lots of STEM—all things science, technology, engineering, and math—with an emphasis on curiosity and learning. The perfect combination for Cleo.

The car crested a hill and continued on Hawking Highway, a surprisingly narrow road. Bleary-eyed from motion sickness, Cleo focused on the twisting road in front of her. CeeCee drove the rickety blue Buick like they were on a rollercoaster ride. As her grandma navigated another hairpin turn, Cleo grabbed the dashboard with both hands to keep from flying into the door.

"Almost there, sweet pea," Grandma CeeCee said empathetically, reaching across the worn blue seat to pat Cleo's leg. Her grandma wore a floral, ankle-length summer dress in bold colours, topped with a soft grey sweater. Her grey and white hair was shoulder length and feathered.

Only days ago, Cleo had arrived on Pandia, in the capital city of Waywee at the northern end of the island, and her grandma had picked her up at the airport. They had driven a few hours south to CeeCee's cottage to spend some time together before school started. They hadn't seen each other for a couple of months, since the opening of Cleo's mom's new museum in Brillianton, England. Cleo was very close with her grandma, so it was unusual for them to go such a long time between visits. That morning when Cleo had left the holiday cottage, she'd been so excited. She couldn't wait to be at her new school. She held her churning stomach and said meekly, "I love science." She then fixed the I HEART SCIENCE cap that was containing her unruly mass of long brown curls. "Chronos Academy will be great. I can't wait," she repeated quietly like a mantra.

"It will be great! When I was a student there, I loved it!" CeeCee gestured with her right hand as she steered with her left. "Think of all the new kids you'll meet. And the adventures you'll—" The sudden sound of blaring sirens came from a police motorcycle behind them. CeeCee swore, pushed on the brakes, and pulled over. But as soon as they were on the side of the road, the policeman pulled out from behind them, waved thanks as he drove past, and turned off his siren and lights.

"Glad we didn't get a ticket, but why bother with the lights?" CeeCee asked the front window as she put the blue 1970s Buick into gear. The car's extended hood pitched forward, and the car suddenly stalled. CeeCee turned the key in the ignition. There was a grinding whirring sound. CeeCee tried again. Once. Twice. No luck. Cleo crossed her fingers the car would start. She looked over at her cell phone nestled between her and CeeCee on an open tear in the blue fabric of the bench-style seat. She checked the text from her mom again. SORRY I COULDN'T BE THERE. LOVE YOU.

Cleo dropped her focus to the floor of the car as different emotions churned through her. She recalled the scene at the airport gate, her mother still angry at Cleo's choice to attend Chronos Academy. Cleo wanted to go to Chronos so badly. She couldn't understand why her mom was so against it. She tried not to think about it.

"Three times a charm!" CeeCee declared as the engine finally turned over and they got back on the single-laned trunk road.

It wasn't long before the town of Glimmerton appeared. A rainbow of two-story narrow houses were nestled between the hills and the ocean. The view disappeared when they rounded a bend on the narrow road, and they were once again surrounded by forest and fields. Cleo clutched her stomach as the car took a final sharp turn before suddenly plummeting down to a marina.

"We made it!" CeeCee declared proudly as the car lurched to a stop in the nearly empty parking lot, right next to a police motorcycle. It looked like the one that had passed them on the highway.

Rolling down her window, Cleo's stomach finally settled with the smell of fresh salty air as she gazed at the dock. Herring gulls were calling and circling the sky. The ocean waves gently bumped the aged branching dock that was wide and long. The far ends of the dock seemed to blur into the blue horizon and the moored boats bobbed lightly on the water. It was all really lovely.

Wait!

There were no kids, no teachers, no ferry! The marina had the ambiance of a fairground the day *after* the fair had left town. Cleo looked back at CeeCee. Her grandma's hands with their soft withered skin on the steering wheel.

"Grandma, we missed the boat!"

4

Luke

The bottom main deck of the *Trillian* was crowded with students lining the white railings. They were grouped together chatting excitedly. Luke made his way to the third upper deck which was less crowded, and had benches and floor boards made of polished wood. The deck ceiling was lined with life jackets. He found a spot under a bright orange Chronos Day–coloured life preserver ring and shoved his duffle under the bench. Thinking about what he would say to his mom when he called her a week from now to let him go home, he plopped into his seat. Looking through the railing Luke watched the waves lapping against the side of the boat.

He put his elbows on his knees and held his chin in his hands, the tick-tick-tick of his watch on his left wrist providing an almost hypnotizing comfort. He felt a slight sway as the boat hit the open water.

Drops of water splashed on the floor between his feet. Without moving his head, Luke turned his eyes up and found Adio wrapped in a towel, water still dripping off the ends of his dark locs. A Black boy, with chestnut brown skin just a tad lighter than Adio's, stood next to him. The boy was holding on to a bulky red and white backpack.

Adio looked up from his clipboard and spoke loudly to be heard over the low humming noise coming from the boat engine and the chatty students. "No problem. Here's a seat, Ollie. Next to?"

"Luke."

"Right, Luke!" Adio drawled easily with his Jamaican accent as he checked the clipboard.

Ollie stood in place, anxiously looking around as though unsure what to do next. He was similar to Luke's height, although next to Adio he looked really short. Ollie's hair was shaved at the sides and faded into short curly black hair on top. He had a cool Z line, a design feature, shaved into one side of his head. His blue-rimmed glasses were kept in place with a wraparound blue band that matched his blue shorts.

Feeling his chest go slightly tight, Luke reached into his left shorts pocket and grabbed his blue and white asthma inhaler. Concealing it in his hand, he breathed in the much-needed medication. His hand was always quick on the draw so as not to attract attention.

But Adio noticed and blinked in surprise. "Asthma?" he asked. When Luke nodded, Adio wrote something down on his clipboard. "Nurse Kelly will have your prescription on file, so make sure you see her whenever you need to stock up."

Ollie spoke up, stuttering a bit with nervousness. "S-S-So do you need your inhaler all the time? How does that work?"

Ollie and Adio were looking at Luke, waiting for him to respond, which made him feel a little uncomfortable. It surprised him that Adio was so patient and waiting to hear his answer.

"I need my inhaler before I exercise or run or anything like that. Otherwise, I take it when my chest feels tight. Because I need to breathe. It helps open up my lung airways."

Adio nodded with understanding as he jotted another note on his clipboard. Ollie stared at Luke as though trying to figure him out.

"Okay, heads up, boys," Adio said. "When we arrive at Castle Bay, you need to get up to the castle and check in quickly, okay? We're a bit behind schedule, and we need to get our first years through the campus tour and out to the amphitheatre for the Chronos Day celebration. So, mind the time." Adio smiled in an easy-going manner.

Hugging his backpack like a life preserver, Ollie sat down on the bench next to Luke and spoke to Adio. "I don't have a watch. I had a smartwatch, but they told us to leave it at home." He held up his wrist. His skin wasn't as dark where his watch band had left a tan line.

"Your buddy has one," Adio pointed at Luke's arm. "Stick together. Now, I've gotta find Miss Cleo Gaven. We haven't seen her yet." Adio dripped off to the next group of students.

"That's a cool watch," Ollie said.

Luke barely nodded. He didn't want to talk about his dad's watch.

"My grandad, he's originally from Ethiopia, but we live in Canada. He has a cool pocket watch, you know, on a chain? It's still ticking. I mean the watch. Although I *can* say the same about my grandad." He snorted a little at his own joke. "His watch doesn't have a cool see-through dial like that. What's that big silver blob at the top?" Ollie asked, squinting through his glasses at the timepiece.

The silver blob was a bird with its wings spread. But Luke just shrugged.

"Is it broken? There's only one hand, and it doesn't even look like it's connected to anything. The hand is just floating in the middle." Ollie pointed at Luke's wrist. "How can you tell the minutes or seconds?" Careful not to touch the watch, Ollie squinted his eyes and moved his head back and forth to get a better look.

Luke replied, hoping to end the conversation, "I just guess. Like right now, it's 9 something."

"There's a bunch of letters around the edge." Ollie read aloud a few of the tiny engraved letters, "M's, C's, and L's. Cool. Do you know what they mean?"

"No," Luke barked. He'd missed out on asking his dad about this and many other things, and now he'd never get the chance.

The boat turned slightly and the angle of the bright morning sun made Ollie squint. He shielded his eyes as he focused on Luke. "There's a horology class at the school. Maybe you can find out," Ollie offered. Seeing Luke's puzzlement he added, "Horology. It's the study of time, clocks, and watches."

Not wanting to encourage any more conversation with Ollie, Luke stayed quiet.

He had to figure out how to convince his mom to let him go home!

5

Cleo

"Don't you worry." Grandma CeeCee's saucy wide smile showed her mischievousness as the 84-year-old quickly touched up her lipstick in one smooth practised motion. Her eyes were now more grey than hazel, a trait she shared with Cleo when their emotions ran high.

Cleo wondered if her own eyes had adopted their grey hue with her rising frustration. "But how am I going to get to school?!" Cleo's voice pitched.

CeeCee glanced at Cleo confidently. "We need a boat."

The marina was full of boats. Could they rent one and find someone to drive it? What if she couldn't get to school and had to return to the cottage with her grandma? She would miss out on everything! A new life, new school, new friends. Cleo bit her lip in worry and glanced at her grandma. CeeCee's life was chock-full of adventures that she happily told Cleo about. And Cleo couldn't help but want one fun adventure of her own, just *once* in her life!

Having parked unnecessarily close to the motorcycle, CeeCee had to shimmy out the driver's side door. Despite trying to be careful, she banged the motorcycle with the car door, then quickly steadied the bike with her hands. Unfazed, she nimbly made her way around to the passenger side and hauled Cleo's bag from the back seat before Cleo had even opened her own door.

"You can't worry about everything in life," CeeCee said loudly through the open passenger side window. "You'll become a stress case. Look at your mother with her perfect hair and not a single crease in her suit. Speak of the devil, better grab the newspaper, kiddo," CeeCee instructed. "There's an article about your mother on page eight. She did a CT scan on a gooey mummy and found tooth decay. Big exciting news for the museum," CeeCee said with a chuckle.

Cleo frowned. She didn't want to read another article about her mother's outstanding museum work and all her discoveries. Work had been her mother's excuse for moving to Brillianton and not being here with them today.

"Oh, and better leave your phone here. It's not allowed at school. Besides, the reception is terrible," CeeCee said. With her flowery dress flowing behind her, she beelined towards the right-hand side of the weathered wooden dock.

Cleo said a silent goodbye to her phone, rolled up her window, and reluctantly grabbed the newspaper before sliding out of the Buick. She ran to catch up with her petite grandma who was checking out a long row of colourful fishing boats along the east side of the marina.

When Cleo slid up beside her, CeeCee whispered, "Something's fishy." Although the air did smell like fish, Cleo suspected her grandma was referring to the conversation unfolding not too far from them between the police officer who had driven past them earlier and a large broad fisherman.

The fisherman had a bushy white handlebar moustache and wore a brown full-body apron and green rubber boots. On the dock next to the boat, he was fiddling with a recently used fishing net.

The police officer was tall and lanky and wore a dark navy blue uniform and aviator sunglasses. He stood rigid like a statue, holding his helmet under one arm.

"We checked your sources, captain. NO ONE has actually seen Recleren!" the policeman shouted at the man in the apron.

"Officer Anders, as ye know," said the man in the apron, "I've reliable sources, an' if a noble newspaper as respectable as the *Glimmerton Gazette* asks me a question, I tell 'em the truth. Recleren is a dodgy fellow. A master of disguise." The fishing captain wiped his hand on his full-body apron. "An' 'e is 'ere on Pandia."

Cleo couldn't pinpoint the fisherman's unique accent. It wasn't strong but she'd never come across it before. It seemed like H's were optional at the beginning of words, which made *here* into *'ere*. And *an'* must mean *and*.

"It's *Detective* Anders! And you have no proof Recleren is on the island." The policeman's face was expressionless. "And you just can't tell the *Gazette* that you're 'assisting on the Recleren case.' You ARE NOT!"

The captain raised his voice to match the detective's. "Well, I CAN ASSIST ye right now! We fishing folks 'ave our ears to the wind for information." The man tipped his head knowingly as if listening to the actual wind. "And those winds say Recleren's in Kingsburg Forest. An' o' course I don't need to tell *ye* why 'e's come back."

"I suppose you'll say it's the Stones," Detective Anders scoffed.

"Aye, o' course it's the Stones!" Suddenly the fishing captain stopped talking. He cleared his throat, smiled broadly at CeeCee and Cleo, and then pointed at them using his thick right thumb as though he was hitchhiking.

It took a moment before Detective Anders whipped his head towards them, his eyes hidden behind his aviator glasses. His golden badge, pinned close to his left lapel, gleamed in the sunlight.

Maintaining his wide grin, the captain spoke to CeeCee. "An' I suppose ye two are looking for a ride to Chronos Academy?" His tone was playful and full of mischief. He waited for an answer as he folded the fishing net once more and placed it in a cooler.

"You guessed right, Captain!" CeeCee answered cheerfully. "Looks like we missed the ferry."

"Aye, but not by much. The *Trillian* gets ye there, but so can *My Betsy*!" He gestured at the whitewashed wooden boat next to them, then introduced himself, "Captain Jumbo at yer service."

Cleo's gaze followed the direction of his hand and she couldn't help but gawk. *My Betsy* wasn't much longer than CeeCee's Buick, and it was just as old! Paint was peeling from everywhere. The anchor on the bow was rusty. The small boat looked like it should be left to decompose and be swallowed whole by the kelp.

Cleo became instantly worried. Surely, she wouldn't be going on the ocean in *My Betsy*. She glanced at her grandma to say so but then stopped.

She took in a deep breath of air tainted with the smell of fish. *Right*, this year was going to be different. Cleo forced a thin smile at Captain Jumbo. She would be positive about the whole thing and was ready for an adventure. It didn't matter that the boat was rickety looking. This boat was fine, great, even. What mattered was that the boat could float, and she would get to Chronos Academy in no time, probably not too far behind the other students.

The captain looked down his long nose at Cleo and smiled back, revealing several gaps next to his yellowed front teeth. "'Appy to take ye, miss."

Cleo thanked the captain and adjusted her I HEART SCIENCE cap lower on her forehead as she waited for her grandma and the fisherman to discuss the details.

"Eh hem," the policeman cleared his throat loudly. They had forgotten the policeman was still there, and he didn't look happy about it. Arms crossed, he tapped his foot impatiently on the dock.

The sound of birds drew Cleo's gaze upwards. Just then a seagull above them squawked and launched a disgusting white gooey poop onto Detective Anders' shoulder. CeeCee's laughter echoed across the water, while Captain Jumbo visibly bit his lip and said, "Don't ye worry, Detective! That there's a sign o' good luck."

The detective, nostrils flaring, walked sharply towards Captain Jumbo. "Remember what I said, Jumbo. You're a private citizen." He paused. "And a respected Glimmician descendent."

"Aye." Captain Jumbo stood straight, acknowledging the compliment.

"But. Not. An. Officer. Of. The. Law," Anders emphasized as he pushed his aviator sunglasses back up his nose. The detective walked away, the white smear still on his shoulder. He strapped on his helmet, hopped onto his motorbike, and sped away from the pier.

"Aye, that man is an arse," Jumbo mumbled under his breath.

CeeCee laughed, looking years younger. "Ah, Jumbo, this sea air brings me back."

"It would that, wouldn't it?" Captain Jumbo said as he winked at CeeCee, his moustache moving slightly.

CeeCee smiled at him and put her arm around her granddaughter. "Cleo, you're going to love it at Chronos Academy! Lots of science, which you love, new adventures, new friends. But if you run into any kids like Stephanie, remember that dealing with mean kids is—" She stopped and waited.

"—an opportunity to grow," Cleo completed. How many times had she heard that from Grandma back when Stephanie had been her best friend but then suddenly wasn't?

"Exactly! It's always an opportunity to grow!" CeeCee echoed. "You learn how to deal with them."

"Just like I 'andled Anders," Captain Jumbo said from aboard the boat as he dropped a cooler onto the deck.

Still on the dock, Cleo stewed. Her parents' separation, the move to Brillianton for her mom's museum job, and her dad leaving to go back to Egypt—it had been a lot. Then another weight had been added on the pile: the problems she'd had at school last year with her former friend and now enemy Stephanie. Why couldn't her mom understand that she needed this change to get away from it all?

Cleo glanced down at the ragged, worn-out backpack that she'd borrowed from her grandma. This hideous backpack with the dented external frame had been on many adventures and had supposedly saved her grandma from an angry camel in Petra, a city of stone by the Dead Sea. And the backpack was waterproof, too. Somehow Cleo felt it would protect her and perhaps bring her luck. Plus, she was sure there wouldn't be any kids at Chronos Academy as mean as Stephanie. New school, new friends, new adventures. This year would be great!

CeeCee's arms wrapped around Cleo's waist, enveloping her in a big hug. Although her petite grandma was a head shorter than her, Cleo felt the hug was bigger than life. CeeCee said, "I'll look for your letters, call me if you need to, and I'll see you at Christmas." Then, as she always did whenever they said goodbye or good night, her grandmother looked at her tenderly and softly added, "Love you more than the universe."

"I love you, too, Grandma." Cleo held on to the hug one moment longer and then let go. She beamed. "Let the adventure begin!"

6

Luke

"Cheer for the Chronos Vikings!" an older boy shouted. The crowd at the bow of the *Trillian* roared, "GO VIKES!"

"That's for the Pandia Games!" Ollie shouted at Luke to be heard over the cheering. They're like the Olympics for students and take place in Pandia every four years. This time they're coming to Chronos Academy in the spring. I can't wait!"

The crowd stopped cheering but Ollie continued on about the Pandia Games, his voice still loud. "There are running sports, relay, long jump, javelin, and then the most awesome is the triathlon with running, archery, and fencing—RAF for short." Looking away from the crowd at the bow, Ollie turned to Luke, waiting for a response.

But Luke changed his focus to his shoes and made no comment. He couldn't care less about the Pandia Games. Feeling a sharp elbow in his side, Luke glanced up. Ollie was rummaging through his red and white backpack, completely unaware that he was bumping Luke. Luke scooted over closer to the railing.

Ollie zipped up his backpack and asked, "Are you from here? Pandia, I mean."

Luke sighed and gave a slight nod, which Ollie misunderstood as a green light to continue with the conversation.

Ollie's words came motoring out. "I'm not from here. I'm from Canada. I've never been across the Atlantic Ocean, or to Africa or anything, but I've researched everything about Pandia and Chronos Academy. Did you know that this southern part of Pandia, where Chronos Academy is, is special? They always have aurora lights, like, all the time. That's because the electromagnetic energy there is strong. Cool, right?"

Luke quickly scanned the benches. Perhaps he could find another seat somewhere?

Ollie pulled out a magazine and turned to a folded page. He showed Luke pictures of aurora lights and scientific cartoon clips that explained how they work. "See this?" Ollie quickly flipped through the magazine to show Luke another diagram. But Luke hadn't even looked at the first picture.

"The aurora lights are caused by—" Ollie began.

"I know about aurora lights! I was born in Wicker, in northern Pandia. I just don't care," Luke snapped tersely as he turned to look at his seatmate. He dropped his gaze when he noticed the surprised hurt on Ollie's face.

Luke was lying. Aurora lights were interesting. Camping with his dad, Luke would watch the glowing green and purple lights dance when they appeared in the night skies close to Wicker. He and his dad would stay up all night sometimes to watch the light show. Luke missed him so much, it hurt. It had been months since he last seen his dad.

Ollie nodded but Luke wasn't sure what he was nodding

about. Ollie put away the science magazine with its glossy cover of aurora lights dancing over a mountainous backdrop, exchanging it for another thin, glossy-covered serial from his backpack. "I also got this."

It was the latest edition of *Knights of Darkness*. He held it in front of Luke for a few seconds and drew his eyebrows together in slight confusion, tilting his head to one side as he waited for Luke to say something. When he didn't, Ollie returned his magazine into his bag. He adjusted the blue band on his head and then held onto his backpack again, looking forward with a straight face. There were a few beads of sweat along his forehead.

Luke hesitated for a moment, feeling remorseful for being rude. He pulled out his own plastic-wrapped *Knights of Darkness* from his duffle bag and showed it to Ollie.

"You're a fan?" Ollie asked, raising his eyebrows high above the blue rim of his glasses.

Luke gave an imperceptible nod.

"Cool."

Suddenly, the ferry turned and a murmur spread like a wave through the crowd. Ollie pulled Luke along with him to gather at the bow with other excited students.

"Chronos Academy. It was once known as Castle Chronos before it became a school! It's just like in *Knights of Darkness*," Ollie exclaimed. "Look at all those towers!"

Luke couldn't help but be in awe.

A massive medieval castle that seemed to float on wisps of mist rising from the sea, overlooked the ocean. Mysterious and foreboding, surrounded by a seemingly impenetrable curtain wall, the castle was framed by two soaring stone towers guarding the castle, like giants ready for action.

Intermittently appearing on the top of the main castle were a few skinnier towers, like pipes of an organ, each with a different height. Where the mist was breaking, they saw green grounds beyond the castle's protective wall.

"Chronos Academy!" Ollie said with nervous excitement. "I can't wait to see it all. It's so old. The campus is supposed to be huge behind that castle. And I can't wait for all the science we'll learn." He paused only briefly. "Every kid in the world wants to come here. And we're actually HERE! This is it! So cool!"

Not every kid wants to come here. Luke trudged to the bench, trying his hardest not to be infected by the giddy atmosphere and Ollie's amazement. He grabbed his duffel bag from underneath the seat. When he stood, he was surprised to see Ollie waiting for him. Reluctantly, he joined Ollie and the rest of the excited crowd. They disembarked and made their way from the Castle Bay dock up a switchback pathway to the imposing home of Chronos Academy.

7

Cleo

With a final wave to CeeCee, Cleo jumped aboard *My Betsy.*

"Watch yer step," Captain Jumbo called just as Cleo's foot slipped out from under her. She nearly did the splits! She quickly steadied herself and adjusted her heavy backpack on her shoulders. Portions of the deck were caked in black, grey, and green slime. She envisioned all kinds of crazy bacteria and amoebae—gross!

"Don't worry," she said to herself, "This is an adventure." Carefully stepping over and around nets, ropes, and stacked wooden crates, Cleo followed Captain Jumbo single file down the length of the boat and up a couple of white steps to a small cabin room. Producing a roll of duct tape from his apron, Captain Jumbo quickly patched a loose plank on the door. Satisfied with his work, he tapped the doorway three times before he entered.

Sunshine filled the tiny cabin through the panoramic windows. Captain Jumbo directed Cleo to sit on a small bench covered with a heaping pile of papers and brown aprons. A grimy coffeepot sat atop the pile like a cherry on top of a cake. Cleo elected to sit on her backpack, which was packed tightly and sturdy enough with its external frame to double as a seat. Captain Jumbo turned on the engine, and for a few moments *My Betsy* sputtered and belched black smoke as she came to life. Herring gulls squawked around the boat as it slowly chugged out of Glimmerton Bay.

On the dash were rolled-up charts, several compasses, and parallel rulers for navigating. The mic of the HF radio hung nearby, an exceptionally long twisted black cord dangling from it. There was also a large bronze medallion hanging next to a built-in display screen. As the medallion clinked against the dash with the motion of the boat, Cleo leaned over and steadied it with her hand. In the centre of the bronze medallion was a silver raven, wings spread, with the engraved words "*Raven Luck*."

Captain Jumbo yelled to be heard over the loud engine. "I come from a long line o' Glimmician people. That's why this town is called Glimmerton. They were the first people on this island two thousand years ago, an' they lived around 'ere. The ancient Glimmicians worshipped the Raven god, an' that raven medallion brings good luck." He shaped his moustache with one hand while guiding the big silver steering wheel with the other. "Sailors get lost out 'ere all the time. The waters can be rough, an' the weather can change at any moment. We sometimes 'ave small magnetic storms, and our GPSes can fail!"

As Captain Jumbo paused, Cleo remembered reading about the area around Chronos Academy. It was quite unique with its higher electromagnetic activity and lots of auroras in the night sky, even more than the rest of Pandia.

Captain Jumbo continued, "We need luck out 'ere!"

The captain pulled on a large black lever, the boat lurched, and the engine shifted from a growl to a loud purr. He glanced at the raven medallion. "From the time o' the ancient Glimmicians, the ravens 'ave been and still are important around 'ere. That's why there are ravens at Chronos Academy. The story goes, if the ravens leave the castle, it'll fall."

Now in the wide open sea, the boat rocked, and Cleo suddenly felt the return of her motion sickness from riding in the Buick. She grabbed the newspaper from the side pocket of her grandma's backpack and fanned her face, hoping it would help calm her stomach.

Captain Jumbo grabbed the microphone of the HF radio, pulling on the long cord. "I'm coming into port shortly, Maggie. Ye'll be able to see us from the light'ouse. I've quite the story to tell ye about Anders. Over."

A female voice replied, "Copy that."

Replacing the mic harshly into its holder, Captain Jumbo stared out into the ocean. A few minutes passed before he spoke, lost in his own thoughts and mumbling angrily to himself, "Anders 'as some nerve, 'just a fisherman.' I'm no liar. I'm a keeper of stories. The *Gazette* asked!" He then huffed out a quick sigh and turned the wheel slightly. "An' I've every right to tell them Recleren *'as* returned to Pandia, Recleren 'as. O' course 'e 'as."

Cleo's stomach lurched as they went over a large wave. Desperate to get her mind off her nausea, she asked, "Who's Recleren?"

8

Luke

Inside the castle Ollie stuck to Luke like glue. He was pulling Luke past their roommates, Andy and Ronan, whom they'd only met moments before in their dormitory. Luke had remembered Andy and Ronan from the dock. Ronan still had gobs of sunscreen smeared on his nose and legs. He held his wide-brim hat in his hand after Adio had suggested he remove it. His hair was shaved on the sides with floppy blond and black streaks falling from the top of his head.

They had moved on from the science tower, but Ollie was still commenting about it. He whispered to Luke, "I hear they have scientists' brains in there and they're experimenting on them."

Adio clapped his hands, grabbing everyone's attention, and finally Ollie went quiet. Adio had large deep-brown eyes that twinkled with mischief. Tall, muscular, and lean, he moved gracefully with a long gait. He was no longer wet and had changed into a tie-dye shirt, shorts, and sandals, which Luke thought were more suited to a beach than a medieval stone castle. His long dark locs were pulled into a low ponytail.

"This is our last stop on the tour before we head back to Knight Hall. This dungeon classroom is Professor Gregor's chemistry and physics class. Lucky you!" he said, grinning a bright white smile.

In the corner of the lab was a tall machine with a robotic arm, which Luke recognized as a 3D printer. Luke noticed glassware all around him, on shelves, on top of large white fridges, on tables.

"There you are!" exclaimed Professor Gregor, entering the classroom from its side door.

"Ah, Professor Gregor," Adio smiled.

"Why are these students still here, Adio?" Professor Gregor asked.

"We still have a bit of time," Adio responded.

"No, you don't. You should've been done with the tour by now. All returning students are already at the amphitheatre for our big Chronos Day celebration. And why haven't you put away this new glassware?" Professor Gregor asked, pointing to the stack of beakers forming a sizable pyramid in a corner on the floor.

"Don't worry, professor. I'll get to it after I read the manual on how to tune up your unicycle," said Adio, smirking.

"I don't give a hoot for your excuses," Professor Gregor replied. At the word 'hoot' Luke couldn't help but smile. Ollie was trying to stifle his giggles. Clearly Luke wasn't the only one who thought Professor Gregor looked like an owl. Wondering how long this conversation might take, Luke glanced at his wrist.

His watch wasn't there!

"My watch is gone!" Luke gasped as panic and tunnel

vision set in.

"What?" Ollie said, scratching at the band holding his glasses.

"My watch. Where is it?" Luke's heart was racing. "I had it on the whole time and then I—" Luke suddenly remembered. He'd taken it off when washing his hands in the bathroom *on the eighth floor.*

Luke ran towards the door. Ollie called out after him, "Meet you in Knight Hall!"

Adio yelled something like "Franklin Lane," but Luke didn't slow to hear anything else.

Desperate thoughts looped in his mind. *Please be there, please be there.* Bolting up the stairs to the main floor, through the saloon with the ugly large straw cowboy hat on the mantle, down the long stone corridor, through Science Tower, and into Knight Hall, Luke ran as fast as he could. He exited Knight Hall, rounding the corner all the way, briefly glancing at the corridor leading to Viking Hall cafeteria, and up the many flights of stairs. He paused on the sixth floor that led to the library, to use his inhaler. Then he raced up to the eighth floor, which housed the arched-ceiling dormitories for the students.

Luke lurched for the bathroom door, pushing it open with all his might. He let out a gasp of relief. His watch was exactly where he'd left it, on the counter next to the copper faucet. He quickly placed it onto his left wrist. *I swear, I'm never taking you off again to wash.*

At the top of the staircase, Luke paused to catch his breath. *I should just hang out in my dorm and skip the boring celebration. Ugh. Mom won't think I've given this place a chance.* He sighed and quickly descended the many stairs.

As he skidded into Knight Hall, he was surprised to find he was alone. Surely the first-year students would have returned from the dungeons by now?! Panting, Luke realized that the entire student body must have left for the amphitheatre without him.

Just then, voices drifted from the far end of Knight Hall, near the big entrance door to the castle. In the murky light Luke distinguished two adults chatting. They were about to exit the castle. Too tired to run, Luke walked quickly to catch up to them. Both men were so engaged in their conversation that they didn't hear Luke coming towards them.

"... ravens are important, Mr. Ringwald," said the short slim Black man with crazy white hair similar to Einstein's.

"Yes, yes, I know," said Mr. Ringwald, who was wearing a weird purple and orange outfit. The enormous heavy door closed behind them, clunking shut like the door of a bank vault.

Luke was there in five steps. He grabbed onto the long vertical iron handle and heaved as hard as he could. It wouldn't open. He put all his weight behind his arms, trying desperately to open the door. *Is it stuck?*

Luke tried again, again, and again. The door wouldn't budge.

Luke yelled, "Hello! Anyone here?" His voice ricocheted off the vaulted ceiling in Knight Hall. The space was huge, larger than two bowling alleys put together, and Luke felt very small.

There was no answer.

Smacking his hand against the door, Luke thought, *I'm trapped inside this massive castle! Come on!* His eyes darted around Knight Hall. *There has to be another exit somewhere!*

Then Luke had an idea.

If he phoned his mom right now, he could catch her before she boarded her plane and he'd be able to go home. It wasn't too late. And even if he hadn't made it to the Chronos Day Celebration, he'd tried. *I've given Chronos Academy—* Luke glanced at his watch—*at least a few hours.*

With no cell phones allowed, there had to be a land line somewhere in the school. He left Knight Hall to start his quest. He headed for the student study area known as the Saloon. Finding only a forgotten book on a table, he continued his search. Not having noticed any phones in Professor Gregor's classroom, he passed the staircases leading to the dungeon, and climbed different staircases, checking around corners, and opening any doors that were unlocked.

About to give up, he finally stumbled into a room with red phone booths. Excited, he entered a booth.

What kind of phone is this? It was a large clunky unit, with a twisting black cord that hung to the side. In the center it had a round plastic circle with holes and numbers wrapped around the edge. He placed his fingers into the holes and pressed hard, trying multiple number combinations. But nothing worked. In frustration, Luke hit the unit with the palm of his hand.

As he made his way back through the Saloon, he heard a sound.

Scritch-scratch. Scritch-scratch.

Perched on the aged stone fireplace mantel was an extremely large black bird! Its head twitched and its dark eyes locked onto Luke's. Luke's mouth went dry as his brain searched for a reason as to why any bird, let alone one as big and scary looking as this, would be *inside* the castle. Standing stock still, Luke felt hypnotized, unable to look away from the bird as the bird looked at him.

It seemed to be searching his soul.

Then Luke noticed the bird had one white foot and one black foot. His mind raced. *Weird phones and weird birds! I gotta get out of here.*

Keeping the bird in his sight, Luke turned slowly to leave the Saloon. The feathered creature spread its wings and glided across the Saloon, coming straight for him. Luke dashed away as fast as he could, running into Science Tower, and straight through the orbiting electrons in the holographic display of an atom.

"CAAAAW. CAW!" The bird's calls were close behind.

He rushed into Knight Hall, slipped on the polished floor, and screamed as he collided with something hard. Looking up from the castle floor, he saw a knight in full armour holding an axe up high, ready to strike. The room spun and tipped.

9

Cleo

Captain Jumbo focused on the horizon. Cleo thought for a moment he wouldn't answer her question about Recleren, but then he spoke.

"Aye, I fished with 'im long ago, in these waters. 'e was just young Richie back then. Loved our stories. Stories only us fishermen told." The ends of Captain Jumbo's moustache dropped slightly as he frowned. "I told 'im one story. Aye I did. The story about the Stones of Destiny." Captain Jumbo's hands gripped the steering wheel hard. "Richie became obsessed. Spent 'is days searching the shores and forests around Pandia looking for 'em. When 'e ran out of money, 'e started stealing. 'Is greed grew and 'e became dangerous. Used weapons to get what 'e wanted, knives and daggers. 'Urt several people, wounding 'em. One almost died." Captain Jumbo glanced at Cleo. "Anders put 'im in prison. But 'e escaped. And aye, if 'e's 'ere on the island, then there's no doubt 'e's back for the three Stones of Destiny. It's been so long since 'es been seen, and sailin' with pirates changes a person, it'll be 'ard to find 'im."

Captain Jumbo paused as he looked at Cleo again, his hands relaxing on the steering wheel. "Ye're looking a bit queasy, young lady." He reached into a small tin can on the dashboard and handed her a set of elastic bracelets.

Cleo stared at the accessories in her hands.

The captain quickly took the bracelets and placed them on her wrists. "It'll 'elp," he said, and then returned to the steering wheel.

Cleo mumbled, "Thank you," even though she had no idea how bracelets would help her nausea. She swallowed some spit. "I don't get it. Isn't the Stone of Destiny under the royal throne in England …," her words trailed off as she tried to remember.

Captain Jumbo jumped in. "Was in England. That stone is now at Castle Edinburgh. CeeCee told ye?"

Cleo shook her head and rubbed her fingers on the beads of the bracelet. "No, my mom. She works at a museum." Cleo felt a wave of sadness on top of her nausea.

Captain Jumbo nodded. "Aye there are different stones throughout the world. Some 'ave the same name and all 'ave their own story. The Stones of Destiny, 'ere on Pandia, come as a set of three. An' they're a lot smaller than ye might think. They'll fit in the palm of yer hand, so the legend says."

Another wave rocked the boat. *I'm going to throw up!* Cleo stood up and looked out the window, hoping that would help her feel better. She could see nothing but blue skies and a never-ending ocean. Not feeling any better, Cleo sat back down on her backpack and started fanning her face again.

"Aye, the legend of the three Stones of Destiny," Captain Jumbo said, staring straight ahead while adjusting the large silver wheel, sometimes a bit to the left, sometimes a bit to the right. "A legend now kept alive by the few Glimmician descendants, mostly fishermen on the high seas. Those inland, not so much. Even smarty pants Professor Agnostos with 'is 'istory lessons at Chronos Academy doesn't understand the legend." Captain Jumbo paused and then continued. "Thousands of years ago the Stones fell from the sky. A gift from the Raven God for the people 'ere."

"Like the raven god, in Norse mythology?" Cleo barely managed to ask, desperate to focus on anything but her nausea.

"Similar to. The Glimmicians 'ad their own beliefs and their own gods, like many ancient people did, Greek, Egyptian, Roman." He stopped and then added, "The ancient Glimmicians guarded these three stones, an' passed 'em down from generation to generation. These stones were powerful, being a gift from the Raven God."

Powerful?

"At some point the Stones of Destiny were lost, though the story of 'em did get passed on." He hesitated before saying, "But it could be a'right that the Stones are lost. I'll tell ye a secret. The Stones are *CURSED*."

He spoke like a storyteller, drawing her in, word by word. "Ye see, long ago, about 800 years past, the dark knight Caelen, a favourite of King Sullivan, tried to get the Stones. 'E disappeared. 'Undreds a' years later a lad named Billy, kind of a bookish fellow, was doing some lookin', and 'e disappeared. I looked for the Stones once m'self, but a lot of bad luck followed me."

He tapped a circular window of a dial on his dashboard and kept going with his story. "I was out one night searching for the Stones at Wreck Cove and not comin' upon 'em, I boarded *My Betsy* to make my way back to the marina 'ere at Glimmerton Bay. It was a fine night for navigatin'. Then suddenly the sky was as dark as any cave, with nary a star an' a vicious storm swirlin'. The seas began to get rough. Out o' nowhere, the boat jerked. So violent it was, I flew backwards 'itting m'head 'ard against the bulkhead. The waves twisted *My Betsy* sideways, rockin' and twistin' somethin' fierce. I got up and planted m'feet onto the floor to keep m'self from flying about the cabin." Captain Jumbo's eyes were large as he stared straight ahead at the ocean, firmly bracing his rubber boots on the cabin floor. "It went on for a long time. The worst storm there's ever been. Nary a stitch of shore in sight. No signals on m' dashboard an' the radio weren't workin' either. I was lost at sea. Gone. My search for the Stones 'ad beckoned the worst o' luck. I could've disappeared. Like Billy and the dark knight. I didn't need any more signs than that to see that the Stones were cursed."

Captain Jumbo paused, for a moment he put both his hands around the medallion hanging from the dash. "But I 'ad the ravens to guide me back to shore."

"Ravens?" Cleo asked. Her nausea was surprisingly almost gone.

"Aye, the ravens," he said, steering the boat again. "In that terrible storm, when the lightning flashed, I saw a raven land just 'ere." Captain Jumbo pointed to the metal rail on the bow of the boat. "The bird looked right at me an' cawed as if telling me to follow. It caught a gust of wind an' 'e fought 'is way into it. I steered the ship through the storm, followin' that raven by the flashes of lightning. When *My Betsy* an' I made it safely to shore, I vowed I'd never again look for the Stones of Destiny."

"Jolly ho! We're already at the pub!" A loud voice boomed on the radio, tossing Cleo out of the magical reverie of Captain Jumbo's storytelling. Captain Jumbo pushed a button on the radio mic and spoke, " 'Ubert! I'm just takin' a delivery to Castle Bay. While I'm 'ere I'll fetch Maggie. Save us a pint. Over an' out." As he replaced the mic, he pointed. "Aye! There's the castle now!"

Cleo looked out the window of the cabin and saw the enormous Castle Chronos looming on the cliff above them. It was beautiful and majestic, a castle steeped in history for a millennium.

As Captain Jumbo expertly manoeuvered *My Betsy*, the boat bumped gently to rest against the dock. He grabbed the raven medallion in his large hand and closed his fingers around it. He shut his eyes, tipping his head forward for a brief moment. Then he tapped on the cabin door three times before opening it, crossed the slippery deck smoothly, and adeptly tied the boat to the dock.

Cleo slid off the anti-nausea bracelets and put them on the dash. She grabbed the newspaper, put on her backpack, and tried not to slip as she crossed the deck of the boat. "Thanks, Captain Jumbo," she said, stepping onto the dock.

"Let me tell ye Ms. Cleo, this world is a magical an' mysterious place. Don't forget it." The boat captain winked.

Now on solid ground and thankfully feeling well again, Cleo hurried past the gleaming white tall lighthouse on the shore. *Let the adventure begin.*

10
Luke

Streaks of fading sunlight emanated from the few stained glass windows adorning Knight Hall. The muted light danced on Luke's closed eyelids, and slowly he came to. When he opened his eyes, he found himself lying on the ground, the back of his head throbbing. He rubbed the ache away gently as he sat up. The creepy white footed bird that had chased him was nowhere to be seen.

Now that Luke had calmed down, he looked around. In each corner of the massive hall stood a knight on display. The one standing over him was brushed silver steel, twice Luke's height, and looked like a giant guard on duty. He hadn't seen any armour in real life before, but he recognized all the pieces from *Knights of Darkness*. The pauldrons on the shoulders reminded him of huge football shoulder padding. The closed helmet with only a slit for eyes, gave the armour a grave and intimidating presence, as though a true knight lived inside. The large gauntlet glove held an axe in the air as though the Knight had stopped halfway through the swinging arc. In the other corners of the hall the sets of armour held swords by their sides.

An ear-piercing screech from the castle entrance suddenly permeated the quiet. Luke turned his head to see the huge door open a crack. A narrow beam of sunshine streaked onto the floor and then grew wider as the doorway swung fully open. Rubbing the back of his head again, Luke blinked at the sun beam and noticed the outline of a girl standing in the doorway. Suddenly he spotted the creepy white-footed black bird swooping down from the ceiling in Knight Hall "CAAAAW. CAW!" Luke felt the wind from the bird's huge flapping wings as it dove towards the open door. He shouted, "LOOK OUT!" and flopped to the floor, covering his head.

Luke strained to detect a sound or a movement, wondering if the bird had mauled the girl to death. But one moment later the girl was walking towards him. "That was a big raven!" she said with an English accent as she adjusted her ball cap.

Luke took a long blink. *A raven? Why was it in the castle? Creepy.*

Sunshine from the door accentuated the top of the girl's head with a halo of yellow. Several strands of curly brown hair sprang out from under her cap. As she came closer, Luke could see the I HEART SCIENCE logo on her hat. She unloaded the backpack she was carrying. It was a puke-green colour and covered in badges. She squinted her large hazel eyes at Luke.

"What're you doing on the floor?" the girl asked, placing her hand on her hip, surveying him.

Trying to sound calm and collected, Luke replied, "Just checking out this knight from a different angle."

The girl laughed. "That's funny! The way you're on the

floor, it looks just like the knight is about to attack you with his axe!" She extended a hand to help him up. "I'm Cleo."

Shaking his head, he got himself up unaided. "Luke."

Shrugging her shoulders, Cleo moved further into the castle and spun in a circle, her arms extended. "I can't believe I'm finally here. I made it! Wow! Look at this place. Four knights in shining armour. Wow!"

"The door was locked or stuck or something. How did you get it open?" Luke asked. The bump on the back of his head hurt.

"Locked? I don't think so." Cleo pointed to the door. "There's an OPEN button. I just pushed it." She approached the door frame and pointed to the button on the right wall.

A button? A BUTTON?! How could I have missed that? If his face got any redder, his hair would catch on fire. He hadn't been able to make his phone call, had worked himself into a frenzy, and had to be rescued by a girl. A *girl?!*

"I guess even ancient castles get updated from time to time," Cleo smiled. "This place is so cool! Where is everyone?" Cleo asked, twisting her body to look around.

"Amphitheatre. Chronos Day Celebration."

"Right! It was in the brochure." She smirked as she set the beat-up puke green backpack at the knight's feet. "I'm just going to leave my backpack here. He'll protect it. Let's go."

Luke looked at his watch. *Ugh. Mom's flight will be in the air by now.* He would have to try later. Luke exited Knight Hall through the castle door.

Cleo followed him asking, "Do you know where the amphitheatre is?" Her hand hovered over the OPEN button as she glanced at Luke. Then she pushed the CLOSE button just below it, a bit more dramatically than necessary.

Luke felt as small as a bacteria on a flea on a mouse. He took a puff of his inhaler and a breath of fresh air, then ran down the front steps to Copernicus Court, the main courtyard.

They passed a giant raven statue in the courtyard, and multiple stone buildings. Together they made their way through the campus, which was as big as a small village. The landscape of the grounds changed from pebbled pathways and manicured green grass to machair grassland covered with wild plants. Tall grasses extended around the campus for a great distance.

The great stone curtain wall outlined the periphery of the school grounds as they made their way downhill. From *Knights of Darkness*, Luke knew that curtain walls were defensive walls used in medieval times. Adio had explained this morning that the stone curtain now protected students from ending up on the rocky cliffs plunging into the pounding sea far below. As they made their way inland, they passed all sorts of sporting courts on the flat areas of the open grounds.

Further away from the manicured grounds of the campus, small wooded areas divided the green slopes that rolled like waves across the landscape. In the distance loomed a massive forest that stretched as far as they could see.

They passed several large black boxes placed intermittently on the grounds, with antennas and red and green glowing lights. A large sign in front of each read

MINI K-INDEX MAGNETOMETER

DO NOT TOUCH

PROPERTY OF CHRONOS ACADEMY

"Magnetometer?" Cleo asked, and then answered her own question, "Pandia has high electromagnetic activity. That's probably what those boxes are for. To measure that or something."

At the bottom of a hill, they came to a fork in the dirt path. There were two well-worn paths of flattened grass on either side of a wooden T-shaped signpost. The tall grass near the post tickled Luke's legs, making him scratch his ankles.

"Pathways named after scientists. So cool! Did you know we know the structure of DNA because of her? Franklin, I mean." Cleo pointed at the gold cursive writing on the wooden sign, "She was a scientist." Cleo plucked a hair tie from her wrist, put her hair in a ponytail, and fed it through the hole in the back of her cap.

Luke suddenly remembered the last words Adio had shouted to him when Luke left the castle tour to look for his watch. "We need to take Franklin Lane."

Luke jogged to get ahead of Cleo, but she kept up and chatted the whole time, telling him more about Franklin. *Why won't everyone just leave me alone?*

"Oh, that must be the famous Eldritch Pitch." Cleo pointed to the stadium in the distance. The stands looked like they could seat at least a thousand.

As they headed east, the path snaked between large hills. It wasn't long before they came up to another fork and Luke stopped to catch his breath. Walking into the sun, they rounded a bend. A short pathway appeared, lined with low shrubs on either side. Luke could hear cheering and clapping. Nestled into the valley ahead was the semicircular amphitheatre which was constructed from large slabs of white-grey rock.

"Wow, there it is!" Cleo said with renewed excitement. She sprinted past him and suddenly fell face first. Before Luke could move to help her, she was wiping the blood from her shin with the sleeves of her shirt and saying, "A new beginning and a new adventure!" She got up and continued running down the hill. "Come on!" she yelled behind her.

I only have to get through this assembly, figure out that crazy phone, and then I'll be going home.

Not wanting to give Cleo the satisfaction of rescuing him from the castle and beating him to the amphitheatre, Luke took off running after her.

11

Cleo

As Cleo and Luke descended from the hillside, they hopped between the trees lining the amphitheatre. Cleo motioned for them to move further down the rows and sit closer to the stage, but Luke adamantly shook his head and chose instead the row closest to the trees from which they'd just emerged. Luke's general *laissez faire* attitude and lack of interest irked Cleo. She wanted to take it all in and sit in the front row. Reluctantly, she motioned to the students sitting at the end of the row closest to them to scoot over. They gave her a passing glance of annoyance and shimmied over to make room for the two of them.

The ash tree next to them had a wide bifurcated trunk. Its green canopy extended downwards and brought with it a lovely shade. Cleo sat down on the thick white-grey stone slab with her eyes fixated on the semicircular stage below.

Director LeCrucia was at the podium. Cleo knew all about her from the academy brochure. LeCrucia was the director and chief scientist of the school and in charge of academic programming. A tall slim woman, her black hair in a tight bun on the top of her head, wore a harsh black suit. She spoke with authority, her words crisp and clear. She took her time as she addressed the audience.

"… turning of the hour glass we will start counting down the days to the Pandia Games, which will take place next spring!" The director waited for the audience to stop cheering. "Thank you, Governor Grossvenor. It's an honour to have you here today. As our elected official in southern Pandia, we look forward to welcoming you to campus more frequently." She paused for the listeners to clap in agreement before adding, "After Governor Grossvenor turns the hourglass, we will relocate it to Viking Hall where it will be a wonderful addition to our school."

"Who's that?" Luke asked loudly next to her.

"Keep your voice down," Cleo said in a whisper as she glanced towards the stage. Students in the rows around them turned back to look at her and Luke. A Black boy wearing blue-rimmed glasses a few rows down also turned back annoyed but then changed his demeanor and smiled, waving at Luke. The two boys next to him turned and waved as well. One of them was pear-shaped, wore a wide-brimmed sun hat, and had gobs of sunscreen on his nose. Cleo noticed Director LeCrucia glaring in her direction. *I hope she can't see us.* Cleo waited a beat and luckily LeCrucia returned to her speech.

Cleo spoke low as she leaned closer to Luke so only he could hear.

"This amphitheatre has natural acoustics. Everyone can hear everything. Can't you tell? No one on stage has microphones." The chirping crickets from the nearby trees were a welcome low background hum that helped drown out her whispering.

Cleo quickly took off her cap and adjusted the hair tie around her curls, and tucked them into her hat again. Still whispering to Luke she said, "And that's the governor of southern Pandia. Director LeCrucia just said that." Glancing down, she noticed a few ants making their way towards the toe of her orange sneaker. Cleo raised her feet to let the ants pass.

On stage, the governor of southern Pandia had moved toward a giant hourglass more than twice his height and filled with blue sand. He was taller than Director LeCrucia, and had short dark curly hair slicked to his head. With the stage radiating in sunshine, Cleo couldn't help but wonder if the governor was hot in his black suit. The governor pulled a rope to turn the hourglass. The blue sand began flowing downward as he adjusted his long white scarf.

"Not him. I know who he is. I'm from Pandia," Luke said curtly. "I mean *that* guy. The one with the moustache wearing that ugly orange and purple"—Luke searched for the words—"costume dress."

Cleo followed the end of Luke's finger. At the corner of the stage was a tall lanky man wearing a yeoman garb. "That's the school's raven master," Cleo said simply.

She had seen similar garb worn by the raven master at the Tower of London. But that outfit had been red and blue, not orange and purple, and the London raven master certainly had looked regal in it. The Chronos Academy raven master's lanky frame was swimming in the ample material of the oversized coat. His pants were too voluminous but also too short, showing a great portion of his orange socks. His head was topped with a ridiculous large purple top hat with the same orange and purple striping as the coat and knickers.

Shoulder-length wavy brown hair stuck out below the hat. Thin moustache twitching, the raven master tugged on his neck collar. Cleo figured he was probably quite hot under all that material. Next to the raven master, the row of teachers sitting on stage was dressed in more suitable summer wear, and the coolest of all was a cheerful man with warm ebony skin, wearing shorts and a tie-dye T-shirt. He tucked a loose loc into his a low ponytail.

"Raven master? Why is there a raven master?" Luke turned his face toward her. She noticed he was slightly ashen.

I can't believe how much he doesn't know about Chronos Academy. "There are ravens living here at Chronos Academy. The raven master looks after them and trains them," Cleo told Luke.

Director LeCrucia was moving away from the podium, the students clapping politely.

I missed something because Luke keeps interrupting!

The crowd switched into an ebullient chant of "Coach Ty-phoon! Coach Ty-phoon!"

The coach, decked out in a head to toe neon orange track suit, approached the front of the stage punching the air triumphantly. "GO VIKES!" The coach shouted. "Okay, okay. Settle down now. As the governor and director have said, we're hosting the Pandia Games next spring. Star players and coaches from schools all over Pandia will come to compete. The main event of course is the RAF triathlon, which is, R for running!"

The crowd cheered.

"A for Archery!"

The crowd cheered again.

"And F for fencing!"

The crowd cheered once more. Coach Typhoon's cheeks puffed and sagged like the jowls of a slightly ageing chipmunk as he smiled.

"Although it has been many years since we've won a medal in the RAF--"

"BOOOO!" yelled the students.

"This year will be different! I am shaking things up!" shouted Coach Typhoon. "The Chronos Viking team will be a force to reckon with. I promise you that! This will be the year of GRIT and GUTS! The Chronos Vikings will ride the wave of victory this year to be champions in every sport in the games! GRIT and GUTS!"

Director LeCrucia returned to the podium. "Thank you—"

"GRIT and GUTS!"

"Thank—"

"GRIT and GUTS!"

As the teacher in the tie-dye T-shirt led Coach Typhoon to the side of the stage, Director LeCrucia added through clenched teeth, "Thank you, Coach Typhoon. The five-day long Pandia Games will begin June 1st. Final exams will follow the games."

"QUACK, QUACK."

Cleo squinted her eyes and arched her head forward, surveying the stage for the source of the strange sound. When she heard the quacking again, she noticed Director LeCrucia bend down to pet a tiny white dog at her feet. The strange sound stopped. The director let a little smile cross her severe face as she looked fondly down at the small puffy cotton ball with legs. She stood up and resumed her poker straight posture. "Introductions are necessary. For all the new students, my dog is called Ducky, for obvious reasons."

The students couldn't help but laugh as the dog started to quack again, a loud piercing sound that was so un-dog-like. Next to Cleo, Luke plugged his ears.

When the dog had ceased his shrill quacking, Director LeCrucia continued, "I want to remind all students that cell phones are not allowed."

Some students groaned.

"Due to local geological anomalies, the earth's magnetic field in this area is stronger than is typically found in other places on earth. This allows us to enjoy frequent displays of the aurora lights. But it can interfere with radio frequency signal transmissions, which the internet, and cellular networks rely upon. Coverage here is poor at best. To demonstrate, Adio and Professor Gregor have prepared a short skit."

The teacher with the tie-dyed t-shirt and the owly looking professor joined Director LeCrucia on stage. The staff member in the tie dyed t-shirt put his hand to his ear mimicking holding a cell phone, and asked, "Professor Gregor, can you hear me now?"

"No, Adio. I cannot hear you," the owly professor said flatly, also pretending to hold a mobile phone to his ear, "There's no cellular network coverage in this area." Adio shrugged and Professor Gregor forced a grimace on his face to resemble a smile while waiting for a small number of students to stop laughing. They left the stage with a quick bow, and the director continued, "We also experience occasional weather-related blackouts."

"Blackouts? Better be during exams," murmured a spectacled boy in front of Cleo. His seatmates snorted and assented.

Cleo was horrified. CeeCee never mentioned any blackouts and they certainly weren't mentioned in the brochure! *What if a blackout happens when I'm studying, or, or, or worse, what if it happens when I'm in the bathroom?!*

"You'll be given instructions later for what to do in the case of blackouts."

Whew.

"On a related note," continued Director LeCrucia, "Placed around the castle grounds and beyond are black computer boxes. We use these tools to monitor local magnetic field strength and disturbances. Please leave these sensitive measuring devices undisturbed.

"Your learning this year will be highly varied, and if you are a first-year, you will find it intense and very different from what you are used to. We have many resources available to supplement your learning, both digital and book based."

A huge smile split Cleo's face, and she quickly forgot about the risk of blackouts.

"That brings us to my very last announcement. At Chronos Academy we remain connected to and honour the ancient local Glimmician folklore. Ravens have always been an important symbol for the Glimmician people, who are from this area of Pandia. A long time ago, the Glimmician people honored Chronos Castle with a gift of ravens and a raven statue to protect the castle. It is the job of the raven master to ensure that these majestic creatures continue to be well cared for at the academy.

"Our raven master Mr. Ludwig Corax is currently on sabbatical to study ravens in the wild, but I am pleased to introduce our new substitute raven master, Mr. Ringwald. He will begin the raven demonstration by reminding us of the raven legend."

Mr. Ringwald stepped from the sidelines and mopped the sweat from his brow with the puffy sleeve of his shirt. He tapped on the archway next to him three times, popped open the door of a wire bird carrier cage, and entered the semicircular stage at the base of the amphitheatre. Director LeCrucia's critical eyes focused on him with laser precision. The raven master took a slight bow to the audience, donned long leather gloves, then turned dramatically towards the bird in the carrier cage he'd placed on stage.

"Mr. Ringwald. The legend?" the director prompted.

The raven master looked at her but said nothing as the sweat dripped down his brow.

Director LeCrucia gritted her teeth. "I will assist you, as I'm sure you're just having a bit of stage fright. The Glimmicians gave the gift of the ravens to protect Chronos Academy and they said, 'If the ravens should leave, the castle will fall.'"

Eyes wide, the raven master nodded, silently acknowledging what he had heard.

Mr. Ringwald held out his arm, looked at the open cage, and said, "Hop!"

"What's happening?" Cleo heard a student from somewhere in the audience ask.

The raven master pulled out a plastic box from the pocket of his voluminous pants. He held out his hand. Cleo couldn't make out what he was holding but he looked like he was gagging. She heard a boy next to Luke say it was probably a blood-soaked cracker. Cleo suddenly felt like gagging, too.

When the bird refused to respond, Mr. Ringwald approached the transport carrier and tapped the raven treat three times on the open cage door.

The bird exited the carrier but ignored Mr. Ringwald and his cracker. Instead, it took flight, landing on Director LeCrucia's shoulder.

The crowd became silent.

Cleo could almost hear a pin drop. But there wasn't a pin, just the light tinkling sound of a tambourine among the chirping background chorus of crickets. When the raven twitched its head, searching for the sound, Cleo got a very uneasy feeling.

The bird suddenly flew from LeCrucia's shoulder to the armrest of a chair occupied by a female professor wearing a white sundress. The professor jerked in surprise but stayed seated. The owly looking professor sitting next to her rose stiffly from his chair and backed away from the bird towards the side of the stage. He made a thin offer of assistance. "Professor Torres, let me know if you need any help. I'll be over here."

A few students chuckled, and Cleo smiled. Next to her Luke had become completely immobile.

Slim and petite, sporting a dark pixie haircut, Professor Torres looked at LeCrucia, then the raven master, and finally at the raven.

She took one of her silver bracelet hoops off her wrist and held it out for the bird to safely investigate it with its beak. As the raven did so, it bit the bracelet and her finger at the same time. The professor gasped and gently scolded the raven, "No, Munnin!" She tucked the bracelet into her pocket, rubbing her finger.

Head downcast, the raven hopped off the chair and back into her carrier. Cleo noticed Director LeCrucia staring at the raven master, her foot tapping slightly on the stage. The sound of the tap-tap-tap was crystal clear to the amphitheatre audience. The raven master glanced around.

The inky-black raven flew out of the carrier again and landed on the armrest of a Black professor who had a crazy shock of white hair framing his rich brown complexion. The raven played up to the crowd, releasing a high-pitched throaty gargle with her beak open. The bird's head tipped back and then bent forward as though giving a pronounced nod. The professor gave a rambunctious laugh and said loudly, "Professor Morlia, Horology."

The bird flapped to the armrest of the next chair over and said, "NEXT!"

That professor announced his name, "Professor Agnostos, History," and Munnin continued to the next chair.

"Is that bird talking?!" Luke asked in a pinched voice. He'd drawn his legs up to his chest.

"The raven? I think so." Cleo nodded her head. She'd read that ravens were very intelligent creatures, so she wouldn't be surprised if ravens were like parrots and could mimic human sounds. The raven hopped from armrest to armrest calling "NEXT!" and introduced the entire staff of Chronos Academy. Cleo couldn't help but laugh and clap along with the rest of the student body. Next to her Luke remained silent. He certainly didn't clap.

What's wrong with him? That was amazing!

After a big round of applause, Director LeCrucia said, "Thank you Mr. Ringwald, and thank you Munnin." The talented raven fluttered to the centre of the stage and, to the delight of the audience, spread her wings wide, fanning the tip feathers, and curtsied. Cleo couldn't believe it!

Munnin hopped off stage and into the transport carrier to eat the blood-soaked cracker Mr. Ringwald had thrown in there. The raven master was smiling ear to ear and waving at the crowd with his leather-gloved hands.

Director LeCrucia squinted her eyes at him sharply and mouthed some words Cleo couldn't make out.

"Look!" A student's shout interrupted Cleo's focus. With feathers extended like fingertips at the end of its wings, a raven soared following the arc of the amphitheatre and greeted the crowd. When it flew directly over her, she noticed it had one white foot. She could almost touch it. Luke yelped and ducked down by Cleo's feet, covering his head with his arms.

The raven master yelled out, "Floki!" and extended his arm out to the side, ready to receive the raven with the white foot. Floki flapped towards Mr. Ringwald, extended its legs to land, then suddenly changed course. After gaining altitude, the raven dove sharply towards the fluffy ball of fur at the feet of Director LeCrucia. It grabbed the dog!

With Ducky in its talons, the white-footed raven flapped vigorously to get away. The dog was beside itself and quacked and quacked his little barking sound.

"Ducky! DUCKY!" Director LeCrucia shrieked.

Luke, with his arms still covering his head, asked, "Is it coming for me?"

"No, it took the dog!" Cleo exclaimed.

In the middle of the stage, Mr. Ringwald stood completely shell shocked in his puffy shift and knicker pants, his leather-gloved arm still extended and waiting for Floki. Suddenly a second raven swooped over the crowd. Munnin. Clearly the raven master had forgotten to close the door of the transport carrier. Surprisingly, the students remained seated although their comments were loud and animated.

Cleo noticed a boy was standing on his stone slab seat. He shook off his large brim sun hat, and stretched a device in his hands as he aimed towards the sky.

"What is that boy doing?" Cleo asked, more to herself than anyone else. Luke opened his eyes and cautiously moved into his seat, "That's Ronan, and he has a slingshot!"

What?!

Mr. Ringwald screamed, "Nooooooo! Not the bird!" right before the tiny stone from the slingshot struck the flying corvid with precision.

"CAW!" Floki shrieked, and released the dog.

Cleo's eyes watched in horror as the fluffy dog hurtled towards earth.

Adio was running across the stage with his arms out, trying to line up with the trajectory of the falling dog. But the raven master ran faster. He held his arms up to the sky, shoved Adio out of the way, and just in the nick of time caught the dog.

Mr. Ringwald swept his left arm back, theatrically holding the fluffy dog up in his right hand while facing the audience. He bowed deeply when returning the prized Pomeranian to Director LeCrucia. The dog stopped barking and licked LeCrucia's face.

Relieved, Cleo jumped up and clapped. All the students cheered! Floki appeared unharmed as he landed on the stage and joined Munnin in the carrier cage for a snack. Director LeCrucia walked past Adio who was dusting off his shorts. She leaned in closely to Mr. Ringwald's ear for a few moments whispering something. She then turned to the audience. "Proceed back to the castle for the remaining festivities. DISMISSED!"

This school is so great! Cleo couldn't wait to see what came next!

12

Luke

It was already the end of September and Luke was still at Chronos Academy. The skies were grey, and it rained more often. Luke missed the warmer drier climate of his home town, Wicker.

Even though he had contacted his mom after the first, second, and third week to come get him, she'd insisted that he give it more time. Luke had tried every argument. In his opinion he had presented a solid case, a great one in fact: scary bird attacks, animals getting shot out of the sky, overly chatty kids, very hard to operate doors and phones. And that was just the beginning. He added a multitude of other concerns and complaints. The castle was gloomy and dreary. His roommates annoyed him, they snored—mostly Ronan and Ollie—and his room was tiny. Chef François' food menu was hit and miss. The pasta was good, but there was too much fish on the menu. Not to mention the entrees of different palettes, textures, and tastes that were so strange Luke couldn't identify the ingredients. Sure, no one had died from it, but still.

Plus, his classes were so different from his old school. They were much more hands-on, and super tough, with a ton of homework most days. There was no homework from gym class of course. But Coach Typhoon's strange workout regimes were exhausting and excruciating so even gym was not much of a reprieve. To confirm his assertion, Luke moved his arms in a circular motion, his biceps and shoulders aching. Worst of all—and he hadn't told his mom this—was that none of it had stopped the recurring dreams he had about camping with his dad. According to his mom, this place was supposed to help Luke feel better. But it was only making him feel worse.

Like a ghost, Luke moved from class to class, absorbing little of the lessons and barely interacting with anyone. When he was able to dodge Ollie, he spent his free time in the library looking for information about his dad. He scoured the newspapers, of which the library had a surprisingly small selection. But there were plenty of past issues of the local magazine-size newspaper, the *Glimmerton Gazette*. Unfortunately it was light on world news.

Leaving the library now, Luke made his way quickly down the stairs. He avoided Ollie who was with a group of students and entered the corridor on the second floor. He hastily rounded the corner heading for horology class when he collided with something half his size.

Rubbing his abdomen, Luke saw a pair of large wheels spinning in mid-air. A monotone robotic voice yelled, "UP!" Luke reached over and pulled the surprisingly heavy robot into a standing position.

The robot was constructed with two solid stacked cubes. On the upper cube, its large dark eyes blinked at Luke.

On the lower cube, red and blue lights flashed across the midsection. The lights reminded Luke of a police car. Above the red and blue flashing lights was a tablet. The robot's name scrolled through the display.

So this is Sir Lancelot. Luke vaguely recalled his roommates discussing a robot the sixth years were working on in their programming course.

"Ow!" the robot complained. The robot's mouth was a drawn red line and Luke couldn't help but wonder where the speakers were. Its head vibrated as it ran some sort of self-check. Sir Lancelot then belted in a monotone voice, "Knock knock."

Ugh. They've set him up to tell knock knock jokes.

The robot rolled back and forth, and side to side. Luke ignored the robot's words and tried to go around, but Sir Lancelot blocked Luke's every move.

Adding this pesky robot to his list of reasons for leaving the school, Luke breathed out in exasperation. "Who's there?"

"Icy."

"Icy who?" Luke said quickly, glancing down the corridor towards the horology classroom doors.

"Icy you looking at me!" Sir Lancelot then announced, "Ducky is bad." Luke could see the same words in blue scrolling right to left across the tablet. The little robot vibrated on the spot, simulating laughing. As it did, Luke bolted around the robot and ran the rest of the way down the corridor.

He swooped into a desk in his horology class. Feeling out of breath and a bit heavy in the chest, he took a puff of his inhaler before pulling the latest *Gazette* from his backpack.

Luke turned to the section headed

A Trip Through Time

He quickly scanned the section's two articles to see if there was anything about his dad's expedition last year. One was titled,

The life of the wanted criminal Richard Recleren

Luke read several sentences:

Captain Jumbo insists Recleren has returned to Pandia. Detective Anders is adamant that isn't so. Who is Richard Recleren and does he still pose a threat? After escaping from the Glimmerton jail, he is rumoured to have joined pirates …

Uninterested, Luke quickly moved on to the next article,

The history of Raven Tower and the ravens in Chronos Academy

Ravens! The bane of his existence. Along with Ducky, Director LeCrucia's tiny quacky dog, and now Sir Lancelot, the pointless roaming robot, ravens were actually part of the school family. With their own home! The Raven Tower was on campus and provided the ravens with plenty of opportunity to torture students.

Frustrated, Luke shoved the newspaper back into his backpack as the other students started pouring into the classroom.

Ollie entered the classroom and sat in the empty desk next to Luke. "I called you when you passed me but I guess you didn't hear me."

Luke didn't say anything and instead turned his attention to the walls in Professor Morlia's class, which were covered with posters and facts.

"Hey Ronan, 'How can you tell when your watch is hungry?'" Andy read from one of the posters as he plopped into his desk behind Ollie.

"I don't know" Ronan played along, heading to his desk at the other end of the row.

"It goes back *four* seconds." Andy snorted at the joke.

Luke turned his attention to another poster, ignoring them,

Wristwatch with listed components.
Can you find them all?

Tugging on his sleeve to expose his own timepiece, Luke ran his finger over the face and brought his wrist closer to his ear to hear the ticking.

His eyes turned to Professor Morlia staggering into the room, his arms full of computers, with cords and a small black magnetometer box dragging behind him. "Sorry I'm late. Just give me two seconds, just coming back from doing a bit of field work," he said. He grinned and shoved aside the papers on his desk and placed his computers down. Needing

69

still more space, he stacked his books: *Watches International, The Longcase Clock*, and several magazines labeled on the spine *Complete Price Guide to Watches Volumes 1–10*. All the while he kept mumbling, "Higher Kp values."

"Professor Morlia, it's not fair that I can't sit next to Andy," Ronan complained from the far end of Luke's row.

"Yah, not fair!" Andy quipped as he drummed his pencils on his desk behind Ollie. "Ollie gets to sit by Luke, like, all the time, and I can't sit with Ronan!"

Professor Morlia said, "Mmm-hmm," as he pulled black drop cloths from his desk drawer.

Andy started tapping on Ollie's head with his pencils while making cymbal sounds with his mouth.

Ronan howled in delight, his black hair streaked with yellow flopping about. With his hair and his shorter, pear-shaped frame, he looked like a rockhopper penguin. Sometimes, he even walked like one.

Ollie turned and yelled at Andy, "STOP IT!"

"No problem." Andy blew his red hair out of his face and scratched his freckled nose with his scrawny arm. Unfazed, he reached over to Nia, who was sitting next to Ollie. Her long black hair fell down her back. Andy started tapping on her head. In one swift move Nia turned around, grabbed his pencils, and snapped them in half. Ollie smiled smugly.

Professor Morlia was taking his sweet time to start class as he placed black drop cloths over the clocks that were displayed around the classroom. The sounds of the clocks throughout the room seemed to invite Luke to rest his tired head. The constant tick-*tick*, tick-*tick*…Luke felt his eyelids droop.

Luke startled from a smack on his head and looked up.

Andy was standing in front of him and staring. "Luke, hello? Here's your assignment!" Andy handed him his papers and added, "You're welcome by the way." Luke ran his hands over his face realizing he'd dozed off. A few students snickered.

"Father Time, are we going to start at any point here?" Andy asked Professor Morlia as he finished distributing papers around the room. Several students giggled.

Luke didn't think the professor was *that* old. Professor Morlia was a short slim man, and although he had crazy Einstein-style white hair, his deep brown skin had no wrinkles, except around the eyes.

Professor Morlia looked up and smiled. "I'm done. I'll ask everyone to bring any personal time pieces to the front." He held up a silver bucket, decorated with the comic character Knight Shade THE BRUTE from *Knights of Darkness*, "You'll get them back at the end of class." Only two kids put watches in the bucket. Luke went up to the desk but couldn't bring himself to remove the watch from his wrist.

He squirmed.

"Come on, Luke. Just add your watch so we can get on with this exercise," Morlia said, shaking the silver bucket while looking at the lesson plan on his desk.

"No," Luke said in a defensive voice that made the professor look up.

Professor Morlia was about to speak but stopped when he saw Luke's watch. His black eyes, framed by thick black-rimmed glasses, focused on Luke in a way that Luke found puzzling. "I'll make an exception this *one time*. But please cover your watch with your sleeve." Professor Morlia then asked the class to get into groups and collect the materials for the exercise from a large plastic bin.

Making his way to the whiteboard, Professor Morlia asked, "What is horology?" He paused for effect and continued, "Many of you, based on last week's assignment, are still not certain. And no, it is not the study of horror."

"I thought my scary story was awesome." Ronan slumped in his chair.

Professor Morlia just grinned. "It was creative, but not what I was looking for. Horology is the science of measuring time, as I mentioned during your first class, and several times after that." He then walked to the side of the room, where the wall was draped with black drop cloths. Luke could still hear the ticking from the many clocks hanging on the wall behind the drapes.

"How can we tell time?" the professor asked. "Today, we take it for granted. Anywhere we look or wherever we are, we know the time. But way back when, people had no idea. So, how can we tell time without a clock?"

Everyone turned to the wall that was covered with black sheets. Ronan, sitting at the end of the aisle, reached over to lift the corner of one sheet and fell out of his desk. Nia snorted and Andy laughed. Then Andy's stomach growled so loudly that Ollie turned around.

"What? I'm hungry," Andy commented loudly.

"Excellent!" replied the professor. "Well done, Andy. Our bodies have a clock. We don't need to see a clock to tell us it's time to eat."

"So I'm a clock?" Andy asked sarcastically.

"In a way," the professor said.

"You sure are," Ronan commented to Andy. "A cuckoo clock!" Ronan laughed at his own joke.

Even Professor Morlia cracked a smile before he continued,

"How else can we tell time?"

"WILL ABDUL PLEASE RETURN TO CODING CLASS?" boomed the PA system suddenly.

"Okay, one more time. How else can we tell time?" The professor refocused the discussion.

"Shadows," a girl shouted from the back of the classroom.

"Right! The ancient Egyptians had the obelisk to tell time using shadows," the professor said.

"What if it's a cloudy day?" Nia blurted out.

"Good point. That brings me to this." Professor Morlia quickly walked into a side closet and disappeared inside. He emerged a few moments later, wheeling a cart that carried a long clay vase. "This is a replica of a clepsydra. Does anyone happen to know what that means? The word is Greek."

Cleo was reaching her hand so high in the air Luke thought her arm would pop out of its socket. When Professor Morlia called on her, she sat rigid straight as she answered, "It means stealing water. I saw one in one of my mother's exhibitions. She's a curator of ancient artifacts at the Brillianton musem."

"Cleo's correct! The ancient Greeks used something like this to tell time." Professor Morlia pointed to the horizontal etches in the vase and zeroed in on one line. "The more water in the vase, the later in the day it was."

The goal of the lab was to make a clepsydra, and they worked at it until the bell rang.

As Luke quickly packed up his things, he heard Professor Morlia's voice amongst the chattering students and shuffling of desks, papers, and books. "Luke, please hang back for a moment."

13

Luke

"Want me to wait?" Ollie asked as he repacked his backpack, trying to fit in a contraption made from several toilet paper rolls.

"No," Luke said. He saw Cleo approach Professor Morlia's desk,

"I have it here." Professor Morlia was handing a thick book to Cleo. "It's one of the best introductory books to the study of time. Enjoy."

"I will." Cleo waved goodbye to Luke as she left.

He never waved back. Cleo had blabbered about Luke's first day being stuck in the castle. Since then, Andy razzed Luke every chance he could with impromptu lessons on opening doors, like he was doing now. The last to leave, he caught Luke's eye and opened and closed the door to the class several times. "That's how it's done, Luke." Andy barked out a laugh and left. The joke was getting old, and only supported Luke's conviction to return home. He couldn't stand any of his classmates, or roommates, for that matter.

Luke checked out one of the posters on the wall.

Why did the boy throw the clock
out the window?
He wanted to see time fly.

When Luke turned around, he found Professor Morlia leaning against his desk and studying him intently. Luke wiggled in his seat, anticipating the worst.

"You can relax, Luke. I'm not a knight about to strike you down." At Luke's confused expression, Professor Morlia continued, "Your shirt. It's pretty cool! I'm a *Knights of Darkness* fan myself," he said as he pointed at the Knight Shade THE BRUTE bucket on his desk.

Glancing down, Luke remembered his shirt read KNIGHTS OF DARKNESS SLAY!

"The history of knights is a fascinating subject. One of my hobbies is learning more about them. I have to keep up with Professor Agnostos, he's a real history buff." Professor Morlia chuckled while adjusting his black thick-rimmed glasses and then turned serious again as he focused on Luke.

"Did your phone call go okay? After I showed you the trick to use the rotary phone, I mean," Professor Morlia asked and smiling, quickly added, "Now I've lost track of the time. That was weeks ago, wasn't it?"

Feeling uneasy, Luke nodded as he grasped for words. "Yeah, thanks."

"Happy to help." Professor Morlia cleared his throat. "Luke, I must be frank. I've noticed you are struggling to pay attention in my class. And lately you've been nodding off." He shifted a bit on the desk. "I know I expect a lot from my students," he paused again, "but I must ask, is everything okay?"

The question caught Luke off guard. Luke dropped his gaze to the ground and stayed silent.

Professor Morlia opened his mouth to speak and Luke stood up, thinking he was dismissed. But the professor motioned for him to sit down again. "Actually, there was one other thing. Something caught me by surprise today."

Luke frowned. He glanced at the marked assignment on his desk. He hadn't done well, but surely he wasn't the only student with a less than stellar grade.

Professor Morlia adjusted his glasses again. "Do you know Antoine Benoit?"

A rush of cold swept through Luke's body, freezing him to the spot. No one had mentioned his father since Luke had arrived at the academy. He stared at the Professor, and then slowly nodded. "He's my dad."

Professor Morlia cleared his throat. "Ahh. But your last name is Alexander, not Benoit."

Luke swallowed and managed to squeak out a response. "Alexander is my mom's last name. I guess because she gave birth to me, I have her last name."

"I see." Morlia nodded and focused on Luke's watch without blinking.

"Did you know my dad?" Luke asked.

"Not exactly," the professor replied. "But I know your watch. Your dad emailed me long ago asking me about it. He sent me a photo and we exchanged a little information. That's how I recognized it. I'm surprised I didn't notice it in class before today." He continued, "Your watch, Luke, is one of a kind. I don't know if you know that. In all my years I have not seen one quite like it, partly because it is very,

very old."

"I know it's old, my dad said so," Luke said pointedly. Protectively, he touched the leather strap on his watch. He quickly asked, "How old?"

"Well, I know it doesn't have a serial number. And because it has one hand, my guess is it's from the 1600s." Luke gasped in response and Professor Morlia nodded. "Yes, it's that old! It's a silver pair case watch with a blue steel tulip-form hand and an early balance spring. You have to wind it manually." He leaned forward and moved his head closer to the watch while adjusting his glasses but didn't touch it. His cautious respectful approach reminded Luke of Ollie. "It has a glass face cover from its days as a pocket watch. But the face is transparent with Roman numerals indicating the hour and on the periphery. Well, I find it interesting. Anyhow, I guess Antoine got it to work again. He cleaned it well, removed the bits of rust. And it now has a leather strap," Professor Morlia said, more to himself as though taking mental notes.

Luke nodded. "My mom added the strap."

The professor touched his finger to his lip in thought. "Your dad told me he found the pocket watch on an expedition,"

"Really? What expedition?" Luke asked. There were so many things he'd never had a chance to talk about with his dad.

After a slight pause Professor Morlia replied, "I don't know. Your father never said."

Professor Morlia continued, "I'm familiar with your dad's work. I was a fan of his, you could say. Antoine was always trying to explain mysteries and had a very analytical scientific way of doing so. He discovered many things in his life's work as a journalist. I'm truly sorry that he didn't make it home from his last trip. This must be"—Professor Morlia paused and ran his hand through his hair, searching for the right thing to say—"an incredibly hard time for you."

Luke sat in his desk and said nothing for a few moments, hearing only the ticking of the clocks and his watch

"At some point, if you want, we could examine your watch and find out more about it." Professor Morlia stood and smiled, though his smile didn't quite reach his eyes. It reminded Luke of his mom's smile. "And if you ever want to talk, my door is always open." The professor put his hands in his bulky sweater pockets and walked back to his desk. "Oh, and one more thing. Your watch is very valuable. It is a rare treasure. Take good care of it."

One of the clocks chimed and the professor looked up at it.

"I've lost track of the hour. You might want to hurry. Professor Gregor is a stickler for punctuality!"

Luke nodded and quickly left the classroom. Professor Morlia's words weighed on his mind.

14

Cleo

Cleo had never been a fan of gym class, even at her old school. Despite Coach Typhoon's spin on the subject of physical education at Chronos Academy, Cleo truly hated these knight-themed exercises. And it was only mid-October, so she had many more months of this to go.

"Grit and guts, people! That's what it's all about. Upper body strength is essential! And there's no better place to build it than the outdoors!" Coach Typhoon bellowed from beside the outdoor rappelling wall which was beyond the courtyard and manicured grounds of the main castle.

The students were trying to stay warm in their gym clothes in the damp and chilly early morning air. They blew on their hands and sat clustered together on the three-tiered bleachers, watching and cheering on their classmates struggling up the rappelling wall. Next to her, Cleo's roommates Nia and Daisy had tea and hot chocolate respectively. Having missed out on getting a hot beverage, Cleo tucked her hands inside the main pocket of her gym strip hoodie and rubbed her hands together to stay warm.

She watched as Ronan and Andy battled it out on the rappelling wall. They were practically wrestling with each other as they climbed. Ronan was three quarters of the way up when he sent a few karate kicks Andy's way. In response, Andy grabbed Ronan's right foot and tried to pull him down. Coach Typhoon, in his bright orange jumper, was yelling, "Good, good, keep going!" After Andy and Ronan made it over the wall and down to the bottom on the other side, Coach Typhoon gave them a huge high five.

Ollie and Luke began pulling themselves up by the rope. Coach Typhoon started yelling his mantra again. "GRIT 'N GUTS, boys! GRIT 'N GUTS!"

Cleo gulped. She was next. She hadn't yet been successful in climbing the wall and she was dreading her turn. Trying to muster all the mental and physical strength she could, she set her gaze on the adjacent other sports courts then glanced at her roommates who were chatting comfortably. Nia was tall and slender, and she had long legs that seemed suited for running. She was very pretty and originally from Taiwan. Daisy was shorter than Cleo, had an adorable, chubby face, and a short nose that turned up a little at the end. Today she had a pink artificial daisy pin above her ear, woven between the strands of her red hair. Nia and Daisy had become fast friends and it seemed all so effortless for them.

Cleo hated to admit it, but deep down she was struggling. Her classes were going well, but she hadn't *really* connected with her roommates yet or made any friends. Even Luke, whom she'd met on the first day, never spoke to her.

But maybe when the new student arrives ..., Cleo thought hopefully as she re-tied her messy curls with an elastic.

Even though they were already a month and a half into

the school year, a new first-year student was supposed to arrive this week at Chronos Academy. All Cleo's classmates were talking about her.

As though reading Cleo's mind, Daisy turned to Nia. "Yesterday Lauren told me the new girl could be here today. Supposedly, a helicopter brought her to Glimmerton yesterday. She was taking part in an archaeological dig, and that's why she hasn't been at school for a month. They found something big and she got a bunch of extra credit. Lauren said her find is going to be in a famous museum in a place called Brillianton in England!"

Brillianton? That's Mom's museum!

Nia nodded. "That's really neat."

For sure this new girl met my mom. I bet Mom didn't give her *a hard time about coming to school here.* Cleo's mind wandered. *I wonder if the new girl will bunk in our room? Maybe we'll be best friends.*

Coach Typhoon's loud yelling interrupted Cleo's thoughts. "Luke! What's the problem? Are you stuck?!" Cleo couldn't hear what Luke was saying from high up on the rappelling wall, dangling over the blue safety mats below. "That's not my problem," Coach Typhoon barked. "You shouldn't wear a watch during training!"

Luke landed flat on his back close to where Ollie lay prostrate. "Oh, poop," Nia said. "Cleo, I think it's your turn." She anxiously rubbed her hands together. "Good luck!"

Grabbing the rope, the roughness rubbing against her soft hands, Cleo mounted her feet on the ready. She heard Coach Typhoon yell, "Go!"

I know I can do this! She arched her neck to look way up towards the top of the wall and then to her right. Usually,

Coach Typhoon paired up people for the climb. But Cleo was on her own for this attempt.

Moments later, Cleo was hanging on for dear life. Sweat dripped down her face. The rope cut into her palms. Her arms screamed, "I can't hold you anymore!" The ravens flying overhead cawed in agreement.

Out of the corner of her eye, Cleo spotted someone next to her. A blond-haired pony-tailed person climbed like a monkey straight up the wall and nimbly over the top. The cheers were deafening. Cleo felt her own grip weaken. WHOOSH. She dropped like a sack of potatoes. THUMP. Her back hit the mat.

Coach Typhoon shook his head at Cleo. Andy and Ronan approached the mat. Ronan lifted four fingers on his hand. "You lasted four more seconds than last time!" Andy laughed. Ronan gave the other girl a high five as she jumped around from the other side of the rappelling wall.

Cleo couldn't make out her face but could see her blond high ponytail.

The new student walked over and leaned down towards Cleo. "Your mom says hi," she said icily.

Lying perfectly still on the mat, Cleo closed her eyes. *She's here! At Chronos Academy! Unbelievable!*

As Cleo opened her eyes, Coach Typhoon introduced the new student. Stephanie! He mentioned how she had been with a team in England on an archaeological dig where they had discovered a decorated drum from 3000BC and the crowd began whooping and hollering.

Deflated, Cleo got herself up and headed straight to the bleachers, climbing the stands to rejoin Daisy who had waved her over. She saw Stephanie join Lauren and Hayden in the front row of the stands. They seemed to know each other. From behind, Stephanie and Lauren had the same hairstyle and were virtually indistinguishable. Hayden, stuck between the two girls and a full head shorter than them, was getting hit in the head by both girls' ponytails as they engaged in a vibrant conversation.

The wind had picked up and now slithered all around Cleo, nipping at her back, chilling her even more through the thick hoodie she wore over her gym shirt. Coach Typhoon shouted, "Let's move it to the next drill, folks."

Jousting. Another knight-themed training exercise that Coach Typhoon had created. Students ran at each other at maximum speed with pool noodles, trying to knock each other off balance. A low impact, minimal contact version of fencing he'd said, to train their GRIT.

Cleo moved mechanically down the bleachers, following her roommates.

"All we do is run these crazy drills," Nia said impatiently. "Coach Typhoon keeps promising to take us to the Eldritch Pitch to try fencing and archery. But we still haven't gone! How can I try out for the RAF triathlon if I don't know how to fence or use a bow?" She pulled her silky straight black hair into a low ponytail that fell halfway down her back and rubbed the palms of her hands on her eyes.

"What's that triathlon again?" Daisy asked.

"It's called the RAF triathlon. R for Running, A for archery, F for fencing—RAF. Anyhow, I guess we'll get to the Eldritch Pitch eventually. Tryouts will start in a couple of weeks," answered Nia. She stretched her legs and jumped up and down to stay warm.

Cleo let her gaze fall upon Stephanie, who was already

chatting with half a dozen kids and laughing as though she'd known them her whole life.

"Let's go say hi to Stephanie," Daisy suggested. "She seems so nice."

"And super cool," Nia added.

Cleo felt a wave of sickness flash over her. *NO! Stephanie's not cool and not nice!*

"You guys go ahead, I don't feel well. Do you know where the phone centre is? I need to call my grandma."

"I can take you after class. But the phones are really old fashioned. Um, I have no idea how to use them," Daisy said.

"I think Luke knows." Nia looked over toward Luke and chuckled. Luke and Ollie were tangled up in the pool noodles Coach Typhoon had asked them to organize for the jousting drills.

As her roommates moved through the crowd towards Stephanie, Cleo's eyes burned as she held in tears. She knew she was lucky to be at this school, but she'd never felt more alone than she did at this very moment. Cleo needed to talk to someone. She'd always planned to write to her grandma. But this was urgent. She left gym class early, telling Coach Typhoon she was sick.

As Cleo walked by herself across Copernicus Court, her thoughts spun in her mind. Her parent's separation, her mom's focus on work, all the fights she'd had with her mom, and now Stephanie.

How is this happening? How can Stephanie be at Chronos Academy AND discover this very old drum that's now in Mom's museum? This is supposed to be a great year of fun adventures, not torture.

Cleo stopped at the three-headed raven statue and

mindlessly let her eyes pass over the words on the sign.

Lost in her thoughts, she no longer noticed the cold air. Cleo carried on walking towards the end of the soaring curtain wall where it merged with the low-lying walls framing the pathway that had first brought her to the castle. Running her hand along the wall she felt the rough-cut stone against her fingertips, and took a deep breath.

As she followed the switchback down towards the shore, she could see the lighthouse in between the fleeting wisps of fog that danced along the coastline. Not too far from there, a small fishing boat was docked in Castle Bay. It was *My Betsy*.

Captain Jumbo must be bringing more fish to the academy or picking up that friend of his. Cleo then remembered being nauseous on his boat and the beads he'd placed on her wrists to help her. *He's a descendent of the ancient Glimmicians of Pandia, so maybe that's why he—*

She stopped on the path. "That's it!" she declared as determination pushed her loneliness aside.

I will have an adventure, even if it's by myself! I'm going to find the three lost Stones of Destiny!

15

Luke

Hiking in the woods with his dad, heading towards the campsite. His dad's voice, "Come on, Luke, just a bit further, you can make it! When we get there, we'll build a campfire." Seated by the fire, his dad wrapping his arm over Luke's shoulder. "I love you, son." Smelling his dad's musky aftershave—

Luke woke suddenly, just before he could tell his dad that he loved him. That horrible day came flooding back when they told his mom they weren't going to look anymore. He didn't know why the search for his dad had stopped. He only knew he wanted to try to find him. He just didn't know how. He blinked at the dull grey light coming through the window above his bunk bed. Rain pounded against the window. Confused and disoriented Luke squinted at his left wrist to see the time but saw nothing. After pressing his palms into his eyes, he looked again at his wrist.

His watch wasn't there!

Immediately, he grabbed his duvet cover and pillows,

shook them twice and dumped them over the edge of the bed. He reached under his mattress. Nothing. The bunk beds across from him were empty. Ronan and Andy were not there.

Ollie's muffled voice floated up from the bottom bunk. "Your pillow's on me."

"My watch!" Luke exclaimed. "It's gone!"

Ollie swiftly climbed out from under Luke's pillow, grabbed his glasses, and wrapped them around his head. Together, they frantically searched the room, including the other bunk beds, only to find Ronan's slingshot stashed under his pillow. Adio had returned it to Ronan a week after the incident at the amphitheatre on the condition it remained in his dormitory and would not be used in any capacity. Any rule breaking and Adio would confiscate it forever.

"Luke! There's a note!" Ollie grabbed the paper next to the old-fashioned alarm clock on the lone desk at the end of the room. Luke jumped down from Andy's top bunk.

"'*On important mission. Borrowed your watch. Andy & Ronan.*' Those kleptos took your watch!" Ollie cried in disbelief as he passed the note to Luke.

"How could they?!" Luke croaked and crumpled the paper, tossing it onto Ronan's bunk. He slumped down on Ollie's dishevelled bed, willing his heart to slow down. "I have to get it back. Did they go to Glimmerton?"

"I don't know. All I know is that you didn't want to go. So I didn't either," Ollie said, glancing at their alarm clock. "The ferry's leaving soon I think."

Panicked, Luke put on his socks and dug through the tall dresser at the end of his bunk to find his favourite cargo pants. "I have to find Ronan and Andy. Professor Morlia said my watch is really old and valuable."

"You never told me that. Friends tell each other this stuff," Ollie said, dressing at warp speed. "But no matter, best friends help."

"I don't need any help," Luke said, tugging down his green sweatshirt over his PJ top.

"I'm coming," Ollie said and grabbed his backpack.

They left the dormitory and ran down the stairs. Halfway down the corridor leading to Knight Hall, Sir Lancelot stopped them, appearing out of nowhere.

"Oh, brother," Ollie groaned, as they both tried to move quickly around the bot. But Sir Lancelot was fast, and his sirens blared painfully. Luke and Ollie covered their ears. The sirens finally stopped when they greeted the bot.

"Knock knock," Sir Lancelot droned, moving back and forth on his two large wheels, following his programmed path-blocking code that required an answer in order to pass.

"Who's there?" Luke huffed in frustration.

"Luke," Sir Lancelot replied.

"Luke who?" Luke asked.

"Luke who got stuck in the castle." Sir Lancelot started spinning in a circle, executing the latest program for robot laughter the sixth years had created, and then sped down the corridor. Luke didn't have time to wonder how Sir Lancelot knew about his trouble with the castle door on his first day; he had bigger problems.

When they entered a crowded Knight Hall, Luke spotted Coach Typhoon near the big ancient wooden door at the opposite end of the hall. He was standing on a tall crate, decked out in his signature tracksuit, today in all yellow. He looked like a plump ripe banana.

"Tryouts will be a bloodbath. Only the BEST will make it." The Coach hurled all kinds of balls—volleyballs, basketballs and soccer balls—with missile precision. He yelled at the students, "Agility, folks!" Students were dodging and screaming with delight. When the coach shouted, "Faster!" The students responded by running in every direction. It didn't help them. Coach Typhoon continued to peg students out of the spontaneous dodgeball game.

Adio had been happily encouraging everyone over the commotion. He now called, "Students going to Glimmerton! The excursion is departing soon. It's pouring rain, but it's better OUTSIDE than inside today. Get your ponchos! Come get your ponchos!"

Luke and Ollie had barely made it halfway through Knight Hall when Coach Typhoon locked eyes on them.

He threw a volleyball that Luke caught in his gut. The ball fell to the floor as Luke gasped for air.

"Grit and Guts, I say!" Coach Typhoon bellowed. "GRIT AND GUTS!"

Ollie grabbed Luke's arm and pulled him through the front door.

"Did you grab any ponchos?" Luke asked, slowly recovering his breath as water dripped down his face. Ollie shook his head but from his backpack pulled a small black umbrella that barely fit the two of them underneath. It was raining at a good pace and Copernicus Court was busy with poncho-clad sopping wet students either headed to the bay to take the ferry or simply evading Coach Typhoon.

"I don't see Andy or Ronan," Luke said frantically.

"Maybe they're at the ferry dock already?" Ollie offered.

Luke ran to the end of the curtain wall and started down

the switchback pathway leading to Chronos Bay. He could see over the low-lying wall lining the path, but he hoisted himself up onto it to see further out. "They haven't loaded the boat yet. I need to get to the dock!"

"Wait!" Ollie said when Luke jumped off the wall. "Over there!"

Luke spotted the two dark figures Ollie was pointing at.

"Andy!" Luke yelled.

Their roommates sped up, scrunching down low and scurrying to the back side of the main castle.

Keeping up with them wasn't easy. Luke glimpsed Ronan and Andy making their way through shrubs at the far end of the castle where a massive round tower tapered into the sky.

Branches jabbed at Luke's arms as he and Ollie pushed through the shrubs and stubby trees. They found a small bronze door in the wall, hidden by the bushes.

"They must've gone through here," Ollie said.

Luke pressed the latch with his thumb and pushed through the bronze door, ducking his head low. Ollie was right behind him.

Once inside, they found themselves in a short stone corridor. They ran down it, staying in hot pursuit. "Do you see them?" Luke asked desperately, as they rounded a corner. He quickly took a puff of his inhaler. He didn't recognize this part of the castle. It was nowhere near their classrooms or dormitory. And it definitely hadn't been on the orientation tour. The walls were decrepit with large fissures that looked like a person could easily fit in them to hide.

Suddenly they could make out adult voices. Ollie crouched, yanking Luke with him into a fissure in the wall.

A man spoke. "I don't like it, Director LeCrucia. The

governor has overstepped his boundary. You know as well as I do that inviting an archaeologist into our school is dangerous. This school has secrets and history that we must protect. You brought me here for that reason."

"I know that, Professor Morlia," Director LeCrucia sighed. "But my experiments haven't been going well. If we could just find more Lambros element—"

"I adamantly disagree. Although the Kp values are holding steady, there have been a few unusual blips. The dig must be cancelled," Professor Morlia replied.

"The dig isn't scheduled until next year," Director LeCrucia said.

"Regardless, I stand by my statement," Professor Morlia replied.

"I'll take this under advisement, Professor Morlia," Director LeCrucia said.

When the voices dissipated, Ollie whispered, "The Ollieaider will show if the coast is clear." He extended the cardboard tube contraption that Luke had seen on Ollie's desk in Professor Morlia's class. It was a sort of spy tool, Ollie had explained, made of cardboard and paper towel rolls and carefully aligned little round mirrors. No batteries required.

"Ok, we're good to go." Ollie pressed a button and the Ollieaider collapsed to the size of a cardboard tube from a bathroom tissue roll.

They exited the fissure and continued down the corridor. "What do you think that was all about?" Ollie asked. "What secrets? What's Lambros element?"

Luke didn't care. He just wanted his watch.

Briefly falling back behind Ollie, he quickly wiped his eyes with his sleeve.

16

Luke

Luke stopped walking. Across from them was a large wooden door recessed in the middle of a wide rounded stone wall. A sign on the door read:

**CONSTRUCTION ZONE
DO NOT ENTER!**

"We've lost them, Ollie!" Luke exclaimed.

On cue, Andy appeared to his left and Ronan to his right. Andy had bright red sneakers that matched his hair. Ronan's sneakers matched his own hair too, black with yellow streaks.

"Following us?" Andy asked, grinning.

"You were hiding in the fissures!" Ollie accused Ronan and Andy in the dim light of the corridor.

"I want my watch back! Where is it?" said Luke.

Andy snickered. "Relax, roomy. We were just borrowing it." He checked one cargo pants pocket, then each of the others, before finally pulling it out of his back pocket.

"You took it off my wrist while I was sleeping!" Luke

yelled. "It's my dad's!"

Ollie's eyes snapped back to Luke with surprise.

"Okay, okay, relax. Here it is." Andy handed it over and squinted his eyes at Luke. He took his index finger and quickly made the circular motion by his temple for "crazy".

Ronan snorted.

Luke ignored them. His hands shook as he tried to place the watch back on his wrist.

"Maybe you should ask your dad to buy you a *new* watch." Andy grinned. "This one only has one hand. I can't tell time with it!"

Ronan gave a harsh laugh. "Right?!"

Still unable to fasten his watch, Luke burst out, "You don't get it!"

Andy snickered again, "Get what?"

Luke sank to the floor with the watch in his hand, his voice trembling. "This watch is all I have from my dad! He's gone, and … and … everyone thinks he's dead."

Ollie sat down next to Luke on the corridor floor. Ronan and Andy looked at each other with confusion. Ronan fiddled awkwardly with the edges of the sign on the door.

"And so, is your dad …" Andy hesitated, scratching his nose while he searched for his next word, "dead?"

Ollie shot a look at Andy, and quietly asked Luke, "What do you mean, he's gone?"

Luke hadn't moved. The cold stones underneath him beckoned for him to stay like a statue forever. However, his mind raced. Images of his father came flooding back. Roasting marshmallows over a fire, playing basketball, reading, showing Luke his pocket watch. Then, Luke wearing his dad's sweater for weeks, even sleeping with it after his father went missing.

The story suddenly poured out of Luke's mouth. "My dad left months ago on a special assignment. He's a journalist and really good at his job. He won a bunch of awards and stuff. But he never came back this time. We waited. And then the phone rang. My mom was crying. They found his boat. And his pocket watch. They searched all over. But they gave up. Everyone thinks my dad's dead but I know he is alive!"

Luke had never told anyone the whole story before. Not Mrs. Abernathy, not the counsellor, and definitely not his so-called friends at his old school, even though they all knew his dad had disappeared. Luke was crying a little bit, but he didn't care. "My mom gave me the watch."

"I bet you really miss him," Ollie said gently.

Luke wiped his eyes.

"Sorry Luke … I … I didn't know," Andy managed to say.

"Yah, it was Andy's idea," Ronan added, "You get the turd award, Andy!"

"Whatever. You said it was brilliant," Andy rebutted. "We needed to keep track of time. But that didn't work out because, you know, the watch only has one hand."

No one laughed.

Luke got up off the floor.

He'd held back the reason he knew his dad was alive: his dreams about him were so real. Somehow he would find his way back to his dormitory, pack his things, call his mom, and insist she come get him. Besides, he'd done what his mom had asked. He'd given Chronos Academy a chance. A seven-week chance.

"Where are you going, Luke?" Ollie asked.

"I'm done! I'm going HOME!" Luke said. *I need to figure*

out how to find my dad.

"Home? As in leaving the school?" Ollie asked incredulously. "Luke, you can't leave me here alone with these wing nuts," he protested.

"We aren't wing nuts! We're brilliant," Andy smiled.

Ollie threw his arms into the air. "Excellent. Whatever. So brilliant but you can't read a watch!" he growled as Andy and Ronan stood grinning in front of them.

The sconce on the wall above them flickered in anticipation as they stood there. Then they noticed a shadow growing larger around the bend. "Shoot! Someone's coming," Andy murmured. "We shouldn't be here. We'll all get expelled."

With lightning speed, Andy produced from his pocket a key ring with two keys dangling from it, one of them was a brass skeleton key with a white tag hanging off the spirally end. He inserted the brass skeleton key into the door with the DO NOT ENTER! sign on it. Andy pushed down on the door handle and it opened with a soft click. Nanoseconds later, Ronan and Andy grabbed both Luke and Ollie, and shoved them behind the wooden door, and piled in after them. The wooden door shut with a click. Andy carefully slid the wrought iron slide bolt latch closed and whispered, "Locked it."

They all held their breath. A few seconds later, someone tried the door handle and then banged at the door.

"Who's that?" Ronan whispered.

"Shush. They could hear us," Andy answered in an even softer voice, pointing at the small barred open window at the top of the door.

Surrounded by darkness and the sounds of breathing in the crowded space, Luke contemplated his options. *I could scream right now and get expelled. Then Mom'll* have *to come get me.* He felt Ollie's backpack digging into his side when he shifted to shout. He stopped. *We'll all get expelled. I can't do that to Ollie.*

Andy whispered, "Follow me." He led the way up a narrow spiral stone staircase. Ronan fell to the back. Ollie and Luke were trapped between them.

As they climbed, light from the grey and rainy autumn day made its way into the staircase through rectangular vertical slit windows that appeared every twenty steps or so. To steady himself Luke touched the outer wall of the staircase on his left. The inner wall was only waist-high, like a handrail. The sandstone bricks were marred by discoloration and felt cold under his touch.

Ollie demanded in a harsh whisper, "Where are you taking us?"

"To the top, of course," Andy replied.

"How many stairs do you think that is?" Ronan asked. "I've counted fifty-seven so far."

Luke fell into step and into a trance while listening to Ronan's persistent counting as they climbed.

Around step one hundred, they stopped to rest, and Ollie asked, "If we aren't supposed to be here, how'd you get that key?"

"Because I'm soooooo awesome." Beaming, Andy pulled out a package of Hubble Bubble signature gum and offered it around. "I got this at the Hubble Bubble candy store in Glimmerton on Chronos Day."

"I can't believe you have any left. That was the first day of school!" Ronan said, taking a piece of gum, then explained, "The store is named after Edwin Hubble. He was an astronomer." Ollie refused to take a piece of gum. Luke also declined and took a moment to use his inhaler.

"Let's get going," said Ronan. He switched places with Andy and took the lead, keeping Luke and Ollie between them.

"Where'd you get the keys?" Ollie repeated as they started climbing again.

"Oh yeah, the keys." Andy blew a huge bubble with his gum, waited for it to pop before speaking. He chewed the giant wad of gum like a cow chewing cud. "So yesterday I was sent to Adio's office for detention. He has the keys to the entire school in there! This ring has two keys. One for the little bronze door by the bushes and see here this larger skeleton key with the tag? BT stands for Bastion Tower. That's where we are."

"And so you just took it?" Ollie asked. "Why am I not surprised? Total kleptos, right Luke? And kidnappers. Not cool."

"Kidnappers?" Andy said. "I saved you all from getting caught!"

"Only because you put us in here in the first place." Ollie was on a roll. "Is this place even safe? The sign on the door said CONSTRUCTION ZONE, DO NOT ENTER! OW!" Ollie said as he stubbed his toe on the stair, stumbled, and bumped into Luke. "See! We shouldn't be here!"

"Don't worry about it. Joe, my older brother, told me this tower has been under construction for more than a hundred years." Andy stopped and jumped up and down on the step he was on. "See? It's fine."

"One hundred and fifty-seven ..." Ronan continued.

Looking down over the inner half-wall, Luke could see

the spiralling shell-like pattern of the staircase winding all the way down to the base of the tower.

"Why do you even care about this tower?" Ollie asked.

"Because Joe's never been here and I for once want to beat him at something," Andy answered. "Besides, me and Ronan have a plan."

"Yeah. A plan," Ronan agreed. "It's a doozy."

17

Cleo

Ever since she'd seen Stephanie at the climbing wall a week ago, Cleo had avoided her like the plague. Although they were in the same classes, they hadn't interacted at all, and Cleo had kept her distance.

She'd heard Stephanie was going on today's off-campus excursion to Glimmerton. Which meant that Cleo was not going.

After having breakfast alone in the Viking Hall cafeteria, she made her way up the stairs to the sixth-floor library. Her roommates were nowhere to be seen. *They must've decided to go together to Glimmerton,* Cleo sighed. Halfway down the corridor, Sir Lancelot projected a hologram showcasing old footage of the Pandia Games: javelin, discus, shot put, running sports, high jump, and the very important pinnacle event of the Pandia Games: the RAF triathlon. Cleo made her way around the few students who stood spellbound watching the film and proceeded towards the library's massive wooden double doors at the end of the hallway.

"Quack, quack, quack!"

"Stop quacking at the robot, you little fluff ball!" Adio stood in front of the doors, struggling to put a leash on Director LeCrucia's little dog. "Good morning, Cleo," Adio said as he looked up. "Ducky escaping was a lucky break for me. Coach Typhoon has a crazy dodgeball game going on in Knight Hall. If I were you, I would avoid the area." He held a quieter Ducky easily in his right hand.

"I will." Cleo grinned at the dog who was now licking her hand.

"You're not interested in going to Glimmerton?" Adio asked. "We do it every year—third weekend in October. It's fun! You still have a chance, you know. The ferry doesn't leave for another 45 minutes."

"Thanks, but I just want to stay here." Cleo petted Ducky one more time, and entered the library.

Chronos Academy's library was beautiful. Dark wooden shelves stacked to the ceiling with books. Small desk lamps perched on long wooden tables. As Cleo moved further into the space, she looked up. The library turret had an amazing glass-domed ceiling that captured the sunlight and dispersed it throughout the space like a prism. Diffuse dust danced in the light. A woody, earthy smell with an underlying hint of mustiness brought a sense of calm and home to her.

Although she'd finally used the old fashioned phone (with help from Professor Morlia), she hadn't gotten hold of her grandma. So as Cleo searched for a table, she composed a letter to CeeCee in her mind. *"Dear Grandma, I didn't think there would be mean kids like Stephanie at Chronos Academy. But she arrived last week by helicopter. The* actual *Stephanie!"*

She went on with her mental letter, *"No adventures yet, but I'm working on something. I think you and Mom will be impressed."*

The sudden sound of voices broke the peaceful library ambience. Two adults were talking loudly at the librarian's desk. As Cleo quickly made her way past them, one of them called out.

"Cleo! Cleo Gaven!"

A woman with a silver-sequined beret covering her lavender hair shrieked, hustled around the desk, and threw her arms around Cleo.

"Barbara!" Surprised and delighted, Cleo hugged her back. The gentle smell of lavender mixed with coffee wafted into her nose. She pulled back a bit and noticed the woman's name badge, *Head Librarian Barbara Barakos*. "How did you? When—"

TAP-TAP-TAP

Cleo recognized the governor of southern Pandia standing next to the tall desk. He was wearing his signature black suit and white silk scarf and was staring at Barbara with a scowl on his face. He kept tapping his index finger hard on the desk next to two large cups, one showing a drawing of an ominous castle, the other a large orange fire-breathing dragon. Cleo knew both mugs belonged to Barbara, a collector of fantasy-themed mugs.

Cleo shifted uncomfortably.

"I used to babysit this girl when she was little," said Barbara. "She was so cute! She dragged this teddy bear around everywhere she went. Do you still have it?" she asked Cleo as she brought her behind the checkout counter. Barbara had an especially cheerful voice. Her eyebrows high on her forehead made her blue eyes large. She looked at the governor again. "Her mother wrote me a reference for this job. Adelaide is amazing. The things she does in that museum. Unbelievable." She then turned her attention back to Cleo. "I can't believe I got this job. It was posted just last week when Ms. Rindle quit. I got in a couple of days ago and haven't had a chance to come find you, Cleo."

The governor sneered and interjected, "Isn't that nice? Ms. Barakos, I was asking if you'd located that manuscript we were discussing the other day?" His voice was deep, sharp, and resonant.

It was weird to hear Barbara's last name. For as long as Cleo had known her, Barbara had always insisted on people calling her by her first name.

"I've been looking," the librarian said. "I have indeed been looking in the few days I've been here. You could've phoned, Governor. You didn't need to make a special trip all the way from Glimmerton."

The governor just glared back unimpressed.

Barbara glanced at her desk, which was covered in books and papers. "This library is vast and there are a lot of documents. I need more information to go on."

"Hm ..." The governor placed his hands in his pockets and gave an unapologetic smile. "I can only tell you what I've told you before: very old—1800s—contains legends of some kind, scientific entries and some personal entries. Evidently written by a former student. It was a part of this library's collection of books, and then it vanished!"

"Ah, it sounds like a diary or journal." Barbara paused, thinking. She picked up a pencil from the desk and tapped it against her lips. "A personal work then? Do you recall the title?"

The governor developed a slight twitch in the corner of his eye. "Of course I don't know the title! If I knew the title,

I would look it up myself! All I know is it has something to do with a former student, a *William Bale*," the governor said with such force that a speck of spit flew out of his mouth. It landed on the stack of papers on the librarian's tall desk.

"Of course, of course," Barbara muttered, jotting down a few notes. "When did it go missing?" she asked as she moved around the desk to her computer.

"It went missing years ago. Before even I began working here. Many years before my first term as governor."

"So you've never seen it or read it?" Barbara asked.

"No, I haven't! If I had I wouldn't be asking you for it," the governor hissed in derision.

"Obviously it's very valuable," Barbara commented, giving a teensy smile.

Cleo was wondering how to get out of there and do so quickly. Her feet, however, would not budge.

"It is valuable! And I need it. I'm working to secure the world's finest archaeologist here next year—"

"Oh, is that the same archaeologist our student was working with? And their find was admitted to the Brillianton museum?" Barbara asked. Cleo cringed.

"Yes! And it would be *nice* if we could provide him with some pertinent historical information about Chronos Academy beyond what he's able to obtain from a simple internet search!" The governor's harsh tone seemed to stretch his already tall frame to an even more intimidating height.

Barbara's eyes widened. "I guess it must be urgent then. I'll do my best. In the meantime, have you thought of checking Magic Awaits in town?" she said encouragingly.

"Of course I have! Mr. Harbinger, his evil cat, and that bookstore, with his 'feel the magic!' An embarrassment to the sanctity of good organizational skills and the academy," the governor rasped. "I thought there was a chance Mr. Harbinger *the IV* had it, but I was *wrong*. The journal must be here!"

"Cleo!"

Cleo jumped. Standing next to the growling governor, Nia seemed completely oblivious to having interrupted an incredibly tense conversation. "Daisy bailed. Couldn't find Stephanie or anyone else. And then I saw you here. I don't want to go to Glimmerton alone. Come with me, please! The ferry's leaving soon."

"You should go!" Barbara exclaimed lightly, quickly mouthing "Sorry" as Nia pulled Cleo's arm. Cleo's letter for Grandma CeeCee and her first research on the Stones of Destiny would have to wait.

"Consider us even," Nia said as they sprinted outside and down to the dock. "I saved you from whatever that was, and you saved me by coming. Is the governor always that grumpy?" Nia asked.

"I don't know," Cleo responded. As they boarded the ferry, Cleo lamented, "I wish I'd had time to get my backpack," while Professor Gregor told them to find a seat.

"No way, we would've missed the ferry for sure," Nia said plopping down on a bench by a window on the lower deck.

Cleo wiped the rain from her eyes. Although she'd decided she didn't need friends, it still bothered her that she was Nia's last pick for the trip.

18

Luke

"... 312, 313, 314! That's a lot of stairs," Ronan said, breathing heavily between his words as he leaned against the wall of the tower landing.

"That's insane! Good training for Vikings tryouts though," Andy said as he doubled over to catch his breath. Luke still felt like someone had tightened a belt around his chest. He reached for his inhaler and took another puff. After a few moments, air began to flow into his lungs and he started to relax.

Having recovered faster than Luke, Andy stood up straight and declared, "I am Andy the Great! Ronan, flashlight."

"What?" Ronan replied to Andy. "I don't have one. You're the brains. Didn't *you* bring one?"

They all turned and looked at Ollie. He reluctantly dug out his flashlight from his red and white backpack and handed it to Andy. Andy swung the beam over the doorway. "Looks like the door got torn right off these hinges," he said and plucked at one of the pieces of shattered wood sticking out of the door frame.

"Dun-dun-dun-DUN!" Ronan added. He flicked on a switch he had found on the inside wall, bringing several dim sconces to life.

"Wow!" was all Luke could manage to say when he poked his head through the doorway. Before them was an enormous grand room with walls of large grey stone bricks. Grey light streamed through the overhead recessed arch windows. The sound of rain hitting the tower roof echoed throughout the chamber. Robust wooden columns and beams supported the vaulted ceiling. The wooden floor was weathered with patches covered in peeling paint.

The place smelled musty as though the windows hadn't been opened in years. There were no signs of construction, but the room did look like it had been used for storage for decades, or even centuries. Cardboard boxes of every size along with wooden crates and storage trunks were stacked between piles of broken furniture, tables and chairs, and rolled up rugs and tapestries. Dusty sheets partially covered furniture: oval-backed chairs with lion paw-footed legs, tables, lanterns, framed portraits, paintings, and sepia-toned photographs. So much stuff was piled everywhere that it was impossible to see how big the room was.

"Let's get exploring. I want to see this ghost Joe told me about," Andy said as he walked through the doorway.

"What ghost?!" cried Ollie.

No one answered.

Ronan purposely walked through the white stringy remains of cobweb hanging on one side of the door frame. They stuck to his face and hair, but he made no attempt to remove them. "I like it here."

Ollie spoke loudly from the doorway over the echoing of

the rain. "Come on Luke, let's go. We don't need to be here with Tweedle Dee and Tweedle Dum."

Andy laughed hysterically. "I— I— get to be Tweedle Dee."

Ollie was right, they should leave. Andy and Ronan weren't keeping them there anymore. Besides, he got what he came for. He had his dad's watch back, and it was safe on his wrist again.

But what is all this stuff? Luke's curiosity drew him further into the room.

With trepidation Ollie followed Luke, "But what about this ghost? I—I feel a weird chill," Ollie said. "I know!" Ollie whipped his backpack to the ground, and quickly produced a medium-sized glass jar containing cotton balls and some gooey gel. He removed the lid and started waving the jar side to side, moving his arm through the full range of motion. "Just in case. This will capture any ghost," he assured Luke.

Then he switched hands and repeated the movement.

BEEP

Luke jumped.

"That was one minute," Ollie said. He pressed a button on a miniature stopwatch in his hand and placed the lid on the jar. "Cool. That should take care of all the ghosts." He shook his glass jar. Luke couldn't see anything in it, just cotton balls and gel. He looked at Ollie quizzically.

"I don't just capture them. They get annihilated. This gel is made of special chemicals. Trade secret. One of my cool inventions." Ollie put the jar back into his backpack.

Andy appeared from behind a row of solid wood maple cabinets and dumped the contents of a small box he was carrying onto the floor. A bunch of rocks rolled out. "Lame."

Andy wrinkled his nose in disgust. After peering into several boxes, he said, "There's nothing here but a bunch of old junk. No wonder Joe never came up here."

"WOOOOO!" said a greyish shape that popped up from behind a wall of crates and boxes.

Ollie immediately karate-chopped the air with his hands and executed a power kick, missing the target by a lot.

"You got me!" the ghost shouted, pretending to be fatally wounded. The grimey grey sheet fell to the floor, revealing Ronan's grinning face.

"Ha ha ha. Ronan, you're very funny," Ollie said sarcastically. Luke smiled.

"I am," Ronan nodded, acknowledging the compliment and then suggested, "Let's make an obstacle course."

"Is this your plan?" Ollie asked Ronan and Andy.

"What plan?" Andy responded.

"You guys said you have a doozy of a plan," Ollie reminded them.

"We don't," Andy said, scratching his nose. "We just say that. Makes us sound smart."

Ollie shook his head.

The wooden floor squeaked in protest underneath their sneakers as Andy and Ronan went to work moving boxes and furniture. Ronan set some of the heaviest boxes up to use as hurdles. They laid a coat rack on the floor for the starting line.

Ronan went first. He jumped over several of the makeshift hurdles then lost his balance and fell right into a crate splitting it open. Slithering metal slunk out of the crate.

"That looks like chainmail!" Ollie said. In two large strides, Ollie was plunging into the broken container while

Ronan extracted his other leg from the crate. Ollie dragged out the chainmail and also brought out a leather sheath for a sword, and a long leather belt with an emblem of a raven on it.

"What else is in there?" Andy asked as he helped Ollie turn the damaged crate upside down. A bunch of tarnished metal objects of different sizes scattered onto the floor.

Luke grabbed a silver ring. "Do you think this stuff is authentic, like from real knights, or is it costume stuff?" Luke asked.

"It has to be real," Ollie said, adding that the castle was initially a small fortress built by Vikings and then later expanded by a king hundreds of years ago. "And kings had knights," he concluded, admiring the leather sheath.

Ronan lifted the chainmail. "Guys, it's sooo heavy! Help me get this on." He tried wrestling the hooded metal dress over his head.

"How much do you think this is worth?" Andy asked as he and Ollie helped Ronan. The chainmail hung well below Ronan's knees.

"A lot," Ollie said. "This is super old; you can't buy stuff like this."

"I look like Ryker in *Knights of Darkness*." Ronan raised his eyebrows and made a strange not quite menacing face at a dusty old mirror propped up against a cabinet. Luke hid his grin. Andy laughed.

Ollie regarded Ronan, eyes wide and questioning, "You know the *Knights of Darkness*?"

"Yeah, of course. Don't you?" Ronan replied. "You know *Knights of Darkness*, right Luke?"

Luke nodded.

Andy added, "Of course he does. Everyone does."

"I can't move! You gotta get this stuff off me," Ronan begged. Andy helped him remove the heavy chainmail and they laid it out on the floor

Luke looked at the ring again and cleaned it with the bottom of his shirt. There was an inscription on the interior. "*Order of Ravens.*" Luke passed the ring to Ollie.

"Maybe this ring belonged to one of the knights," Ollie said enthusiastically, turning the ring in his fingers. "This tower would be a great hiding spot for treasure. Knights always had treasure."

"Let's spread out and look. If I find treasure, Joe will be so jealous," Andy said. "I'll be able to buy whatever I want!"

"We could go to Glimmerton whenever we wanted to get candy. Lots of it," Ronan agreed.

"Right—we would buy the *Trillian* to get there," Andy offered.

"I would be captain," Ronan said.

"You don't know how to drive a boat," Andy reminded him.

"I would hire a captain to teach me," Ronan suggested. "And we would have a fridge in our room full of the best snacks!"

"We would hire another chef at the school to make pancakes, all day, everyday," Andy said, rubbing his stomach.

"We wouldn't have to eat fish," Ronan grinned.

"But we would eat pasta!" Andy beamed.

Ollie's mouth gaped open as he followed along with the silly banter.

Luke remained quiet. If he had all the money in the world, he would only want one thing—to find his dad. He looked around the grand chamber room. There were tons of boxes, cabinets, and crates to dig through. If he found treasure in the tower he could use it—to fund his own search expedition.

That's it! That's what I'm going to do!

Luke squeezed his way through some stacks of boxes and moved further into the chamber. He found a large brick fireplace tucked into the very back corner of the room. The bottom of the fireplace was charred. He ran his finger over the mantle and removed a thick layer of dust. Rubbing his finger on his pants, he stuck his head inside the chimney and looked up. A chunk of old dusty ash fell into his face, making him cough.

"Guys, over here!" Ronan called a few minutes later from behind a mountain of piled-up furniture.

When Luke joined Ronan, he saw a long wooden ladder leading up to a round opening in the ceiling.

"We need to move these cabinets so we can get up there," Ronan said.

The boys strained to move two ornate heavy oak cabinets away from the ladder. They went up the ladder and through the opening in the ceiling, one at a time. Andy and Ronan quickly cased the room. The attic was a lot smaller than the lower grand chamber. It was sparsely furnished with one small cabinet and a couple of wooden chairs. The light coming in from a few small recessed windows was so dim that darkness loomed at the edges of the room. Just like in the grand chamber below the attic, there was a brick fireplace.

"This room is B for Bust! There's no treasure here at all, not even junk," Andy lamented closing the cabinet door. "Ollie, if knights had treasure, where is it?" Before Ollie could reply Andy answered his own question. "I'm going back downstairs to search." Ronan followed closely behind him.

"I don't like it up here," Ollie whispered and moved toward the ladder. Luke started to follow Ollie, when out of the corner of his eye he saw a flash of blue light coming from the fireplace.

"Did you see that?" he asked. But Ollie was long gone.

Luke gave his head a shake. He moved cautiously towards the small fireplace. A set of iron hearth tools were hanging on sturdy hooks mounted beside it. He grabbed the fire poker with his left hand, crouched down, and poked at the charred base of the fire box. The motion reminded him of roasting marshmallows on camping trips with his dad. He dropped the poker, stood, and took a step back. What was he doing? He was being ridiculous. There was nothing to see here, it was just an old fireplace.

Must be my imagination.

When he regrouped with Ollie and his other two roommates at the spilled crate of chainmail in the obstacle course, Ronan asked, "Anything upstairs Luke?"

Luke shook his head.

"Where's the treasure, Ollie?" asked Ronan, looking up from another upended box. Its meagre contents were spread out on the ground. He made an exaggerated pouting face, pushing the old textbooks and a few pencils with his foot. "We've found nothing!"

Andy said, "Well, I guess that's it for Bastion Tower."

"What do you mean?" Luke asked.

"There's no treasure here, so let's go," Andy said. "I'm hungry, and I don't want to miss the mac n' cheese lunch at

Viking Hall. Plus, whoever was at the bottom of the tower will be long gone by now."

"We have to come back," Luke said louder and with more determination than he had intended.

"Why?" Ronan asked.

"Ahh ..." Luke hesitated. He was sure there was something in this tower worth a lot of money. The place was big, with lots of boxes, cabinets, and hiding spots. It would be a way faster search if he could convince his roommates to help him look. They didn't need to know he was going to use any treasure he found to fund a search for his dad.

Ollie looked at Luke quizzically, then jumped into the conversation, "Knights wouldn't just hide treasure in a cardboard box, right Luke?"

"Yeah," Luke said, grateful for the assist.

"Good point, Ollie. They didn't even have cardboard in medieval times," Ronan commented.

"Right. So we'll have to look harder," said Ollie. "We need to work together, and we share what we find."

"Makes sense," said Andy. "And this place is a sweet hangout spot."

They all nodded in agreement.

That worked for Luke. The more they found the better. Looking pointedly at Andy, Luke said, "No one can know about our treasure hunt, or that we've been to the tower. Not even Joe."

Ollie jumped in, exclaiming, "Of course not, we don't want to be expelled!" Ollie continued, "Remember that scene in *Knights of Darkness number 5*? Let's take an oath as a secret order."

"Order of Ravens!" Ronan offered, grabbing the ring from

the broken crate where they had found the chainmail. "That should be our name."

"I like it," Andy said.

"I don't like the ravens part," Luke frowned.

"I think it's cool." Ollie adjusted his glasses. Then he handed the ring to Luke.

"Okay," Luke swallowed.

"Everything has to be top secret," Andy said.

"We do not discuss Order of Ravens business outside the Order," Ronan said.

"We need to keep this place, Bastion Tower, a secret," Luke added.

"And with this oath, we will protect, share and keep secret any treasure we find," Ollie proclaimed.

"If anyone breaks this oath it will be their doom," Andy said as he rubbed his hands together.

"Yah, a wicked death!" Ronan grinned. "They will spend eternity with John Bones." Ronan held up the arm of a skeleton from under a sheet next to him and waved it.

Ollie nodded, his eyes large. "No. What? Where did you get that?"

"Over behind those rolled up rugs," Ronan said with glee. "It's John with no skin on. John Bones, get it?"

Ollie rolled his eyes. "So we all agree?" Ollie asked, holding up the ring.

"Let's swear on it," Andy said, then spit in his hand and wrapped it around the ring. They stacked their spit-covered hands to make a binding contract.

Luke felt like an actual knight when Ollie added the *Knights of Darkness* command, "Order of Ravens, go forth to adventure."

As the boys moved toward the door of the grand chamber, Ollie asked, "Luke, does this mean you're going to stay at Chronos Academy?"

"Yes," he answered. He just didn't know for how long.

19

Cleo

Cleo shouldn't have come to Glimmerton. Not only had she been Nia's last choice, but Cleo had also thrown up on the ferry ride. "On the boat Stephanie said everyone will be meeting at the bakery. It should be fun," Nia said.

"I'm not hungry." Cleo couldn't even think about food, and she certainly didn't want to hang out with Stephanie. Cleo quickly came up with an alternative. Instead of going to the bakery, she would check out the bookstore Barbara had mentioned earlier.

She accepted Nia's offer to join her under the umbrella as they walked up the street of the pretty town. It was raining gently and the sky was still grey and cloudy. At a little kiosk in the middle of a pedestrian-only street, Cleo bought a bottle of water and asked about the bookstore. Nia inquired about the main bakery in town.

"The Magic Awaits bookstore and the Keys bakery should be across from each other at the end of the main street," Nia said. Then she started laughing, "Look at the actual street name. It's called 'This Way'! So, let's go this way!"

Cleo gave a half smile and sipped her water. She stepped to the side to let Professor Gregor zoom past them atop his unicycle. He waved a thank you. The owly professor wove expertly between the rows of tall lamp posts, each topped with a raven head, beak open with a light bulb inside. The cobblestone streets of the quaint town were filled with poncho-clad students roaming the stores and shops that were tucked in tightly next to one another. Cleo peeked through one window, The Time Store. The ceiling was covered with hourglasses that flipped in unison.

"Can we check these stores on the way back? I'm too hungry." Nia pulled on Cleo's sleeve as she set a brisk pace. "Chef François' cooking is good, but he doesn't make Taiwanese wonton or sticky rice like Mom. Her cooking's the best! I miss her. Do you miss your mom?"

Not wanting to talk about her mother, Cleo evaded the question. "I guess," she replied. After sipping some more water, Cleo said, "I wish I had my backpack to put this bottle in." Mentioning her lucky backpack made her miss her grandma and their conversations. She also wished she had a warmer coat instead of just the thin poncho that they had grabbed at the castle door.

"Cleo, I told you. We didn't have time to get it," Nia replied tersely.

With that, Cleo moved out from under the umbrella and they walked in silence.

At the corner of the streets This Way and That Way, Nia said, "Bye," and crossed the intersection to join the crowd of students gathered outside Keys, waiting their turn to get inside the bustling bakery.

Cleo closed her eyes and opened them again. *This. Year.*

Definitely. Sucks.

As she pushed open the bright yellow door of the Magic Awaits bookshop, warm air rushed out. Cleo entered the shop and had to wait a moment for her eyes to adjust to the darker interior.

On the main floor there were books everywhere. Books were stacked, on shelves, tables, and on the floor in towering columns. It was impossible to see through to the back of the store. Cleo noticed the ceiling was tall and wide with wooden beams that crisscrossed from one end of the store to the other. Narrow carpeted curved stairs with brass railings wound up to the second-floor circular loft that overlooked the main floor. Lining the exterior wall of the loft, small round stained-glass windows interspersed between the bookcases let in the soft hue of natural light from the rainy day.

Keeping her arms tucked in tight, she weaved her way around the vertical columns of books that looked like skinny highrises. As she rounded a corner she bumped into her worst nightmare.

"You spilled my coffee, Cleo*patra*!" Stephanie, with a blonde ponytail high on top of her head, was staring right at Cleo and pointing to the whipped iced coffee in her hand.

Cleo felt a flash of panic in her belly. Whenever anyone, especially Stephanie, said her *full* name, she *truly* hated it! But her grandma's words echoed in her mind, "*Dealing with mean kids is an opportunity to grow.*"

"Sorry," Cleo stammered, "I was just looking for the history section." Stephanie puffed air at her blonde bangs. She was flanked by her sidekicks Hayden and Lauren. A mirror image of Stephanie, Lauren's long blonde hair was also in a ponytail high on her head. Hayden, the solitary boy in this group, was at least a foot shorter than Lauren, had dark hair and was stout compared to Lauren's tall and lean body type. The sidekicks looked like a mismatched pair of salt and pepper shakers.

"Hmmm, this looks like a history book," Stephanie said. She pointed to a tiny book wedged fifteen deep in a tower of books forty-five high. Hayden elbowed Lauren and they snickered. Stephanie started pulling the book out of the vertical pile. The column swayed like a tree in the wind.

Cleo froze.

Stephanie gave a final yank and jumped back.

Like a film played in slow motion, the towering stack collapsed into the next book pile, which then toppled into the one beside it.

One by one the towers fell like dominos in quick succession, releasing a large plume of dust. Customers ran and jumped to get out of the way. A couple of unlucky patrons got hit by a flying book or two.

Seconds later, when the dust settled, Cleo could make out the carnage of books, scattered all over the floor. The centre of the store had been transformed from a maze of towers into a lava field of books.

The sound of a bell chimed at the entrance of the store. There was a clear line of sight now from where Cleo stood to the yellow front door. Stephanie was hurriedly exiting the store, calling, "It was Cleo's fault!" The door closed behind Cleo's nemesis and her entourage of two.

Within seconds, the little bell on the door was ringing again as the remaining academy students quickly filed out of the bookstore, their eyes moving judgmentally between the mess and Cleo, who stood frozen and trapped in the heap of books.

A few adult patrons ambled past her. "Tsk, tsk. Kids these days. So misbehaved." Cleo wanted to shrivel into nothingness. When she blinked again, she was the only customer left in the store.

"Sullivan's luck! You kids need to be more careful!" an elderly man barked angrily as he hobbled towards her, leaning on his cane. The man was mostly bald with a furry strip of white hair around his head. He wore dark blue slacks and a short-sleeved, grey plaid button-up shirt. His trousers were cinched at the waist by a brown leather belt that matched his brown leather shoes. The shoes and belt were as worn as used book covers.

Cleo stammered, "I-I-I didn't. It wasn't me." Tears pooled in her eyes. She wanted more than anything for a massive hole to appear wherever Stephanie was and swallow her and her whipped coffee. And her two sidekicks too!

"Blah, blah. Tears won't help me clean up this mess!" he hissed angrily, "I have in mind to kick you out." He bent over very slowly to gather a book from the floor. "What's your name?" he asked as he wrestled with gravity to straighten up, his hands empty.

"Cleo." She swallowed. "Cleopatra."

Why did I give him my full name?

The elderly man turned towards her slowly. He retrieved his glasses from his shirt pocket, placed them on his wide nose, then squinted his eyes at her. "Well now." The terse tone in his voice had softened considerably, and his old, weathered face looked a bit younger as he unscrunched his nose. "That's a unique name. I like it. Well, Cleopatra. Don't just stand there. You made this mess, you'd better help clean it up."

Despite wanting to shout, "It wasn't my fault!" Cleo nodded.

A beautiful white cat with piercing blue eyes meowed and approached her. Cleo smiled a little. "Maybe you can be my friend," she said, as she crouched down to pet the cat.

"That's Purrl. She showed up one day and never left," the little old man scoffed.

Remembering the library conversation with Barbara from this morning, Cleo surmised that Purrl was the "evil cat" the governor had mentioned. Purrl rolled on Cleo's sneakers.

"My name is Mr. Hubert Harbinger, *the fourth,*" the elderly man said. "You may call me Mr. Harbinger. I am the owner of this *exquisite* treasure trove."

It certainly wasn't an exquisite treasure trove at the moment.

What a mess! How long will it take to clean this up? What if I miss the ferry?

She didn't even want to think about having to ride back to the castle on *My Betsy!*

"Um, is there a system for putting these back, Mr. Harbinger?" she asked hoping it would be quick. "I used to help my dad when I was little. He had a bookstore. It was a lot smaller than this one." Thinking back to her father's store in England, made her nostalgic. Since her parents' separation, she only saw her dad now on the rare occasion when he flew up from Egypt for business.

"Did he now?" Mr. Harbinger said, sounding less and less annoyed. "No fancy system. Just stack them up, Cleopatra."

Cleo grimaced. *My full name again!*

She gathered the books from the floor and stacked them

the best she could. But her stacks only got to waist height before they toppled over.

"Well, now you see there is actually a system for stacking. Big ones at the base," Mr. Harbinger said as he topped his shoulder-height stack with a small red book.

With this in mind Cleo restacked her book tower. She liked the calming repetitive motion. Mr. Harbinger gave her a brisk approving nod when he examined her first stack through his glasses. Still, the silence was a bit unnerving.

"I don't see any signs anywhere in the store. How do you find books here? There are so many," she said.

"In over two hundred years of owning and operating this little enterprise, my family has curated more than 300,000 books."

"Really!"

"Indeed! We have a book for everyone. As my great-great grandfather used to say, 'The magic awaits. The reader just has to find it.'"

"And so customers just look around?"

"And believe they will find it," Mr. Harbinger replied matter of factly.

She shook her head in disbelief. *This is one crazy system.*

As she stacked the books into columns, the floor began to reappear. When Cleo finally finished, she glanced at the clock on the wall. It really hadn't taken long at all. It helped that Mr. Harbinger had stacked several columns himself.

When Mr. Harbinger made his way over to inspect her work, he eyed her with curiosity. "Your eyes have changed colour. They are now more hazel than grey."

Cleo felt her face warm. Her eyes only changed to grey when she felt powerful emotions. "That's just something they do. My grandma's eyes do it, too."

"Really? That's a rare trait. What did you say your last name was?" Mr. Harbinger asked.

"Gaven," Cleo replied.

"Gaven … Gaven," he repeated as he went to his desk and grabbed one of the many framed photos on it. He put on his glasses and examined the picture. He then turned over the frame and motioned Cleo to come over.

He passed the picture to her. "Here is my Mary, with her two friends at the beach, more than sixty years ago." His eyes went misty. "She kept me in line." Three pretty teenage girls were laughing in the black and white photo as they pointed to something outside the frame. In the background was the lighthouse at Castle Bay and in the top-right corner of the photo Cleo could see Chronos Castle.

"Notice anything familiar?" Mr. Harbinger asked curiously.

"This is at Chronos Academy," Cleo said.

"Anything else?" he asked.

"Ummm …" Cleo shook her head.

Mr. Harbinger placed the picture back on his desk tucking it behind several books.

"Why the name Cleopatra?" he asked.

"My mom, she's a curator at the Brillianton museum. She loves all things ancient history, ancient Greece, ancient Egypt," she explained.

"Cleopatra was an astounding figure, and no doubt a favourite of your mother's," Mr. Harbinger said, still studying Cleo. "Now that you have finished helping me, is there anything I can help you with?"

The question caught her off guard. She paused in thought. *Maybe I can find something here about the Stones of Destiny!*

20

Cleo

Cleo's heart skipped a beat. "Do you know Captain Jumbo?" she asked Mr. Harbinger.

"Of course! Good man. Full of sea-lore. And he brings me fish. Why?" the bookseller replied.

"Captain Jumbo, he told me about a legend—the three Stones of Destiny. Do you know anything about it?"

"Well, let's see. The stones, ah yes, the Stones." Mr. Harbinger paused and looked at her again. "A few of us from around these parts remember the old Glimmician legend." He tapped his lip with his index finger. "If I recall correctly, these powerful stones belonged to the ancient Glimmicians, but were lost long ago." He hesitated and then continued. "Over the centuries, some have looked for them, but no one has ever found them."

"What does the legend say these stones look like exactly?" she asked. Captain Jumbo had only told her that the Stones would fit into the palm of your hand.

"I have no idea, Cleopatra. We are talking about a legend that dates back to at least the 1200s, probably even earlier. It's the fishing folks that are our storytellers here in Glimmerton. And there are only a few known descendants left. Captain Jumbo is one of them. The ancient Glimmicians passed down their stories, orally. Nothing was written." He cleared his throat. "But … this is the Magic Awaits bookstore after all. There are a lot of unusual books here. And if someone did write something down about the legend, then it could be here. Who knows? Maybe you'll find what you are looking for. The magic awaits!" He pulled a novel from his desk, sat down on a stool, and sipped from a mug. He looked up at her one last time. "Don't knock over any more books."

"But I didn't," she said, though Mr. Harbinger was no longer listening. She sighed and headed to the bookcases at the back of the store to avoid the towering columns. She didn't need a repeat domino event. She scanned the titles quickly by running her fingers along the spines, but found nothing of interest and moved on to the next bookcase.

She paused. Remembering what Mr. Harbinger said about believing and finding the right book, she closed her eyes and plucked a volume from the shelf.

Fungi need Mush-Room to Grow by Albert Gardner.

She tried again and selected a book made of cheese. The pages were created from individual cheese slices, vacuum sealed in clear pouches and it had a funky smell. She quickly returned it to the shelf. Cleo proceeded to the curved stairs to try her luck upstairs.

When she looked over the loft railing to the main floor, she could see Mr. Harbinger sitting at his desk. The light from the wall lamp reflected off his mostly bald head.

"MEOW!"

She looked down to see Purrl rubbing against the rail next

to her. Cleo picked up the cat as she scanned the incredible wall of books before her. "Did you come to help me? Do you know where I might find my book?" she said to the feline as it pawed at the books closest to it.

Then Cleo noticed something weird. A faint shimmer of blue light, coming from deep inside the bookshelf high above her. Cleo set Purrl down. She walked over to the wooden ladder attached to a brass railing just below the ceiling, slid it close to the blue shimmer, and climbed upwards, trying to zero in on the strange blue sparkle. Suddenly, out of nowhere Purrl leapt onto her arm as though it was a tree branch.

Surprised, Cleo jerked back and her feet slipped.

"GASP!"

"MEOW!"

Cleo frantically grabbed for the ladder rung to prevent herself from falling onto the loft floor. Purrl went flying through the air.

Oh no!

From the ladder she looked over the loft railing to the main floor. Purrl had landed on Mr. Harbinger's desk, feet side down, and seemed okay.

Trying again, Cleo reached up as far as she could to where the shimmering was coming from. A smaller book was wedged between two large books and stuck deep into the shelf. She dug in a bit more and wiggled it, pulling it forward. The shimmering moved from side to side. *This must be the source of that light!* She tugged with more gusto. Finally the smaller book popped out from the shelf and into her hand. She made her way down the ladder and sat on the floor.

The brown leather book looked very old, and the cover

was creased in spots. She was surprised at how heavy it felt. Three leather straps were interwoven around the cover to keep it closed. The spine had no markings or title, and it was no longer shimmering blue as she moved it around in her hands. *So strange.*

She tugged on the leather straps one at a time, memorizing how they were positioned, and finally opened the book to its middle. The paper was thick with rough edges and yellow with age. The pages were handwritten in black ink, some of it faded. As she flipped through the pages, the entries reminded her of a journal.

She was about to close the book and return it to the shelf when roman numerals and other strange markings at the top of the pages caught her eye. In between the numerals and markings were dates from the 1800s. Cleo turned to the first page of the book.

Research Findings of William Bale

William Bale?! The governor said that name today in the library! I'm sure he did.

"Cleo!"

She jumped and quickly moved to the loft railing. Nia was staring up at her.

"There you are! We gotta go! The ferry's leaving in fifteen minutes. I came to get you, and to say sorry. You're my roommate. You shouldn't have been the last person I asked to come with me. That was rude. I got you a cupcake." She smiled and waved a paper to-go bag at her.

Cleo smiled at the peace offering. "Thanks, Nia," she called down.

"It's a little crazy in here," Nia commented, looking around with concern at the chaotic book displays. "If these book towers fell, sheesh, that would be a mess. I'll just meet you outside, okay?"

Cleo hurried down the curved narrow staircase towards Mr. Harbinger's checkout counter and heard the sound of chiming bells as Nia left the store.

Mr. Harbinger moved his glasses up his nose and lifted Cleo's find from the counter, staring at it for a few moments. He stood surprisingly quickly and spoke in a hurried and quiet voice. "The governor was in here a few times looking for a book *just like this*. Never did find it though."

So this is the book. I was right! I can give it to Barbara when I get back.

"Cleopatra, I *strongly* advise that you keep this to yourself," Mr. Harbinger said. It was almost as if he had read her mind.

"But-but-but why?" Cleo asked. "The governor is looking really hard for it."

"And he *must not find it*," Mr. Harbinger said in a very low voice.

"But … I don't understand," Cleo said, her enthusiasm suddenly deflated.

Squinting his eyes, Mr. Harbinger spoke in a whisper. "In time you will. There is more than one secret at Chronos Academy.

"Young lady, you better hurry up or you'll miss the boat. Isn't your friend waiting for you outside?" Mr. Harbinger added.

Right! "Um … how much?" Cleo asked, reaching for the money in her pocket.

"This one's on me, Cleopatra. For helping me stack the

books."

Cleo was about to defend herself. Then, remembering her manners, she said, "Thank you, Mr. Harbinger."

As she and Nia sped towards the pier, Cleo's mind raced.

What is so special about this book? And what did he mean by more than one secret at Chronos Academy?!

21

Luke

Luke tilted Ollie's flashlight to reread the news article about his dad for the umpteenth time. His dad had disappeared around Bovet Island in the southern hemisphere near Antarctica. A cold, unforgiving island with icebergs and no cities or towns. *That's where I'll start my search.*

Luke readjusted the pillow behind his head. It was late. Their dorm room was completely dark because of another school-wide blackout. He glanced at Ronan in the lower bunk across from him and could only see a partial silhouette.

"I cannot believe there's no Halloween in Pandia!" Ollie said from the bottom bunk below Luke. He was still disturbed that Luke had no idea about this Halloween thing.

"I can't live like this. I need decorations, I need costumes, I need candy. Halloween is only a week away!" Ronan said.

Professor Torres had held a lunchtime seminar on the importance of the *Dia de Los Muertos*, day of the dead, for Latin American cultures. Ronan had felt that Halloween was an important part of his American culture, especially the dressing-up-and-scaring-kids-and-getting-candy part. So after supper he'd taken it upon himself—with some help from North American kids like Canadian Ollie—to educate Luke, and Adio, who was from Jamaica and didn't celebrate Halloween either.

"We don't really have Halloween in Denmark either," Andy had told them. "We do have *Fastelavn* where kids dress up and go door to door singing a song for treats, but not in scary costumes. And it's not till February or March."

Ronan had been shocked. "How is it even possible that you guys can live through the fall without getting a bag full of candy from your neighbours?"

Ronan and Ollie now had a plan and permission to decorate portions of the castle with some cobwebs, and a skeleton or two. Wanting to up the wow factor, the two of them were brainstorming to get more ideas.

"Maybe Chef François can give out candy?" Ollie offered, his voice muffled from underneath his covers.

"Great idea. It could be a candy buffet instead of fish. Yah! I'll ask him," Ronan replied with a large yawn.

Several moments of quiet ensued until Andy disturbed the peace. "For my birthday in December, I will finally be thirteen, and I'm asking my parents for a headlamp. Joe never told me it was so dark here during all these blackouts."

Ronan thumped the bottom of the bunk above him. "Be quiet. I wanna sleep."

Luke re-folded the article and placed it back under his pillow. "Ollie, here's your flashlight," he said quietly as he lowered his arm to the lower bunk. He felt the flashlight being grabbed with a muffled thanks.

"You know what? No, I won't sleep!" Andy seethed on the top bunk across from Luke. "I'm still mad at Director

LeCrucia and Coach Typhoon after last week! First years are not allowed to learn fencing. I can't believe it! It's so arbitrary."

Here we go again, Luke thought. *How long will he keep us up this time?*

He heard Andy tearing paper and ripping it to pieces.

Andy imitated Coach Typhoon's deeper voice, although he squeaked a bit. "First years will not be allowed to try fencing. The Pandia Games are a serious competition and I need to focus on the older students." Resuming his normal voice, he continued, "Just because he's the coach, he gets what he wants? How are we going to make the RAF triathlon team for the Games if we can't fence with an actual sword? Those pool noodles are useless as weapons. What happened to grit and guts? And then Director LeCrucia replies NO to my letter asking to change it. I will never sleep." Luke was about to turn in his bunk to tell Andy to let it go—"Anger will fuel … ZZZ … ZZZ … "

Luke looked out the window, listening to Andy's snores. The purple aurora lights dancing in the clear night sky were dazzling.

His eyelids drooped.

Hiking in the woods with his dad, heading towards the campsite. His dad's voice, "Come on, Luke, just a bit further, you can make it! When we get there, we'll build a campfire." Seated by the fire, his dad wrapping his arm over Luke's shoulder. "I love you, son."

Luke woke with a start and felt for the watch on his wrist.

22

Cleo

In the stillness of her dorm room Cleo looked over at the glowing face of the small mechanical wind-up clock that was topped with double bells. Two a.m. Thoughts of the book spun in her mind. She'd discovered the leather-bound volume several days ago, but she still hadn't figured out what secrets Mr. Harbinger had been talking about. And she still didn't understand why she shouldn't give the book to the governor.

Outside the window the purple lights from the aurora borealis danced through the dark sky, oblivious to the blackout in the castle. Cleo closed the curtain. She'd been invigorated by the call with her grandma the other day. But Cleo hadn't mentioned anything to her about the book she'd found in Magic Awaits. Instead, she'd shared her drama with Stephanie. Her grandma had listened to Cleo's woes and encouraged her to give her roommates a chance; they might surprise her. Then CeeCee had mentioned an unexpected trip had come up and she'd be leaving immediately. Although Cleo was happy for her grandma, she was also sad that she wouldn't be able to call her or write to her for a while.

Cleo pulled the blanket over her head like a tent. Her book light clicking on sounded as loud as a bomb going off. Nia rustled above her in the top bunk. Cleo held her breath. When she was finally satisfied that Nia was still asleep, she opened the book as quietly as she could and looked at the first page again. The Chronos Academy crest was at the bottom of the first page with the year 1878. Above it she read

Research Findings of William Bale

Turning through the first couple of pages, her mind raced with the same thoughts she'd had since leaving the bookstore days ago. *Why is your book so important, William Bale? So important for the governor, anyway. And why did Mr. Harbinger want me to keep it a secret?*

She flipped further through the book. The cursive handwriting was hard to read. Her eyes fell on a sentence at the top of one page:

> *I continue to suffer through the torture delivered to me by my classmate Desseron.*

I guess I'm not the only one who's feeling tortured.

Cleo turned to another page. It was rather thick. Realizing two pages must be stuck together, she gently peeled the two corners and carefully separated them. She smoothed the pages down with her palm.

An intricate drawing with harsh, strong lines was sketched in pencil on the right-hand page. It was a 3D rectangle with a knight and other drawings on each of the faces. Next to the images inked in pen were the words:

arca of Athlia

What does "arca" mean?

Knight Athlia showed up in the margins, a couple of times.

Athlia must be a person!

Underneath "arca of Athlia" was a straight arrow drawn vertically. Cleo traced the line with her right index finger down the length of the page. At the arrowhead were three words:

Stone of Destiny

What?!

She quickly scanned the front and back of the two pages that had been stuck together and found something else:

This journal contains my research and findings on the three Stones of Destiny.

William Bale searched for the Stones of Destiny when he was a student here in the 1800s. Cleo half closed the book, using her fingers as a bookmark, and ran her other hand over the old leather cover.

The Stones of Destiny!

135

A loud THUMP sounded from the hallway outside their room. Startled, Cleo immediately turned off her booklight. In the stillness of the night, she waited, frozen, wondering if her roommates would wake up. Nia turned over in the bunk above her, but Daisy remained motionless, buried under her covers on the lower bunk across from Cleo. The quiet was so loud she couldn't bear it. Mr. Harbinger's words about secrets and warnings ran through her mind, *"He must not find it."*

Wait! Does the governor want the book because of the Stones?

When there wasn't any more thumping from the hall, and she was certain her roommates were still asleep, she released her breath.

Finally, Cleo clicked on her book light again.

Clearly one of the Stones had to do with the arca of Athlia, whatever that was. One thing was certain: she had to keep the book safe. Until she decided what to do with it, she'd keep the book with her at all times, inside CeeCee's backpack. When she wasn't in class, she'd examine the book and find out what else Bale had discovered.

Cleo smirked. She was on the track to finding the Stones of Destiny after all! She fell asleep repeating the words "arca of Athlia," in her mind.

23

Luke

It was Halloween day! Ronan and Ollie had successfully increased the wow factor of their decorations with Adio's help. The castle was covered in large fake spider webs, skeletons, scary drawings, and carved pumpkins, all competing with the "Go Vikes!" banners and the Pandia Games posters. Spooky organ music echoing in the background piped through the building, and fog machines filled the corridors with an eerie mist. Ronan was really happy, especially now that Chef François had relented and would have candy available for the students after dinner tonight.

Professor Logos' Bugs 'n' Such entomology lab aligned with Halloween.

"You'll have to pick up your handouts at the front, of course!" Professor Logos reminded them. He was a portly man and wore large dark glasses and a suit and tie. He had a goatee, and dark poofy hair in the shape of a mushroom on top of his head. "I am but a hologram." The projected professor waved his hands through his desk to demonstrate his point. He was a well-known and sought-after zoology professor. Being a hologram allowed him to teach worldwide without being anchored to one school.

Luke couldn't begin to understand the technology that put the professor in their classroom. The image was so lifelike, students often forgot Logos was a projection. Andy could never resist getting out of his seat to pass his hand right through the professor's round midsection. Professor Logos would joke, "Hey! That tickles!" then tell him to sit back down and stop interrupting.

Being a hologram wasn't the only reason Professor Logos was the strangest of all the professors at Chronos Academy. It seemed he always found time to maintain his personal grooming during class. Today he appeared sitting at the desk at the front of their classroom, trimming his fingernails and inspecting his cuticles as the students completed their Bugs 'n' Such assignments.

Andy was tapping his finger on a jar, holding it up to Ronan across the aisle behind Luke and Ollie. "It's a phasmid. Also known as a walking stick bug."

Ronan retrieved a container with a cricket in it.

"Make sure you're considering the anatomy and habitat of the species," said Professor Logos from his desk. "Would these two species ever meet in the wild? What are their food sources and predators? What role do they play in their ecological systems?"

Ronan held up his jar. "Since Luke won't join, let's go, Andy: cricket vs. phasmid! Who would win?"

"DO NOT put two species in a jar together to watch them fight! ANDY and RONAN! I REPEAT! DO NOT!" the professor insisted.

"I can't believe he heard us," Luke heard Ronan say

behind him.

"Of course I heard you! Your classroom is outfitted so I can see and hear all of you with great clarity."

Ollie snickered beside Luke. Luke wasn't sure if he was laughing at the professor or at a joke in the *Knights of Darkness* he was currently reading. Ollie had already finished his work.

Luke stretched his left arm by bringing it across his chest and using his right arm to tug on it. He was quite sore. They had their first archery lesson in gym class yesterday. Drawing the bow had used all his arm and back muscles, and striking the target had been impossible. He had no idea that archery could be so hard.

"Now that we're all nearing completion of the assignment," Professor Logos said, as he gathered his nail trimmings and placed them in a projected trash can. "We're going to depart from entomology this morning only for a brief rendezvous with the study of ornithology. We'll have a visit from a Halloween-themed scavenging species. So it's of the utmost importance that you put all your bugs 'n' such back into their jars."

Andy leaned across to poke Luke. "What's orbitcology?"

Luke shrugged but Ollie answered as he placed his comic into his backpack. "*Ornithology.* It's the study of birds."

"Remember, Ollie, I get the *Knights of Darkness* after Luke," Andy reminded.

"No, I do," argued Ronan.

Ollie had just turned thirteen, two days ago. And Ollie's birthday present, the latest issue of *Knights of Darkness,* had just arrived by mail. "You can flip a coin to decide who reads it after Luke," Ollie said. "He called it first."

One row over, Hayden complained loudly to no one

in particular, "I can't find all my worms." He held up two worms and an empty container.

Daisy, Cleo's roommate, answered Hayden's plea for assistance. She joined him at his desk, holding a worm in her hand. "Here's one. I found it back there," she said. She then plucked each of the worms off his hand and placed them all back into their container.

Hearing knocks at the door, Professor Logos rose from his desk. "Cleo, can you get the door, please?" he asked.

When she opened the door, Sir Lancelot zoomed right in. "Boo. Boo. Halloween animals. Ducky is scary." The robot stopped and wheeled slightly back and forth and continued, "Missing: Gregor's Unicycle, Torres's wallet, and Ludwig Corax."

The class murmured at Sir Lancelot's news but stopped when the robot belted out its next words. "Knock knock."

Andy jumped out of his seat. "This guy is hilarious." He moved in front of Sir Lancelot and Professor Logos gladly let him.

"Who's there?" Andy answered.

"Stopwatch."

"Stopwatch who?" Andy grinned.

"Stop watcha doing and let Mr. Ringwald in."

Andy whooped with laughter and returned to his seat.

"Thank you, Lancelot!" Professor Logos said as the robot left the classroom. The raven master entered, wearing an eyepatch.

Luke's focus quickly shot to Floki. Mr. Ringwald held the one-white-footed raven on his leather-gloved arm. The raven spread his wings widely. Luke gulped as he flashed back to the terrifying experience of being trapped with the bird in the castle on his first day.

"We'll be learning about ravens from our very own substitute raven master," Professor Logos said, as his translucent portly form made his way to the back of the class.

Mr. Ringwald frowned. "I'll answer some questions. But I can't stay long. LeCrucia—er sorry, Director LeCrucia—has me on a tight schedule."

"What happened to your eye?!" Ronan blurted out

The raven master adjusted his eyepatch. "Oh, my eye?" he said, "Yeah. Just a bit of bad luck. I, uh, ran into the, ah, door at the aviary."

The raven cawed and flapped onto Professor Logos' desk, moving papers around with its feet as though riding a skateboard, raven style. With its long hard black beak, it grabbed a pencil from the pencil holder, and began tapping it hard on the desk. The pencil broke in half.

"Floki! No. No. No!" Mr. Ringwald reprimanded the raven.

Luke wanted to retreat to the opposite end of the room, but his desk was in the front row.

And now the agitated raven was looking at him.

Floki extended his neck, fluffing his throat feathers. "Caw!"

Professor Logos, now somehow at the back of the room, called on students to ask questions quickly.

Cleo raised her hand. "How many ravens are on campus?"

The rest of the students chimed in belting out their own questions.

"How long do ravens live?"

"What's the difference between a crow and a raven?"

"Are they smart?"

"Do they take baths?"

Daisy followed with, "Um why does this one have a white foot? Can students come to the aviary? For my art project, I'd like to draw the ravens in their home."

Luke could see Mr. Ringwald was sweating. "There are, ah, seven—no six, yes, six on campus. Ravens are really big, they live a long time, they hate baths and this one is ah—Bad bird!" he shouted as Floki flew and landed on Luke's desk. Luke pressed his back hard against his chair, trying to push away from the terrifying scavenger. He felt trapped again.

"Do you have to trim the raven's nails? Floki's nails look pretty sharp," Ronan said, reaching out his arm to entice the bird to fly to him. He dragged his desk along the floor, trying to get closer to the bird. "Do you use clippers like Professor Logos' clippers or do you use scissors?"

Floki was turning his head side to side looking at Luke as though he recognized him. Luke stayed perfectly still, hoping the raven would fly onto someone else's desk.

"I found another worm!" Hayden said cheerfully, waving it in the air.

Floki flapped away from Luke and dove for Hayden's hand.

Hayden tossed the worm like a hot potato.

It landed on Luke's head.

Luke flapped his arms and tried to shake the worm from his hair. Suddenly he felt a breeze and something sharp pierce his scalp. He froze.

Ollie's dark skin blanched in terror and his eyes widened, the effect enhanced by his glasses. Pointing to Luke, he whispered, "Floki's on your head," stating the obvious.

Hayden shrieked, "The raven ate that worm—whole!

Holy Raven!"

Floki was digging into Luke's scalp with his talons. The pain was searing.

"Cacaw!"

Luke shook his head violently trying to shake the raven off, but the bird gripped his skull harder. He could answer Ronan's question definitively. This raven's nails had been trimmed by a razor sharpener!

"Stop moving, Luke!" Daisy commanded. "You're making Floki angry."

What about me?! He thought.

"Just sit still," she repeated calmly, "Or Floki will rip at you worse."

"Good idea. Everyone, stay still." Professor Logos spoke in a quiet voice from the back of the class.

Luke slowly looked up through the tears forming in his eyes. Maybe Daisy was right. If he stayed perfectly still, Floki would leave him alone. With all his will power, he stopped and sat still as the raven's sharp claws gripped his head like a perch.

He could hear the other kids in the class fidgeting, freaking out, commenting, and Professor Logos trying to regain control of the classroom. Floki's beak was rummaging through his hair.

"I think um, he's playing," Daisy said. "Maybe he's looking for more worms?"

Luke felt a poke. A trickle of liquid slid from behind his ear.

"Oh no Luke, his beak cut you," Nia added.

Luke swallowed. Through his tears, he watched a blurry Daisy open Mr. Ringwald's bag on the floor.

"Floki, want some of this?" Daisy said sweetly to the bird as she carefully placed something on the professor's desk.

"Blood crackers, a well-known raven treat. Well done, Daisy!" Professor Logos said, his voice faint as though far away.

"Come on, Floki. Yum," Daisy said. Cleo was now beside her, looking rather nervous. Daisy approached Luke and called to Floki again, inviting the bird onto her outstretched arm. Luke was grateful when the raven jumped to her. She carefully took the bird to the snack she'd put on the desk.

Luke shook his head vigorously and rubbed it with his hand. Ollie saw Luke's bloodied hand and started to gag.

"Caw! Caw!"

Daisy gently stroked the bird's head, keeping it calm.

Professor Logos had moved to the front of the room. He said, "Good job Daisy, can you look after the bird? Alas, I can't grab it." He turned to the other students near his desk. "Cleo, can you stay to help Daisy? Everyone else, give Luke space. That's better. Luke, those cuts look like they could use some attention from Nurse Kelly. Ollie, please accompany him. I will contact Director LeCrucia." He raised his eyes to the class. "Everyone else is dismissed. And please exit calmly, do not agitate the raven."

Ollie grabbed his backpack and moved next to Luke as he stood.

"Where's Mr. Ringwald?" Luke managed to squeak out. His legs felt like jelly as he moved further away from Floki.

"He left after the worm fell on your head. Probably to go to the bathroom. It must be a number two, 'cause he hasn't come back," Ollie said. He stood on his tippy toes trying to examine the top of Luke's head. He gagged again. "It's not that bad," he said reassuringly.

Walking quickly down the corridor, they passed the horology classroom and then took the stairs two by two from the second floor, to the nurse's office on the third floor. Luke was glad Ollie was with him. The nurse's office was a long narrow white room, with white walls and floors, white framed beds, and white tables that made it look like a hospital room. Open floating shelves all around the room held first aid kits, bottles of medicine, and equipment. In between were randomly distributed miniature skeletons in celebration of Halloween.

"Holy Halloween!" Nurse Kelly exclaimed when she saw the trickles of blood from Luke's cuts. Her long black hair was in a side braid, exposing a large tattoo of a skull on her neck under the edge of her white lab coat.

While she examined Luke's head, Ollie explained what happened and finished the story saying, "It was really Daisy that saved Luke. She's so great with Floki. She was better than everyone there."

"Thanks, Ollie. You have a good friend here, Luke." Nurse Kelly said, and Ollie beamed. "Sit down on this," she added, grabbing a rolling stool from under her small wooden desk and pushing it toward the patient.

Luke sat, shook his inhaler, and took a puff.

A few seconds later when she spoke, she sounded irritated. "We need Ludwig Corax back. Poor man. Mr. Ringwald cannot control those ravens one iota. You know, he came here to get that eye patch just a week ago or so. The ravens nicked him. Again."

Luke eyed Ollie, who nodded. That's not what Mr. Ringwald had told them in class today.

"What happened to them?" Ollie said, now noticing the other kids in the infirmary. Two students were lying on cots. A boy had his ankle wrapped with a brown elastic bandage, and a girl her wrist. Both were sleeping.

"It's been non-stop since Coach Typhoon changed up his gym classes in preparation for the games. He's pushing the kids too hard. I had to bring in extra cots," Nurse Kelly sighed loudly, and pulled gauze from a jar. "These are mostly scratches, so you won't need stitches. But they must be cleaned." She poured alcohol on several pieces of gauze and gently tapped on the wounds on Luke's head. He squirmed and yelped. Before he could say that he didn't want to be treated anymore, Nurse Kelly straightened up. "There. Done. But I need you to wait here for a second. I'll grab you another inhaler. Be right back."

Once she'd exited the room, Ollie came up to Luke and spoke quietly. "Luke, look at this." He had grabbed the *Gazette* from the nurse's desk and was pointing to a story on the front page. Relieved to be distracted by something else, Luke silently read the article alongside Ollie.

Bad Luck Befalls Chronos Academy

In addition to the string of thefts at the academy, Ludwig Corax has been reported missing. The renowned raven master of Chronos Academy was on sabbatical in England, researching ravens in their natural habitat. He failed to return to the Abton Nature Reserve Center after scheduled field work. Foul play is suspected at this time. "We're all hoping for his safe and quick return," said Roy Ringwald who has been filling in as raven master at Chronos Academy. He also added "All the thefts at Chronos Academy, and now poor Mr. Corax missing, well the pressure on Director LeCrucia must be enormous."

Anyone with information on the Ludwig Corax case or the string of thefts at Chronos Academy is asked to contact Detective Anders, Glimmerton Police.

"What thefts on campus?" Ollie asked quietly, quickly taking an inventory of his backpack

Luke meekly added, "I wonder what happened to Mr. Corax. Foul play?"

"Maybe that's why the ravens are acting extra strange lately." Ollie added, "Or maybe that's why Mr. Ringwald is acting so strange!"

Luke didn't know anything about Ludwig Corax, but he wondered if foul play might have been a factor in his father's disappearance. It was something he'd never considered. He had to find his dad. Luke could only think of one way to do that. He needed to get back to Bastion Tower and find treasure. Besides, he couldn't shake the feeling that he had missed something in the tower attic.

The nurse returned not only with a refill of Luke's inhaler but also with a syringe, needle, and a small vial. "Your records say you're due for a tetanus shot. Best we take care of it Luke, so time for a wee bit of a poke," she said cheerfully as she cleaned a spot on his upper arm.

Liquid squirted out of the needle as she pushed the air bubbles out. She lined the needle up with Luke's upper arm with one hand and held his T-shirt out of the way with the other, gripping his deltoid muscle.

As the needle stung his arm, Luke looked away and towards Ollie. His roommate's eyes were wide and focused on the needle. Ollie collapsed onto the floor.

24

Luke

It had been a frustrating two weeks. After Luke's head had been ripped apart by Floki on Halloween, a spider infestation had spread over a huge swath of the west wing of the main castle. A wide out-of-bounds perimeter had been set up outside for the two weeks of fumigation, and even the corridors leading to Bastion Tower had been sealed off.

The spider infestation was finally declared over at the end of the second week of November. It was a Sunday afternoon when Luke, Ollie, Ronan, and Andy finally pushed their way through bushes that had shed their colourful fall foliage. They passed through the little bronze door into the castle. Making their way to the wooden door with the DO NOT ENTER! sign, they climbed up the spiral stairs of Bastion Tower.

Andy shouted as he entered the tower room, "I'm checking the boxes over there by John Bones." Clearly Luke wasn't the only one who was excited to be back at the tower.

Luke made his way to the attic ladder.

"Why are you going there?" Ollie asked. "That attic is

scary. It feels weird up there."

"That attic's B for bust, Luke," Ronan added before veering off and joining Andy.

Luke wasn't so sure. He kept thinking about that blue spark he had seen. Luke stopped at the bottom of the ladder for a second, "Ollie, can I borrow your flashlight?"

Ollie whipped the flashlight out of his backpack. "Thanks," Luke said as he pushed past his roommate and started to climb the ladder.

He moved to the attic fireplace, following the path of the flashlight. He squinted his eyes trying to remember where he had seen the spark. He looked up the chimney. After examining the fireplace for several minutes, a sudden swirl of cold air blasted Luke, forcing him to step back. White looping wisps began to appear from the floor and walls of the firebox, growing together to form a ghostly translucent image. A woman in a long white dress was removing a brick from the floor in front of the fireplace. Her long silky hair trailed down the back of her flowing gown. Luke's heart thumped loudly against his chest as he stood frozen in mid-step.

Luke watched the woman place a red object in the space under the brick. After she had replaced the brick in its original spot, she stood, turned in Luke's direction, and said, "For those who seek the gift of time. May this treasure return to you the ones you've lost." Then the woman dropped to her knees and wept as the mist dissipated and the image vanished.

Luke felt a rush of cold leave his body.

CREAK.

Luke stifled a scream as he jumped and turned around.

Ollie was staring at him with large eyes from the ladder at the attic entrance. "Did you see that?" Luke asked.

"See what?" Ollie responded. "Did you find something?"

"No," Luke lied, not wanting to sound crazy. "Did you?"

"Nope," Ollie said and began wandering around the attic. Pulling open a drawer on the wood cabinet Ollie asked Luke, "Can you feel that chill? It's way worse than downstairs. This attic is eerie."

Ghostly, actually.

Shaking a little, Luke crouched down and started looking for a loose brick in the fireplace. Holding the flashlight with his left hand Luke ran his right hand along the bricks and found one. To pry it up, he grabbed the fire poker he'd left on the floor last time. A very upset spider shot out at him, but nothing else lay underneath. It took a while before he found another loose brick. He pried it upward. Nothing.

"What are you doing, Luke?" Ollie asked, confused.

That ghost lady said treasure. It has to be here.

"Help me find the loose bricks," Luke directed him, "There might be treasure under them."

Ollie crouched down next to him to help him search.

"Why do you think there's treasure under the bricks?" Ollie asked.

"I don't know," Luke said. He couldn't tell Ollie about the ghost lady. That would be so weird.

After some time, they had only found a few bricks they could pry up and none of those had treasure underneath them.

"Nothing under this one either," Ollie said, wiping his dusty hands on his pants.

Disappointed, Luke put the fire poker aside and leaned

back on his heels. *The ghost lady seemed so real, just like when I dream about Dad.*

He was about to tell Ollie that they should head back down to the grand chamber when he decided to lift up one more brick. As he lifted it, a small cavity appeared. Luke leaned forward and examined it more closely with the flashlight. A rectangular dust-covered metal box was nestled inside the cavity. As he moved the light, he saw a blue shimmer.

"Ollie, there's something here!" Luke shouted in disbelief.

Luke was ecstatic! He leaned forward, placed his hand inside the cavity, and picked up the red box. He showed it to Ollie.

Ollie took in a deep breath, his cheeks puffing. He snapped forward, blowing at the grey layer of dust on top of the palm-sized box. The dust broke loose and flew into Luke's nostrils. Luke scrunched and stretched his nose in response.

"Sorry," Ollie said.

Luke released a powerful sneeze that nailed Ollie in the face.

"Me too," Luke said as he wiped his nose with his sleeve and Ollie cleaned his glasses with the bottom of his shirt. They both laughed.

Wiping the rest of the box clean with his sleeve, Luke could now see that the treasure he was holding was a deep red metal box. "This is it," Luke said out loud.

"What do you mean this is it?" Ollie asked.

"The treasure she put under the brick," Luke said, forgetting himself.

"Who?"

"No one!" Luke said. Hoping Ollie wouldn't ask any more questions he said, "We found our first treasure!"

"You're acting strange," Ollie said. "How did you know there was a treasure hidden by the fireplace?"

Ollie squinted at him with his lips pursed, "Did you tell someone about the tower?"

"No! Of course not." Luke would never do that.

"Then how did you know where to look? Who told you?" Ollie demanded.

"Fine. I'll tell you. I don't know what I saw exactly." He turned the metal box over in his hands, "I don't really get it." Luke explained his vision of the ghost lady.

"Can you see her now?" Ollie asked, looking hesitantly at the fireplace. "I can't see her."

"No, " Luke said.

Ollie was a little shaky. "I'm getting my ghost annihilator." He was reaching into his backpack when Luke grabbed his arm.

"No!" Luke said again. He didn't know if he had seen a ghost or if the ghost capturing jar would work, but what if it did and they captured and annihilated the ghost lady?

"She might be able to tell us about more treasure," Luke said, trying to reason with his roommate.

Ollie nodded, considering Luke's argument. "We better tell Andy and Ronan," Ollie said, putting the jar away.

"We can't! They'll think I'm crazy," Luke said.

Ollie nodded slowly. "And they'll bug you nonstop about the ghost lady," Ollie said, his face contorting in thought.

Luke gave a quizzical smile and then understood that Ollie was using Canadian English, in which bug meant teasing. He gave a small nod.

"Cool. I swear I won't tell about the ghost lady," Ollie said and crossed his heart. His eyes widened and he did an extra step of gleeful anticipation. "But this treasure is cool! We gotta show them the treasure. It's in the oath."

Luke remembered the oath for the Order of Ravens. Ollie was right, he needed to stay true to his word to share his find with the others. "Yeah, we better. But I don't want to talk about the ghost lady yet." Ollie made a gesture of locking his mouth closed and throwing away the key.

They made their way back to the big tower room where Ronan was dancing with the skeleton.

Ollie announced, "Luke found something."

"Dun-dun-dun-DUN," Ronan bellowed. "What is it?"

"Some kinda antique box." Luke turned the small rectangular box in his hand. It was about the size of a four-pack of Hubble Bubble Gum.

"It's in really good shape," Ollie added. "There's no dents or anything in the metal and these drawings are so cool."

Each side of the box was embossed with coloured medieval images that had faded only a little.

"It's kind of heavy for something so small," he said as he ran his hand over the palm-sized red metal treasure. "It feels like there's something in it."

Luke put the treasure onto a sheet-covered table so they could examine it. The box appeared to be solid, without any sign of a lid, keyhole, or latch of any kind. Ronan grabbed the box and gave it a good shake. "I don't think there's anything in here, Luke. It's not rattling at all," he said. He tried to force it open anyway, pulling on two sides.

"It doesn't look important. It's probably just a decoration. My uncle has tons of baubles like this around his house," Andy said with a shrug. Having lost interest, he and Ronan moved on to examine the contents of a tall black cabinet.

Ollie observed, "The pictures on it are really interesting. They look like they tell a story. Like a comic strip."

"But where does the story start?" Luke asked.

Ollie held the box close to his glasses and squinted at it. "I can see knights here. There's one on each side. Each one has a sword."

"Not every knight." Luke took the box. "Look here, this one doesn't have a sword. This one has an axe. This—wait a second. That's like the knight in Knight Hall!" He recalled the looming axe of the swordless knight, ready to strike him on the first day of school.

"A swordless knight," Ollie said curiously. "That's weird. I always think of knights having swords. I wonder what was on the top side of the box." Ollie held the box again and scratched some of the worn out black that covered the top with his nail. Not making out anything, he shrugged and turned the trinket over. "Hey, on the bottom here, there's a tree with a sword leaning against it. Cool."

Ronan called from across the room, "I just found a hammer. Maybe we should smash it to see what's inside?"

"Then you'd smash what's inside, too," Ollie replied disapprovingly.

"I guess." Ronan turned his focus back to the cabinet in front of him.

Andy approached them with a large frown on his face. "Today was a bust," he said. "No gold coins, no cool stuff! The coolest thing we found was this decoration. It's not even half as cool as the chainmail we found weeks ago. Let's just go. I'm getting hungry!"

Ollie looked at Luke, eyes wide like he might want to say why Andy was wrong and the box was way cooler than the chainmail. Luke shook his head. Ollie understood.

"Do you want to carry that in your backpack?" Luke asked Ollie, motioning to the red box.

Ollie straightened and beamed, "It would be an honour, fellow knight. But you found the treasure. You must guard it." Ollie nodded in approval when Luke tucked the red trinket into the pocket of his jacket.

As Luke continued down the spiral staircase his questions multiplied. *The ghost lady said that this treasure could bring back someone who was lost. But how? How do I get from here to my expedition and finding my dad?*

25

Luke

For a classroom in a dungeon, Luke found Professor Gregor's lab to be quite bright. There was one long lab bench in each row, and stools for seats. He noticed the glassware; Erlenmeyer flasks, oblong glass tubes, and conical flasks were no longer on the floor. Adio had *finally* stacked all the glassware onto the shelves. It was *only* mid-November after all.

Professor Gregor clapped his hands, to quiet the classroom. "I want to call your attention to the posters I've put up on the wall. And I have an important question," Professor Gregor said. The Pandia Games posters had now been replaced by MISSING posters showing a picture of Professor Gregor's unicycle and offering a cash reward. "Has anyone seen my unicycle? Or did any of you borrow it? Do you know if anyone expressed an interest in borrowing it or taking it? Have you noticed any suspicious activity around campus?"

"That's more than one question," Andy remarked.

Professor Gregor stared at him. After an awkward pause he continued. "Fine, we shall move on. You've just finished your mid-November unit test yesterday, so today we're doing something different. The name of the game is Serious Science. *Light-ning* round," Professor Gregor hooted.

"*Hola, todos!*" An exuberant feminine voice came from the side of the classroom.

"Ah, excellent timing, Professor Torres," Professor Gregor said, with a stiff almost-smile.

Much younger than Professor Gregor, Professor Torres wore her dark hair in a short pixie. She sported a casual look of jeans and, under her lab coat, a T-shirt decorated with black and white cartoon fireflies that were glowing in yellow. Sir Lancelot was hot on her heels.

"Ding dang dong. Ding dang dong," Sir Lancelot drawled out. Luke had heard that the students in the robotics lab had a new menu of sounds to choose from whenever they reprogrammed the robot.

Professor Torres quickly walked to the back of the lab, grabbed a small plastic container from a shelf, and handed it to Sir Lancelot who took off in a hurry. Making her way to the front of the classroom she said, "I am a biology teacher here at Chronos Academy. This year I am not teaching because I am helping Director LeCrucia with a special project. Today I am here to help Professor Gregor with a most wonderful surprise. Ready, professor?" Professor Torres was now at the chalkboard, her wrist jingling with delicate bracelets as she created a score sheet.

"Yes. Lightning round begins!" Professor Gregor cried. A buzz of excitement filled the classroom as the students tried to grasp what was going on. Professor Gregor walked down an aisle between the lab benches. "Tell me what an atom is."

Cleo answered, "An atom is the smallest unit of everything,

both living and nonliving."

"Correct, Cleo. Two points." Professor Gregor said, pointing to the chalkboard.

"Why is it bad to trust atoms?" prompted Professor Torres as she wrote on the board.

Cleo giggled, "They make up everything!"

The class groaned.

"Exactly!" Professor Torres laughed, "Give me an example of things composed of atoms."

"I'm made of atoms, and so is the desk I'm sitting in," Cleo beamed as she answered the question.

"That's two more points. For answering the question and getting the joke," Professor Torres smiled.

"What are atoms made of?" Professor Gregor asked.

"The nucleus is made of protons and neutrons, and electrons orbit the nucleus," Stephanie piped up from the back of the class.

"Very good, Stephanie. Three points. And what are protons and neutrons made of?"

"Quarks!" Cleo and Stephanie said in unison.

"Two points for each of you."

Luke turned to look at the back of the room. Stephanie stuck her tongue out at Cleo and glared, but Cleo just turned stiffly to face the front of the classroom.

"Hair is typically 50 micrometers in width," Professor Gregor said, plucking a strand from his own head and holding it up for the class to see. "How many times smaller than a millimeter is a hair?"

Hayden lifted his desk with him as he stood. "A million! 1000. 913. 475. 500. 14— no—20."

Professor Gregor looked slightly more exasperated than

usual, although it was hard to tell. "The correct answer is 20. Give Hayden two points."

Professor Gregor continued with his barrage of questions, "Now, how many atoms could fit in the width of a hair?"

Luke felt a tug on his head. "Ow!"

Ronan was holding up several strands of Luke's hair against a ruler as he mumbled a calculation under his breath. Andy was laughing.

Luke rubbed his head and noticed that the scratches Floki had inflicted had healed. Next to him, Ollie was scribbling a calculation longer than his paper onto his desk.

"Two million atoms in a millimeter!" Stephanie shouted from the back.

Ollie smacked his pencil on his desk, just under the printed number 2,000,000.

Stephanie got three points.

"How many types of atoms make up an element?"

Luke shot his hand up as he spoke. "Each element is made up of only one type of atom."

"Good, Luke! Two points. Example of an element?"

"Alpha, no, beta. No! Omega. No—carbon!" Ronan managed to shout before Luke could say anything.

"Greek letters no, but carbon is correct! One point." Professor Gregor waved his hand briefly in Ronan's direction.

"Nitrogen and oxygen," Luke said quickly before anyone else could answer.

"Good! Two points for Luke," Gregor said. "What is it called when more than one atom combines with another?"

"A molecule!" Cleo got two points.

"Give an example of a molecule."

"Water! H_2O," Cleo offered.

"DNA," Stephanie quipped, hot on her heels.

"A complex molecule! Two points for that answer, Stephanie. And one point to Cleo. A bonus of three points to anyone who can name the molecular shape of the double-stranded DNA molecule!" Professor Gregor said enthusiastically.

"Octagon!" Ronan shouted.

Professor Torres chuckled at the board as she drew the shape of the molecule.

"Anyone else?" An alarm on Professor Gregor's watch beeped. "Never mind. Time's up, everyone. DNA forms a double helix, as drawn by Professor Torres on the board. Anyhow, that was a tough question. Professor Torres, who's the winner of today's Serious Science *light-ning* round?"

"The top scorer is Stephanie! She will be the nucleus, or team captain. The other four who will join her, the orbiting electrons," said Professor Torres, laughing, "are Hayden, Ronan, Luke, and Cleo."

Professor Gregor blinked at her and addressed the class. "Well done everyone. Stephanie's team is first up. The rest of you will be chosen at random."

"Chosen for what?" Andy asked.

"Getting a chance at the fencing team?" Nia asked hopefully.

Professor Gregor said, "Ah. No. The locked room escape challenge, of course. A joint project between myself and Professor Torres. It's STEM—*science, technology, engineering, math*. And it's fun! You have to work together to figure out the clues to escape confinement—"

"ALIVE!" Andy yelled. "Nooooooooo! Ronan I will miss you, goodbye, goodbye my young friend, too young. Too young."

"Oh brother," Nia rolled her eyes and then added, "Good luck, Cleo."

"Stephanie!" Professor Torres called, ignoring Andy who had fallen to the floor, squealing in mock agony. "For your group, the STEM locked room event begins NOW! And be good. Remember we are keeping a positive i-on you. Get it? Positive ION?"

Professor Gregor groaned along with the class.

Ronan grabbed Luke's shirt. He had him out the door by the time Luke heard the beep of Gregor's stopwatch and Torres's comment that Andy's cheekiness had earned him the place of captain for the next team.

The lightning round had actually been kind of fun and pretty exciting. For the first time in days, Luke had momentarily forgotten about the red box in his pocket.

26

Cleo

Following the instructions on their STEM challenge handouts, they raced across campus, down the hill, and to the fork in the road. Instead of taking Franklin Lane they took Faraday Lane to the Blacksmith's cottage, workshop, and armoury. On the outside, the historic building looked like a cute stone cottage, with a modern-day banner draped across the top of the door

Pandia Games, we soar to incredible heights

The cottage was trimmed with large wooden beams and the roof sagged just a little bit. Cleo could see the vast Kingsburg Forest well behind the cottage, and she could just make out the peaks of the castle towers in the direction from which they had come. Not too far from the cottage was a cart holding the black mini-magnetometers and computers with a sign that read

DO NOT TOUCH
PROPERTY OF CHRONOS ACADEMY

The cold and cloudy November morning made Cleo shiver in her hoodie. She was happy with how fast she could run—easily keeping up with Ronan, and not becoming breathless— thanks to all Coach Typhoon's crazy gym classes. But now any thoughts about running, the Stones of Destiny, and the book were usurped by more pressing matters. Cleo couldn't believe she'd gotten assigned to the same team as Stephanie. How many "opportunities to grow," could she possibly need?

At the bottom step of the three-step staircase that led to a small landing, Cleo was surprised to see a knight holding a spear in the air and displaying a sword tucked in his belt.

When the face shield lifted, Mr. Ringwald was revealed. Ronan approached the armour-clad raven master. "How come you're dressed like that? This is just like the armour in Knight Hall. It's so cool! Is it from medieval times? Is it heavy? Is it hot in there? Can I try it on?"

Mr. Ringwald scratched his twitchy brown moustache and scowled at Ronan. Responding only to the first question he said, "Ludwig Corax always did it. Raven master tradition." His tone suggested he wasn't a big fan of the dressing up traditions for raven masters at the academy.

A raven pecking at the ground said, "Bee boop." It sounded just like a human speaking. Luke immediately took a few steps back. Cleo guessed he was still traumatized by his encounter with Floki during the Bugs 'n' Such lab. She giggled a bit to herself.

"Are you a ventriloquist?" Ronan blurted out, pointing at the raven master and then the raven.

"Munnin, right?" Cleo asked. As Mr. Ringwald nodded, she turned to Ronan. "Remember the Chronos Day celebration at the amphitheatre? Munnin talked. Ravens can speak when they're trained to do so," Cleo said as she crouched and approached the bird. "Munnin also has one blue eye and one black. Daisy told me. She's working on an art project drawing all the school ravens."

Stephanie piped up imitating Cleo, "'Daisy told me.' Whatever, Cleopatra."

No matter what Stephanie said, she could always make Cleo blush with embarrassment. And now Stephanie was whispering to Hayden. It was just like back at their old school. Stephanie whispering secrets and excluding Cleo. When Cleo stood up, she felt like shrinking back into the ground.

"Is that raven flying upside down?" Ronan asked, pointing upwards.

They all looked up at the bird.

Mr. Ringwald responded gruffly, calling to the raven in the sky, "Show off!" His armour creaked on his climb up the three cottage stairs. Using the little landing as a stage, the raven master called, "Hear ye, hear ye!" and began reading from a scroll:

"Hear ye a few clues to solve this medieval mystery.
Keep track of the time, call upon science and history.
Clues are not elementary, but answers they'll yield,
Using knight vision, in darkness all will be revealed.
Work letters and numbers to find a pattern repeater,
Will you escape this medieval STEM classroom
theater?"

"Dun-dun-dun-DUUUUUN," Ronan added.

"Who's the team captain?" Mr. Ringwald asked.

"I am!" Stephanie said, bounding up the stairs to join the raven master on the landing.

He handed her the scroll, then tried to plant his heavy spear ceremoniously on the step. He missed the step and caught his toe poking out from the armour. "Mangled milk-livered mammet!" He dropped the heavy spear and bent down to rub his foot. The heavy weight of the armour shifted and upset his balance. He tumbled down the steps and lay splayed on the ground.

Unfazed, Stephanie read from further down the scroll:

"Through these doors your quest awaits. Solve all the puzzles to make your escape."

Stephanie tried to open the door. "It's locked, Mr. Ringwald."

When the raven master finally made his way back up to the landing, he unlocked the door and gestured for the students to pass through. On his way into the cottage, Ronan accidentally bumped him, and the face shield fell over Mr. Ringwald's face again. "Curses!" Mr. Ringwald's muffled voice said as Cleo passed.

After they'd all entered the cottage, Cleo heard the door lock behind them. She tried not to freak out that she was locked inside the cottage with Stephanie. Fate was cruel sometimes.

The building felt cool. Muted light came through the round window above the door. There was an old wooden table, one chair, and an open trunk at the foot of a bed with a small wooden stool next to it. Above the bed hung a tattered tapestry in earthy colours. To the left of the table was a fireplace made of stone. It had a thick mantel lined with a few small objects and metal boxes. At the back of the living quarters, an arched doorway led to another room.

Cleo made her way through the arch and entered a larger room that was only weakly lit by a single naked bulb hanging from the ceiling.

"This is the Blacksmith's workshop!" Ronan said in surprise when he entered, followed closely behind by Hayden and Stephanie. The room felt dark and dingy. A large forge stuck out from the wall with a cauldron on top of it. There was a stool next to it. On the floor, several large iron tongs leaned up against a solid wood toolbox filled with hand hammers, a variety of chisels, punches, and a selection of tongs with different pincers. A sledgehammer leaned against a wooden barrel in the corner. Two more barrels sat beside the first, and a set of shelves hung on the wall above them. Three knight's helmets lined the wall adjacent to a cabinet by the hearth. Double sliding wooden doors were padlocked and set into the long side of the room.

Cleo spotted an information placard on top of one of the shelves:

Blacksmith's workshop used in medieval times, during the reign of King Sullivan. Burnt in the Great Reckoning and restored many times since. Still used at Chronos Academy for recreating historical implements, repair of artifacts, and custom iron work for the castle.

"*Still* used! I wonder who the blacksmith is?" Cleo asked.

"It's not Mr. Ringwald!" Ronan chuckled as he examined

a set of large iron tongs. "Adio, maybe? He seems really strong."

"Where are all the clues? I don't see any!" Hayden cried. He hastily turned around in a circle, trying to get his bearings.

"Everything is pretty medieval. Tough to see the STEM here," Stephanie commented, arms folded as she leaned against a wall.

Cleo ignored her desire to correct Stephanie that forging is a technology of its own. She looked around one more time and made her way back into the living quarters to search. There she suddenly spied their first clue.

An hourglass the size of a large flashlight stood on the floor beside the bed. It contained black iron filings. Cleo placed her backpack on the bed, grabbed the hourglass, and flipped it over. The filings began to flow downward.

That was when she noticed Luke. He was taking a puff of his inhaler as he stared at the fireplace's mantle. She was surprised he hadn't made his way into the blacksmith's workshop with everyone else.

"'*Keep track of the time.*' That was an easy one," she called over to Luke.

"Huh?" he asked. He shoved something red into his pocket.

"I got the first clue! Keep track of the time." She pointed out the hourglass.

"Oh. Good."

"Uh, everything okay?"

He nodded and went to join the team members in the other room. Cleo followed him and placed the hourglass on the hearth. As she did, she noticed an inscription written on the bottom of it. *A second clue.*

"It says three rings."

"Great job Cleo," Ronan said. "Three rings? Where?" and he started rummaging around the blacksmith workshop.

"I'm team captain!" Stephanie's shrill voice brought Cleo's attention to where her nemesis was standing, arms akimbo, by a barrel. "The next clue on the scroll says *clues are not elementary!*"

"Whoa!" Ronan cried, pulling three rings from an open metal container on one of the shelves above the barrels. "Three metal rings, with a tag on each one."

"What's on the tag?" Hayden asked.

Ronan tossed a ring to Luke. Hayden caught the other.

"A single letter. '*C*,'" said Ronan.

"'*N*,'" said Cleo, leaning over Hayden's shoulder to read the tag.

Luke cleared his throat, "Mine has a letter, too," he said, "'*O*.'"

"What does that mean?" Cleo was puzzled.

"I'm team captain—I'll figure it out!" Stephanie commanded.

Hayden huffed, put the ring down and grabbed a placard from on top of the barrel that described the history of forging.

"There's something on the back," Ronan said. He grabbed the card out of Hayden's hands and showed it to Luke and Cleo.

It was unreadable gibberish with random letters. Cleo tapped on her forehead with her forefinger. "*NOT elementary*," she paused. "So not an element?"

Stephanie snatched the placard from Ronan and moved towards the forge oven. She grabbed a pencil-sized piece of wood from the forge that was black at one end and started to rub it on the placard.

"That's actually smart," Ronan commented, and Stephanie

scoffed.

"Not elementary. So cross off the letters that are elements. Like," Stephanie paused.

"C, N, O are the elements carbon, nitrogen, and oxygen," Cleo offered.

Surprisingly, Stephanie didn't resist her suggestion and she began crossing out the letters. Stephanie looked up. "It says 'What is a medieval lamp?'"

"I know! It's a knight-light," Ronan said, raising his eyebrows and grinning.

Cleo could feel her pulse increasing with excitement. "That must be the *knight vision* clue!"

Stephanie clucked with a superior and sour voice, "Well, aren't we clever?"

"Knights, that means—" Cleo began.

"Helmets!" Ronan and Hayden said at the same time. They raced across the room, and leapt for the three knight helmets on the wall. Stephanie sneered at Luke and Cleo.

The two boys wrestled with each other, each trying to grab the helmets first. Hayden flew hard onto the ground, landing a few feet away. Red in the face he got up, his hands balled into fists, and stared at Ronan.

Ronan glared back, just as red. He walked over to Luke with two helmets in his hand. He shoved one over Luke's head.

"Ow!" Luke said.

Ronan noticed something inside his helmet and pulled out a small beige flashcard. He read it out loud, "*It glows like a worm or a firefly.*"

"Bioluminescence," Cleo and Stephanie said at the same time.

"That's two points!" Ronan laughed.

"Professor Gregor kept saying *Light-ning* round." Stephanie explained, and darted towards the light switch, her long blonde ponytail swooshing back and forth.

The boys dropped their helmets to the ground just as the light went out. In the dark of the windowless workshop, Cleo smelled the charred coal and wood in the forge and a hint of cedar from the barrels in the corner. She felt the weight of the cool musty air around her, and she could see a glowing in the distance. She moved cautiously towards the faint green light, shuffling her feet on the floor. She could hear the others making their way clumsily in the dark, too.

THUMP

"Owww," moaned Ronan.

"Not cool!" Hayden added from somewhere in the dark.

"Scared, Hayden?" Ronan taunted. "I'm not. I have the nocturnal vision of a raccoon."

"Whatever, Ronan," Stephanie's shrill voice cut through the dark.

Cleo's foot bumped into a barrel. Then she leaned over and grabbed the glowing objects from the top of the barrel. They felt soft and crinkly. "I found it."

Suddenly the light came back on. Cleo blinked as she examined the find in her hands. "It's leaves. Four of them. Each one has a letter on it. X, I, T, E."

"XITE," Ronan said, and scratched his head.

"EXIT... it must be this door that looks like a barn door! This must be it," Stephanie said excitedly, pointing to the padlocked double doors.

Luke was closest to the hourglass and mentioned, "We're almost out of time. The hourglass is nearly empty."

"What does the scroll say?" Cleo suggested.

"Just some dumb rhyme about a pattern repeater, but we don't need to figure it out. Let's just break the lock and get out of here," Stephanie said.

Cleo looked at the barrel, where the leaves had been on the lid. When she shimmied aside the lid, she saw more leaves inside. If more letters or numbers were imprinted on those, the team could use them to find the scroll's pattern repeater.

Hayden held the large silver padlock connecting the two handles of the warped and rotting barn doors. "Let's use the hammers over there to smash the lock open."

"I think there are clues in this barrel," Cleo insisted.

"That makes sense," Ronan said, making his way to the barrel to help.

Stephanie approached Cleo aggressively, her eyes hard and narrow. "I'm the team captain! I decide."

"But we are missing the pattern repeater clue from the scroll," Cleo said meekly.

Stephanie stared right at Cleo and gritted her teeth. "If we want to win, we have to beat the timer. There are no more clues! Do it, Hayden."

Hayden returned with a hammer and started pounding on the lock, while Stephanie grabbed another tool and joined him.

Stop! Cleo pleaded in her mind while Ronan grabbed at the hammer in Hayden's hand. Luke came to help him.

Hayden resisted but Ronan finally freed the implement from his fist. The hammer went flying, missing Cleo's face by a centimeter.

Hayden screamed in frustration and shoved Ronan back into Luke, both boys tumbling to the ground. Ronan disentangled himself from Luke and jumped back up. He and Hayden started circling each other like boxers in a ring.

27

Luke

As Luke got up from the floor of the blacksmith's workshop, he spotted his red box. It had fallen out of his pocket. The zipper of his jacket must have come undone!

Cleo moved with lightning speed. She grabbed the box, retreated from the Ronan–Hayden showdown, and started examining it.

Stephanie approached her from behind and snatched the tiny treasure from her hands. "Oooh, what's this? Seems interesting."

Luke shouted in a surprisingly tough voice, "It's mine!" Hayden made a break from Ronan and took the box from Stephanie. "Important, is it?"

"Give it back, Hayden," Ronan said, lunging for the box. He pulled at Hayden's fingers, trying to pry it loose. Luke joined him and pulled on Hayden's arm.

Moments later the red box went flying, just like the hammer had only moments ago.

Hayden yelled and shoved Ronan again. Ronan shoved back. Hayden took a swing at him. Ronan ducked and Luke caught Hayden's fist in the face.

Cheek stinging, Luke felt an arm wrap around his neck, putting him in a headlock, and pulling him up off his feet. He lost his bearings as his vision blurred and the assailant spun him around. Luke grabbed hold of the attacker's arm, trying to loosen it. As he spun, he could see nothing but a passing blur. Suddenly that blur transformed into figures.

A man, wearing a brown tunic and trousers under a long brown apron, was sitting on a stool in front of the forge holding large iron tongs. A peasant woman in a long dark cloak was kneeling in front of him.
"Did you give the arca to her?" she asked gently.
"Yes. But with my actions I have doomed her to die."
"We had no choice. It was her last request. You had to obey her."
The blacksmith dropped his tongs, lowered his head, and sobbed.

The figures faded back into the spinning blur. Dizzy, Luke struggled to understand what was going on. He heard Ronan yelling. With one final yank Luke released himself from the headlock, and his momentum propelled him into the rotting wooden doors. Seconds later Ronan and Hayden smashed into him. Under the weight and momentum of all three boys, Luke heard a loud crack and felt the door give way. He went hurtling through the door, followed by Hayden and Ronan, who landed next to him.

Luke glanced back. One of the wooden doors now had a massive splintered hole in it. Stephanie had been wrong. This wasn't the exit. This was another room! The room had low ceilings, with walls lined with swords, lances, and shields.

Just then an alarm sounded, with three red oval lights flashing on the wall.

Luke heard Cleo yelling, "We have to stop!" and saw her follow Stephanie through the damaged doors. Something was wrong with his left eye. It felt puffy and painful, and he couldn't fully open it. Luke looked around frantically.

Where is the red box?! His mind flashed back to the small metal boxes on the mantle in the cottage. They'd seemed so similar to his red one. He hadn't had a chance to compare them side by side because Cleo had come in, and he hadn't wanted Cleo to see the Order of Raven treasure.

The blaring alarm suddenly stopped. "What is going on here?" a loud voice boomed through the splintered door. Professor Gregor made his way in. His jaw was clenched, his owl eyes had become slits, and his cheeks were very red. Following him were Adio and Mr. Ringwald, who was still dressed in knight armour.

Gasping for air, Luke grabbed a puff from his inhaler. He scanned the damage around him as he looked for the red box. Cleo was next to him, looking panic-stricken. Ronan had a bleeding lip and Hayden had a black eye. Stephanie was glaring and sighed so hard she blew her bangs off her forehead.

"It's all their fault!" Stephanie pointed to Luke, Ronan, and Cleo.

Even though Luke's eye hurt and he knew they were in trouble, really big trouble, what mattered most was the treasure.

Where is it?

"Yah, what Stephanie said. And Ronan hit me," added Hayden.

"Enough!" Professor Gregor shouted. "You broke into the armoury?! It was locked and has a security alarm for a reason. You were supposed to follow the EXIT clue, and there were more clues after that! You are *all* responsible for this outcome!"

"But—" Ronan began.

"I don't want to hear it," the professor cut in. "Your behaviour, all of you!"—the visor on Ringwald's helmet fell over his face with a clank, which he didn't bother raising— "In all my years I have never seen anything like this. It's absolutely horrific! Adio, these students. There are no words!"

"Well, the story must be interesting," Adio said calmly. "Too bad Professor Torres missed all of this."

Professor Gregor gave Adio a weary glance. "I am very disappointed in all of you."

Adio suppressed a grin.

They were ushered out of the armoury and into the blacksmith shop. Stephanie was already giving her very animated version of the fight to Adio and Professor Gregor, Ronan and Hayden were verbally sparring, while Cleo stood there looking dumbfounded. Luke suddenly spotted the red box in Mr Ringwald's armour-clad hand.

"That's mine," Luke muttered, stepping closer to Mr. Ringwald.

The raven master barely glanced at him through his visor. "Not according to Stephanie. And because it was the source of this incident today, I'm confiscating it."

Luke couldn't understand how all of this had gone so very wrong for him. Grasping his head with both hands to control the ache, he hung his head in agony.

28

Cleo

Cleo crossed off her last day of detention on the calendar, November 22. Cleo would have preferred to serve detention for the antics at the STEM challenge with anyone but Stephanie. She'd been stuck with her for the last week.

They'd helped Chef François prepare raven food in the Viking Hall kitchen. It was mostly ground beef smooshed with hard-boiled eggs. According to the chef the food mixture should be served *étouffée,* which meant that they stuffed the food mixture into fun containers that were designed to challenge the ravens to get their food. Chef François, petite with a stylish long brown moustache, instructed them with his strong French accent. "Make sure you girls clean all this up, *oui?*" He pointed to the exit door at the back of the kitchen. They grabbed a compost bag and shoved remaining bits of food inside, then grabbed the paper bags and cardboard boxes. Stephanie lamented again about missing her free Saturday before letting the door slam in Cleo's face on her way out. Cleo clenched her teeth and pushed at the door with her back.

As she added the compost bag to the green bin, she heard a loud belch from the blue recycle bin. A crumpled silver bag shot out of the now shaking blue bin. "THAT IS NOT RECYCLABLE!" it cried.

Unfazed, Stephanie yelled back, "Well IT SHOULD BE!" The bin stopped shaking and went quiet.

Afterward, Cleo sat down in the Saloon, happy to be free of Stephanie and the funky smell of raven food. Three students in the corner were holding a not-so-quiet conversation, wondering who would make the Vikings team for the Pandia Games. Nestled beside the crackling fireplace, she kept one eye on her surroundings while stealthily opening William Bale's book under her table.

She'd visited this page many times in the last week, trying to understand how Luke could possibly have the arca of Athlia in his possession. Although the diagrams were drawn with charcoal pencil, it was clear that the small box she'd held for a brief moment in the STEM challenge was the same as the one in the drawing. While some of the details in the drawing were smudged, she could still make out the knights on the four sides, and a tree with a sword leaning against it on the bottom of the box. Cleo had so many questions.

"The rumours about Recleren were started by a bored fisherman. There is nothing to them," said a sharp deep voice across the room.

Abruptly Cleo froze.

"Now, this part of the castle dates back at least 800 years, to the days of King Sullivan. I always imagined the king meeting with his knights around this fireplace to discuss battle strategies. In present years, the students have nicknamed it the Saloon. An appropriate name for a place that displays the ugly cowboy hat placed here long ago, I suppose. What started as a prank has remained as a nickname."

Cleo slowly looked up and saw the governor. He stood next to a man who wore an Indiana Jones type of hat, brown leather jacket, hiking shoes, and carried a black leather cross-body satchel. The man was a foot shorter than the governor and had a bulkier build.

"Yes, I see," the governor's guest responded, chuckling. "A very large cowboy hat. Straw. And are those miniature cowboy figurines tucked into the crevasses of the stone?"

"Yes, I suppose." The taller man stood straighter, almost gaining another foot to his already impressive height, and adjusted his white silk scarf, which glowed against his jet-black suit. "Shall we move on?" he asked briskly.

Cleo glanced down. The book the governor wanted was perched on her lap! Trying not to panic, she snuck another look up at the two men. As the governor stepped back, he spotted Cleo and began making his way over.

Her heart and mind raced. If the governor spotted the book now, would she be suspended, or worse, expelled? Should she tell him about the book and Luke's arca? Would her mom be proud? Would her discovery be in the museum next to Stephanie's? What about the secrets Mr. Harbinger mentioned? What about Barbara?

The governor stopped only a few feet from Cleo. The book was still hidden on her lap underneath the round wooden table. The man wearing the Indiana Jones style hat stood beside the governor.

"Ah, here is apparently one of our brightest students." The governor sneered and addressed Cleo, "Professor Gregor informed me about the STEM incident, and if I recall he said your performance was rather lackluster. Am I correct?"

Cleo's heart was pounding as she spoke, "Um, I-I-I …" She couldn't believe she was stammering.

"I hope you are brushing up on your science," the governor added. "You have a lot to live up to since your mother has quite the reputation as a curator. Brillianton Museum, Ms. Barakos said?"

Shocked, she could do nothing but nod and hold her breath.

"Well, sometimes the apple does fall FAR from the tree." The governor turned to his guest. "Let's continue on our tour, shall we?" he said, leaving the insult filling the air of the saloon. The students in the corner left too, glancing at Cleo as they wandered out.

Finally, after a long time, she placed the book into her backpack. Any internal debate she'd had about handing over the book had suddenly been snuffed out. The governor had seen to that.

Cleo made her way to her dormitory. As she rounded the corner on the eighth floor, she found Nia standing in front of their room's open door with a shocked expression on her face. "What the heck?!" Nia said, springing into their room, her athletic wear sweaty and dusty from Vikings tryouts for the Games. Cleo quickly looked through the doorway. Stephanie, Lauren, and Hayden were inside their room! Several drawers of their wardrobes were open. "What're you guys doing here?" Nia asked.

"Adio had a letter to give to Cleo. I offered to bring it. The door was opened," Stephanie said, suspiciously smiling at Nia. Cleo huffed in disbelief. If her roommate believed that, she would ask to be relocated to another dormitory immediately.

Stephanie plopped down on Cleo's bed, grabbed an envelope off the pillow, and held it up to the light.

"Give me that!" Nia snatched the letter out of Stephanie's hands and handed it to Cleo. "I better not find any of our stuff's gone," she continued in a low and intense tone, inclining her head towards the open drawers of their wardrobe.

Daisy arrived in the doorway, holding a small painting in one paint-streaked hand and brushes and a palette in the other. Today her hair was parted on the side, little white flowers woven through her pinned-back hair. "Oh. Hi, Stephanie. What are you doing here?" she asked.

Nia was fuming as she brought Daisy up to speed.

Stephanie interjected, "As if, Nia! How dare you accuse us of stealing?!" She shot Nia and Cleo a snooty look, then turned and touched their roommate on the arm. "Daisy, you can't believe these two. We were just here looking for you. To see if you wanted to join us for lunch," she added with a sickly sweet voice. Hayden and Lauren made agreeing sounds.

"Oh, AS IF we believe that!" Nia shouted.

"We're leaving!" Stephanie harrumphed. "Daisy?"

Daisy blinked like a deer in headlights and didn't make a move either way.

Stephanie shrugged and left.

"Toodles," Lauren said as she whipped her ponytail around and followed Stephanie out. Hayden stumbled behind them and grimaced as he touched his slowly healing black eye.

"Don't come back!" Nia called through the wide-open door.

Cleo couldn't believe it. She'd never seen anyone stand up to Stephanie before. Maybe she'd misjudged Nia.

"Sorry, Daisy. I know they're your friends," Nia apologized.

"It's okay," Daisy said. But her eyes glistened as she tried to look busy. She laid her painting and palette on her chest of drawers and popped the paintbrushes expertly into the jar where she stored them, like flowers in a vase.

Through their open doorway, Cleo heard a sound coming down the hall.

"Ding dang dong. Ding dang dong. Unicycle missing. More items missing on campus."

As Sir Lancelot wheeled off in the opposite direction, Nia slammed the door. "Somebody needs to fix Lancelot's computer chip. It hasn't told us anything new lately."

Cleo glanced at the letter in her hand as she sat on her bunk. It was from her grandma! She brought it close to her chest. "How did those three even get in here?" she asked. "The doors to the dorm rooms only open with our thumbprints."

"I'm so sorry!" Daisy hung her head down low and gently closed up the dresser drawers left open. "This morning I was in such a hurry, um, maybe on my way out I didn't shut the door properly."

"Oh poop, Daisy," said Nia. "It doesn't matter! Even if the door was *wide* open, they had no right to snoop around." She gave her most encouraging smile to Daisy, who shyly returned it. Daisy turned, picked up her newest painting, a pineapple for the fruit-themed decoration of their dorm, and handed it to Nia. Nia held it up to show Cleo, commenting on how great it was. Cleo nodded her head in agreement.

Cleo glanced at her own things and started checking to make sure Stephanie hadn't taken or damaged anything. Thank goodness she kept William Bale's book in her backpack! What if she'd left it under her mattress and Stephanie had found it?

"Okay, none of my stuff is missing," Nia said as she shut her wardrobe drawers.

"I'm good too," Cleo said after she had checked hers, relieved.

"Me too," Daisy added meekly, as she slid her art box under her bunk bed and grabbed the library book that lay on top. She had forgotten to return it and it was past its due date. She quickly left with it.

While Nia fumed in the bunk bed above her, Cleo opened her letter. CeeCee was in a small village, building houses for those in need. A picture of CeeCee next to two little kids fell out of the envelope. Behind them was a house with a wooden frame. Cleo smiled and continued reading.

I've been thinking about our last call a lot. That was way back at the end of October. I have missed you! Be brave, sweetie. Fear of failing or fear of rejection will isolate you and stop you from making great relationships and achieving great things. I know Stephanie being there is a setback but be brave! I believe in you and I know this year will get better for you. You are a wonderful soul. Never forget that.

I'll be traveling from village to village, so I still won't be able to receive letters for a while. But I will write or call when I can! I love building houses and I'm thinking about doing this for a year. But I promise to come back for Christmas first and I can't wait to catch up. Remember that I love you more than the universe.

She missed her grandma so much! A sense of isolation swept back over her. Cleo read the letter again.

Be brave. It's now or never.

"Nia, I …" Cleo began and took a deep breath. "I need

your help."

Nia's long silky black hair draped over the top bunk like a curtain. "What is it? Sounds serious." She jumped off the bunk and sat next to Cleo. "Is it about Stephanie?" Before Cleo could answer she continued, "I know she talks to everyone in class except you. And she's said mean things about you. I should've stood up to her earlier. I'm sorry."

Surprised by Nia's honesty and hurt by Stephanie's nastiness, Cleo could not respond. Her roommate waited patiently. After a few moments Cleo spoke. "We went to the same school together. We used to be best friends." Cleo focused on her hands as she tangled them together. "And then Stephanie stopped talking to me. I never knew why. Then other girls stopped talking to me, too."

"I get it," Nia answered. "Something like that happened to me once. And I guess I never wanted it to happen again. To me, with Stephanie. You know what I mean?"

Cleo turned and looked at her with surprise. "Really? But everyone likes you! You know so many people here. And you stood up to Stephanie."

Nia smiled. "Yeah. Better late than never. My mom always said to be brave."

Cleo nodded. Her grandma said the same thing, but it was always easier said than done. Yet for some reason being brave did feel easy right now. Before she could change her mind, she told Nia everything about the book, the arca she saw at the STEM challenge, the governor, and even Captain Jumbo and the legend.

Nia listened intently. She was quiet for a few minutes after Cleo finished. "How is Luke involved in all of this?" she finally asked. "I don't get it,"

"I don't know," Cleo replied.

"Can I see it?" Nia asked

"The book?" Cleo asked.

"Yes," Nia replied.

Cleo hesitated.

"Oh. Is it Stephanie?" Nia asked. She abruptly went to the door, opened it, and poked her head into the hallway with concern. "She's long gone." She closed the door and returned to Cleo's bunk.

Cleo shook her head and looked tellingly at the bunk across from hers.

"Oh! Daisy? I trust her, we're friends. But you don't?" Nia said, furrowing her brow in thought.

Cleo quickly added, "She's nice and everything but—"

Nia interjected, "But she's also friends with Stephanie. I get it. And this is a big secret. I promise not to tell anyone!"

Cleo sighed with relief. "Thanks, Nia." As Cleo pulled the book from her backpack to show her new friend, she did not notice the blue spark that glinted along the spine of the *Research Findings of William Bale*.

29

Luke

After learning about the inside of watches for weeks in horology class, observing Professor Morlia take a watch apart, and having done a few hands-on labs, it was finally time for the exam. Each student had been assigned a watch to disassemble and put back together. The opera music in the classroom overlapped with the tick-tock of the many asynchronized wall clocks. Students collecting supplies from the tool bench created another distracting tune. Luke tried to block it all out, choosing a table at the back of the room so he could focus.

He looked briefly out the window at the grey and dreary day. It was the beginning of December. The hills around campus were now covered in frost, and the trees had long lost their leaves. It had been two weeks since the STEM challenge when Mr. Ringwald had confiscated the red treasure box. Luke kept revisiting the same thought over and over.

I need to get that red box back. But where is it?

No. He had to concentrate. This exam was important. Ever since Morlia had told him his watch was so valuable, he had even more reason to maintain it for when his dad returned. If he could prove to himself that he could disassemble and reassemble a watch in this exam, he might let himself do the same to his Dad's watch. He really wanted to know what made it so special. He was also worried he had gotten moisture in the watch and it may have some internal damage. Several times already the face had fogged up. He looked at his wrist to check. The watch face was normal.

He returned to the task at hand but still had a hard time concentrating. *Maybe Mr. Ringwald put the red box in a special room where teachers put confiscated items.* Luke imagined a room full of cell phones, and all other stuff students weren't supposed to have. Like slingshots. *I asked Ronan but he has no idea.*

Gently lifting the exam-supplied watch's face, Luke found and removed a tiny screw from inside. Holding the screw carefully, he moved his arm towards a little grey dish to drop it into for safe keeping. Suddenly something blocked his light. Cleo's face was only a few inches from his. Startled, Luke dropped the miniscule grey screw on the dusty, grey stone floor. He cursed silently. Cleo was trying to get his attention, but Luke ignored her. He sank to the floor and placed his hand palm down, searching for the tiny camouflaged screw.

Cleo crouched to the floor and came closer. She looked annoyed. "Are you listening to me?"

"Cleo! You made me lose a screw. I need to find it," Luke told her. *If anyone has the right to be annoyed, it's me!*

Cleo gave him this funny look as though *he* had a few screws loose in his head.

Luke knew it was the other way around.

"I don't have much time before Professor Morlia comes

back to class, y'know. And it's already been a week. And," she paused, "I haven't found a good time to talk with you. You're always with your friends. I need to talk to you alone."

"Now?" Luke paused, imitating her. "We're in the middle of a test!" He was frantic. The screw must be here somewhere! Maybe Professor Morlia had extra watch parts that he could use.

"I want to see the red box you have," Cleo said.

Luke gave her a sidelong, wary glance.

She quickly added, "The arca, the arca of Athlia. "

He had heard that word arca before! In the cottage during the STEM challenge, the blacksmith had said it.

Was the red box this arca thing? And how did Cleo know anything about it?

Confused and his concentration on the exam completely disrupted, Luke snapped, "You can't." He could've kicked himself as the words came out. He could've said a million things, like, "What're you talking about?" or "We're in an exam!" or even "Leave me alone." Certainly a member of the Order of Ravens should deny knowledge about any secret treasure they'd sworn to protect.

"What's going on, you two?" Professor Morlia's legs came into view. His dusty, tan-coloured boots were tapping the floor.

"Um, Luke lost a screw. I was helping him." Cleo's eyebrows drew together.

"That's nice of you Cleo. But you and Luke both know the rules. No help allowed during the exam. I do have a broom in the back closet. That might help." Professor Morlia smiled as both kids came out from under the table. "And if that doesn't work, you can also use a magnet." The professor continued walking around the classroom looking at the students' work and nodding in encouragement. Luke grabbed the broom *and* the magnet, just in case.

She made me lose a screw, I might fail this test and now Professor Morlia probably thinks I'm cheating!

He never found the screw, and the possibility of failing this horology test was only one of the reasons he was upset as class ended. Cleo obviously knew more about the treasure box than he did. She'd come out of nowhere, claiming it was some arca of Athlia, whatever that is. Plus, it was entirely his fault that the box was gone. PLUS, now he'd violated his oath as a protector of treasure.

This was serious.

He had to discuss this with the Order of Ravens.

Viking Hall was bustling with students talking and clanging cutlery and plates as everyone hunkered down to the lunch provided. Ronan, having finally made it through the buffet line, had returned with two plates. He sat down with a fork in each hand, ready to chow down. He waved one hand in front of Luke. "Your ice cream's melting."

Luke asked his easiest question first. "Ronan, are you sure you don't know where Adio kept your slingshot before he returned it? Like a room somewhere, or maybe his office?"

"Luke, we've been through this. Ronan doesn't know." Andy replied on Ronan's behalf. "The confiscated stuff isn't in there. I would know! I'm in there a lot for detention." Andy turned to Ronan and changed the conversation. "Coach Typhoon just announced he's picked his team. He said we'll know on December 5th. That's just two days from now! I can't wait."

They discussed who would make the Chronos Viking

squad for the Pandia Games.

"I'll make it, and you will too," Andy said, nodding to Ronan. Andy rotated his head slightly and grinned at Luke. "But not Luke. He never tried out. Which I find crazy."

"I might make it, too," Ollie said, pointing his fork at Andy.

"Not sure. I beat you in the 60 meters," Andy said, puffing his chest out slightly.

"I wasn't in the 60 meters," Ollie shook his head. "I was in the 300 meters."

Ronan chuckled and said with his mouth full, "And Ollie beat you, Andy, 'member?"

"Barely," Andy said, slouching a tad. "That was after the 60 meters! I was worn out." He sat up straighter, "All this running Coach is making us do in gym class is exhausting."

"But he's keeping track of our times in class. That's how he'll make the final cut," Ronan said, wiping his mouth with his sleeve. "Which is why we're running in the gym and not at the pitch. Also, it's kinda wet now."

"But to pick a team this late, it's crazy," Andy added.

"Not really," Ronan reasoned. "He did say he was shaking things up."

Luke looked at the pink pool of cream in his bowl and the two pink mini icebergs slowly diminishing into the surrounding liquid. "We need to get the red box back," Luke announced, interrupting the conversation.

"What are you talking about?" Andy asked.

"It's not just a decoration. Cleo called it the arca of Athlia. She knows something about it. It must be worth something!" Luke said. He had to win their support. "C'mon, we need to find it. It's our only treasure so far!"

"Yeah, some treasure," Andy said sarcastically. "Even if it *is* treasure and we knew where to find it, I can't risk any more detention," he said.

"Well, I'm in!" said Ollie, giving a firm nod.

Ronan added, "I want to make the team, Luke. That's all I can think about. So I can't help right now."

"Well, maybe I should ask Cleo for help?" Luke wanted to see what the others might think of that idea.

"Help from a girl?" Andy snorted in disgust and looked at Luke again. "*Although,* she did rescue you on the first day."

Ronan laughed and even Ollie chuckled, his hand cupped over his mouth. Luke turned beet red.

"Seriously. Girls aren't allowed in Order of Ravens business," Andy said.

"There are no girl knights!" declared Ronan. He added another cheese string wrapper to his growing pile at the end of the table by the napkin holder.

"I have to agree." Ollie shrugged. "Knights are boys. Look at the *Knights of Darkness.*"

"Right!" Ronan agreed.

"Besides," Andy continued, "Order of Ravens business is secret. Remember the oath? So you can't talk to her about it."

Luke didn't want to upset the Order. They might think differently if they knew about the ghost lady and his daydream in the blacksmith hut. But he definitely couldn't tell them about all that.

"Fine," he said.

Just then, the power went off. Luke couldn't see his bowl of ice cream or anything else for that matter. *Ugh!* When the lights flickered to life a few moments later, he blinked a few times, adjusting to the brightness.

"Let's get to the gym, Andy," Ronan said, jumping up.

"Great idea," Andy said. "See ya."

Watching his friends leave, Luke spotted Cleo. She was sitting with Nia only a few tables over, their heads together, talking. He noticed their conspiring stopped abruptly when Daisy interrupted them and showed them her latest painting. Stephanie waved at Daisy and she went to join Stephanie's table.

Ollie leaned close to Luke and whispered, "Daisy's a pretty good artist, don't you think?"

"Sure," Luke said dismissively, "But look at Cleo." She was silently eating her soup, her mind clearly miles away.

"You're right," Ollie said. "She knows something. For sure!"

If the rest of the Order won't help me get the red box back, then Cleo might be the only one who can.

"You can't ask her," Ollie said, reading Luke's mind, "without breaking the oath."

Luke nodded, thinking hard. He might not have a choice.

30

Cleo

"Today marks your final chemistry class. Next week we will do a magnets lab, the following week will be the winter holiday break," Professor Gregor announced to mixed reactions.

"What stinks?" Nia asked, fanning her face with their worksheets. The windowless dungeon classroom was pungent.

The professor dropped a huge potted flower onto the lab bench at the front of the classroom. It had enormous red petals with whitish dots and a large tubular opening in the middle. It was the largest flower Cleo had ever seen and the funkiest flower she had ever smelled.

"Rafflesia is truly rare," Professor Gregor said. "It is found in the forests of Indonesia. This one weighs fifteen pounds. It's perfect for our chemistry of odours lesson." His face and upper body disappeared behind the potted bloom. "Here's a fun fact: this flower is also known as the rotting-corpse flower. The corpse flower's scent is a chemical combination of wonders, dimethyl trisulfide, dimethyl disulfide, and trimethylamine. And there is so much more to learn! You all have your worksheets."

Several students made their way over to the giant odorous flower, including Andy and Ronan, both quickly scribbling on their worksheets. "Wow that really reeks!" Andy declared through a pinched nose. Ronan pulled his nose out of his shirt to gag. He quickly followed Andy back to their desks.

"I'll take down the notes, okay?" Cleo said, turning to Nia. They joined other students up by the specimen. Plugging her nose with one hand, Cleo began writing notes with the other, while her lab partner made indistinguishable observations through her own plugged nose.

At the next table over Daisy was partnered with Stephanie.

"I don't get it," said Nia through her pinched nose. "Where does Professor Gregor find these things? Winter vacation is only a couple weeks away. Why not a Christmas cactus or a poinsettia?" She took in a small quick breath and grimaced.

Professor Gregor overheard her and responded, "Nia, this is a rare opportunity. We are lucky this unique flower is in bloom. Its odour imitates the smell of decaying animals to attract fascinating pollinators like dung beetles, flesh flies, and carnivorous insects."

"Gross." Nia examined the plant from a safe distance. Cleo did the same, wondering if there were any hidden flesh-eating insects on the plant.

When they returned to their table, Nia told Cleo, "Anyway, I hope I make the Vikings team tomorrow. I'm so nervous."

"Right, tomorrow is December 5th. The big announcement. You'll make it," murmured Cleo around her pinching hand. She gave Nia a thumbs up before returning to her worksheet. The sooner they finished the better.

The sound of retching made Cleo whip her head around. Hayden was vomiting into a bright yellow biohazardous waste bucket, which was unfortunately too close to Cleo and Nia's table. She slowly turned back to Nia. Her lab partner was glancing back and forth from their table to Simon, holding her breath with puffed cheeks, while adding gobs of hand sanitizer to her palms.

"Cleo!" Luke whispered. His face appeared out of nowhere, one inch from her own.

Cleo sprang back. Her skull hit Nia right on the bridge of her nose. The force of the blow caused tears to spring from their eyes. Nia was moaning slightly. Cleo rubbed her head and immediately began apologizing to Nia.

Nia nodded and regarded Luke with murderous eyes. "This is your fault," she snapped at him as she gently pinched her nose to defend herself against the stench in the room. Cleo quickly replugged her nose, too.

Luke grabbed Cleo's bent arm and moved her to the side, while keeping his nose closed with his other arm. "Meet me at the raven statue," he said. "Tomorrow after the team announcement." He paused, perhaps responding to the irritated look on her face, quickly adding, "Please."

Stephanie breezed past, spraying perfume in the air and, in a flash, spritzed Cleo's face. Her eyes now stinging, she wiped them with her sleeve. When she looked up Stephanie was gone and so was Luke. He hadn't even waited for her response! She wished he'd stayed around to hear it: a resounding NO. He'd refused to show her the arca and had been rude to her from day one.

Cleo squinted her eyes, which were now full of tears. When she returned to her table, Nia leaned over and whispered, "What was that all about?" Daisy glanced back at them.

Rubbing her eyes again, Cleo whispered, "Tell you later." The end of chemistry class couldn't come soon enough.

31

Luke

The next morning, the Order of Ravens made their way to Knight Hall after breakfast. It was finally December 5th and time for the big announcement of who made the Chronos Viking team.

The hall was packed with students, and so too were the stairs leading to it. Sir Lancelot was standing at the end of the hall, projecting a hologram of an orange scroll from the hand of the swordless knight, just below his raised axe.

Luke heard whooping and hollering and then a scream. "You did it, Alisha!" A girl was hoisted onto someone's shoulders. The crowd chanted, "A-li-sha, A-li-sha!"

"Hey, little brother."

Luke turned and saw Joe giving Andy a playful noogie, messing up Andy's hair. "I made the team. Whoo hooo!!!"

"Good for you, Joe," Andy said in a monotone voice, unimpressed, as he squirmed out from the hold, and smoothed out his hair.

The Order edged their way through the shifting crowd of students. Andy ran his finger down the list of names on the orange tinted hologram and back up again, creating tiny pixelated ripples. Sir Lancelot didn't move or make one ding dang dong noise as it projected the hologram of names. "Although Coach never let us first years try fencing, I'm sure I made the team in the running sports," Andy said confidently.

Andy's face turned beet red. "My name isn't here." He ran his finger back up through the list. "This can't be. How is it I'm not here? I'm one of the best!" He wouldn't budge to let the others get a good look at the scroll, making them gaze over his shoulders.

Luke was the only one in the Order who hadn't tried out for the team. He was focused on his mission: find treasure, find his dad. But that didn't mean he was completely uninterested in who made the team. He leaned in a bit closer and recognized some of the names from around the school: Jocelyn, Maria, Christopher, Ishaan, Jacob, Rebecca, and Farid.

"I'm not on the team either," Ronan said, his mouth open in shock.

"Me neither," added Ollie matter-of-factly. Ollie had confided to Luke that he wouldn't be too upset about missing out on the team.

"So, none of us made the team?" said Andy in disbelief. "Not me, not you, Ronan, not Ollie. Not even Nia! She was really good in relay. Don't tell her that." He scratched his head as he reexamined the list again.

"Most of the team are in sixth year," Ronan said while consulting the list again.

"What about the other grades?" Andy protested, clutching his head.

"Oh, Farid, he's in third year. He made the team," Ollie

said, shrugging his shoulders.

"That's 'cause Coach said he's amazing at parkour and the skills transfer. So I guess we all need to learn parkour," Andy said, rolling his eyes.

"They better work hard. The Vikes just have to win!" Ronan said.

"Doesn't it bother you?" Andy asked when he finally stepped back from Sir Lancelot, "Not one first-year!" His fists were balled at his sides. His face was a deep red. "I. Am. MAD!"

Luke and Ollie glanced at each other. They'd never seen him like this.

"Yah. But what can we do?" Ronan asked genuinely.

Just then, Coach Typhoon, in a bright yellow track suit, appeared in Knight Hall.

"Well for starters I'm going to find out why no first-years made the team. This is outrageous, it's a-gis-ism!" Andy shouted, staring at the coach as he lunged in his direction.

Typhoon's sneaker squeaked as he quickly pivoted to avoid the students and jogged toward the castle exit.

"You mean ageism!" Ollie called after Andy and Ronan who had moved just as quickly towards the open castle door, calling out the coach's name. Luke had never seen the coach run before.

As the door clanked shut behind their roommates, Ollie grabbed his arm. "Luke, I know you're meeting Cleo now. But it's a bad idea. It breaks the oath."

Luke turned sharply on Ollie. "You don't have to come."

"As an Order member, I have to tell you if I think you're doing the wrong thing. But as your best friend, I'll still come with you," Ollie said.

Minutes later, Luke and Ollie waited in the crisp damp air at the three-headed raven statue. Even though there wasn't any snow falling yet, Luke shivered in his hoodie. *I should have worn my coat.*

A few students ran past the two roommates and into the castle to get warm. Luke could see his breath and couldn't really feel his toes. He was re-reading the statue's inscription again. Cleo had still not shown up.

Ollie elbowed him in the ribs. Cleo and Nia had exited the castle and were approaching them. *Finally.*

Luke huffed out, "Thanks," when they stopped before him and Ollie.

"You're a poop, you know that? You've been so rude to Cleo!" Nia blasted Luke. "And I didn't make the team, so I'm even more mad. About everything."

Luke turned red. "Sorry," he said. Ollie stood silently beside him.

Cleo looked around and moved closer to him when a professor walked by. She lowered her voice considerably. "Do you have the arca of Athlia on you? I'd like to see it."

"How do you know what it's called?" Luke asked with suspicion and excitement at the same time.

Cleo replied, "I have a book. A tell-all book. A journal, actually. I—" Nia was giving Cleo the cut sign, moving her hand rapidly back and forth across her throat. "Ix-nay, the governor," she whispered. Cleo adjusted her puke-green backpack and looked at her feet. The governor glowered as he swept his way across Copernicus Court and toward the castle, completely ignoring them. Luke and Ollie exchanged puzzled looks as the imposing man entered the building.

"Let's see this book," Luke said impatiently.

"Please," Ollie quickly added, admonishing Luke for his lack of manners.

"No. I can't show you out here," Cleo said nervously.

"The governor might come back," Nia added.

None of this made sense to Luke. He glanced at Ollie who just shrugged his shoulders.

Nia spoke quickly. "Mr. Ringwald's coming. Act normal."

The raven master strode into the open space of the courtyard. Not far from them, Floki and Munnin swooped to the ground.

Luke tensed up. He'd stayed as far away from the ravens as possible ever since the first day and especially since Floki had used his head as a scratching post.

Munnin hopped her way closer to the group, and Floki followed with a swagger. Luke took multiple steps back to maintain a safe distance.

"Boop boop," Munnin said.

"Caw," Floki barked.

"Mu and Floki, let's go. Time for your morning nap." Mr. Ringwald came over and pointed his fingers at both ravens.

"No, no," Munnin said, hopping in the opposite direction with Floki following close behind.

The four of them watched as the raven master chased the two birds, trying to corral them closer to Raven Tower. "Boop boop," Munnin would tease just before she flew or hopped away just out of Mr. Ringwald's reach. Floki continued to strut in whatever direction he wanted.

Finally, Mr. Ringwald pulled out a box of crackers and dropped a few by his feet, counting each of them. "One, two, three. Good things come in threes."

Luke couldn't relax while the ravens were out of control.

It was clear they couldn't talk here and needed a safe place to share this secret information. He whispered in Ollie's ear. His friend nodded.

"There's somewhere we can go. But it's a secret. You have to swear not to tell," Luke said.

Cleo and Nia looked at each other and nodded.

"We swear," Cleo said solemnly.

"You can't tell anybody," Ollie said.

"We won't!" Nia answered.

"It's in Bastion Tower," Luke said.

The girls' mouths dropped open.

32

"What are they doing here?" barked Andy.

After the monstrous climb to the top of the tower, Cleo was still trying to catch her breath. They hadn't advanced any further than a few feet from the doorframe, but she was gobsmacked by what she saw. Arched windows brought in the muted grey daylight that grazed the walls and a trove of objects in the grand room.

What is in all these crates and cabinets?!

"Girls aren't allowed here!" Ronan said as he quickly blocked the two girls from advancing any further into the room.

"How rude!" said Nia. She took an aggressive step forward.

He quickly took one back.

"You two betrayed us!" Andy was livid, flicking his eyes back and forth between Ollie and Luke. "If I'd known, I would've locked the door."

"Oh, please," Ollie said as he rolled his eyes. He took off his backpack and placed it on the floor.

Andy stomped his right foot. "I'm so mad at Coach for not making the team and now I'm really mad. So mad. This is my happy place. Or was! Now it's ruined. You brought them here!"

"ACHOOO!" Ronan's projectile sneeze washed over Ollie, just missing Nia.

"Gross," Ollie said as he quickly wiped his face and lenses with the bottom of his shirt.

"Eww." Nia took a step back. "If it makes you feel better, Andy, I'm mad too. I didn't make the team either."

"No first years did," Ollie said. He retrieved hand sanitizer from his backpack, used it, and handed it to Nia.

"Really?" Nia asked, using the sanitizer and passing it back.

Andy gave a quick nod, still shooting daggers from his eyes towards Luke and Ollie.

Luke said, "You wouldn't help me with the box. Cleo wants to. And she has a book—"

"Wow! A book!" Andy squinted his eyes at Luke defensively. Then he turned to Cleo, "We don't need you here," he said. "We can get books at the library."

"Rude!" Nia replied.

But Cleo wasn't listening to Andy. Help with the box? *Help how?* She moved closer to Nia and whispered, "I'm confused."

"What're you whispering?" Andy came closer.

"I know," Ronan said, pointing at them accusingly. "They're telling secrets!" Before the girls could reply, he added, "About treasure!"

"Treasure?" Nia asked Cleo, looking at her with a puzzled grin. Cleo shrugged.

Pulling a dusty sheet off a pile of furniture, Ronan found a few chairs and unstacked them. He sat on one and offered the other to Nia. Shaking her head, she sat on the floor. Ronan took advantage of the open seat, slipped off his shoes and pulled off his socks. "There's a rock in my sock." He wiggled his toes and waved his bare feet in the air. Nia suppressed her laughter and feigned disgust as she moved further away.

"Fine, I guess we're doing this." Andy grabbed a seat.

Cleo turned to Luke, "Can I see the arca, please?"

"No, you can't," Luke said flatly.

Cleo's face went red. She couldn't believe it. She had planned to share William Bale's journal with Luke, and yet he still wouldn't show her that little box! She started towards the door.

"I can't show you because Mr. Ringwald took it. At the STEM escape room," Luke called after her.

That stopped Cleo in her tracks. "That was more than two weeks ago!" she said. Luke nodded. "Mr. Ringwald has the arca of Athlia? I can't believe this."

"The what?" Ollie asked as Cleo sat on the floor, crossed her legs and dropped her chin in her left hand.

"The box is called the arca of Athlia," repeated Nia.

"But wait," Cleo piped up with renewed energy. "It doesn't matter about the arca. You have the Stone, right?"

"The stone?" Luke asked.

"There was no Stone inside the arca?" Cleo's mouth gaped open.

Everyone started talking at once, excitedly firing questions. Nia put up her hand to stop the discussion. She turned sharply to Luke. "There was nothing inside the arca, at all?"

Luke squirmed. "It doesn't open," he said.

"Kinda like the castle door on the first day, hey Luke?" Andy teased.

"You didn't open it?" Cleo and Nia asked in unison.

"No. None of us could," Luke explained.

"There has to be a Stone of Destiny inside the arca," Cleo insisted. "I don't understand why you couldn't open it."

Luke folded his arms across his chest. "I don't understand why you keep talking about a Stone."

This was supposed to be Cleo's big adventure. She was so close to finding one of the lost Stones when no one else had been able to. Now there was nothing! Cleo let out a breath of frustration.

She removed the thick leather-bound book, with its crisscrossing straps, from her backpack and placed it on the floor in front of her. The boys watched her carefully as she picked the middle leather strap and tugged on it. She opened the book. "This is William Bale's journal from the 1800s. He was a student here, at Chronos Academy." She flipped to a page with a drawing sketched in pencil and pointed to it.

"It's the red treasure box!" Luke said. "With the knights and everything."

"No way!" Ollie said as he moved closer to the book, squishing in between Cleo and Luke.

Cleo outlined the words 'arca of Athlia' next to the drawings with her index finger. "I think this arca belonged to a person named Athlia. Arcas contained valuables during the medieval times. And inside this arca," she slid her finger down the page, following the arrow drawn there, until it reached the bottom, "there should be a Stone of Destiny." She looked at Luke.

"Stone of Destiny?" Luke asked.

Cleo nodded. "The three Stones of Destiny are part of a very old local legend."

Nia jumped in, "The Stones fell from the sky and were given to the ancient Glimmician people by their God, the Raven God. There's three Stones. The Stones are supposed to be powerful, and they're really old. At least 1000 years old. Probably older."

Ollie added, "Usually things that are really old are really valuable, right Luke?"

"Yeah," Luke said, glancing at his watch.

"Right, worth a lot of money," Andy said.

Why does that matter?

"So what does a Stone of Destiny look like?" Luke asked. Cleo flipped to another page in William Bale's book. "It says here the Stones are black with blue streaks, and small enough to fit in the palm of a hand."

"I can't believe I lost the arca!" Luke slumped, "I knew it was a special treasure!"

"So did I!" Ollie said.

"Is it though?" Andy asked.

Cleo knew he was just being difficult, so she ignored him and carried on explaining what she had learned from Captain Jumbo and the journal. "The Stones were passed down from generation to generation. Then at some point the Stones were lost."

"How?" Ollie asked.

"No one knows," Cleo replied. "But lots of people have looked for them."

"The governor's looking for the Stones—we think," Nia said. Cleo nodded and recapped her first encounter with the governor at the library and Mr. Harbinger's warning.

"Maybe Mr. Harbinger just doesn't like the Governor—the Governor does seem like kind of a jerk," Andy commented, grabbing the book from Ollie and flipping through the pages. "Besides, the governor does have a job, you know. He's the governor. He's not running around looking for stones," Andy said.

"They're impossible to find. Captain Jumbo tried and failed. Even a criminal named Richard Recleren tried, but no one has EVER found them." Cleo didn't mention the supposed curse that Jumbo associated with looking for the Stones. While she spoke her mind was reeling.

There has to be a way to get the arca back.

Luke interjected, "I know that name Recleren. I saw it in the *Gazette* loads of times. Recleren escaped from the Glimmerton jail, and joined pirates.

"Pirates!" Ollie interjected. "Have you guys ever seen movies about pirates?" asked Ollie. "They're not nice!"

"But about the arca—" Cleo began and was interrupted by Andy loudly flipping the pages of the book.

When Ronan sneezed and wiped his nose on his sleeve, Nia moved even further away from him. "You're sick," she accused him. He denied it, "Nope."

"Just so you know Cleo," Andy said, "half of this book has blank pages and the author of your book is Billy Bale."

"Billy's a nickname for William," Ronan chimed in. "My cousin in Cincinnati is named William and we all call him Billy."

Cleo's mind snapped back to the boat ride with Captain Jumbo. He said a bookish fellow named Billy had looked for the Stones more than a hundred years ago and had disappeared.

Is this the same Billy?

The name, the 1800s. It has to be!

Is that the reason for all the empty pages? Billy never got a chance to finish looking for the Stones or write in his journal again, because he disappeared?

Andy's laughter brought her to the present, "This Billy guy is a joker. He writes about chimpanzee fire. This is a fairy tale book, Cleo. Like Bale tales. Hey, that rhymes!" he laughed. "*Bale's Tales!*"

"*Bale's Tales*," Ronan chuckled and sneezed. Andy was mimicking a chimpanzee, scratching his armpits and making ape noises. Ronan's version of ape vocalizations and gestures sent him into a coughing fit. Ollie just shook his head.

Cleo had lost control of the situation.

She swallowed hard. "I don't think this book is a joke." She was about to mention the arca again and that they need to find it, when Luke beat her to it, "We need to get the arca back!"

"Exactly," Cleo said, relieved.

"But how? Mr. Ringwald confiscated it and we have no idea where it is," Ollie reminded them.

"We know it's not in Adio's office," Luke said, "and we don't think there is a special room for confiscated stuff."

"If Mr. Ringwald took it, it's probably in the aviary. Right? That makes sense," Nia said logically.

Thank you, Nia. Cleo stood, thrilled that everyone was back on track. "Right! We need to check out the aviary."

Ronan tapped Luke on his head. "I bolunteer Pluke," he said, struggling with nasal congestion.

"Ah, nooo," Luke groaned and rubbed his head.

"I will go," Cleo said.

"But you can't go by yourself. One of us has to be there." Andy chimed in. Cleo knew he meant the boys.

"It's our arca." Luke nodded emphatically.

"Ok, Andy you should come," Cleo said.

"Ah, nooo," Andy grinned, imitating Luke.

"So none of you want to go?" Cleo said. "You know what? It doesn't matter, Nia and I can do it."

"Oh poop. We can't just show up, it will look suspicious," Nia tapped her finger on her lips in thought. "I know. Why don't we just ask Daisy?" When the sounds of protest rang throughout the tower, Nia held up her hand. "She was amazing that time in class with Floki, remember, Cleo? And she's told me she's gone in a few times to sketch the ravens for her art project. So it wouldn't be strange that she is there. And she could bring a plus one. She said Mr. Ringwald is always looking for helpers."

"I'll go," Ollie stepped up. "I can offer to help Mr. Ringwald with some chores at the aviary." Ollie added, "And Daisy can just play with the ravens while I look around. Good idea, right? Cool?"

Nia grinned, glanced at Ollie, and looked around the group. "Daisy doesn't need to know what we're doing or why."

Cleo couldn't think of a good reason why that plan wouldn't work.

"What if d' arca's not der?" Ronan asked, now breathing loudly out of his mouth and slumped across two chairs he had turned into a makeshift bed. He rubbed his neck and let out a small cough.

"Then we go with plan B," Andy offered.

"Which is?" Cleo asked.

"It's a doozy," Andy said, and the boys laughed, even Ollie. Nia and Cleo regarded them with confusion.

"Forget about it," Luke assured them, "We can always figure something out. For now, we have a plan," Luke said. "Ollie needs to get into the aviary."

Although it felt like a minor setback, Cleo knew she had to work with the boys. It was her only way to get a Stone of Destiny.

33

Luke

Three days after the big Vikings team announcement, Andy and Nia were standing at Luke's desk with a small crowd milling around them. They were gathering signatures for their shared petition to protest that first years had been excluded from the Chronos Viking team. Since Andy's letter to Director LeCrucia requesting first years be allowed to fence failed, Andy thought he would up the ante. With power in numbers, he and Nia figured attaching a petition with many names to a letter of request would pack more punch. Andy insisted repeatedly that it was their democratic right. Most of the class had made their way over to sign.

Luke was growing impatient.

The Order of Ravens is about treasure, not petitions!

The group of students scattered back to their seats when Professor Gregor entered the class with Sir Lancelot. "Why are we missing more than half the class today?"

Luke huffed out a breath of frustration and said, "Ollie and Ronan are sick."

So no aviary, no arca, and no Stone of Destiny.

"And Lauren," Stephanie blurted from the back of the room.

Another student called out, "And Tony!"

"Same with Charles."

"Layla."

Names continued to ring out.

"Are they now?" said Professor Gregor. "Hmmm. Clearly a virus is making its way around, jumping from host to host. And children are walking incubators of germs."

A few students commented on being called incubators. The professor dismissed them with a wave of his hand. He then scribbled something in his notebook and turned to the blackboard.

"Today, we are talking about magnets." Professor Gregor rubbed his hands together in delight. "Here are two very powerful magnets." Two brick-sized magnets, each with a red cap on one end, sat on the professor's lab bench at the front of the class. The magnets were spaced about half a meter apart and separated by a thick block of wood. "We will use Sir Lancelot as a battery to make a large circuit and see how these magnets affect it."

Sir Lancelot was wheeling around the back of the classroom.

"Awesome. Dibs on that one," Andy said, pointing to the magnet on the right.

"I'll have the other one," Stephanie added loudly.

"Ding dang dong. Yippee," the robot said.

Professor Gregor held up his hand. "I alone will handle these Herculean magnets." He called on Daisy to grab a stack of papers from his desk and distribute them to everyone. Then he grabbed something from his lab coat pocket and held it up. "First, you will work with these less powerful neodymium magnets to begin to understand their physical properties." Luke could just make out the magnets between Professor Gregor's fingers. They were the size of a small coin. "You are not young children, so I know you won't swallow these. But just in case—they are NOT candy."

The class let out a unified moan.

Unfazed, Gregor continued, "While you are working, you should discover you don't need that much magnetic strength to make ferrous objects levitate."

"Right. It's magic," Ibish said from the back of the classroom. His wild black hair was sticking up every which way, similar to Ronan's.

"Noooo, Ibish. It's science." The professor walked slowly between the tables as he spoke. "Magnetic force might seem like magic because it is invisible. But I assure you it is simply electrons rearranging in the same spin direction that causes the magnetic force. Magnets are fascinating. The world itself has a large magnetosphere that protects us from the sun's rays and solar winds." He paused his walking. "When the solar winds are strong, they interact with the earth's magnetic field. And we get aurora lights, or what is known here in the northern hemisphere as aurora borealis. The lights are beautiful to look at, and occur often in this area of southern Pandia because the magnetic field is particularly strong. Some of the professors at Chronos Academy study the auroras with equipment you may have seen out in the fields. These magnetometers collect data about the aurora borealis, and magnetic strength, which is measured in Kp units." Professor Gregor returned to the front of the classroom.

There was a knock on the door. That same instant the

door was opened by Coach Typhoon, wearing a bright lime green and cherry red tracksuit for the holiday season. He ignored the class and looked straight at Professor Gregor. "Morlia showed me some data," he said. "He's in my office and we need your opinion."

"Do you now?" Professor Gregor beamed.

"Regrettably so," the coach muttered as he quickly disappeared into the hallway.

The professor drew his eyebrows together and addressed the class. "I will be back in ten minutes tops. In the meantime, fill out the worksheets in front of you." He briskly left the room, leaving the door open behind him.

Luke glanced at his watch. Thankfully this was the last class of the day. He, Andy, Nia, and Cleo would be heading to the Saloon afterwards. He hoped he could convince one of them to go to the aviary as a substitute for Ollie. He grabbed his sheet and turned to ask Andy a question.

Andy however, was standing by the doorway, peering out and down the hall. He darted back into the classroom to Professor Gregor's lab bench and began examining the large magnets. Immediately Hayden approached the other side of the lab bench along with Stephanie.

"Those aren't yours," Stephanie said to Andy, wrapping her hand around one magnet.

"Nope, and they aren't yours either." Andy grabbed the other brick-sized magnet and pulled off the red cap from the end.

Not to be outdone Stephanie did the same. Hayden snickered.

"You're not supposed to touch those," Nia said, moving with large strides to the front of the room.

"You're not the boss of me," Stephanie quipped.

Luke joined Daisy, Cleo, and several other classmates who had congregated around the lab bench.

Hayden knocked away the wooden block from between the two magnets.

Andy pushed his magnet across the bench surface towards Stephanie's, playing a game of magnet chicken. But they couldn't push the bricks together. There was an invisible force keeping them separated. "Luke, the force is against us." Andy laughed, "Get it? Like in *Star Wars*?"

"They're repelling. Great demonstration. Now put them back," Nia said. She was standing next to Luke.

Sir Lancelot was frantically wheeling forwards and backwards in the middle of the classroom repeating a message on a loop. "Danger! Danger!"

The students were all fascinated by the wide space forming between the two large magnets. No matter how hard Andy and Stephanie tried, the magnets couldn't be forced closer together. Daisy waved her hand through the space between the two brick shapes. "Look at this! My hand doesn't block the repelling," she said and giggled in wonder.

Then Hayden grabbed Stephanie's magnet and flipped it. Andy jerked forward from the pull of the brick in his hands. The students watched in horror as the two magnets slammed together with a loud THUNK.

Daisy screamed. One of her fingers had been caught between the two magnetic bricks.

"You're hurting Daisy!" Nia yelled at Andy and Hayden as each scrambled to pull the magnets apart.

"OH NO," droned the robot. Sir Lancelot left the classroom at warp speed, sirens on and lights flashing.

"Pull, Hayden!" Stephanie yelled.

"I'm trying!" Hayden replied.

Daisy kept screaming.

Andy and Hayden were pulling hard. "Help us!" Andy yelled.

Stephanie grunted as she pulled Hayden's arm.

Nia and Cleo pulled on one of Andy's arms.

Luke grabbed for the magnet but couldn't get any leverage. Grabbing Andy's other arm he pulled hard. He lost his grip and fell backwards. Unable to stop his fall, Luke crashed into the open shelved glassware cabinet.

He scrambled to get up. He turned his head to see glassware toppling from the shelving behind him and onto the floor.

KRRSHHH. SMASH. KSHHH!!

"Enough! What is going on here?" Professor Gregor's voice suddenly boomed from the doorway.

"What on earth?" Coach Typhoon said from behind Professor Gregor.

Nia shouted, "Daisy's finger is caught between the two big magnets! We can't get them apart."

Professor Gregor rushed over, pushed through the students, and grabbed Andy's magnet. He instructed Coach Typhoon to do the same with Hayden's. But Coach Typhoon was immobilized staring at the blood on the table. He'd gone as white as the professor's lab coat.

"Coach Typhoon, FOCUS!" Professor Gregor bellowed, "Grab the other magnet." He turned to Luke. "Luke, take hold of Daisy's arm. Get ready to pull it free as soon as we move the magnets apart. Then keep her arm elevated."

Luke did as he was told, waiting for the magnets to part. Daisy was almost as limp as the flower tied to her ponytail.

She was moaning softly.

Typhoon said meekly, "You're lucky I'm here, Gregor. I'm strong. I have grit and guts."

"Pull on three, Coach. Luke, get ready. One, two, THREE!" Professor Gregor yelled. Luke watched a blood vessel bulge in the professor's temple as the two men pulled against the magnet force.

The two magnets came apart an inch.

Luke pulled Daisy's arm with a jerk and raised it up.

Daisy fell against him as the magnets thumped together again and dropped onto the lab bench. He glanced at Daisy's finger above him. Blood was pooling and dripping down the side of it as a thick piece of skin flopped over and hung by a thread. Luke looked away, queasy.

Andy came up and quickly looked at the wound. "That is awesome. I can see inside your finger," he said.

Luke knew that wasn't true. How could anyone see anything with all that blood?

Daisy groaned. She slowly pulled her arm from Luke's grip and held it up herself. Luke took a puff from his inhaler.

Professor Gregor slumped in his chair breathing heavily. Coach Typhoon had collapsed against a desk. "That was easy," he said.

Nia moved toward Daisy but Stephanie got there first with a stack of paper towels from above the lab sink. She wrapped it clumsily around Daisy's finger. "I'll take her to Nurse Kelly," Stephanie said, her ponytail whacking Daisy's head as she helped her up.

"Professor Gregor, I think Simon fainted." Cleo nodded towards the middle of the classroom. Luke looked over and saw their classmate on the floor in the fetal position.

Nia stared in surprise and quickly said, "I'll help Simon."

"Good good," commented Professor Gregor from his slouched position in the chair.

"Professor Gregor," Hayden said, gesturing at Luke, Cleo, Nia, and Andy, "They broke a million of your flasks."

"Enough, Hayden. I will not tolerate another episode of the STEM challenge debacle!" Professor Gregor declared loudly, managing to point his finger in the air. "Everyone stay away from the broken glass."

They all had detention after class—Nia, Cleo, Andy, Luke, and Hayden, with Stephanie joining them after she returned from the nurse's office. They cleaned up all the broken glassware and scrubbed the lab bench, removing the spots of blood. They washed the floor with a mop and helped the professor replenish his stock of glassware.

When they finally got to Viking Hall for a bite of dinner, they were exhausted. Nia, Cleo, Andy, and Luke, slumped together at a table. On a small stage, a large Christmas tree was decked out with twinkling lights next to the gigantic Pandia Games countdown hourglass. Suddenly, a commotion came from the back of the cafeteria. They watched as Chef François stormed out of the kitchen, followed by Adio. Then the lights went out. Luke waited. One two, three, four, five. When the lights returned Chef François shouted, "I CANNOT WORK IN THESE CONDITIONS," his French accent stronger than ever.

"I can't believe what happened in class today," Luke said, half watching Adio chase after the chef as he stormed out the hall doors. Several tables away Stephanie and Hayden sent dirty looks at their group. Stephanie had been very clear that she blamed Andy for starting the whole magnet debacle.

"At least Daisy's gonna be okay," Nia said. Stephanie had reported that Daisy was resting in Nurse Kelly's office while getting her finger treated.

"Did you see her finger? A piece of skin was hanging off. Gross," Luke added.

"Not skin, a chunk of her finger you mean," Andy said, and shoved a heaping spoonful of pudding into his mouth, finishing the last of it. He pointed his spoon to the middle of the table at the thick pile of worksheets Professor Gregor had assigned as detention homework. "Extra homework sucks! Who wants to do that? And we have to do it all tonight."

"Honestly, that's your fault Andy," said Nia, pointing her finger at him.

"Exactly!" said Luke.

"You started it with the magnets," continued Nia. "And then you got us in trouble when we came to help."

"You're right," Andy smiled around the table. "Wouldn't have it any other way." He nonchalantly played with a quarter-sized coin, flipping it along the tops of his fingers, running it from his forefinger to his pinky and back again.

Nia squinted her eyes at him.

"Fine," Andy said. "Sorry guys. I'll apologize to Daisy, too."

While the others changed topic and finished their food, Luke glanced over at Cleo. He was amazed to see her focused and quietly working away, their homework worksheets in front of her. Her dishes were shoved to the side, the food untouched.

"Cleo, how can you be reading all that?" He then noticed *Bale's Tales* on her lap, half tucked under the table. He leaned over and whispered, "What are you doing? Someone could see!"

She whipped her head towards him, her eyes wide. "I know why you couldn't open the arca and I think I know how we can!"

34

Luke

It was Saturday morning, one week before winter holiday break. Ollie and Ronan were still in the sick bay with the flu along with many other students, and the academy hallways were quieter than usual. Inside Bastion Tower it felt bone-chilling cold. Ice crystals covered the recessed windows of the grand room. Cleo, Nia, Luke, and Andy tried to keep warm by wrapping themselves with the dusty sheets that covered some of the furniture. Luke had unrolled one of the old rugs onto the floor for them to sit on. The wind, a whipping howling force, battered the tower and its windows. Luke wished there was a roaring warm fire in the fireplace.

Andy was seething as he and Nia reviewed their letter from Director LeCrucia. In response to their petition and in typical Director LeCrucia style, it had started with a resounding NO. She would not override Coach Typhoon's decision on the Chronos Vikings team and Andy and Nia should cease and desist with this endeavor.

"Anger will fuel me!" Andy declared.

Luke sighed. The Order of Ravens had heard this tirade

before. Often right before bed.

"Me too. I can't believe this!" Nia said as she reread the letter. Andy lay back on the rug with a plop, his sheet over his head, defeated.

Luke looked away from the duo having a Pandia Games crisis, shook his head, and shifted closer to Cleo. *Bale's Tales* was open on the floor in front of them. She wrapped her sheet tighter over her sweater and read aloud the clue she had found.

> To open the arca
> the strength that you seek
> shall be found in a force
> both powerful and weak
> Invisible
> Gods of dawn will purr
> to the Greek north wind
> and keep the arca secure

"So you think a magnet could open the arca?" Luke asked.

She nodded. "We can't see the electrons rearranging and causing the magnetic force, so it's invisible." Cleo shifted on the rug. "That's what Professor Gregor said."

"And it seems magical. A force both powerful and weak. Okay, but what about the Gods of dawn and the Greek north wind?" Luke asked as Nia crawled over to them on her hands and knees, her sheet draped over her back, leaving her petition partner behind.

"Aurora is the name of the Roman goddess of dawn and borealis is the Greek name for north wind. I looked it up. The scientist Galileo Galilei named the lights 'aurora borealis' because he thought they were caused by sunlight reflecting from the atmosphere. Which was wrong," Cleo said and scooted over so Nia could sit next to her. Andy began slowly rolling his body toward them, blindly encased in his sheet like a spring roll.

Nia looked at the open journal. "Oh, I'm getting this. Professor Gregor also said that the earth has a magnetosphere."

"The key is the magnet part of that word," Cleo explained.

"Exactly." Nia continued, "The *magnetosphere* is hit by charged particles from the sun and that causes auroras. But they didn't know that in the 1800s. Yet Billy Bale has this clue? It doesn't make sense. And, he never had the arca, right?"

"I don't think so. If he did he would have had the Stone," Cleo confirmed.

"But he did draw the arca," Luke said, looking pensive.

"Whatever," Andy said, who had just re-joined the conversation and was lying on his side, his face poking out from his sheet. "He probably got the information from someone. Who cares? So a magnet will open the box!" He paused. "So it only took a mountain of homework to figure this out!" He rolled his eyes. "And all those facts like birds have iron in their beaks and follow the magnetic field. Why did I need to know that? I'm not a bird."

He is extra grumpy today, thought Luke.

Ignoring Andy, Cleo said, "We need a magnet."

"I have one right here," Andy said, and he pulled a quarter-size coin from his pocket, flipping it over his knuckles. "I grabbed it when we were cleaning up the lab."

Cleo looked at him accusingly.

"What?" he said, "I'm being careful with it. It's not like

I put it in my mouth." He flipped it over his knuckles one more time and plopped it back into his cargo pants pocket. Luke stood, letting his sheet slide to the floor. He placed his arms behind his back and started pacing, "Now we just need to get to the aviary."

"For the last time. We can't just show up there, Luke," Nia replied. "Ollie already spoke to Mr. Ringwald and Daisy about it. We'll have to wait till Ollie is better."

Luke grunted. He knew he'd just have to wait but that didn't mean he liked it.

Cleo suddenly sneezed.

Nia shimmied further away. "You're not getting sick too, are you?" She leaned toward her backpack, pulled out a bottle of hand sanitizer, used it, and held it up on offer to the others. Luke stepped closer and lowered his hands. SQUIRT

"Thanks," he said.

Cleo ignored them and then sighed when Nia insisted on doing the same for her.

"You probably need a bath in this stuff, Cleo. Ronan and Ollie are so sick. We don't want what they have," Nia said.

Luke walked over to the window. It was sleeting, and the icy pellets hitting the windows created a loud pitter-patter sound. The wind howled loudly, vibrating the windows. He motioned Andy over, who wormed up to a standing position in his sheet and shuffled over.

"Can we include the girls in the Order of Ravens?" Luke asked. "I've been thinking about it for a while. We could use their help to find the Stones, and more treasure."

Andy thought about it for a second. "I do like treasure. And Nia has helped with the petition. So ya, why not?"

"We should get going. Tons of homework," Nia announced as she made her way towards the staircase. Cleo was packing up *Bale's Tales* into her hideous puke-green backpack.

"Nia, wait!" Luke called. He and Andy walked over to the two of them. "We've formed a top-secret order, me, Ollie, Andy, and Ronan. The Order of Ravens. And we want you two to join."

Nia watched Andy. "Really?" Both boys nodded. She smiled and unwrapped a piece of gum she'd found in her jean jacket pocket and popped it in her mouth.

Cleo was lightly bouncing in her shoes and shaking her hands slightly by her side. "I've always wanted to be part of a secret group," she beamed at Luke. "Thanks."

Andy spit into his hand, "Come on, we all need to shake. That's how this works, and then you can be in the Order." He held out his hand with mucus dripping from the middle of his palm.

"Gross, keep that hand away from me. It's flu season!" Nia grimaced.

A compromise was finally reached when Nia suggested the oath would be taken using *Bale's Tales*. All four piled their hands on top of the book. "We are now united in the Order of Ravens," announced Luke. "Treasure seekers!"

"Protectors of secrets!" Andy added.

"And guardians of artifacts!" Cleo said.

"Protectors of the world!" Nia added.

"Fine. Okay, are we all agreed?" Luke asked, wondering how the rest of the order would feel about the "protectors of the world" and "guardians of artifacts" bits.

The three others nodded solemnly.

Ollie wasn't there to finish off the oath, so Luke did.

"Order of Ravens, go forth to adventure." They all grinned at each other and collected their things to leave.

When the newly expanded Order approached the bottom of the narrow staircase of Bastion Tower, Luke told everyone to shush. He could hear something. The others froze on the steps. He slowly looked over the railing and down into the spiralling stairwell that ran through the centre of the tower. He crept down a few more steps listening intently, the other three inching down closely behind him. Voices. But from where? He prayed they weren't in the stairwell, too. Then he remembered Andy had the only key to the tower door and always locked it behind him using the sliding bolt. No one could be on the stairs below them.

"Roy, did you hear me?" There was a pause. "Is everything alright?"

"Adio?" Cleo mouthed. She was pressing against Luke's side. The step didn't fit four of them side by side, but they'd managed it by leaning against each other, toward the outer wall of the staircase. The inner wall rail was only at waist height, and nobody wanted to risk falling down the spiral shaft as they strained to hear. Luke could hardly breathe. He felt like someone was squeezing him like a tube of toothpaste.

"Ah, Adio. Good. Lucky for me you've come along just in time. I'm uh, a bit lost, I'm afraid. I came into the castle from a side door and got turned around." It was Mr. Ringwald. The two men weren't speaking loudly but the sound traveled up the stairwell enough so they could just be heard. *They must be standing right outside the tower door*, thought Luke.

"I see you have some papers there," Adio said.

"Uhh yes, I've been keeping an eye out for signs of mischief, unusual happenings around campus, you know," Mr. Ringwald replied.

"And have you noticed anything unusual?" Adio asked.

"Actually, I did see some suspicious footprints in a flowerbed below one of the castle windows," Mr. Ringwald said.

"Well, show me where!" Adio demanded.

"Yes, yes! I was on my way to tell Director LeCrucia, but now I don't know if I'll be able to find that same window again. This castle is so darned confusing. And which tower is this then?" Mr. Ringwald asked.

Nia and Andy pressing on her, Cleo leaned more heavily on Luke. Luke had to re-brace himself against the stone wall of the staircase as Cleo's backpack dug into his side.

"This is Bastion Tower," Adio said. "Still under construction. Quite a project going on there."

"Sure, a one-hundred-year project," Andy scoffed.

"Shhh," Luke reminded him

"I guess we shouldn't be here then?" said Mr. Ringwald and laughed.

"Well, the DO NOT ENTER! sign does give it away," Adio said. "Come on then. I was headed back to the armoury to fix the door when I saw you from afar. Let's go to Viking Hall and get you a bite. You really look awful, Roy."

"The ravens ..."

"I can't imagine it's easy, especially with Ludwig still missing." Their voices diminished in volume as they moved away.

The group waited, squeezed together on the same step. The hallway finally fell silent. When Luke squirmed to get some air into his lungs, he felt the stone wall under his shoulder give way with a sharp crack, followed by a grinding noise. Then Luke felt himself tumbling.

His left shoulder hit the ground and Cleo fell on top of him. He wiggled out from under her and tried unsuccessfully to get up as Andy fell on top of them both.

"Andy, you're squishing me," Cleo complained. She raised her head, her crazy curly hair highlighted by the dim light streaming into the space from the stairwell. "Did we break the wall?" she asked Nia.

Nia was still standing out on the staircase, looking up at the edges of the opening. "No. It looks like a secret tunnel! Where does—"

The light from the stairwell vanished. The door in the wall had slammed shut. Suddenly the floor underneath Luke gave way.

35

Cleo

Cleo screamed and screamed and screamed, the sound echoing all around her. Sliding uncontrollably headfirst down a steep incline she tried to slow herself, but there was nothing to grab onto in the pitch black. Her thoughts swirled: her grandma, the call she never made to her mom (to say sorry maybe?), her new friends, the life she was just starting to make.

"OOFFFF!" She was jettisoned from the slide and her momentum came to a full stop as she hit the ground. Dizzy and trying to get her bearings, she noticed hazy natural light. Coming from somewhere behind her Andy barrelled out of the slide with Luke right behind him. Cleo couldn't get out of the way before the boys slammed into her, rolling all three of them over from the boys' momentum. Cleo suddenly halted from a jerk at her back. She was awkwardly lying on her backpack. One of the boys was wedged next to her. Her right arm ached, its skin feeling raw. But why was her arm dangling like that? Tilting her head to look down at it she saw ocean waves crashing wildly against huge rocks far below her. She was on the edge of a cliff! Correction: she was hanging over the edge of a cliff!

"Oh no, no, no, no," Cleo said, trying to retract from the cliff's edge. Her backpack was caught on something and she couldn't move back.

"Don't move!" shouted Andy's voice to her left. His voice mingled with Luke's in muffled conversation while she inhaled deeply, trying not to scream or cry.

It smelled of rain, like after a storm. She looked up at the sky again and blinked her eyes twice to adjust to the grey light. An enormous icy cloud stretched above her. In the center of her view a small ball of orange haze was trying to shine through the thick grey clouds. Seagulls flirted with the ocean drafts, their wings spread lazily over them. A freezing cold wind blasted her face.

Luke's head and upper torso appeared to her left. She felt a yank on her backpack and her left arm. But she didn't move.

"She's stuck," he said over his shoulder. She heard Andy say something unintelligible.

She felt another unpleasant yank. This time her left arm scraped against the rocky surface as her body was slowly dragged away from the cliff's edge. Once safe, Cleo pushed herself to a sitting position and shimmied hurriedly backwards on her butt, putting a body's length between herself and the sheer drop.

Luke was visibly shaken as he sat next to her, his face pale.

"That was close," Andy said. He collapsed into a sitting position on the other side of her.

She undid her pack. She pressed back against the wall with her backpack on her lap, wanting to be as far away from that cliff edge as possible. Cleo rubbed the nasty ache from the scrapes on both her arms.

Surveying their surroundings, she noticed the three of them were sheltered by a rocky canopy that extended all around them. They were in a tiny cave. It wasn't tall enough for any of them to stand up straight. Cleo twisted around and looked up into the circular opening in the wall from which they'd emerged and had almost plummeted to their deaths. It was too steep and narrow for them to climb back up to return to Bastion Tower. A shiver of fear rippled down her spine.

"Sorry about your arm," Luke said.

"I guess you two are even," Andy said with a half grin. "You saved Luke from the castle and now he saved you from …" He nodded towards the cliff, not grinning so much anymore.

"Thanks," Cleo said. She managed to smile at Luke.

"Your backpack got caught there somehow. On that pointy rock," Luke pointed to the right corner of the cliff's edge. "If your backpack hadn't stopped you, and us …"

"We'd be dead," finished Andy.

Her grandma's backpack was lucky after all! It had saved all of them. Five small steps and one would walk right out of this shallow cave and plunge into the ocean below. Cleo shivered at the thought. She hugged the pack tightly in silent gratitude.

The wind swirled around the edge of their enclosure, whipping up loose dirt and pebbles. As Cleo watched the swirl, she remembered something important. "Where's Nia?"

"Probably safe and sound in Bastion Tower on the OTHER side of that secret door!" Andy said as Luke moved on to all fours, then on his belly, and made his way cautiously to the cliff's edge. His head disappeared as he cranked his neck, looking over the edge. He turned on his back and looked up. Luke carefully shimmied back inside and squished himself next to Cleo again. "We're closer to the top of the cliff than we are to the bottom," he said breathlessly.

Cleo imagined herself as a baby eagle stuck in a nest way up high, waiting for mommy and daddy to come take care of her. She swallowed hard. "Nia must've heard us," she offered. "I mean, we were all screaming."

"Speak for yourself." Andy placed his chin on his knees.

"I heard you, Andy!" she replied. "You were the loudest."

"It doesn't matter," Luke stated. "There's no way she'll find us. How would she even know what happened to us?"

Andy shrugged his shoulders and kicked at a loose stone. As it tumbled over the cliff's edge, Cleo gasped. She quickly unzipped her backpack. *Bale's Tales* was still there, leather straps holding it closed. Phew. She sealed the zipper again.

Andy straightened up. "Hey, this must be Traitors' Gate!"

"Traitors' Gate," Cleo repeated.

"What's a traitors gate?" asked Luke.

"Joe told me about it." Andy stood to give his sermon, and hit his head on the ceiling of the cave. He hunched his head and neck down and explained, "Chronos Castle has a long history, right? It was first built as a fortress and ruled by Vikings. Then a king and knights came and built up the castle."

"We know this, Andy." Cleo was annoyed with this unnecessary history lesson.

"Joe said traitors to the king were, ah, pushed down a tunnel to their death. In this castle. But that was just a rumor," Andy said, sitting down on Luke's other side, "until now."

Cleo shivered as she remembered the huge rocks breaking the water's surface below them. She wondered how many skeletons were layered on the rocks in the ocean at the bottom of the cliff.

36

Cleo

Icy damp air shot into the cave in gusts. All three of them sat with their knees up to their chests. Cleo shivered next to Andy and gazed out at the grey stormy sky. Andy tapped on his knees, entertaining them with different rhythms. Luke leaned his forehead on his crossed arms. They huddled closer together, attempting to stay warm in the December cold of the cliffside cave. They stayed like that for a long time.

"Luke, what time is it?" Cleo finally asked, glancing at Luke's wrist.

He looked at his watch. "Twelve something," he said.

"Lunchtime," Andy lamented, rubbing his stomach.

Cleo gasped. "We've been here for over an hour! That means Nia's not coming. No one is. Okay, I'm freaking out now!" She needed to distract herself from her fear and hunger by focussing on something else.

"Why does your watch have only one hand?" Cleo asked as she leaned over to look at Luke's wrist.

"Don't get him started," Andy said. "Here, I'll help. His watch is ancient. It was his dad's. Don't ask him about his dad."

Luke's face reddened. He cast a dark glance at his roommate.

"Why? What about your dad?" Cleo asked.

"My dad is …" Luke gulped, "he's missing." He nervously looked away. "Everyone thinks he's dead."

Andy shrugged.

Cleo looked at Luke with concern. "I'm so sorry, Luke." He seemed to be shrinking in size with all their attention on him.

Andy got up, crouched over, and inched his way a wee bit closer to the mouth of the little cave. "Maybe we could jump for it. Like a high diving board."

"Right, except for the churning ocean and the big rocks at the bottom," Luke replied.

"If Ollie was here, he would have, like, an inflatable trampoline or something in his backpack. He'd throw it onto the rocks below, and we'd jump out and bounce to safety on it," Andy said. Cleo giggled.

Luke asked her, "Do you have anything like an inflatable bouncy castle in your backpack?" Cleo laughed, thinking of *Bale's Tales* and the few assignments she had in her bag. She shook her head.

Andy turned and motioned to the round hole they'd fallen from. "We could try to climb back up."

"It's way too steep. We'll come flying back out and y'know." She inclined her head to the cliff's edge.

After a few minutes Andy spoke again. "I've been thinking," he said. "Maybe this tunnel is one huge toilet for pee and poo to flow down. One big poop chute!" He wrapped his arms around himself trying to get warm. He carried on speaking his thoughts, "I wish I had the flu, then I'd be safe and warm in bed! I blame Nia and her hand sanitizer for keeping us healthy. And she even escaped this whole thing! In a few days she'll be home for winter break eating those noodles and dumplings she always talks about, getting presents, and having a good life. And I'll never open a Christmas present again."

He's right! We can't stay here forever. We'll die from exposure, hunger, and thirst.

Then Cleo thought of something even worse.

What if we have to go to the bathroom? That would be mortifying! Andy's jokes about the poop chute would never stop.

Andy moved closer to the cave opening again and cupped his hands around his mouth. "HELP!"

Cleo and Luke plugged their ears.

"H-E-E-E-E-L-L-L-L-P-P-P!!" Andy continued, his cry drowned out by the crashing waves and wind.

"It's no use," Luke said. "No one can hear you."

Andy slumped against the side of the cave and yelled one more time for good measure.

When he stopped, Cleo unplugged her ears. "Andy, my ears are ringing!" she said.

"Mine too," Luke said, tapping both ears with his palms.

The wind was howling at the opening of the rock face. Andy returned to the back wall and they huddled together again.

After a while Luke looked at each of his friends and said, "We have to get outta here. Maybe we can climb this cliff somehow."

"That's impossible!" Cleo squawked.

"Not really. The cliff is not totally vertical. We would just have to be SUPER careful!" Andy said.

Undeterred, Luke wriggled back to the edge again, this

time making his way further out. He called back, "Andy, help me." Andy went and held Luke's legs.

Cleo shook with fear. Luke could plunge to his death at any moment. What was he thinking?!

Luke screamed out and Cleo jumped.

"I see something!" he called, gesturing with one arm. "Out there to the side. Andy, make sure you've got me."

"I'm trying but don't go out too far," Andy said.

Horrified, Cleo watched as Luke pushed his way out further over the edge, moving his shoulder blades beyond the ledge.

"Cleo, help me," Andy demanded.

She couldn't budge.

"Any time now! Come on!" Andy commanded. "Luke could fall."

She scooted over on her butt and put her weight on one of Luke's legs. Andy did the same with the other. Luke leaned even further out.

Cleo yelled, "Stop Luke, before we all go over!"

"Got it! Pull me back," he said. He sounded winded. Andy and Cleo shifted their weight and tugged on his legs, bringing Luke back inch by inch until he could shimmy the rest of the way back into the cave on his own.

"A rope!" Luke said, proudly holding a weathered rope in his hand. "I didn't see it the first time. I barely saw it this time! And there's lots of it. It must be hanging all the way down the cliff, to the ocean. Help me pull it up."

They began pulling the rope up over the lip of the opening and into their little cave, creating a large mound of rope until they finally pulled up the frayed wet end that had been in the ocean below.

Andy flopped onto his belly, shimmied to the edge and then rolled onto his back. "I want to see if it's REALLY anchored up at the top of the cliff."

Cleo's eyes followed the line of the rope from the pile in the cave to where it was rubbing along the rock at the top edge of the cave. She watched Andy tug on the part of the rope hanging above their cave. "The rope goes all the way up. It's anchored all right," he shouted from the cave opening.

Cleo rubbed her hand on her face. She did not like where this was going.

"We go up. It's like Coach Typhoon's climbing wall. Simple," Andy said when he was safely back inside the little cave.

"There is nothing. Simple. About that," Cleo commented. Andy could climb his way up, no problem. Luke could even complete the rappelling wall more than three quarters of the way now, so he'd probably survive this, too. As for her, there was no way! She'd never once made it over the rappelling wall. And when she had fallen there had always been a spongy foam mattress at the bottom to land on, not huge rocks and violent crashing waves. She couldn't believe it, but maybe Coach Typhoon was right. Upper body strength was vital to life.

"When I get to the top, I can go and get help," Andy offered, tugging on the rope again.

"How could we possibly explain how we got here without being expelled?" Cleo asked.

Luke nodded. "We'd have to tell about Bastion Tower, Andy."

The reality was that they all had to climb.

Cleo hugged her backpack. "That cliff is really high. If

any of us fall …" she said, shaking her head.

"Then what difference does it make? We die if we stay and we can die if we go. It's been a good life," Andy said nonchalantly.

"Cleo, we can do this. You can do it," Luke said.

She took a deep breath and exhaled slowly.

"Maybe you should leave your backpack here," Andy suggested.

"No way!" she said.

"Cleo, you can't even hold yourself up," Andy said. "Your backpack will drag you down."

"I need this bag. It's my grandma's, and it already saved us once," she insisted. "Plus, it has *Bale's Tales* in it." She wasn't giving up on the Stones of Destiny until they plunged to their deaths trying to get out of this cave.

"Fine. I'll take it then," Andy said.

She figured that was her best chance of survival, so she reluctantly accepted his offer.

"I'll yell when I get up. Then you can go," Andy said to Luke.

Luke nodded and turned to Cleo. "We'll go closer together. Follow me. Step where I step."

Andy grinned at Cleo as they stood crouching, the cave ceiling scraping his red hair. "Luke, hold on to the rope. Actually, there's so much here—" he looked at the pile they had wound onto the cave floor and revised their plan, "—we can tie it around ourselves, like a safety belt, as we each go up." He got to work creating a makeshift harness, drawing and tying the rope securely around his waist. He glanced at the other two.

Luke nodded and Cleo pursed her lips.

Andy looked out the cave opening. "Just one thing left. I need to check that the rope can hold us." He grabbed onto the rope. "Don't try this at home!" And he leaped out in the air over the cliff like Tarzan swinging on a vine.

37

Cleo

"Go Cleo!" Luke called faintly in the howling wind from just above the cave.

It was finally her turn. She looked down at her waist. She had tied lots of rope around herself and there was still plenty of rope in the cave curled up like a snake. She grabbed the rope leading up and wound some of it tightly around her right arm. She willed herself closer to the ledge. Looking down, she saw the wild swirling of the ocean waves, foaming against the large sharp rocks. She could barely hear their crashing sound over her incredibly loud beating heart. *Don't look down!* her brain screamed.

"Come on!" Luke yelled from the cliffside.

Cleo looked up. Andy had made a fair bit of progress and was nearing the top. Luke was above her and to her right.

Luke tried to reassure her, "Step where I'm stepping. It isn't totally vertical. And there's lots of hand and foot holds."

The cliff looked vertical to her. Fear gripped her and she couldn't breathe. Perhaps expulsion was the better option? She could stay here in the cave until her friends came and rescued her.

Her grandma's voice shook Cleo from the inside, *"Be Brave!"*

Cleo tightened her rope harness. Okay, she had to be reasonable and logical. If she was being honest, the cliff wasn't exactly vertical. She could place her feet on the cliff and sort of scramble up. But without the rope, she would fall for sure.

She edged out of the little cave, holding on to the rope for dear life. As she started upwards her palms quickly became hot and sweaty, while her fingers and knuckles were freezing because of the cold December wind. Placing her feet where she could find a rock ledge to alleviate the discomfort, she pushed with her legs and pulled with her arms. The wind whipped around her.

After what felt like forever, Cleo paused and angled her head upwards. She could now see the castle's curtain wall looming above Andy and Luke's figures. The cliff top still seemed far out of reach, and she was already exhausted. With her body pressed against the rock, she knew she couldn't go any further. Warm tears fell down her face, freezing to her cheeks in the wind.

Out of nowhere, a raven flew towards her and perched on an outcrop of rock close above. It was Floki with his one white foot. She couldn't believe it. He cawed at her. She watched him ruffle his inky black feathers and caw at her again. It was as though he was yelling at her to keep going. Finding a rock ledge the width of her big toe, her legs pushed her up, and she moved her hands just a bit higher on the rope.

Her eyes on the raven, Cleo kept inching her way up and she soon noticed the strangest thing. Floki slowly moved *his* way up too.

Keep going. Be brave! her grandma's voice echoed in her head.

Cleo continued, watching the raven. It was better to focus on the bird than on the thundering waves below, or her frozen hands, or her painful, tired body. Each time she passed Floki, he turned his head as though studying her. He stayed eerily close as he flapped his way to each next outcrop of rock.

The rope was burning her hands. She was exhausted and terrified. Cleo focused on her breath as her heart beat inside her ears. She followed the raven to the next perch and then the next. Keep moving, she pleaded with her stiffening limbs.

Don't look up, or down!

"Cleo, come on!" Andy said.

"You can do this!" Luke and Andy yelled over each other.

"*Caw!*"

"Heave ho. She's almost at the top," Andy shouted. There was a pull on the rope, and Cleo felt herself moving with no effort. Her friends were now pulling her up. She gripped the rope tighter while shutting her eyes.

"Okay Cleo, hang on!" Luke yelled.

Stay alive, her teeth chattered. Her eyes squeezed shut. Her arms and legs scraped against protruding edges as Andy and Luke pulled her upwards. Holding on tight, her arms ached terribly. The palms of her hands stung madly from rope burn.

The alarm in Luke and Andy's voices made Cleo open her eyes. The rope was snagged along a jagged edge and wouldn't go any further. Andy was straining, leaning back with full effort, holding the rope taut. Luke squinted against the wind as he reached over the cliff's edge for her arms. Grabbing her, he pulled hard.

Clinging to the rope and scrambling against the ridge, she tried to move up. She found a foothold, but it quickly crumbled under her feet. Luke adjusted his grip on her arms, while Andy grunted and braced himself a little more.

"That's it, Cleo, come on," Luke said through gritted teeth.

Desperate, she scrambled for another foothold and found one. With one final push from her legs and Luke pulling hard, she made it over the top of the ridge.

"Move over here," Luke commanded as he scrambled back from the edge on his behind.

"Careful! There isn't much room," Andy gasped, out of breath. He'd fallen backward to the ground when Cleo cleared the lip of the cliff and was now sitting with his back pressed to the castle's towering curtain wall. Only a few feet lay between the wall and the cliff edge with the pounding sea below.

"There's no way to get over the curtain wall," Luke said as he joined Andy. He took a puff of his inhaler.

Cleo collapsed beside him. She twisted around slightly and let her gaze sweep up. The castle's defensive wall was massive and of an unscalable height. It had been designed to guard against invaders but was now keeping them at the cliff's edge.

Andy spoke between gulps of air as he got up. "We have to find the end of the wall. Let's move."

"Careful!" Luke glanced at his friends, his eyes filled with worry.

Andy cautiously slid Cleo's backpack off and moved it in

front of him so he could wear it on his chest. With their backs tight against the curtain wall, they shimmied sideways. With just a few feet between them and the cliff's edge, the wind blowing at them, and the tricky footing—it was terrifying.

After surviving the murderous tumble down Traitors' Gate shaft and the climb back up the cliff, Cleo couldn't believe that this was her predicament. Shimmying along this ridge, she could slip and die!

Luke, who was closest to her, said "Don't look down, just focus on where you're putting your feet."

Floki reappeared, catching the updrafts, and staying with them.

It seemed like she'd taken a million steps, her hands and face completely numb from the cold wind, her back sore from scraping along the curtain wall, when Andy finally yelled, "We made it!" Cleo slid around the wall's stone corner and fell to her knees. The cliff's edge and the sound of the ocean waves were now behind her. The fields extended forever in front of her and further in the distance, partially hidden by a fog of the low-lying grey clouds, she could make out Kingsburg Forest.

38

Cleo

Cleo wept. The boys were slumped to the ground out of sheer exhaustion. Then, out of nowhere, Nia almost mowed her over in a hug. She kept asking if Cleo was okay. Cleo nodded between sobs. Nia placed a warm sweater around Cleo's shoulders. Cleo was grateful that Nia always dressed in layers.

Nia demanded to know what had happened to them. "I freaked out when that secret door slammed shut. I had no idea what happened to you guys! I pounded on the wall trying to get it to open again, but it wouldn't. Then I screamed to see if you guys were alright, but I couldn't hear anything. I was going crazy. I searched Bastion Tower, but you weren't there. Then I didn't know what to do. So I searched all over. I moved further and further away from campus but I couldn't find you anywhere. I was about to give up and turn around and go tell Director LeCrucia when I saw you. Nia paused and took a breath, her eyes filled with tears. "Oh poop." She wiped her sleeves against her eyes.

Andy shifted slightly, unconformable with all the emotions

on display, and started telling Nia everything that happened from the moment the door shut in Bastion Tower.

Nia nodded when Andy was done. "Could this rope be a weird Coach Typhoon thing?"

"No," Andy said, "the rope was different from gym class. It was a climber's rope. Much better for the hands."

Cleo scoffed at that. Her palms were still red and hurting, and blisters had formed at the top of her palms.

"Professor Gregor's maybe. He is crazy, you know. Always doing push-ups," Nia offered.

"He does ride the unicycle," Andy offered as evidence of being crazy. "Well, he did before it was stolen, as he's told us a million times in class."

"What if it was someone else?" Cleo interrupted. Her mind was racing. Jumbo's comments about Receleren returning to Glimmerton, Mr. Ringwald talking about suspicious footprints at the castle, the Order looking for the Stones. She could only jump to one conclusion.

"Like who?" Andy asked. "Who would climb a rope up to this curtain wall from a boat in the ocean?"

"A pirate!" Luke said, suddenly understanding.

"Recleren!" Cleo whispered, her eyes huge.

"Recleren?" Nia asked.

"He could've climbed up this cliff right from the water," said Cleo, her hands shaking. "The rope goes all the way down to the ocean."

"But how could he anchor and attach a rope at the top of the cliff from way down there?" Andy asked. "I don't buy it."

He had a good point. Deep in thought, Cleo and Luke squinted their eyes at each other and simultaneously responded, "Maybe he had help."

Everyone paused for a moment, as they considered the possibilities.

"Recleren could be hiding somewhere here, near Chronos Academy," Cleo said, looking at Kingsburg Forest in the distance.

They all followed Cleo's gaze. The broadleaf trees that had displayed different shades of oranges and reds only a month ago, had lost their leaves. But the evergreen coniferous trees stood strong and full, protectively forming a large green canopy. And somewhere in that forest, could be a dangerous pirate criminal.

Cleo's nerves were fried and she needed a break. She didn't know how much more adventure she could take. *How did grandma CeeCee do it?* Cleo chose her next words carefully. "We need to tell the police."

"About what?" Andy said.

"Traitors' Gate, the rope, the tower," Cleo said.

"Oh great, and then the school will expel us for being in Bastion Tower," Andy said.

"Oh, poop," Nia said.

"I can make a call anonymously," Cleo piped up.

"Only tell them about the rope," Luke said.

Andy asked, "Do the phones in the phone centre even work? I tried pushing all the numbers. It doesn't do anything."

"They are rotary phones," Luke said, demonstrating by pointing his finger and drawing a circle to the right, his movement sharp.

"No way!" Andy replied. "It rotates! Rotary. I get it now!"

"We need to get going," Luke said. "We should probably tell Ollie and Ronan about all this."

Cleo could see Luke's breath as he spoke. The boys stood

and slowly started walking toward the castle. The days were very short on Pandia as the calendar approached the winter solstice. The sun was already starting to go down and the temperature was dropping. As Nia helped her up, Cleo could see the silhouette of the main castle behind her roomie. She could make out Bastion Tower, too. She realized how far they'd fallen vertically from the tower through Traitors' Gate, and how far they'd come along the curtain wall.

Nia helped Cleo get her backpack over her aching arms. Just before they fell in line behind the boys, Nia stopped Cleo. "You still have *Bale's Tales* in your backpack, right?"

Cleo nodded.

"That's good. But this whole thing is weird though. Like, bad luck," Nia commented.

Cleo didn't answer because she was slightly flummoxed. She'd never mentioned to Nia, nor to the Order, the supposed curse that Captain Jumbo had associated with searching for the Stones. It hadn't been worth mentioning. But Jumbo *had* told her that no one who ever looked for the Stones had found them. Billy and the dark knight Caelen had even disappeared.

Maybe there is *a curse? Captain Jumbo had big trouble when he'd searched for the Stones. And today we were in real danger. We could have disappeared forever!*

Cleo shivered at the thought of what would have happened if they had plunged from Traitors' Gate into the ocean.

But curses aren't real!

They gradually walked their way up the gentle slope towards the castle grounds. The wind had died down. It was dusk now. They reached the castle without running into any professors to ask questions about their dirty and dishevelled appearance. However, outside the castle's main entrance a few students stared at them curiously. Adio called out a greeting as he pulled holiday lights out of a box to decorate a grouping of trees. He did a double take and gave them all a perplexed look, his eyes wandering over their faces and clothes as they scurried through the doors.

After quickly changing their clothes, they made their way to Viking Hall. They were the first ones to arrive for dinner and they were starving. Chef François was happy to serve them early, perhaps because he knew they wouldn't stop pestering him. After filling her plate twice, and now fully satiated, Cleo made her way to the phone centre with Nia. She made her anonymous call to the police about the rope and the Order's suspicions about Recleren. The instant Cleo hung up the phone she felt a wash of relief that the police would take care of Recleren. The last place the Stones belonged was in the hands of a pirate criminal!

Cleo walked back to the dormitory with Nia. As they entered their room, Daisy looked up from her sketchbook at the desk, thick gauze still wrapped around her crushed finger, and asked where they'd been. They gave a vague response and Nia and Cleo exchanged a knowing glance. Daisy barely gave a nod and returned to her drawing.

Cleo could hear sleet starting to come down again as she got into her PJs. She slipped into bed, relieved to be alive. She slept like a rock.

39

Luke

In the abysmal daylight of the following morning, three policemen in uniform had responded to Cleo's anonymous phone call. They were now standing together near the raven statue.

"That was quick," Luke said, feeling nervous. Luke and Cleo were watching through the wide-open door of Knight Hall with other students curious about the activities outside in the courtyard.

"Excuse us," Professor Morlia said as he and Director LeCrucia made their way out through the students gathered at the Chronos Castle main door, which was decorated with lights and a large Christmas wreath. Sir Lancelot was close behind Director LeCrucia, bumping into Ducky who was wearing a garland collar and yipping at the director's heels. LeCrucia scooped her dog from the ground, fixed its little Santa hat, and turned angrily towards the robot before moving on. They stopped next to the three-headed raven statue, which Adio had decorated with a red scarf. Sir Lancelot was still inching closer to LeCrucia.

Cleo and Luke crossed the courtyard to discreetly watch the action from behind the trimmed hedge halfway between the castle doors and the raven statue. Cleo whispered to Luke that the tallest policeman was Detective Anders. Both students made their way a wee bit closer towards the adults. The hedge, just sharp spiky twigs at this time of year, was not great at concealing them.

"Knock knock," they heard Sir Lancelot say.

Director LeCrucia remained silent, narrowing her eyes at the robot.

"Who's there?" Professor Morlia answered.

"Razor."

"Razor who?"

"Razor hands. This is a stickup. Happy Holidays."

The professor smirked and the director turned around to face the three policemen. "You were saying?" She stopped and looked back at the robot. Sir Lancelot turned towards the school and left without any more comments. Ducky, safe in LeCrucia's arms, began quacking at the receding robot.

"The call was anonymous," Detective Anders said. "Strange thing, though. It was traced back to the phone centre here at Chronos Academy," he added, raising one eyebrow.

Luke looked over at Cleo. She was staring at the detective, biting her lower lip. Director LeCrucia briefly glanced in their direction. For a brief panicked moment Luke thought Director LeCrucia knew it was Cleo who had made the call. But Cleo had told Luke she and Nia were alone in the phone centre when she placed the call, and that she had even disguised her voice. There was no way the director could know it was Cleo.

The director swiftly turned her gaze to the sky, following

the helicopter that was now headed towards Kingsburg Forest. The director shifted her eyes back to Anders and the two other policemen. "I don't understand your implication," she said to the detective as she zipped up her jacket, tucking Ducky inside, "but we must not digress, Detective Anders. I have asked you to assess the cliff area for—"

"My men checked," Anders interrupted. "There is indeed a rope dangling from the cliff. On the other side of the curtain wall. Just as the caller described it."

"Do you really think it's—?" Director LeCrucia quickly lowered her voice so that Luke couldn't hear the end of her sentence. But he knew she was thinking of the same person the Order of Ravens did—Recleren.

"We are of course being cautious. And have the helicopter about. But I really think the rope was anchored to the cliff some time ago and no one noticed," the detective said, straightening his shoulders even more to stand perfectly straight.

Professor Morlia spoke. "Possibly. But we cannot ignore the string of thefts at this school either. A unicycle, Professor Torres's wallet, and more."

The sound of the helicopter had brought many students out from the castle, pointing to the sky and exchanging theories on why it was there.

"Yes, all true," Director LeCrucia agreed, and ushered the detective and fellow policemen back towards the castle. "Detective Anders, let's forget the tour for now and continue this discussion in my office."

Professor Morlia gave a feeble smile to the students as the adults passed them to enter the enormous castle front door.

Cleo whispered to Luke. "Remember the article in the

Glimmerton Gazette you mentioned about Recleren, Captain Jumbo, and Detective Anders?" Luke nodded and Cleo continued, "I looked it up early this morning in the library. Detective Anders arrested Recleren ten years ago! And I found out how he escaped from prison. He dug a hole in the wall of his cell, right behind the toilet! He used a teaspoon from the prison cafeteria."

"Really? That must've taken forever," Luke whispered back.

After glancing around nervously, Cleo added, "Recleren is bad news. Captain Jumbo said that first he stole stuff but then he became dangerous, hurting people! And then after he escaped, he joined pirates. And that he's probably looking for the Stones."

Luke spoke in a hurried manner, "If he's looking for the Stones, then the sooner we get the arca and the Stone, the better. We only have a couple days before the break. Ollie is better. We need to do this now."

Cleo looked aghast, her eyes grey. "Luke, Ollie still has a fever and can hardly stand up! And how can we possibly snoop around the aviary with the police and this helicopter around?"

She was right. Luke looked at the police heading into the castle and the helicopter overhead. It was a pretty serious situation. He would have to wait.

40

Luke

It was the new year and everyone was back from winter break. The Order members were in Viking Hall, enjoying the Chronos Academy welcome back breakfast buffet. They sat at their usual table behind the last stone pillar at the back end of the room, near the entrance to the kitchen. Ronan had chosen it, because he preferred to be close to the food. Nia had a healthy smattering of fruit and lots of bacon. Cleo's plate was similar to Luke's—just pancakes. The other three had a bit of everything and as usual Ronan brought back two plates from the buffet table, each piled high with sausages, scrambled eggs, bacon, toast, and pancakes. The buffet was also stocked with plenty of hot chocolate and warm pastries.

As they ate, they exchanged stories about their break. Luke didn't really want to think or talk about his trip home. He'd been miserable. Auntie Marquette, his dad's younger sister, had come for a weekend. It was always fun when she visited, but it was the first Christmas not having his dad home. His mom had done her best to make the season lively but it just wasn't. His dad's empty chair during Christmas dinner had been almost more than Luke could bear. He even overheard his mom talking with his aunt about a possible memorial service. That, coupled with his ongoing vivid dreams about his dad, had only escalated his desire to get back to Chronos Academy and recover the arca. He needed to find and sell the Stones of Destiny fast so he could start looking for his dad!

"The school grounds look so different covered in snow!" Nia remarked, sipping her hot chocolate. "We don't have snow in LA, so it was a nice warm Christmas. My parents' friends and their kids visited us and my grandparents were there, too. It was chaotic." Nia reached over and dabbed her bacon in Cleo's syrup.

"We had family visiting from out of town, too. We took them ice skating and went to at least ten Christmas markets in Copenhagen," Andy said. "Joe and I totally pranked our cousin Henrik. It was hilarious!" He grinned, and Ronan high-fived him in appreciation. "And the nissemen brought me the headlamp I asked for."

"What's a nissemen?" Cleo asked him.

"They're little mischievous Christmas gnomes," he replied.

"Like you!" Ronan joked.

"Ha ha," Andy replied sarcastically.

"What about you Cleo?" Nia asked.

"Um, it was quiet," she said, "Just stayed in Pandia. Spent it with Grandma CeeCee at her cottage. My dad stayed in Egypt. So it was just the two of us and a few deer and wild hares. There was an owl that hooted every night by my window."

"It must've reminded you of Professor Gregor," said Andy, as he laughed with his mouth full.

"Your mom wasn't there?" Nia asked with surprise.

Luke noticed that Cleo turned her gaze back to her food as she responded, "No. She was working. It's all good."

Cleo doesn't seem good.

For several moments everyone was quiet and then Ronan asked, "Ronan, what about you?" He answered, "Well, Ronan, thank you for asking. We went to Hawaii for a family trip." He tapped Ollie on the shoulder. "What did you do, Ollie?" Ronan grinned and, looking pointedly at all of them, said, "See how I did that?"

Ollie didn't miss a beat. "First I just relaxed with Mom and Dad and my sister at home in Vancouver. It's a huge time change from here. I was jet lagged for days! We played a lot of board games and watched movies. Then they came with me on my flight back to Pandia, but we stopped in Scotland, which is kind of on the way, and celebrated New Year's Eve there. They called it Hogmanay. It was a massive three-day street party, with dancing, fireworks, and even a costume parade. It was cool," Ollie said. He tapped Luke on the shoulder. "Tag, you're it," he said.

Luke's friends were all looking at him, waiting for him to answer.

"Um, I was home in Wicker. It was just my mom and me. My aunt visited for a weekend," he said. He decided to change the topic. "We need to find the arca of Athlia," he said, reminding the Order of Ravens of their immediate mission.

After all the catch-up stories, Luke was happy to focus everyone's attention on something more important, something he'd thought of every single minute he'd been home. He was just about to go over the plan they'd made before the holidays—Ollie working with Daisy to see if the arca was in the aviary—when Director LeCrucia, with Ducky in her arms, strode into Viking Hall to start the welcome back assembly.

Assemblies were always held indoors at Viking Hall during the winter months instead of at the outdoor amphitheatre.

"Awww! Ducky looks so cute in those tiny winter boots!" Nia said to Cleo.

The director was accompanied by Adio, who, despite his Caribbean heritage, seemed indifferent to the frigid weather outside the castle. He was casually dressed in a long-sleeved T-shirt and shorts, and had his locs pulled back. Coach Typhoon followed them, wearing a new lime-coloured tracksuit and a matching lime knitted hat.

"Welcome back! I hope you're enjoying the breakfast buffet," Director LeCrucia said from the stage at the back of the hall. She paused the exact amount of time it took the students to cheer "Woo hoo!"

Luke squirmed in his seat, desperate to keep discussing the Order of Ravens' mission.

LeCrucia exchanged Ducky for the clipboard Adio passed her, and put on her reading glasses. Checking her clipboard, the director continued her speech, "We are on track with our countdown to the Pandia Games," she gestured to the hourglass at the corner of the stage. Luke saw that just about half the blue sand had fallen to the bottom. Students cheered again, "Woohoo!"

"We want to address the rumours circulating about a certain criminal that may be on Chronos Academy grounds. The police have given us the utmost assurance that Chronos Academy is absolutely safe and there is no threat to our school. Now moving on—"

Luke was stoked. One less thing to worry about while they searched for the Stones. He noticed Cleo give a huge sigh of relief.

"In response to the petition against the exclusion of first-year students on the Chronos Vikings team," the director glanced over the rim of her reading glasses at Luke's table, focussing on Andy, "we have created an opportunity which I believe will be acceptable to all parties. Coach Typhoon?"

Coach Typhoon was repeatedly adjusting his knitted hat. He looked like he felt the same way Luke had when he was a little boy, forced by his mom to stand still for a photo.

"Ehhem. Ah, yes." Coach Typhoon stepped forward. "We have positions, jobs, that need to be done. For the Pandia Games." Director LeCrucia handed him the clipboard and tapped the middle of it pointedly with her finger. "Right." Coach Typhoon started to read from the script on the clipboard. "We need a crew to do these important jobs. And it can only be first-year students, so they can," and here he paused to look closely at the words on the clipboard and finished woodenly, "develop foundational skills for sport and life."

The crowd groaned.

"Wait a minute, now. These VIP jobs will need a lot of Grit and Guts!" Having said his signature line, Coach Typhoon seemed more like the coach they knew from gym class. He started listing the jobs at top volume. "We need a VIP mascot!"

The crowd responded with cheers.

"A VIP Spirit Crew!"

More cheers.

"A VIP Equipment Crew!"

"Wooohoooo!"

"And VIP Coaching Assistants!"

Even Luke got caught up in the resounding final cheer from the crowd.

Director LeCrucia took over the podium and closed the assembly by saying, "Adio will gather names of all who are interested. Go Vikes go!"

Coach Typhoon gave out high fives to everyone on his way out of Viking Hall.

"Well, it's better than nothing," Andy said. "At least we know democracy works at Chronos Academy."

Sure, democracy worked at Chronos Academy, but Luke's plan to find the arca of Athlia was not working at all!

Luke

In the following two weeks, interest in searching for the arca waned among most members of the Order. They'd become busy with their new Pandia Games crew jobs. Andy got a position as coaching assistant. His head got so big, it was nearly impossible to bring him back down to the real world. Speaking of big heads, Ronan was learning to be the Vikings mascot. The costume included a giant foam viking helmet that couldn't fit through a regular door frame. Now on the equipment crew, Nia was spending more time at the gym. Even Ollie was busy with the spirit crew, creating banners and putting them up all over campus. Daisy was on the spirit crew, too. When Ollie wasn't doing spirit crew work, all he talked about was Daisy this and Daisy that. Cleo, who didn't sign up for any crew jobs, was the only one besides Luke that still seemed dedicated to finding the Stones of Destiny. It seemed as important to her as it was to him.

With several dozen other students and teachers, Luke, Cleo, and Ollie were now sitting on the spectator stands in the oversized gym watching the Vikings' open practice. Luke watched Coach Typhoon head to the bathrooms. While he was gone, coaching assistant Andy went power-crazy, blowing the whistle at everyone and barking out instructions. When Coach returned, he took Andy's whistle away.

Next to Luke, Cleo and Ollie were laughing at Ronan bumbling his way around the gym in his oversized plush viking helmet and bright orange Chronos cape. Despite his focus on his mission, Luke had to chuckle, too.

"We need the arca and that Stone. Mr. Ringwald is here watching the practice. Maybe this is our chance," Luke said quietly, glancing over at the raven master several rows away and not wanting to draw any attention from the surrounding students.

"For sure," agreed Ollie who turned to Cleo. "Luke already knows this. I went to the aviary last week to help Mr. Ringwald. Daisy came, too. But Mr. Ringwald said he was busy and to come back another time. So I never had a chance to look around. I was only inside for a second. He stood up. "If we're going now, I'll go get Daisy," he said.

Cleo stopped him. "That's not going to happen now." She gestured to where Daisy was talking with Stephanie a few rows over. "It will sound weird, asking her in the middle of practice."

"Okay," Ollie said, a bit crestfallen. "I guess I can do this on my own."

"We'll do it together. Come on," Cleo said. Luke jumped up and together the three friends left the gym.

Since they'd been back at school, the sky had maintained a crisp blue, with the sun shining brightly off the ice crystals in the air. Running through the ankle-deep snow in the still frigid January temperatures, Luke, Ollie, and Cleo made it to

Raven Tower in record time. Raven Tower was a stand-alone tower at the far east side of campus, and hardly anyone ever came this way unless they wanted to visit the aviary.

Ollie and Cleo quickly entered the tower. Luke stayed outside and kept out of sight behind the tower. Ollie exited a short time later. "We found it!" he exclaimed.

Luke was relieved, but it was too early to celebrate. He really wanted Cleo to be right and for there to be a Stone of Destiny in the arca.

Ollie continued, "It's way up, but I saw a long ladder in a storage room."

"Are the ravens flying around?" Luke asked. Despite the cold, sweat beaded on his forehead at the thought of being in a confined space with all six birds roaming at will.

"No, they're in their cages. They can't get out," Ollie said.

"Are you sure?" Luke asked, rubbing his forehead.

"Yes," Ollie answered.

"Are you *sure*, sure?" Luke asked again, his voice pitching slightly.

"I can go in there instead, and you could be lookout," Ollie offered.

It was a reasonable plan but Luke had to do this. He'd been responsible for losing the arca and failing to protect the treasure, so he should be responsible for retrieving it, not just for himself, but for the Order. And Ollie would be best for lookout; Mr. Ringwald had seen him just last week at the aviary. If he was spotted he wouldn't seem out of place.

His throat dry and stomach flipping, Luke entered the aviary. It had one large room connected to two smaller rooms within the base of Raven Tower. The large room had tall ceilings and the walls had a few windows that let in the morning daylight. The bright sun cut through the air showing dust, feathers, and tiny floating debris. The aviary smelled like birds, with a hint of citrus. On the ground were toys that would typically be found at a daycare centre: soft small balls, squeaky toys, a colourful mat with the letters of the alphabet on it, a toy piano, and an abacus. On the walls, placed so the ravens could see out the narrow windows, were perches covered with green turf. There was a chair and desk tucked into the corner just to the left of the door which Luke guessed was the raven master's office space. The back of the aviary opened into the two separate rooms through arched doorless entryways, one with windows and deep shelves with oversized cages on them where the ravens were now perched, the other the windowless storage area Ollie had mentioned.

Luke quickly went to the cage room and from the doorway scanned the ravens' cage doors to make sure they were locked. All six ravens cawed a greeting from their cages when they saw Luke. Luke stiffened. Then the ravens went quiet. He wasn't sure what was worse, the cawing or the silence. Either way, he was sure Floki was watching him. Cleo called out to Luke for help with the ladder. He hurried into the adjacent storage room.

Cleo pointed out the arca in the main room. It was on the highest open shelf, right on top of a stack of *Bird Care* magazines.

Together they set the ladder in the right spot against the wall. Cleo held the bottom of the ladder while Luke climbed to the top rung. But he still couldn't reach the top shelf! "We need a stick or something! I can't reach it," he said.

Cleo quickly left the base of the ladder and stepped outside, leaving Luke alone at the top of the ladder in the aviary. He felt a wave of intense panic in the lonely presence of the birds. His senses were on high alert. His hands started to sweat, and his chest tightened. He could almost feel the cawing of the ravens in their cages in the adjacent room. Cleo hurried back in and passed a stick up to Luke.

Finally!

Stretching, he batted at the little box, while she held on to the wobbly ladder. With a final whack, the arca flew off the shelf and fell into a bucket of water.

Luke practically slid down the ladder as Cleo removed her mittens to fish the arca from the bucket. "Ew" she said, holding it out and shaking it off. Luke took a puff from his inhaler and placed the magnet he'd borrowed from Andy on top of the box.

Nothing.

"No, no, no," Cleo muttered. "It has to work."

Luke was devastated. "Maybe we ruined it in the water."

She shook her head. "Magnets work underwater, it shouldn't matter. Try again."

Luke took the box from her hands, placed the magnet on the box, and ran it along the black top again. *Why isn't it working?* "Maybe we should just take the arca?" he said in desperation as he turned the box around in his hands.

"No! Mr. Ringwald knows it's your box. He will know it was you who took it, Luke." Cleo pressed her fingers to her forehead, as though willing her mind to think. "We've talked about this. We stick to our plan."

"What if we're wrong? And the clue from the poem in *Bale's Tales* doesn't mean magnet?" Luke said. His hands shook a little as he squinted at the arca in his hands.

SQUEAK!!

They both froze at the sound of the aviary door opening.

Ollie stuck his head in. "Hurry!" he implored just as the ravens struck up a cacophony chorus, "I can see a bunch of students walking around. Practice must be over! Mr. Ringwald will be back soon!" He watched from the doorway as, panicked, Luke ran the magnet over the entire arca, back and forth on each face of the box, like he was wiping it clean. He kept the blackened top of the box upright as he did so. The screeching chorus of the ravens pierced his skull.

A seam appeared along the blackened top. Click. The two halves of the lid sprung apart and the box opened like the wings of a butterfly. The ravens quieted.

"You did it!" Cleo exclaimed as Ollie rushed over, the door automatically shutting behind him.

Luke tipped the box into his hand. A jagged raw-cut oval stone tumbled onto his palm. It was black with blue streaks. "Is this the Stone of Destiny?"

Cleo nodded with excitement. "It matches exactly what Bale wrote, black with blue streaks!"

"Wow," breathed Ollie, staring at the rock.

"Are you sure?" Luke asked again. He really wanted it to be a treasure.

"Yes!" Cleo was beaming.

Munnin was now speaking, "Next, next, next!" It seemed like the bird had picked up on Cleo's excitement.

"We should get moving," Ollie reminded them.

"Ollie, put this in your backpack," Luke said, and passed the oval stone to his roommate, who took it carefully. While Ollie tucked their new find into an inner pocket of his pack, Luke pressed the flaps of the box closed and quickly made his way back up the ladder, to put the now empty arca back in its spot.

The ravens started cawing again.

TAP-TAP.

"Mr. Ringwald, are you in there?" Director LeCrucia's voice penetrated the closed aviary door. Luke froze on the top rung. Ollie's eyes were huge and Cleo was as still as a statue, holding the ladder.

Director Lecrucia pushed the aviary door open a crack, allowing sliver of light in.

They were toast!

"Ah! Professor Morlia, have you seen—" The door to the aviary shut again while the muffled voices of the director and horology professor continued outside.

"Throw it!" Cleo hissed while glancing at the door.

Luke tossed the red arca upwards. It landed on the top shelf, not on the stack of *Bird Care* magazines, but close by. Hopefully Mr. Ringwald wouldn't notice.

Ollie quickly helped Luke place the ladder back. They cracked the aviary door open just a tad and peeked outside. Professor Morlia was no longer around and Director LeCrucia was standing fifty paces away in her long black parka, her back to them. She was looking towards the main castle. This was their chance. They bolted, just making it to the back of Raven Tower as the raven master walked up to the director. The three students stayed hidden, but could hear the adults speaking.

"Mr. Ringwald, there you are. Several times in the past few weeks, I've come by the aviary but I haven't found you here," the director reprimanded. Her breath hung in the frigid air like a speech bubble in a comic strip.

Mr. Ringwald stuttered, "I-I-I'm surprised you have time

to come by, with so much going on."

"Frankly, I make the time because I'm quite concerned with the state of the ravens." Director LeCrucia sounded vexed. "You shouldn't be leaving them unattended for long lengths of time in this cold weather, and you simply must do a better job of entertaining them," she said. "I'll be visiting you again soon. See that you are prepared." She stormed off, her stylish black winter boots leaving footprints behind her in the snow.

Mr. Ringwald opened the aviary door. "Curse you, ravens!" he shouted and slammed the door behind him.

Luke was vibrating with excitement. He had finally gotten the treasure back. They had found a Stone of Destiny!

42

Luke

The Order of Ravens were meeting in Bastion Tower on Luke's request. There were no classes or Chronos Viking practices during the annual Chronos Academy study break that always took place during the first week of February. So it was an opportune time to resume their mission. Since they'd discovered the arca of Athlia and taken the Stone from it, Luke had spent lots of time in the library and he had finally figured out the Stone's value. It was crucial for the Order to go along with his plan. He was certain that wouldn't be a problem. With the information he and Ollie had discovered a few days ago, Luke was sure they'd all be as excited as he was.

He presented their idea to the group. "The Stones fell from the sky, right? So this stone could be a meteorite!"

"So cool!" Ollie added supportively.

Luke pulled out the note paper he'd tucked into the latest issue of *Knights of Darkness* that his mom had recently sent him. He'd already finished reading the comic, so he tossed it to Ronan who wanted it next. Luke unfolded the note paper and placed it next to the oval-shaped arca of Athlia stone. "Ollie and I did some research on geology—y'know rocks and stuff." Luke began to show the scientific evidence for his theory, something he'd learned in Professor Gregor's classes.

"Can we hurry this up?" Ronan asked, rubbing his hands together. "It's cold in here and I wanna find out what happens to Ryker!"

Luke nodded and continued his presentation to the Order. "Meterorites are black and have a burned shiny exterior from falling through the atmosphere. Meteorites are also heavy because they contain many minerals including iron. Our stone is black, heavy, and has these blue veins." Then he pressed the jagged edge of the black stone hard against the bottom of a mug that they had found in one of the attic boxes. "See? There's a light grey streak! That only comes from a meteorite."

"That's called the streak test," Ollie said quickly before Andy could jump in with one of his quips. "It helps tell what kind of minerals are in rocks. Meteorites leave weak streaks. So it's not a stone from earth."

Nia, Cleo, and even Andy were listening intently, while Ronan half watched Luke and half studied the cover of the comic.

Luke grabbed paper clips from Ollie's backpack and held them a centimeter from the jagged stone. "Meteorites are also usually magnetic." When he let go, the paper clips instantly jumped to the surface of the rock.

Intrigued, Ronan removed the paper clips and re-did Luke's demonstration. "It's magnetic for sure!" he observed.

"Lemme try," Andy said.

"Me too," added Nia, as Andy repeated the paperclip test.

Ollie jumped in. "And that's why a magnet was needed to open the arca. The stone is magnetic and kept the metal lid of the box closed. But the magnet we used was strong enough to pull up the lid. Or something like that."

"So this Stone of Destiny. It's from a meteor, for sure," Luke said. He saw Cleo cross her arms across her chest.

"People pay a lot of money for meteorites," Luke added. "I looked it up. Meteorites are more rare than gold or diamonds! One pound could be worth a million dollars! This stone feels like it's one pound. And when we have all three, that's three million bucks."

Ollie giggled with glee. Ronan sat open-mouthed, staring at Luke.

"Three million?!" Andy said excitedly. "And these could be worth WAY more because they are the Stones of Destiny. This is crazy! It's brilliant!"

"I saw this ad in the Gazette. Someone in Glimmerton buys meteorites," Luke said, and the boys nodded in approval.

Suddenly Cleo shouted, "Sell the Stones?! No way!"

"What?!" exclaimed all four boys.

Cleo stood and faced them, while Nia watched, clicking and unclicking paperclips to the stone. "The Stones and *Bale's Tales* belong in a museum. We can talk to my mom later, I'm sure she'll help us."

Luke was stunned. This was a no brainer. The money from selling the Stones would launch his expedition to find his dad. Although he hadn't mentioned what he wanted to do with his share of the money, it wasn't necessary. The boys understood that selling the Stones was the best way forward. Cleo needed to get on board.

"I spoke with my grandma during Christmas," Cleo

continued. "Don't worry, I didn't say anything to give us away. I just mentioned the legend that Captain Jumbo told me. And my grandma said it would be the find of a millennium." Cleo's face turned beet red. "These stones belong to the ancient Glimmicians. Like Captain Jumbo. Don't you get it?"

"Get what, Cleo? Find the Stones and pack them into a museum?" Andy was aghast. "No way! The Order of Ravens is about treasure."

Ronan was nodding so hard that he looked like a bobble head, "Exactly! Treasure! What do you think we've been doing here?" He swept his arm across the tower room, indicating all the turned-over boxes and stuff that had been sorted into small mountains as they'd sifted through everything to determine what had value.

"It's not all about money and treasure, you know," said Nia, moving closer to Cleo and crossing her arms in defiance. "We took the Order of Ravens oath."

"That's right and we said treasure seekers," Luke said. "Trea-sure."

"And protectors of secrets," Andy added. "Not showing our secrets in a MUSEUM."

"We also said guardians of artifacts," Cleo said.

"And protectors of the world," Nia added.

"No, you two said that," said Andy, pointing at them.

"Uh, and you two agreed to that?" asked Ronan, looking from Andy to Luke.

Luke felt there was a lesson in all of this: pay attention to the details when swearing an oath to an Order. He took another stab at trying to bring the girls around. "But we all agreed. Treasure and secrets."

"No! We said guardians and protectors!" Cleo said.

Now Luke was mad. Cleo was being bullheaded. And he couldn't understand why Ollie, his best friend, wasn't saying anything.

At that moment, his best friend cleared his throat. "All of that doesn't sound so bad," said Ollie, glancing from the girls back to the other boys. "We can figure this out. We must stand together," he pleaded to the group.

Stand together, they did not.

There was no way Luke was going to let anyone derail his plan. He needed the money. He was not going to spend another holiday without his dad. Adults may have given up, saying his dad was dead, but Luke never would. He would never deviate from his plan to bring his dad home, and he knew the only way to do that was to sell the Stones.

"We have one Stone already. I found it," Luke said, "Without it, your museum collection won't matter."

"You never would've found that Stone without us!" Cleo said. Luke saw her eyes do something crazy, changing colours to more grey than hazel. She marched towards the door to leave with Nia right behind her.

"If you leave now, you girls won't be allowed back in Bastion Tower," Andy called, waving his keys to the tower in the girls' direction.

"The other Stones are probably here in the tower, just like this one was!" Luke said in a quick burst, hoping that would convince the girls to stay and drop their crazy ideas.

"You can all keep your stupid Stone and your stupid tower because we have *Bale's Tales*. Good luck finding the other two Stones without us!" Nia barked over her shoulder.

And with that, the girls stomped their way down the

stairs.

Luke rubbed his face. This was not part of his plan.

43

Cleo

Since the big fight in Bastion Tower two weeks ago, Cleo had set out, with resounding new purpose, to find the remaining Stones. She had to admit she missed being part of the Order of Ravens. Having a group of friends had meant the world to her, especially with Stephanie lurking in the shadows with her cold shoulder and mean glances. But Cleo still had Nia, and the mission.

Searching for another clue in *Bale's Tales*, she'd found "chimpanzee fire" written a second time in the book. Andy had spotted the first entry when she'd first shown them *Bale's Tales*. But this second entry was next to a picture of a tree with a sword leaning against it, just like one of the drawings on the arca of Athlia. She'd racked her brain, trying to figure out what it meant, and finally hoped that sometimes the simplest explanation was the right one. So, Cleo reasoned, chimpanzee fire had to be some sort of tree.

Although it was mid-February, it was just as cold as January had been. During the day, the sun was hidden behind a thick layer of clouds which had made Cleo feel even more miserable. At the library late into the evening every night, she combed through books about trees, looking for anything about chimpanzee fire: *All About Trees, 100 Famous Trees, Trees with Fruit,* and many more.

Tonight, the dreary cloud cover had dissipated. Cleo cast a glance out the library window. The robotics building had most of its lights on. She wondered if students there were working on Sir Lancelot. Probably they were, as a team. Cleo leafed through *World's Oldest Trees: Yes, They Do Talk,* fascinated that the book said trees "communicate with one another through their elaborate root system: a fungal network."

Suddenly all the lights went out on campus. The only thing Cleo could see through the library windows were the green aurora lights that filled the night sky. She could just make out the shape of the shelves and tables in the dark library. Perhaps she should call out to Barbara. She got up from the chair and started feeling her way along the edge of the table. The lights blinked back on.

Whew. I'm glad that's over.

Cleo saw Barbara approaching her table. Barbara spoke. "These blackouts are something, aren't they?" the librarian yawned "—It's almost 10 p.m. I should close the library, Cleo. Normally I don't mind staying late but I'm tired. I was up late last night—saw a band play in Glimmerton. Thankfully the library doesn't open tomorrow until noon. I'm going to sleep in!" Barbara adjusted her blue beret, which matched her now blue-streaked hair. "Have you spoken to your mom at all since December?"

Barbara had been encouraging Cleo to reach out to her mom, ever since Cleo had confided that the situation with her mom was not good.

Cleo shook her head and glanced down at her books. It had been great spending time with CeeCee at her cottage over the holiday break, but when she and her mom had spoken over the phone during Christmas, it had been brief and shallow, nothing more than talking about the weather. Cleo hadn't seen her mom since the summer. That felt like an extremely long time ago. Cleo was still really hurt with all that had happened with her parents' separation and the daily fights she'd had with her mom before coming to Chronos Academy. They just didn't seem to see eye to eye on anything. And with the Order breaking up, Cleo was very sad. She pressed her fingers to her eyes. She would not cry.

"Don't worry, kiddo, it'll get better," Barbara said, and leaned over to give her a hug. "You know what? It would help me if you could put some of these books back. I need to find some items that I misplaced. I am clearly more tired than I thought. Up for it?"

Cleo gave Barbara a small smile and nodded.

When Cleo entered the biology section, a tapping sound towards the end of the aisle caught her attention. Director LeCrucia was sitting at a small desk drumming her pencil in thought as she stared out the window. Ducky was lying at the Director's feet. On her desk, a medium sized plant emitted a green glow that matched the streaking aurora in the night sky.

"Quack."

Ducky came running up to Cleo and jumped up against her legs. Cleo couldn't help but smile. Placing her books on the table, she picked up the fluffy dog and was surprised how light he was.

Director LeCrucia turned her head towards Cleo. Her normally tight bun was lopsided with several flyaways at the back of her neck and side of her head. Her face was soft and thoughtful, and she smiled at the sight of her dog in Cleo's arms. This was not the same stern, stately, and intimidating Director LeCrucia that Cleo encountered in the hallways, whose suit and hair were always perfect. Like my mom, she thought.

"Sorry, I didn't mean to disturb you," Cleo said, and she giggled as Ducky licked her fingers.

"Oh, no worries," the director said as she got up, closed her notebook, and carefully placed the glowing plant inside what looked like a cupcake carrying case.

"What is that?" Cleo shifted her eyes from Director LeCrucia to the carrying case.

"Oh, it's my glowing green plant. I created it by introducing DNA for bioluminescence—specifically Luciferin and Luciferase—into the plant. Unfortunately the plant is not as bright as I had hoped. It's a work in progress. But imagine having glowing trees instead of streetlights." Director LeCrucia's eyes twinkled. "The first step of course would be to replace the lamps in the library with these plants. That would be amazing!" Just then the lights went out again. Cleo gasped and focused on the faint glow from the plant. LeCrucia laughed a little as the lights came back on. "And it would help out with the blackouts we have."

"Quack. Quack."

Ducky wanted more attention, so Cleo started petting him.

"Looks like you've been doing some research of your own." The woman glanced at the stack of books Cleo had set on the table, "Books about trees. Interesting. Did Professor Gregor change his curriculum?"

"Um, no. Just curious," Cleo said. "Are there trees like your plant in nature?"

"Hmmm. There are no trees with naturally occurring bioluminescent genes that we know of. But some trees have glowing fungi attached to them. These fungi have a few names, like fox fire, fairy fire, or my favourite, chimpanzee fire."

Cleo caught her breath and slowly repeated the words. "Chimpanzee fire?"

"Yes, chimpanzee fire," Director LeCrucia said, as she tilted her head to one side to stretch her neck. "It's a quirky name, isn't it?"

Cleo nodded, trying not to convey her excitement at her discovery. But she wanted to scream at the top of her lungs, Chimpanzee fire does mean something! And it wasn't the name of the tree, it was the name of the fungus on the tree.

Trying to remain calm and cool, Cleo asked, "Are there trees like that in Kingsburg Forest?"

"As a matter of fact there are," the director said, smoothing the flyaways of her hair. "A small section of the forest has a few trees with glowing fungi species living on their bark. Chimpanzee fire is unique to this area and is dormant now, hard to see. The spores will sprout when the weather warms, around May." She raised her eyebrows and looked past Cleo then said to her conspiratorially, "It seems we are not the only ones keeping late hours at the library." Director LeCrucia projected her voice, "Good evening, governor."

Cleo did her best to keep her eyes from widening with fear. She had been doing all she could to steer clear of the governor. She really didn't want him to join them now.

"You'll have to excuse me," Director LeCrucia said quietly to Cleo as she collected her plant-carrying case. "Good night, Cleo."

Cleo nodded, relieved, and put Ducky down. "Good night."

Ducky quacked a goodbye as he followed his owner.

Cleo put her books away and quickly searched the aisle on plants. She found what she was looking for. She quickly checked the book out using an automated scanner and blew past the front desk, where Barbara, the governor, and Director LeCrucia, all with their heads down, were talking quietly. She had barely left the library when she began formulating a plan. It would be impossible to find the right tree until the glowing fungus was blooming in May. She would have to wait to get the second Stone of Destiny. Feeling bummed she redirected her thoughts. There was still a third stone to be found. She had work to do.

44

Luke

Taking the route to Bastion Tower, Luke noticed the weather seemed to have changed overnight when the calendar flipped to March. The sun was brighter in the sky, and there weren't as many clouds. The sun hadn't set yet, even though it was after dinner. The ice and snow had melted, the smell of spring was in the air, and the fields surrounding the castle were once again green.

Luke was still angry at Cleo and Nia. He'd finally felt like he belonged at Chronos Academy, with a group of friends who cared about each other and him. When he wasn't fuming at what the girls had done to their group, he felt out of sorts and alone, as though he'd failed somehow. Failed the group that he'd formed and failed his dad. He thought back to the friendship he'd had with Cleo and Nia. The truth was that he missed them. He hated what had happened to the Order of Ravens three weeks ago. He wished he could go back and change things somehow. But he couldn't. *Why are the girls being so difficult?*

Whatever! He had to stay focused on his plan. Since they

were going to split the money, they would need all three stones to make sure Luke had enough to fund his mission. He'd need a boat, probably an airplane. And definitely a lot of snacks. He and the guys would find the other two Stones of Destiny. He'd found the first one, hadn't he? Luke was certain the other two stones were also in Bastion Tower. *All I have to do now is wait for the ghost lady to appear and show me where they are.*

A week ago he'd explained the plan to Ronan and Andy, telling them for the first time how the ghost lady had appeared in the attic of Bastion Tower and how he'd discovered the arca. Andy'd said it wasn't fair because he wanted to see the ghost. And Ronan now constantly made mysterious warbling ghost sounds around Luke, "Wooooooo." The boys spent days searching the rooms in Bastion Tower, looking for cracks in the walls or loose bricks in the floor that might signal another hidden cavity. Andy had tried to summon the ghost lady by yelling, "Ghost lady, show yourself." When that failed, he and Ronan had announced they were done with chasing ghosts and resumed sifting through boxes and crates.

Luke met the other three Order members for the second time this week, outside at the locked little bronze door. When Luke and his friends finally reached the top of the stairs and entered the main tower room, Andy started rooting in a corner cabinet for valuables and Ronan took a rest with Mr. Bones. Ollie and Luke headed up to the attic room, or room B for bust. Luke sat on the floor, waiting for the ghost lady to reappear at the old fireplace where he'd first seen her. Ollie sat next to him, his ghost capturing jar open and ready, just in case. Luke looked at his watch, frustrated to see it was clouded over again. He made a mental note to find Professor Morlia later.

Something else was bothering him. He didn't understand who the ghost lady by the fireplace was, or why she'd hidden the arca under the brick in the fireplace. *Who had she been hiding it from?*

From an envelope, Luke took out a magazine that he'd ordered over the study break. It contained an article, written by his father, about one of his dad's expeditions from long ago. His dad had scaled Mount Kilimanjaro, seeking a precious gem called tanzanite. Luke took a puff of his inhaler and thought about the million times he'd read this very same article in a frame sitting on his dad's desk, next to the press award trophy.

"You know, if we find the Stones, you can have my share of the money," Ollie said, jarring Luke from his thoughts.

"What? Why?" Luke asked.

"Because I only want a few *Knights of Darkness* special edition comic books. They don't cost too much. So you can have the rest to help find your dad." Ollie placed the jar on the ground next to him.

Luke thought of his dad all alone somewhere, cold, hungry, and afraid, waiting to be rescued. "Thank you, Ollie." His voice wobbled a little and he squinted to keep the tears back.

"Sure," Ollie said, acting like nothing emotional was happening. He truly was a great friend. "If my dad went missing, I'd do anything to find him. My mom, too. But my sister, I'm not so sure." They both cracked a smile and then Ollie's faded. "Luke, I think we should still be working with Nia and Cleo."

"No. They don't get it," Luke replied.

"The ghost lady hasn't come back. And we don't know

how to make her appear. Do you think Cleo was right, and *Bale's Tales* has the clues for the other two Stones?" Ollie asked.

"I don't know. Maybe," Luke conceded. "But Cleo's not going to share it with us now. She's still really mad."

Ollie nodded.

"Maybe we can borrow it," Andy said, his voice coming from the attic entrance. He hopped up, Ronan climbing behind him, and joined them by the fireplace.

"He means we should steal it," Ronan said, plopping down next to Ollie and Luke on the floor.

"No! *Borrow* it! We'll give it back," Andy defended. "At some point."

"Are you kidding me?!" Ollie said, "The Order of Ravens took an oath! And that does not include stealing!"

Luke, on the other hand, had to admit he was tempted by the idea. They could just peek through the book quickly, see if there was any information on the other two Stones. But the book was always in that horrendous puke-green backpack Cleo constantly wore! Luke knew she'd never let that pack out of her sight. Especially now that they were on the outs.

45

Luke

The Order of Ravens had been debating the merits and downsides of borrowing *Bale's Tales* from Cleo for the last couple of weeks. Now, at the end of March, it seemed like a lost cause. The debate just kept going on with no final agreement.

"If you don't give it back, it's stealing," Ollie reminded the other three in a low voice. They were chatting in hushed tones, waiting for Professor Agnostos to arrive at their history classroom.

"She never leaves that backpack out of arm's reach!" Andy said, "I can't believe I'm saying this, but maybe we should sneak into her dorm room while they're all sleeping."

"We'd have to get their thumb prints," Ronan reminded him of the technology that kept their dorm rooms secure.

"Right, that's a problem. I just don't think we can get that book," Andy said.

He's right. It's way too risky, and way too complicated. Almost as complicated as trying to convince the girls they should re-join the Order.

Professor Agnostos, a tall man who was always slouching, entered the classroom and with a thump dropped his briefcase on his desk. "It is too loud!" his voice boomed, silencing the class.

After sorting through several sheets of paper, Professor Agnostos freed his dark-streaked-with-grey ponytail that was tucked into the back of his shirt. He turned to face the class. Luke had a hard time listening in history class because he found himself focusing on the professor's eye twitch. The left one would sometimes twitch during the entire class. Trying to count the number of twitches was impossible.

"Pandia through the ages. We begin today in the 1200s." Professor Agnostos turned to the board and wrote *Crossing the Rubicon*.

"What in the world does that mean?" Andy asked loudly.

Luke glanced across the room at Cleo. For once she was quiet, which meant she didn't know either.

"It means, Andy," Professor Agnostos answered, "to pass a point of no return. Once a decision is made you can't go back."

Luke squirmed in his seat. Forming the Order of Ravens and then losing part of it felt like a point of no return. And if they didn't find the other two Stones soon, Luke was worried he would pass the point of no return on finding his dad, too.

"The king of Pandia in the 1200s was King Sullivan," Professor Agnostos continued. "He lived here. The king and his knights expanded the original Viking fortress into Chronos Castle. It was changed over the centuries and in the 1800s it became Chronos Academy. There are four questions for you to choose from to write a report on. In this manner you will learn some history about our little island of Pandia.

Some of you are from here, some of you are not. Either way, this exercise is good for all of you. But you must stick to the time of King Sullivan. I do not want a history report about other things, like the history of Viking Hall." He looked sternly around the room. "And you must state in the report how your topic relates to the conundrum of Crossing the Rubicon. This is a large assignment and an important one. It will count for fifty percent of your grade and it is your last assignment for this class, due May 15. Final exams will be held after the Pandia Games." He looked to a raised hand on the left side of the room. "Yes, Nia."

Nia blurted out her question. "Were there women knights during King Sullivan's reign?"

"Not that I know of," the Professor said.

Andy turned towards the class and barked loudly. "Women knights?! There's no such thing as girl knights."

"There's no girl knights in *Knights of Darkness*," Ronan gave as an example.

"Exactly. No girl knights," Andy said definitively.

Luke agreed, but kept it to himself.

Stephanie shouted, "There should be, 'cause girls are better than boys!"

The classroom volume increased as several students weighed in on the topic. Nia stuck her tongue out at Andy.

"It is too loud!" shouted Professor Agnostos as he handed out the list of questions. He stopped at Andy's desk. "Andy, this assignment has barely begun, yet you are already on my radar." Andy took the handout with an innocent expression on his face. The professor stared at him a moment longer before moving on. "Nia, if you want to investigate the answer to your question, you may. If any of you have any questions that you want to research that are not on my list, you must seek my approval beforehand."

When Luke glanced up from the handout, he saw Cleo approach Professor Agnostos at the front of the class. Agnostos then clapped his hands together loudly. "That is a fantastic question, Cleo! Well done."

Luke was instantly worried, and not just about the complexity of the assignment. Cleo and Nia didn't know or care at all about knights. Nia's question about girl knights made Luke wonder if her and Cleo were researching about knights as part of their search for the Stones. Would her report help her find the other Stones of Destiny before the Order did?

But then Luke thought of something he had that Cleo did not—the ghost lady. He'd been wondering for a long time who the ghost lady in the attic was and why she had hidden the arca of Athlia. This assignment was his chance to figure it out. Maybe he could even learn about the blacksmith he'd seen in that vision from the STEM escape challenge.

This assignment couldn't have come at a more perfect time!

46

Luke

"Go Vikes go!" Members of the Chronos Vikings team chanted as they paraded through the library, pumping their fists into the air. It was a daily occurrence now that there were only five weeks to go until June 1st and the Pandia Games.

The days were warmer now and the fields surrounding the castle were green. The sun shone through the library's windows. All the boys of the Order of Ravens were spending more time there than anywhere else, when they weren't at the Eldritch Pitch working as the crew and watching the Vikings' practices. In addition to their other assignments, their reports for history class were turning out to be a monstrosity.

Andy had one leg on the chair seat and another leg anchored to the ground, absorbed in a large book. Luke didn't know how he could read like that. Ronan was napping on his book, wearing ski goggles that he'd found in Ollie's backpack. Luke had no idea why Ollie carried goggles in his backpack.

They hadn't found another Stone yet, but with this assignment Luke felt they were getting closer. He dropped a book on the table. "Ollie, look at this!" Luke moved the library book closer to Ollie, who was sitting across from him. "This is a portrait of Queen Avelina." He paused and lowered his voice. "This looks just like the ghost lady in Bastion Tower. She's Queen Avelina! This is her, her dress, and everything! And she was married to King Sullivan!" Luke paused and then asked, "Did you find anything?"

Ollie nodded his head, and turned his book to Luke. "King Sullivan *killed* his queen."

Luke's mouth dropped open.

"What?" Andy asked, setting his own book aside.

"He hung her." Ollie turned the page and continued summarizing what he had read, "for treason. She knew the identity of a rogue and rebellious knight, Knight Athlia, but wouldn't tell the king."

"Knight Athlia, as in, the arca of Athlia?" Luke turned his focus to Ollie's book.

Ollie nodded. "Knight Athlia," he paused and read from the book, "*'incited a full-scale revolution against King Sullivan, aiming to end his reign of tyranny.'*" Anyhow, the queen wouldn't say who this Knight Athlia was, so he imprisoned her in Bastion Tower and then hung her." Ollie lowered his voice, "I think that's why she's still there. She's mad and she haunts the tower." Ollie's eyes were nearly as wide as the frames of his blue-rimmed glasses.

Then Luke remembered his vision of the blacksmith talking about the arca. He looked around and lowered his voice. "I had a weird daydream, vision, or whatever. When we were at the STEM challenge. I never thought it mattered and didn't mention it because it was weird. I don't know." He took a deep breath and continued, "That day, I saw a blacksmith in the cottage, but way in the past, and he said something like by giving the arca to some woman, he had doomed her to die."

Ollie leaned even farther over the table. "Was he a ghost like the ghost lady you saw in Bastion Tower?"

"Maybe," Luke shrugged. "I don't know."

Ollie queried very seriously, "Why would the arca doom anyone to die?"

"The arca had the Stone of Destiny in it." Luke paused, trying to put the pieces of the puzzle together, and then continued, "The ghost lady—Queen Avelina—had the arca." Luke squinted his eyes in thought. "What if the queen was hanged not for treason but because of the Stone of Destiny?" Luke paused and looked down at Ollie's book and then up again, "Because she hid it from the king." He swallowed hard. "What if she was hung because she wouldn't tell the king where the Stone was? What if King Sullivan was looking for the Stones of Destiny?"

"And the queen didn't want him to have it?" Ollie asked. Luke nodded.

"This is big," Andy said.

"Dun-dun-dun-dunn!" Ronan sat up.

"You heard that? I thought you were sleeping," Luke said, and took a nervous puff of his inhaler.

"I have the ears of a fox," Ronan replied. "Now what do we do?"

47

Cleo

Groups of students were seated at tables throughout the library. The aisles were full of students searching for reference material, and a long row of students had lined up to talk with Barbara. The library hours were going to be extended May first, which was only a couple of days from now.

"Anything?" Nia asked.

"Nothing," Cleo huffed in frustration and closed the book in front of her. Another dead end. She had been looking for months and not found out anything about the third Stone of Destiny in any library books, nor in *Bale's Tales*.

"Maybe Luke's right and the Stones are in the tower?" Nia offered.

"No. I'm sure the chimpanzee fire is a clue for the second stone. But the third one, I don't know. But I do know we are not going to the tower. Let's just stick to our plan to get the second stone in Kingsburg Forest," Cleo said.

Cleo turned her attention to another stack of books on their table.

The project for Professor Agnostos was taking a lot longer

than Cleo had anticipated. And the looming deadlines of her other homework were piling up too. Tense, she shrugged her shoulders, moving them up and down as she tried to relax. She'd been studying at this table for hours. At the next table over, Stephanie, Daisy, Lauren, and Hayden were working. For the most part they ignored Cleo and Nia, although Daisy had looked up several times at them before returning to her own work.

Seeing this, Nia sighed. Cleo tapped Nia's papers with her pen to refocus her friend on their own investigation for Professor Agnostos' report. Sunlight was beaming through the windows, several of which were letting in fresh air, and the chorused melodies of numerous birds were pleasantly loud. The occasional CAW could be heard as well. Cleo smiled thinking of the song making ravens flying around, enjoying the warm spring day.

"Do we know yet who Knight Athlia was?" Nia asked.

"No, *Bale's Tales* doesn't say. Not that we could put any of that in our report. Some of these textbooks say Athlia was a French knight supported by the French king to cause trouble for King Sullivan. But nobody knows for sure. One thing is certain," Cleo read from the book in front of her, "'*King Sullivan's actions unleashed the event known as the Great Reckoning.*'"

"That's what I found, too." Nia pulled her notebook closer and reading from her notes said, "After the queen was hung there was a rebellion. I guess they really loved their queen. The rebellion grew and got so bad that the kingdom ended."

Cleo added, "There was a fire during the Great Reckoning. A big one. Look at this painting."

Nia nodded. "A big fire. How sad. Many villages were

burnt to the ground."

"King Sullivan died in the fire, and so did his most trusted and loyal Knight Caelen who tried to save him. Caelen—the Dark Knight. Cool name huh?" Nia commented.

"What?" Cleo said, focusing now on Nia.

Nia pointed to the page on the *History of Pandia* book. "It says, '*In this period, there were three famous knights that served the king: Caelen, Thomme and Goffridis. No one knows what happened to Thomme and Goffridis, nor Caelen, the dark knight. Some historians believe he perished with the king in the fire.*'"

"Nia, I have to tell you something." Cleo relayed Captain Jumbo's story of two people looking for the Stones of Destiny and then disappearing—someone named Billy and a dark knight named Caelen. "Captain Jumbo also said he looked for the Stones himself and had bad luck. He thinks the Stones are cursed," she added.

"Cursed?! You should've told me!" Nia exclaimed.

"I just don't believe in curses. I didn't think it was a big deal," Cleo replied.

"Well it is. Oh poop." Nia became pensive and then said, "So that means Caelen the dark knight was looking for the Stones. And he went missing, probably because he died in the fire, all because of the curse?"

"Or because of the rebellion," Cleo corrected Nia and added, "If Caelen was looking for the Stones, that would mean King Sullivan was probably after them, too."

"The king also died in the fire." Nia rubbed the back of her neck. "And after the fire there was famine and then a plague, called Black Death, in the 1300s. After that there was no king. That's a lot of bad luck."

Cleo wasn't superstitious and didn't believe in curses, but searching for the Stones certainly didn't seem to bring anything good to the people who'd looked for them.

48

Luke

Luke entered Professor Morlia's classroom. Director LeCrucia stood next to the professor, pointing at a computer screen. Several black mini magnetometers from the school grounds were hooked up to the computer.

"For the first few days of May, the Kp number has been hovering around 7, slightly higher than in May of last year. We do have pockets of higher electromagnetic activity close to the Eldritch Pitch. But overall the activity is stable," Professor Morlia said.

"Anything else?" the director inquired.

"Not at this time," Professor Morlia responded. "Professor Gregor is also looking at the data and—"

Director LeCrucia interrupted him, "But the stable Kp data suggests all is well even though NASA warned about high coronal mass ejections—" She leaned forward on the desk as she examined the computer screen closer.

Professor Morlia shook his head, stretched his back, and said, "Though CMEs are a concern—" he glanced up, and stopped mid-sentence as he spotted Luke by the door. "Ah, Luke."

"Um, Professor, is this a good time?" Luke asked.

Director LeCrucia answered, "Of course. Professor Morlia, we can discuss this later." She quickly left.

The horology professor stood up and stretched again. "I'm sorry I had to cancel our previous appointment."

"That's okay, I've been busy with tons of homework." And with finding the other two Stones of Destiny, Luke thought.

"Are you excited about the upcoming Pandia Games? Less than a month away."

Luke nodded.

"Will you try out for the team next year?"

"Oh, yeah, I love the RAF triathlon event" Luke said, hoping it would provide a good cover. Next year he wouldn't be at school. He'd be on a boat headed to Bovet Island, using the money from the sale of the Stones of Destiny, to start searching for his dad.

Professor Morlia leaned on his desk. "Are you still concerned your watch is not working properly?"

Luke nodded. "The face has fogged up a few times again. I just want to make sure no water has gotten in it." He held up his wrist, keeping the watch on.

Morlia put on his miniature head lamp and used a loupe to examine Luke's watch. After a few moments he said, "It looks fine to me. But to make sure we'd have to open it up."

"No!" Luke said, louder than he intended to. That sounded risky.

Professor Morlia paused. "It seems like you aren't ready for that yet, and that's okay."

Luke nodded. The watch seemed fine. A huge weight had been lifted off his shoulders. He thanked the professor and left for Viking Hall to join his friends for lunch. As he entered the hall, he spotted Nia and Cleo's table and steered clear. His eyes went up to the small stage at the back. The large hourglass was still there, and the amount of blue sand piling up at the bottom was much greater than the amount slowly falling from the top.

Just then Director LeCrucia entered Viking Hall with Ducky seeking safety by her legs.

The dog frantically quacked at Sir Lancelot, who trailed a safe distance behind. Adio paced next to Director LeCrucia, writing quickly on a clipboard as he went. They paused behind Luke and Ollie's table, waiting for other students to clear the aisle.

"I'll be spending more time in Glimmerton to help the council prepare for the Games," the director said. "Make sure you clear my calendar. Oh, and we need to prepare for the dignitaries. Some might want a tour of the school and grounds." She raised her voice slightly at the students talking, nudging, and shuffling into and out of their seats. "Excuse us."

Sir Lancelot sped up from across the aisle, sirens blaring, and blocked Director LeCrucia's path. Now, all eyes on the robot, the sirens stopped while Ducky quacked more rapidly. A strange spout extended from the top of the robot's chest. Suddenly a jet of water came shooting out from the spout. Director LeCrucia danced out of the way to keep from getting wet. The squirt of water hit Ducky square in his face and immediately silenced him, his fluffy fur sagging. The hall erupted in laughter, and Sir Lancelot bolted away at warp speed.

49

Cleo

Cleo was more than a week ahead of the history report's due date of May 15th, just like she'd planned. She'd finished hers that morning and was excited to hand it in to Professor Agnostos. Wasting no time, she placed her bound essay into her backpack alongside *Bale's Tales* while speed walking down the corridor from the library to the staircase. She glanced up just as Sir Lancelot passed right in front of her. She yelped in surprise as she collided with the robot and her open backpack flew from her hands. She tumbled to the ground, joining Sir Lancelot who had fallen onto its side, wheels whirring at maximum speed.

Cleo hastily got up and saw her backpack was only a few feet in front of her but *Bale's Tales* had fallen out and was now teetering on the lip of the staircase! Just then, Ducky's little head appeared over the top step and he started quacking at the downed robot. As he climbed the last step, his little front paws landed pitter patter on the cover of *Bale's Tales*, pushing it down the stairs. Shocked, Cleo ran towards the stairs and watched as the journal tumbled down the staircase.

The leather straps came undone and the book flew open, pages splaying, as it bumped down the steps. She donned her backpack and sprinted down after the journal, leaving Sir Lancelot to be helped by the students who'd witnessed her embarrassing kerfuffle.

At the landing she found her *Bale's Tales* lying completely open, cover side up, straps splayed out and a bunch of pages bent against the floor.

And right next to it, the feet of her nemesis Stephanie.

Stephanie bent down to grab the book, her eyebrows lifting with interest.

Cleo lunged for the book, too. "That's MINE!" she hissed.

She had hold of the back cover, Stephanie the front. The open pages fanned out and dangled down. A tug of war ensued that Cleo had to win. She would not lose *Bale's Tales* like Luke had once lost the arca. And she could NOT let the book fall into the wrong hands!

Yanking with all her might, Cleo pulled the journal away from Stephanie. Ignoring her ex-friend's insults, she changed direction and ran up the stairs to her dormitory, clutching *Bale's Tales* to her chest.

"What's going on?" Nia asked, in the midst of changing her socks when Cleo burst into the room.

Cleo glanced around. Luckily, Daisy wasn't there. "The journal," she said, her voice full of worry.

It was definitely damaged. She quickly told Nia what had happened. Holding Bale's journal in her shaking hands, she passed it to Nia. Nia placed the book carefully in her lap, and flipped through the pages quietly, examining the damage. Several pages were bent and the cover seemed lopsided. The pages were all still bound together but the inner part of the spine with the bound pages had detached from the outer part of the spine that was part of the cover. Cleo was crushed. She'd always planned to submit the book and the three Stones for display in her mom's museum. The condition of the book mattered! She had just ruined a precious historical record.

"Maybe Daisy has some glue or something in her art supplies that could help fix it?" Nia offered and passed the book to Cleo.

BANG! They both jumped up with a start when a raven's beak tapped on the window and flew away. *Bale's Tales* flew out of Cleo's hands and landed on the ground with a loud thump.

"Oh no!" Cleo said, picking the book up from the floor. "The spine's cracked now!"

Fix it, fix it! Cleo's brain screamed. She ran her finger along the cracked spine.

"Glue might still work?" Nia offered again.

Cleo tried to push the crack in the spine together with her fingers, but that made it worse. Panicked, Cleo tipped the book over, crushing some of the splayed pages.

"Or a stapler!" Nia said.

The situation was getting worse every second.

Cleo's eyes filled with tears and she squeezed them shut tight. The journal slipped down her lap, and she felt a chunk of it slide to the floor with a thump. She had destroyed William Bale's book!

"What's that?" Nia gasped. Reaching down she picked up what Cleo's watery eyes saw as the chunk of the book. "Cleo?" Nia said in wonder.

When Cleo wiped her eyes, she saw that her roommate was holding a jagged raw-cut rectangular stone. It was about five centimeters long and just a tiny bit narrower than the width of the spine of *Bale's Tales*. It was black with blue streaks.

They glanced between *Bale's Tales* in Cleo's hands and the stone in Nia's hand. The black rectangular stone had been bound into the spine between the page threads and spine itself.

"It's a different shape, but it definitely looks like the arca of Athlia stone!" Cleo said, her panic morphing into jubilation. "Billy Bale must have found the stone and hidden it in the book." Cleo's mind raced. *Why would he hide it?*

"Let's test it like Luke did, to make sure," Nia said. She grabbed Daisy's mug from her desk and a paperclip from Daisy's bin of art supplies under her bunk bed. They did the streak and magnet tests. Nia's mouth gaped open, then spread into a smile that stretched from ear to ear.

"It *is* a Stone of Destiny! I can't believe we found the second one!" Cleo wanted to scream with delight but stopped herself.

Nia asked. "Do we tell the boys?"

Cleo beamed. "No way. We're going to find the third Stone and we don't need them to do it." Cleo bit her lip. "I'm positive that the chimpanzee tree will lead us to it. We are so close!"

50

Luke

The Order of Ravens were working in the library after dinner. Their history reports were due tomorrow. Ollie was talking about the ghost of Queen Avelina who was doomed to haunt Bastion Tower forever. He snickered that he would include an interview with Luke for his report. Luke reminded him that certain details of what they'd discovered about the queen belonged to the Order of Ravens, and therefore had to be secret. That included the tower, the ghost lady, the Stone and the arca, and the real possibility that King Sullivan had killed his queen for hiding the Stone of Destiny.

"What is Cleo up to?" Luke asked.

"I heard she handed in her assignment over a week ago!" Ollie answered.

"Do you think she knows how to find the other Stones?" Luke asked his friends.

Ronan chomped on a mouthful of candy to keep his sugar levels up and mumbled, "Probably. She might get them before you. She has *Bale's Tales*."

That was not what Luke wanted to hear.

Luke typed in the last few lines on his report as to what caused the rebellion (famine, raise in taxes, and the king's greed). He was grateful they had access to computers to type up this huge assignment.

"Done!" he said. He looked up at his roommates who were still frantically typing. "I'm gonna print this now and hand it in before I go to the Tower."

"Lucky you. I am nowhere near done!" Andy said and Ronan sighed next to him. "Better take the keys," Andy said tossing the keys to Luke.

"Thanks," Luke said.

"I just finished, too!" Ollie said. "And there's no spirit crew duty for me tonight, so I can come with you."

Two hours later, after prying up more bricks from the fireplace in the grand chamber, Luke and Ollie returned to the attic B fireplace to wait for the ghost lady. The firepoker rested on a pile of bricks.

"Oh no." Ollie jumped up. "I forgot! I have a call with my family tonight! Sorry, Luke. My parents said my little sister really wants to talk with me because she misses me. But I think it's my parents who really do. We planned it a while ago, so I need to be there. Will you be okay?"

Luke nodded supportively. Ollie grabbed his backpack, waved, and hurried out the door.

Luke then returned to the grand chamber and spent another hour alone going through a cabinet. Glancing at his watch he saw it was getting late and decided he should probably go. He headed down the tower's staircase and locked the wooden tower door behind him. After he locked the little outer bronze door, he looked up.

The green and purple auroras were moving about in the

night sky. As he pushed his way out through the bushes, his right foot smushed into mud. "Ew!" Luke said, and wiped the bottom of his sneaker against the grass.

Suddenly, Luke was grabbed from behind. A man's voice rasped next to his left ear. "Don't turn around and don't yell if you want to live." Luke couldn't yell if he wanted to. His vocal chords were paralyzed in fear. He could feel the man's rough cold hands on the back of his neck pulling on the nape of his sweatshirt, choking him and lifting him up so he could barely touch the ground with his tiptoes. The man was very strong. Luke could hardly breathe. The man shook him and then lowered him to the ground, so his feet were once again on the grass. Luke's legs felt like bags of cement. He couldn't will them to move at all! The man still had a firm grip on the back of his sweater.

In the shadows of Bastion Tower, even with the sky partially lit with auroras, Luke knew it would be impossible for someone to spot them from any castle window.

"Where are the Stones of Destiny?" The man whispered. He could feel his attacker's warm breath at the back of his neck and smell its nasty odour.

Luke sputtered meekly, "I-I-I don't know—" Luke gasped for air as the stranger pulled harder. The collar of Luke's hoodie cut into his skin.

"You *do* know," the voice interrupted.

Well, that was true. In his jeans pocket was the Stone of Destiny they'd retrieved from the arca in the aviary.

The attacker lifted Luke onto his tiptoes once more. "Tell me what you know about the Stones! Answer me!" he demanded, shaking Luke harder and making his lungs burn for air.

Terror seized Luke's heart as he suddenly remembered.

Mr. Ringwald and Adio worried about strange footprints by the castle windows.

The thefts at school.

The rope dangling from the cliff at Traitors' Gate.

Recleren!

"Ding dang dong!" Sir Lancelot's voice sounded nearby, around the castle corner.

Luke felt his attacker's weight shift as the man looked around. Luke kicked one of his feet back at the man's legs. Surprised, the attacker yelped, and clutching his kneecap he let go of Luke. Luke staggered to keep his footing, sucking in air. The man lunged to grab him, but Luke was just beyond the man's reach.

Luke ran and ran.

51

Luke

The next morning, the Order of Ravens had all dropped off their history reports and were having breakfast in Viking Hall. They'd been talking about last night's incident since Luke had collapsed on his bunk bed in their dorm. Desperately clinging to his inhaler, Luke had told his roommates everything. Now they were distracted as Ronan poured a bowl full of maple syrup and, piece by piece, dunked his pancakes and bacon into it.

"So, you really think it was Recleren?" Ronan asked, shoving another piece of bacon in his mouth.

Andy opened his mouth to speak but then closed it and shook his head.

"One hundred percent," Ollie answered. "It was Pirate Recleren. It had to be. Who else?"

Luke agreed.

"Maybe it's the governor. Nia would say so," Ronan said.

"Do you think he's hanging around the bushes?" said Andy. "He's busy. He's the governor and he doesn't sneak around at night attacking students."

Luke glanced at his roommates. "Cleo said Recleren wants the Stones of Destiny," he said. "That's what Captain Jumbo told her. It makes sense that it was Recleren."

"Shouldn't we tell Director LeCrucia?" Ollie said, becoming animated.

"And lose everything? The Tower, the Stone, everything?!" Andy said passionately. "I think NOT!"

"We *can't* tell her," Luke said adamantly. "And same with Nia and Cleo."

"But," Ollie was pleading now, "they're looking for the Stones too, so they are in danger. This is PIRATE Recleren we're talking about!"

"But they don't *have* a Stone, so they are NOT in danger." Luke said, trying to convince Ollie, and himself.

"What about *Bale's Tales*? It mentions the Stones," Ollie said

"No one except us knows about *Bale's Tales*," Andy said.

"That's right," Ronan said, pushing his plate away.

"So we don't have to worry about the girls," Luke said. He was almost convinced. But truthfully, he was worried about the whole Order of Ravens, including the girls. "If anything changes, I'll tell them."

"Luke, I think you're wrong. We need to tell them." Ollie looked sternly at Luke. "The police were wrong and so is Director LeCrucia. They need to know."

Luke lowered his voice even further, "Ollie, we went through this last night. If we tell Director LeCrucia or anyone, we'll lose everything. The Stone, the Tower, everything!"

Andy glanced over at the Games hourglass. "Yeah. Besides, Cleo and Nia are not in the Order anymore," he said, gobbling up his scrambled eggs.

"They don't need to know. They don't have a Stone. They are not in danger," Luke repeated.

"You have a Stone so that puts you in danger. You should leave it in the tower." Ollie shook his head in frustration.

"No, the girls could get it," Luke pointed out.

"Really?" Ollie raised his eyebrows. "Without the keys?"

Ronan spoke up, his mouth full of smushed pancakes, syrup and bacon, "Maybe. Those girls are too smart. You never know."

"The Stone of Destiny stays with me," Luke said.

Andy wiped his mouth with his sleeve. "Don't worry, Ollie. We're going to be his bodyguards. Luke will go everywhere we go."

"That's not how bodyguards work. You're supposed to follow Luke." Ollie shook his head.

"Not how we do it," said Ronan as he gulped a glass full of orange juice. "And we have a weapon." He reached back under his shirt and showed them his slingshot tucked into the top of his pants.

Ollie rose and pushed his chair away from the table. "I will give you one day, Luke. If you don't tell Director LeCrucia, I will. It's not safe for you—or any of us!—if Pirate Recleren is hiding at Chronos Academy."

"Don't worry so much Ollie," Andy said. "We've got this!"

"Let's go Luke, we gotta get to the pitch. We'll protect you," Ronan said.

"That's all nice and everything, but I'll be okay. Besides, I don't feel like going to the pitch today," Luke said. Having hardly slept at all, the thought of running around a pitch was not very appealing. Then again, perhaps it was what he needed to take his mind off last night.

"We need to keep you safe," Andy said. "Besides, going to the pitch has been planned for days. We booked it, remember? The Vikes are at Glimmerton all week to get pictures taken and interviews and stuff. For two hours the pitch is ours! We have to go. I'm exhausted from staying up so late last night. Professor Agnostos's assignment almost killed me," Andy said and made an exploding sound as he brought his hands to his temples. "But I'm not missing this."

"Definitely need to burn off some steam," Ronan agreed.

"Okay, okay, I'll go," Luke said.

"Besides, I want a re-race with Ronan and you Ollie. You should come. If you feel like getting whipped," Andy gave a genuine smile. He was very good at switching topics to lighten the mood.

Ollie said he'd join them in a bit. He had something to do.

52

Cleo

How could the boys not tell us? Cleo was fuming. Luke had been attacked by Recleren in the middle of the night! And Luke knew she was totally worried about Recleren, especially after finding the cliffside dangling rope. That's why they had made the call to the police in the first place! And he'd been with her when the helicopters had been flying overhead searching the school grounds and forest. They had both been unnerved.

This attack confirmed that Recleren was on Chronos Academy grounds right now! Not only were their lives in danger, but what about the Stones of Destiny? They could be lost to a criminal pirate! Her worst fears were coming to fruition and the boys had decided to say nothing. Thank goodness Ollie had told her and Nia.

With a picnic lunch packed carefully next to *Bale's Tales* and the Stone of Destiny in CeeCee's backpack, she and Nia had been on their way to Kingsburg Forest to find the tree with chimpanzee fire fungus when Ollie had found them. After he told them what happened, Cleo quickly developed a new plan. To rip a strip off the boys, Luke in particular.

With Ollie chasing after them, the two girls stomped through the Eldritch stadium archway and entered the pitch. Nia pointed straight ahead at the Order of Ravens members running on the track. "There they are!" she seethed. "Our lives are threatened, and the boys are playing and having a good old time."

If that wasn't bad enough, the Order of Ravens was hanging out with Cleo's arch nemesis, Stephanie, and her posse.

"Daisy's here?" Nia asked, frowning.

"Luke! What took you so long?! This isn't a dancing competition!" Stephanie's voice resonated across the stadium as she got first across the finish line, flipping her ponytail. Daisy made it second across the finish line, followed by Andy and Ronan who were busy as usual trying to sabotage each other. Hayden and Lauren were chiding Luke who came in dead last.

Stephanie spotted Cleo. "What're you doing here?"

"Don't be so rude," Nia said as they moved in closer, "New sidekicks?"

"I have a lot of *friends*." Stephanie sneered and levelled her gaze on Cleo. Next to Stephanie, Daisy pulled nervously on her ponytail. Ollie shifted uncomfortably side to side.

Stephanie stomped her foot. "You two aren't invited. Come back another time."

Fists by her side, Nia moved a few steps forward, ready to pounce on Stephanie. "We are not here to play!" Nia said, crossing her arms. "We're here to talk to Luke." The boys seemed uncomfortable. Andy and Ronan were fixated on their shoes as they over-exaggerated their stretching.

Stephanie regarded Nia with a confused expression. Cleo shot a look of accusation at Luke who quickly evaded it by looking up at the sky.

Three ravens, wings spread, were floating on a current as the wind picked up. Cleo watched as one raven dropped a small stick from up high and one of the other two ravens flew to catch it. In the endless blue sky, a few dark clouds were now gathering above them.

"You know what? Forget it," Stephanie said flipping her long blond hair. "I'm going. I don't need this. Are you coming, Daisy? Ronan?"

"Um …" Daisy said, looking at Nia and then at Cleo. Luke was using his inhaler as he stood close to Ronan and Andy.

"Daisy, decide! Me or them," Stephanie commanded. "Remember, I was nice to you when they weren't."

"What? We've never been mean to Daisy," Nia replied and glanced at Daisy who didn't say anything. Instead, she tugged softly on her high ponytail that she'd braided and woven with a flower. She nodded to Stephanie.

With that, Stephanie stormed off through the gate, Daisy next to her, Hayden and Lauren trailing behind. Just then the three ravens circling overhead glided down gracefully and perched on the stands. "CAW, CAW, CAW!" They took turns in a raven conversation.

More dark clouds coalesced menacingly. The wind blew harder, whistling past the stands.

The boys didn't move. It was like a western standoff, each side waiting to draw their weapons. Cleo and Nia versus Luke, Andy, and Ronan. Ollie was in the middle, literally.

For the longest time, no one said anything.

Had the Order of Ravens come to this?

They couldn't even talk to each other.

Finally Cleo spoke, "How could you?"

"What?" Luke said as he looked between Cleo and Ollie.

The wind picked up out of nowhere and roared to a howl pushing on all of them, making it hard to stand straight. Cleo could no longer clearly see the stands at the other end of the pitch.

"What's going on?" Cleo said, shouting to be heard over the gale.

As though answering, the ravens cawed and took off.

Like wings of a monster, darkness had spread over the Eldritch Pitch and a ferocious cloud was developing against the black sky at the end of the field. Hypnotized, Cleo watched the cloud spin and extend its length, stretching down vertically.

"OMG!" Nia cried, pointing. "That's … a funnel cloud!"

"It's coming this way!" Luke shouted.

"RUN!" Andy and Ronan screamed in unison.

"Cleo!" she heard Ollie yell and felt someone pull her from behind.

The six students raced away from the tornado and out of the stadium through the closest archway exit. Cleo looked back over her shoulder just as Ronan blew past her. A loud humming noise was percolating around them. She felt the hairs on her arms arch back. The funnel cloud was now accompanied by bright lightning flashing against the dark skies. One lightning bolt zigzagged down to earth.

BOOM!

A lightning rod, placed on the tops of the stands to protect the pitch from lightning, was hit and snapped in half like a toothpick, rendering it useless.

The air, now static and deadly, fizzled around them.

Another lightning strike zapped down the first goal post and moved into the field. Cleo stood mesmerized. Small flashes of blue electricity were jumping through the field as though playing hopscotch, snapping with sound as they went, and moving towards the second goal post. The electricity seemed alive as it traversed the Eldritch Pitch. She'd never seen electricity move like this. And right behind it was the ferocious sparking tornado. "Keep going!" Nia said, pulling Cleo's arm.

Turning rapidly, both girls ran behind the boys. Running at top speed, a loud BOOM knocked them off their feet. The girls flew forward, landing on their knees in the field outside the stadium. Cleo quickly scrambled up from the ground and turned around. A huge lightning bolt struck the middle of the pitch. The pitch exploded into an enormous ball of fire!

53

Luke

Outside the stadium the tall grass bent under the strong winds. As lightning cracked above them, the six students ran at top speed, away from the roaring fire in Eldritch Stadium. When they tried to circle back to get to the castle, the sparking tornado changed trajectory, razed a hole through the stadium, and then blocked their path.

The only way to escape its wrath was to head to Kingsburg Forest.

Panicked, Luke raced along with the rest of the group. The arca of Athlia stone bumped against his leg from within his jacket pocket. He tripped over a rock and fell hard to the ground. Out of breath, he struggled to get up.

Cleo had stopped next to him. "Are you okay?" she yelled.

Luke fumbled with his inhaler, quickly taking a dose.

"Cleo! Luke! Hurry! That tornado is right behind us!" Nia shouted back at them. Luke quickly glanced over his shoulder. The tornado was moving in their direction. They had to get somewhere safe!

Heart pounding, Luke ran for his life. Up ahead he could

see the three inky-black ravens again. They were struggling to fly, flapping their wings as fast as they could against the wind, and heading towards the forest. He pushed even harder towards Kingsburg Forest, where the massive, thick and ominous trees were standing on guard, waiting for them. Andy and Ronan got there first and stood at the edge of the woods, panting. "Over here!" Andy called and ushered his friends toward a hole that he and Ronan had found in the dense brush.

Luke felt a sudden yank on his arm as Ronan pulled him through the opening. "Follow that path!" Ronan instructed with authority, turning back to pull the next person through and onto the narrow strip of flattened dirt that wove through the trees. A moment later, the brush wriggled as Nia appeared, then Cleo, followed by the rest of the group. All Luke could hear was the swishing of the leaves and groaning of the enormous branches above them as they were pushed by the wind. *Can we outrun this storm?*

With Andy leading the way, they stumbled along the rough path and went deeper into the forest. Luke felt his chest growing tighter and tighter. It was getting harder to breathe. He stumbled on his feet. He had to stop. His asthmatic lungs burned with pain. *My inhaler.* Frantically he searched his pockets, finding it in his inside jacket pocket. He popped off the blue lid and welcomed the mist that would relieve the burning. He waved at Ronan and Andy to keep moving forward.

"Luke, are you okay?" Ollie yelled next to him.

Luke nodded. He tried to shout, "Go!" but it came out as a wheeze. They had to get deeper into the forest.

As he caught his breath, he tipped his head up to try to see a piece of the sky. He saw the three ravens flying in and out of the forest's high canopy. They were flying with purpose, like they knew where they were going. He remembered how Floki had hopped along with Cleo as she climbed the cliff. The birds were usually so terrifying to Luke, but now the sight of them somehow reassured him. He tried to yell, "follow the ravens," but it came out as a mere gasp and he stumbled again.

Cleo and Ollie came to his side and held onto Luke's arms to keep him steady. He felt oxygen flow into his lungs again as the medicine from the inhaler kicked in. "I'm good now," he said, and the three of them dashed to catch up with Ronan, Andy, and Nia, who were a little ahead of them and veering left at a fork in the pathway.

"No! Not that way!" Luke called. All heads turned to look at him. "Follow the ravens!" He pointed at the three ravens still bobbing and weaving among the trees, heading off over the path on the right. Ronan gave Luke the thumbs up and he, Andy and Nia quickly veered to follow the birds.

The forest grew denser and darker the further in they went. The ferocious swirling wind of the storm pushed through everything. The giant trees groaned around them. Branches crashed through the canopy and fell like daggers to the forest floor.

Luke jumped over rocks and tree roots, dodged the falling tree limbs, and pushed other branches out of the way. Twice he felt the sting of a switch scraping his cheek as Ollie pushed through the brush ahead of him and sent a small branch flying back into Luke's face. Single file they moved deeper into the forest, following the ravens swooping overhead flying from tree to tree. The trees were becoming more gnarled and twisted and the forest more damp. Luke noticed green moss covering parts of the forest floor and decaying logs that had fallen long ago. They finally came to a small clearing. The group of six filled the space with no room to spare. They all hunched over to catch their breath, Luke coughing.

"Maybe we're safe here," Andy said, panting.

KRRRRACKKK.

A massive tree was coming down nearby.

"GO, GO!" Luke yelled.

54

Cleo

In the thickness of the woods, it was eerily dark. Whatever daylight normally squeezed through the green canopy was obliterated by the black skies of the storm. Cleo could barely see her footing. Debris was falling from the trees all around them as the wind whistled an eerie tune through the branches. An unstable tree came crashing down and she narrowly got out of its way as it hit the ground beside her. Some of the smaller trees had fallen over like dominoes. She made her way over the downed branches. It was like racing hurdles on the longest track in the world. She did her best to get over them as they kept appearing, again and again. The thinner, flimsy branches on the hurdles whipped at her, slowing her down with a thousand cuts.

She knew Nia and Luke were behind her, Andy just up ahead with Ollie and Ronan. She had no clue where they were going. None of them did. But they needed to find shelter from the storm, and fast.

Without warning, Cleo ran into Andy's arm. "Stop!" he said. He was holding her back from falling down a steep bank and into a fast-moving river.

"Look over there!" Ronan called as he pointed across the river. The three ravens were cawing on the roof of a structure that looked like a hut. Ollie was next to Ronan, his flashlight honed onto a door. The hut was barely bigger than a four-person tent and was well-camouflaged under an overhanging ridge, twenty steps up the riverbank on the opposite side of the river. If it wasn't for the ravens it would've been easy to miss. Old and unkempt, it was made of river rocks held together with cracked mortar. The solid wood roof was layered with tree branches that gave it the appearance of a thatched roof. The door was made of wooden planks and swung loose on its hinges.

Behind them, trees were bowing their heads and branches continued snapping from the wind. They had no choice, they needed shelter.

"On three," Andy said to Nia. "One. Two. Three!" He tossed Ollie's backpack across the river and Nia tossed Cleo's. Andy's toss was higher than Nia's, but Cleo's bag was safely on the opposite riverbank and Ollie's pack was caught on a tree branch, dangling in the water. Nia pumped her fist in the air. Ollie shouted, "Oh no!"

One by one they formed a chain, holding hands to cross the river. Ronan ventured first down the bank and into the water. Cleo watched as the water edged up higher and higher above Ronan's knees. Luke was grappling to hold on to him, with Ronan struggling to find his footing in the strong current. Ollie was third in the chain. Andy held Nia's hand, edging step by step. Cleo would be the last link, and Nia gradually pulled her into the rushing river.

The spring water was shockingly cold as it pushed against

her. Cleo squeezed Nia's hand tightly. She struggled to stay up, slipping on the rocks at the bottom of the river. She didn't want the strong current to pull her under. Ronan shouted, but the surging water drowned him out. She saw Ronan exit the other side of the river, grabbing Ollie's backpack from the branch as Luke came out behind him.

Cleo took a deep breath as the water rose higher and higher, reaching her thighs. As she moved her feet along the riverbed, she slipped off a large rock and lost her balance but Nia's tight grip on her hand saved her from going under. Nia gave one final pull to yank Cleo out of the water and they clawed their way up the muddy riverbank.

55

Luke

Luke's eyes took a moment to adjust to the dim gray light in the safety of the hut. The storm had now morphed into a torrential downpour with howling winds. The wind and rain squeezed into the hut between the cracks of the aged mortar, and the wooden plank door rattled with each gust. "What's going to happen to us?" Ollie asked

"Do you think the tornado is gone?" Andy added.

No one knew the answer to either question so no one answered.

"I have some snacks," Cleo said. She borrowed Ollie's flashlight to look inside her backpack, then passed around some sandwiches and water. She then turned off the flashlight to conserve the battery, as Ollie requested.

"Why didn't you tell us that Recleren threatened you last night, Luke?" Cleo asked. It was so dim in the hut Luke couldn't see Cleo's face. He could only make out the dark silhouette of her crazy curly hair when she turned towards Ronan and Andy. "And you two agreed to it! Recleren could've attacked Nia and me." Her voice was now intense and sounded angry.

Luke spoke up, his words bursting out as he defended himself, "He's only after me because I have the Athlia stone. You're safe because you don't have one. All you've got is *Bale's Tales*, and no one but us knows that."

Cleo didn't reply, but Luke could tell she was still angry.

"Cleo, Nia, I'm really sorry," Luke said, and he meant it. "I should've told you. I just … I don't know. All I can think of is finding the Stones and then—" he stopped. He heard nothing but the wind and the rain. It was now or never. "I need to fund an expedition. To find my dad and bring him home. That's why I want to sell the Stones. I can't have anything stopping me."

He knew there was more to the story of his dad disappearing. He could feel it. The ghost lady, the vision of the blacksmith, and his dreams of his dad, all of them felt so real. He knew his dad was alive, no matter what anyone said. But he also knew that with each passing day, the chances of finding his dad were getting smaller and smaller. It was now almost a year since his dad had gone missing. Luke's mouth went dry but his eyes were teary. He tried to swallow the lump in his throat.

"I didn't know that," Cleo said. There was less anger in her voice. But when she spoke again she used a serious voice, like a grown up would use, and it kind of annoyed him. "But Luke, our *lives* depend on knowing this stuff right now."

He was angry that Cleo implied that their lives were more important than his dad's.

They all sat close together as the wind and rain pummeled the forest around them. Their angry silence filled the little stone hut.

Ollie broke the silence. "Luke, you're my best friend, and I get why you want to find the Stones and look for your dad. But Pirate Recleren is dangerous for all of us, not just you."

Luke felt a sudden wash of remorse. He knew he hadn't reported the attack because he was being selfish. He hadn't been thinking about the Order of Ravens at all, or anyone else for that matter. He'd only been thinking about his own plan to find the Stones so he could rescue his dad.

"You have to report the attack when we get back to the castle," Ollie insisted.

"If he does that, we lose everything!" Andy piped up.

Ronan who had been uncharacteristically quiet spoke up in a meager voice, "Maybe Ollie is right."

"What?!" Andy said but after Nia hurled several choice comments his way, he relented. "Fine! Alright!"

Luke touched the band of his wristwatch. As much as it hurt, Luke knew he had to do the right thing. "Cleo, Nia, I'm really sorry. Ollie too." Luke continued, "I was just being selfish. I'll report the attack when we get back."

"Good!" Ollie said. "Then I won't have to."

BOOM! Thunder cracked right above them, shaking the hut.

"If we get back!" Ronan said.

"Do you think we're going to die here?" Ollie asked, as another bout of thunder rolled over the hut.

"We are not going to die!" Nia said. "We're going to stay here."

"It's safer in this hut than it is out there," Luke said, trying to reassure his best friend.

"That's for sure!" Ronan agreed. "Outside the pitch blew up, we were chased by a tornado, almost killed by falling trees, and we nearly drowned in a river. I'm staying here."

"Oh, poop." Nia added.

"And this is way better than being stuck at Traitors' Gate," Andy said. "At least the entire Order of Ravens is here to suffer this time," Andy said. "Ouch! Nia! Why'd you hit me?"

Luke could make out Nia leaning toward Cleo's curly hair. She started whispering something to her roomie.

Ronan scolded them, "No more secrets!"

Cleo asked Ollie to turn on his flashlight. He clicked the light on and focused on Cleo. She dug through her backpack and then opened her hand and showed them a raw-cut narrow rectangular stone. It was black with blue streaks.

In unison the four boys gasped.

"We found it yesterday morning, in *Bale's Tales*," Cleo said.

"*Bale's Tales*?" Luke asked incredulously. He pulled the oval Stone of Destiny from his pocket to compare it with hers. Except for their shape they were virtually identical.

In the beam of the flashlight, Cleo brought out *Bale's Tales* to show them the spine of the book where the stone had been bound.

"So we had the Stone all along and we didn't know. That's crazy," Andy said.

"What happened to the book?" Ronan asked.

Cleo frowned. "I had a bit of an accident with it."

"I'll say," Ronan added.

"I'm still hoping to fix it somehow." Cleo paused. "Anyway, that's why I freaked out about Recleren attacking you."

"But I didn't know you had a Stone," Luke said.

As Luke moved the stones closer together, he could feel

the magnetic attraction between them. Not overwhelmingly strong, but it was there. To see how strong the attraction actually was, he placed both stones on the floor a few feet apart while Ollie trained his beam on them. They all watched the stones slowly move closer together.

"I'm sorry, I guess we should've told you when we found it." Cleo looked at Luke.

"Yeah well. Let's call it even?" he proposed.

"Maybe, but it's not exactly the same," she said and then grimaced when Nia said, "Tell them about the curse."

"Curse?!" Ollie's voice went up two octaves.

Cleo took a deep breath and told them about Jumbo's description of people's bad luck when searching for the Stones. "Billy Bale disappeared in the 1800s, and way back a knight named Caelen also went missing. But we think he probably died in the fire of the Great Reckoning. I just don't believe in curses," she added, "so I never mentioned it."

Ollie was beside himself. "We're searching for the Stones and we have had *a lot* of *bad luck!* I mean, *real* bad. It must be this curse! That's why Traitors' Gate happened, Pirate Recleren's attack, and now this crazy day! And now that we have two Stones?! We're doomed." He moved as far from the Stones as he could, handing the flashlight to Ronan, who then put the flashlight under his chin, casting spooky shadows over his own face.

Over the last while, Luke had been wondering if his weird visions of the blacksmith and the ghost lady were somehow caused by having the Stone of Destiny. Now, he was wondering if they were caused by this curse. Luke focused on Cleo. He just had to ask her, "Do you have weird visions, too?" Ronan moved the spotlight onto Cleo.

"No?" She sounded confused. Cleo shook her head, "What do you mean, visions?" she asked.

"Tell her, Luke," Ollie encouraged him. "No more secrets."

Luke hesitated, Ronan shining the light into his face "I had a daydream, kind of a vision, once. Well, twice actually. I don't really get what I saw. The guys know." Andy tried to catch the light with his hands, to make shadow puppets while he listened. Luke continued, "Remember the STEM challenge? I saw a blacksmith inside the cottage. No one else saw it. He said he gave some woman the arca, and because of that, he doomed her to die."

"We think that the doomed woman was Queen Avelina. The wife of King Sullivan. You know, from the 1200s," Ollie interrupted. Luke continued, "Right. And I also saw a ghost, a lady ghost, in Bastion Tower. I saw her hide something under a brick in the fireplace. In the tower's attic. That's how I found the arca."

"And we figured out the ghost lady is actually Queen Avelina. She haunts the tower," Ollie added, his eyes huge in the flashlight beam.

Cleo looked at Luke with a shocked expression on her face in the glow from the flashlight, as Ronan quickly moved it around like a camera man catching everyone's response.

"A ghost?" Nia said, "Like, woooo woooo, ghost?"

He nodded.

"Oh poop, Luke! Are you saying you saw two ghosts?" Nia asked.

"Maybe? I don't know," Luke said.

"I do!" Ollie said. "The ghost lady—the queen— she's definitely a ghost." His eyes widened even further as he gasped, "She had the arca, Luke! With the Stone in it! It all makes sense. That's why she was doomed. The CURSE. She was a cursed queen."

"Did you see the queen, too?" Cleo asked Ollie, her eyebrows raised in disbelief. "Because I never saw the blacksmith."

Ollie started to shake his head, "No. I don't really want to see a ghost. I had my ghost annihilator jar with me when we were there, so I might have accidentally captured her. And that could be why we never saw her again." Luke didn't think so but wasn't going to say anything to his friend.

"Jar?" Cleo asked. And then when Ollie opened his mouth to explain, Cleo cut him off. "Whatever. It doesn't matter. I don't believe in ghosts," Cleo said flatly.

The wind shook the hut. A few members of the Order gasped in surprise and concern.

When Cleo spoke again her voice sounded shaken, "I wondered how you'd found the arca, but these visions…I don't get it."

"Me neither," Ronan said, speaking Luke's thoughts.

"Anyone have any more secrets or apologies they need to get off their chest?" Andy asked, making a shadow rabbit with his fingers on the wall when Ronan had returned the beam of light towards him.

"Just one more," Cleo said. "I think I know where the third Stone of Destiny is."

56

Cleo

It was late afternoon, according to their check of Luke's watch. The last of the lightning and thunder had subsided, and the torrential rain had stopped. The threat of the tornado had never materialized. The sky had lost its ominous darkness, and the occasional bird twittered. As they made their way out of the hut, Ollie had given the blessing, "Order of Ravens—go forth to adventure." Cleo was happy that the group was together again.

They quickly followed the rushing river downstream. In no time at all, they found a natural bridge made of trees that had fallen long before the storm. It connected to the other side of the river.

"Well, this would've helped earlier," Andy said.

They all watched their footing as they crossed the slippery natural bridge. When they'd made it safely to the other side, Nia commented, "If we keep moving away from the river, we should find our way back. I hope."

Fallen trunks and branches were strewn between the trees from the winds. On occasion they came across a tree blackened by lightning, now soggy from the deluge of rain.

They walked in silence for a great distance. Somehow, Cleo couldn't shake the feeling that they were being followed. She kept checking behind her to make sure. The forest was alive, and animals were scurrying around making her feel skittish.

"What if Pirate Recleren is roaming the woods right now?" Ollie asked.

"Dun-dun-dun-dunn!" Ronan said.

"Oh poop, Ollie," Nia said.

"People! If Recleren was out in the forest during that storm, it got him, for sure," Andy answered, picking up a switch from the ground.

"And if it didn't, the police will find him," Luke added. "Because I will tell Director LeCrucia about the attack, when we get back."

"Right!" Ollie nodded. Cleo was not quite convinced they didn't need to worry about being attacked. She jumped when she heard a woodpecker, jackhammering the bark of a tree. When she spotted something moving between two trees, she screamed as a cute little deer bounded off. "Come on Cleo, these are just animals!" Andy laughed.

She nodded nervously. She needed a distraction.

As though reading her mind, Luke reminded her, "Just focus on the chimpanzee fire fungus you told us about. You're the only one that knows what it looks like."

It was a long shot, but maybe they could find this tree and the third Stone on their way back. Cleo hadn't paid attention to the types of trees on the way into the forest, since they had been blindly running trying to survive. Now she noticed various trees that had maple leaves, and others she recognized as trembling aspen.

"I wonder what that is?" Cleo asked aloud, staring up at the tall tree extending into the green canopy above. Cleo couldn't see the top of it.

"That's the black cottonwood tree," Luke said. "It's used for lumber and toilet paper."

"Nice," Ronan said.

"How do you know that?" Nia asked.

"I camped a lot with my dad," Luke replied. "He taught me about trees." Luke gave a pained smile and pointed at another tree, "See these white flowers? This is the Black Hawthorn tree. It grows to eight meters tall."

"Wow!" Nia added.

"A lot of these trees are Douglas maple. See the wide canopy?" Luke added. Water was dripping slowly off the leaves.

As they continued, Cleo noticed some of the trees had really thick trunks, thicker than three people standing side by side. Moss covered many sides of the tree bark.

"How can these trees get so big?" Ronan asked.

"All the water and humidity," Luke replied.

After a long while, Ollie stopped short and thumped his muddy sneakered foot into the ground in frustration. He pulled down the hood on his sweatshirt. "Why isn't anyone looking for us?!" he asked.

Cleo had to admit Ollie had a point.

"The curse! Maybe like Billy and Caelen, we have disappeared and we just don't know it," Ollie said. "We have to leave the two Stones here! Just get rid of them! Throw them into the river!"

"No way!" Luke barked.

Nia chimed in, "That makes no sense, Ollie."

"Maybe no one knows we're missing," Andy suggested.

"Stephanie and her gang know. They would tell, wouldn't they?" Ronan offered.

"Daisy would, hopefully," Cleo added, remembering how at the pitch Daisy had chosen to go with Stephanie instead of her and Nia.

How could Daisy even stand hanging out with Stephanie? Stephanie's so bossy and she's always screeching!

The Order walked on in silence, each with their own thoughts. Ronan kicked a stick that hit Nia in the back of the leg.

"Ronan!" she admonished him.

"Sorry," he apologized, and kicked a rock instead. Lucky for him it just missed her.

As they moved forward, they came across a different grouping of trees that obstructed their way.

"These are red cedar trees," Luke said. He placed each hand on the tree trunk to steady himself as he moved around it. "Ew," he said, quickly drawing his hand back from something fleshy and wet on the tree trunk.

Cleo stopped and gazed at the tree. *It's a Red Cedar. With yucky stuff on the trunk. Wait a second!* "I think this is it!"

"You mean we found it?" Nia said.

"What?" Ronan asked, running up to them.

"This tree is gnarly!" Ollie said. "And black."

"And dead!" Andy added, craning his neck to look way up. "Really dead."

"Look at the trunk," Nia added. "It's huge. All of us together wouldn't even be able to make a circle around it."

Cleo was busy examining the fungi on the tree, running her hands softly along the slimy blobs. Checking to see if they were glowing, she created a shadow over the fungi and even cupped her hands around it. They all gathered in close.

"I can't see!" Ollie said, "Is it glowing?"

"It is!" Cleo was excited. "It's faint, but it's there. This is chimpanzee fire. I don't see other trees with this fungus. And this tree looks just like the one from *Bale's Tales* and the one on the arca," Cleo said.

"Wow!" Ollie said when he finally got his turn to look at the glowing fungus.

"What good luck!" Ronan said.

"See Ollie? Good luck. No curse," Nia said, touching the fungus on the tree with her hands. "So what do we do now?"

"Find the Stone, of course!" Andy said. "It's gotta be here somewhere."

"Where? I don't see anything!" said Ollie, biting his nail. "And Recleren could still be in this forest! We need to get back to the castle and report that Luke was attacked," he insisted. "We can come back later, after Recleren's been captured."

Cleo was looking at her feet and biting her lip. *Maybe Ollie's right?* Cleo took a long look around them, her feelings suddenly conflicted. The thought of Recleren made her very anxious but the thought of not getting the third Stone made her feel worse. She had been waiting for this moment for months.

"You just wanna leave the Stone here?" Andy said incredulously.

"How can we come back, Ollie?" Luke said, pressing him. "We have no idea where we are! This forest is huge."

Nia, Ronan, and Andy agreed.

The Order took a vote. Cleo was the last one to make up

her mind, but in the end, Ollie was outnumbered five to one.

"It'll be quick," Luke assured Ollie. "I promise."

Ollie shook his head. "Everyone keeps forgetting that these Stones are *cursed*. And therefore, SO ARE WE."

"Everyone keeps forgetting that these Stones are worth three million dollars!" Andy added.

Ronan said, "Oh yeah! We need to get looking!"

In all the excitement of the day, Cleo actually had forgotten about the value of the Stones. She could see she still had some work to do to convince the boys not to sell them. But now was not the time. They had to find the third Stone. They couldn't let this opportunity go to waste.

"Let's spread out," she instructed. "Hurry."

Cleo circled the tree looking for anything that might lead to the Stone. Moments later, she felt again as if they were being watched and she glanced behind her. A raven cawed in the far distance and a smaller bird twittered from a nearby bush. *I'm sure it's nothing.*

Nia, Andy, and Ronan started coordinating their search actions, Ollie listening glumly. Luke disappeared under a large exposed raised root that made a cave-like opening. Cleo crawled in after him.

Inside the tree it was darker and cooler. They had to crouch because the space had no headroom. The two of them squished in there, on their hands and knees. As Cleo ran her right hand along the rugged wood of the interior of the trunk, a bug crawled on her hand and she yelped. She shook her hand towards the opening of the trunk and watched the creature take flight.

"Can you get Ollie's flashlight?" Luke asked.

Cleo nodded and headed back out. She returned quickly,

leaving her backpack with Ollie so she'd have more room to move in the hollow

Andy, Nia, and a reluctant Ollie were looking for anything suspicious sticking out from the ground in the vicinity of the tree.

"I'm going up," Cleo heard Andy announce loudly. "In case the stone is hidden up in the branches."

"I'm going in!" Ronan tried to squeeze into the hollow. Half his body was practically laying on top of Cleo. "It smells in here, like my socks when I've forgotten to change them," he said, scrunching his nose.

"Ew!" Cleo asserted. "There's not enough room here, Ronan." He wiggled himself into the hollow anyway as Luke took the flashlight from Cleo. Luke zipped the light around. They saw creepy crawlers and ants scuttling.

Nia popped her head into the hollow. "There's nothing out here."

Cleo said, "There is nothing in here!" All her research on bioluminescent fungus was for nothing. Chimpanzee fire wasn't a clue after all.

Cleo was about to exit the tree when a straight line below Luke's knees caught the circular beam of the flashlight.

"Look!" Cleo cried and pointed.

Cleo swept the dirt on the ground, moving it left and right. Luke shone the flashlight to where she was sweeping as he started to do the same. Ronan joined in. Dirt was flying everywhere and everyone started sneezing.

They dug, their fingers following the line. As they moved the dirt to the side, they revealed a metal square and a piece of root sticking up out of the ground. Luke and Ronan scraped away more dirt. It wasn't a root. It was a handle.

"There's a trap door here!" Luke shouted excitedly.

"Open it!" Andy yelled, suddenly peering inside the hollow.

"Hurry up!" Ollie pleaded from outside the tree. "I want to go back to the castle." From inside the hollow of the tree, Cleo could only see him from the waist down, shoving his hands into his pockets.

The three Order members in the hollow tugged on the handle but nothing happened. "We can't open it!" Ronan shouted. "It's stuck!"

"Is there an open button?" Andy grinned, as he poked his head into the hollow.

"Ha, ha," said Luke, while Cleo and Ronan giggled.

"Now hurry up!" Andy barked. "I agree with Ollie."

"Finally," muttered Ollie as he shuffled his feet.

Andy continued, "We need to find that Stone already and get back. I am so hungry."

Cleo was hungry, too. They hadn't eaten since she shared her and Nia's picnic food in the hut.

"What's going on in there?" called Nia from outside.

Luke quickly tried pushing the panel down. "Still stuck," he said in frustration.

"Let's pull all at the same time," Ronan instructed. "One, two, heave ho!"

CRACK!

The trap door inched up a bit. "It's really heavy," Ronan said, straining. The three of them heave hoed again. The door opened more. Now Cleo put the flashlight down and pulled on the handle while both Luke and Ronan moved around her towards the tree opening so they could push the panel upwards. With all their strength, they got it open as far as it could go, the leading edge of the door resting against the inside of the tree. Luke shone the flashlight into the hole. It was only big enough for one of them to go down at a time.

"The Stone must be down there," Cleo said. "Right?"

Luke rubbed his hands together. "For sure," he said.

"There could be dead bodies, too," Ronan mused, as he eyed the opening.

Ewww. Creepy!

Andy was trying to squeeze himself into the trunk hollow. Giving up, he asked, "Who's going first? Luke?"

Cleo leaned over and poked her head down into the dark hole. Although she was scared by the darkness and what lay at the bottom, the possibility of the third Stone being down there made her consider leading the way. CeeCee would say, "Be brave." But Cleo just couldn't do it. Someone else could go first.

Suddenly nudged from behind, she unexpectedly found herself falling into the dark void.

57

Cleo

"Cleo!" Luke called from somewhere above her.

Rubbing the back of her neck, she slowly moved. Other than a couple of aches and pains here and there from her terrifying tumble, she was surprisingly alright. She sat on the ground and looked around but couldn't see anything in the dark. The musty air made her scrunch her nose. She rose to her feet, slowly, a still blackness surrounding her like a blanket.

"Cleo!" Luke called again. He was shining the light down. Although the light wasn't very bright, Cleo was relieved to see she wasn't at the edge of a cliff! She could see the shadows of Luke's face as he gazed down from the hole. The light showed that she had just tumbled down stairs created with the underground roots of the tree. They were covered with glowing fungus.

Chimpanzee fire.

"Are you okay?" Luke yelled as Ronan's face appeared, asking the same question.

"It's really dark down here. I'm freaked out a bit," she

shouted and wrapped her arms around herself. She was about three meters below the trap door. Her imagination went wild with what creatures big and small could be down here with her. "What happened?"

Ronan grabbed the flashlight and shoved Luke to the side. "You bumped into me and then fell in," he shouted down the hole.

Cleo stared up at Ronan through the beam.

"Fine. Sorry," Ronan managed, "I bumped you."

"Cleo, he really didn't mean to," Luke said, his face reappearing beside Ronan's. "He bumped me and I almost fell, too."

"Are you good?" Ronan yelled back down.

"Good? No! I could've died!" she yelled back. "But I'm okay, I think."

"Yah, with a gazillion bruises," Ollie's voice added from above. "What's down there? Are there spiders? Monsters?"

Cleo's heart raced. Except for the dimly glowing fungus on the stairs, it was super dark. "None of that, I think," Cleo added, her jitters abundant. "I don't see the Stone. But I can't see anything except there's some chimpanzee fire on the stairs."

"I'm coming down to help you find the Stone," Ronan said as he bumped down the slippery fungus-covered steps on his butt.

"Wait for me!" Nia cried, and followed him. "Whoa," she said when she landed beside Cleo. Then she shouted up, "Luke, make sure the trap door stays open. So we can get out."

"Good point," Luke yelled down. "Just wait for us there."

Nia asked Cleo, "Are you sure you're okay?" Cleo assured

her friend that she was alright as Nia hugged her and Ronan repeated his apology.

Cleo took a deep breath and repeated her grandma's words in her head, *"Be brave, be brave."* They heard muffled sounds and then Luke's face reappeared. "We're getting a big branch to secure the hatch. We'll be right down." After what felt like forever, Luke slipped his way down the mossy stairs with Ollie's flashlight zipping light into the void. Ollie followed, taking his time to find his footing. After checking once more that the trap door was securely propped open, Andy joined them.

All eyes on the beam of the flashlight, they assessed the area. Tucked away near the last step, Cleo spotted a grimy antique-style lantern. She grabbed the handle and examined it. *Someone else has been in this cave before!* Her mind raced. *The door was really buried. It had to have been from a long time ago. Maybe William Bale?* She shivered.

"Here!" Ollie said, handing Cleo her backpack and a small box of matches from his own bag. "They're even waterproof" he said, puffing up a bit with pride.

"Thanks," she said and put on her backpack. She retrieved the lantern from the ground and tried to light it but nothing happened.

"Maybe you need this," Andy said. He was holding a filthy glass bottle full of liquid in his hands. "Found it over there with another two empty bottles." Andy smudged away the thick layer of grimy dust on the bottle exposing the label: *Whale Oil.*

"Really? Whale oil?" Nia said. "That's gross! And cruel."

"They used that in the 1800s. That or kerosene—for the lanterns," Cleo said.

Andy added, "1800's! That's the same time as Billy Bale. Maybe it's his whale oil?"

"Maybe," Luke said.

Cleo held the lantern, Andy filled its reservoir and moved the wick around, and Ollie set the wick on fire.

They were pleasantly surprised when the lantern lit.

Whoosh!

Burning brightly, its warm yellow light joined that of the flashlight casting a halo around the group below the glowing tree. It was quiet, peaceful, and very dark outside the reach of the light. All they could hear was the sound of water dripping, their own breathing, and the faint ticking of Luke's watch.

Cleo held the lamp above her shoulder.

Nia yelled, "Hello!"

"'ello, 'ello, 'ello, 'ello, 'ello," her voice echoed back.

Andy repeated Nia's experiment, "Fart!"

"'art, 'art, 'art, 'art, 'art," the echo replied.

Ronan and Luke snickered.

"What is this place?" Ronan asked, bending over to tie up his shoelace.

"It's a cave," Cleo said.

"But where's the Stone?" Nia asked.

Somewhere here. It has to be!

They walked in two lines as they advanced. Ollie stuck close to Cleo, and carried his flashlight.

"Maybe this is a tomb," Ronan said, only half-joking, his voice sounding shaky.

Andy answered, "Nah, we'd have seen a body by now. We just need to find the Stone."

"I'm kinda freaking out," Nia said, hooking arms with Cleo.

"Yeah. What else could be down here? Animals? Ghosts? Or worse!" said Ollie, and he gulped. "We could just disappear down here and no one would ever find us." Then he whispered, "Because of the CURSE."

Cleo didn't want to fall victim to Ollie's curse talk, so she kept her opinion to herself. She tapped her lantern as it flickered. "How far do you think we should go?"

"All the way," Luke answered.

Inching forward to the edge of their illumination, Luke gestured to Cleo to move the light over the cave wall. There was a narrow lip on the rocky wall. On it were a few buckets.

Nia looked into each of them. "There's some tools in here, but that's it," she said.

"No Stone," Ronan said, peering into the buckets.

"Well this was a waste of time," Andy commented.

"Great! Let's leave," Ollie said.

She thought they'd been on the right track. The tree from the arca, the glowing fungus. Cleo sighed, and she nodded in agreement.

Luke seemed as disappointed as she was. He kicked the floor and stuffed his hands in his pockets. As they walked back to the fungi ridden stairs, Cleo saw Luke pull the oval Stone of Destiny from inside his jacket pocket. He rubbed it between his thumb and forefinger, grimaced and put it back.

They'd struck out. The Order of Ravens was no closer to finding the third Stone.

58

Luke

"The hatch won't budge," Luke said, out of breath from the effort of climbing up and down the slippery glowing steps. "I don't get how it closed."

"We're locked in here?!" gasped Ollie.

"Maybe it was the wind?" Andy said.

"Or a bird or something knocked it shut?" Ronan offered.

Luke remembered the heavy trap door and the good-sized branch they'd shoved in there to make sure it didn't close.

"There's no way the wind or a bird could have moved that branch," Andy said, echoing Luke's thoughts.

Ollie shook his head. "This is happening because of the curse," he said. "Because we're looking for the Stones." He nervously chewed his fingernail.

Luke reassured all his friends, "We just need to figure out how to get out of here."

They were on their own in the cave. They took stock of their supplies: one lantern, one flashlight, and a few tools in a bucket. No food. No water.

"Let's get those tools and try and bust the hatch open,"

Ronan suggested.

After retrieving the tools, the Order of Ravens took turns trying to open the hatch again. When they couldn't, Andy asked, "What now?"

Luke heard a crinkle of paper as Ollie passed around a chocolate bar he'd found at the bottom of his backpack. Luke broke off a piece gratefully. Savouring his chocolate, he found some hope.

"There has to be another way out," Luke said.

"Luke's right," Nia agreed.

"Let's go!" Ronan said.

The Order went deeper into the cave. The six of them could stand side by side comfortably and there was still enough room to add another three people on either side. As they continued, the cave floor got less smooth and the elevation changed, sloping up and down, the cave narrowing and widening. In narrower spots they had to walk single file. At other times the route was wide enough for all to walk side by side. The character of the cave transformed again. The ceiling became lower.

"This is the end of our nice stroll," Andy said.

Ronan pointed the flashlight to where their passageway ended in a narrow, round opening a few feet above the floor. "It's like a laundry chute," he said.

"Or a birth canal," Andy said. Nia grimaced.

Luke noticed Cleo check behind them for the millionth time before she peered into the opening and quickly recoiled.

"I'm not going in there," said Ollie.

Luke looked through the round opening. *That is really narrow!*

"I'm not either! We don't even know what's on the other

side!" Cleo said, standing with Ollie, together, arms locked and a look of defiance on their faces.

"We have to try," Nia said to her. "Otherwise we'll be stuck in this cave forever!"

After a moment of debate, Andy volunteered to check it out and report back.

Andy got in the chute with the flashlight, squirming and slithering out of view. Moments later a voice echoed up from the opening. "Okay, it's not too long. On the other side there's more cave. But I can see light and I can hear water or something. There has to be an exit, for sure." Andy gave a small cough. "You guys can do this. Just pretend you're a worm."

There was no further discussion. It was a tight squeeze but they all had to go through or risk being left behind.

Ollie dragged his backpack behind him as he followed Ronan. Nia went in front of Cleo, pulling Cleo's backpack behind her as she called back, "Imagine writing about this to grandma CeeCee. Here I go!"

Cleo took three deep breaths before she followed Nia into the chute.

Luke took a deep breath himself and hopped in after Cleo with the lantern.

This is it. No going back.

59

Cleo

Cleo could feel the skin on her elbows and knees scraping as she made her way through the narrow tunnel. She felt like she was being buried alive in rock, but this was the first time since they left the hut that she hadn't felt like she was being followed. She closed her eyes for a moment. Everything inside her screamed. But she had to keep going. Cleo had wanted adventure at Chronos Academy, but she'd had no idea how much bravery it required!

She must have shimmied three body lengths when at last she plopped out from the chute. She squeezed her eyes tight to keep in her tears. Then she heard Nia exclaim, "Wow!"

Cleo opened her eyes, looked up, and saw the ceiling. Dotted with millions of mystical round blue flecks of light, it was beautiful. Somewhere in the distance she could hear a trickle of water. She marveled at her surroundings

"What is this place?" Andy asked.

"An underground milky way," Nia said.

Luke joined Cleo in taking in a 360 degree view. He was looking up, missed a step and stumbled.

Cleo answered Andy's question, "They're glow-worms. Bioluminescent glow-worms."

"Bioluminescent?" Ronan asked, "Like the leaves in the STEM challenge?"

"Yes! And the chimpanzee fire on the tree!" Cleo said.

"So that means?" Ollie asked.

Luke replied quickly, "The third Stone must be here!"

Cleo felt a surge of excitement.

"To the Stone!" Nia said.

They moved along the cave under the glowing ceiling, sticking close together.

The ceiling seemed almost like streetlights marking their path forward, guiding them around a narrow bend. Their path soon opened into a spectacular wide cavern still lit by the luminescent glow-worms. Off to one side, a small pond, completely still and translucent, reflected the glow-worms' blue light throughout the cavern. Their flashlight and lantern added a layer of warm light over the blue, revealing a breathtaking almost alien landscape of striated rock formations.

Then Andy called out, "Over there." He pointed the flashlight beam dead ahead. In the middle of the chamber was a large egg-shaped rock with a sword running through it. Cleo thought about the drawing on the arca again. There had been a sword leaning on the tree, but no drawings nor any mention of a sword embedded in a boulder.

So what does all of this mean?

All six of them quickly gathered around the rock. The sword was covered in cobwebs and dirt. As they started to clean the sword using their sleeves and blowing at the dirt, Ronan ran his index finger along the blade. He'd barely begun when he flinched. A small amount of blood oozed out of his finger. "It's still sharp," he said, sucking on his index finger.

As they cleaned, the details of the sword were revealed. The black pommel at the top of the hilt was shaped like a bird's head with an open beak. From the open beak, a bronze rapier guard traversed the pommel in a circular winding pattern around the bronze hilt and stopped at the top of the blade. The bronze hilt had an intricate woven pattern.

"I've never seen a sword like this. Not even in *Knights of Darkness*," Luke commented, setting the lantern down as he leaned over and grabbed the pommel of the sword and ran his hand over it. Cleo picked up the lantern and stepped in for a closer look. Andy and Ronan moved to the other end of the rock.

"How did they stab a sword into a rock?" Andy asked.

"Magic," Ollie offered. He eyed the sword with awe.

"The sword in the stone, it's just like the sword of King Arthur," Luke exclaimed excitedly. "Remember? It's mentioned in *Knights of Darkness*."

"Right!" Ollie said wide-eyed. "Maybe it's Excalibur!" Commanding the flashlight, Ollie moved closer to the sword to get a better look, too.

"If I pull it out, I'll be king, the great chosen one," Ronan said. He nodded at Luke and Luke nodded back.

"It's not Excalibur!" Cleo pointed out. "Look!" Using the light from the lantern, Cleo read an engraving on the sword, "It says *Goffridis*."

"Goffridis! " Nia commented, "The knight who was with King Sullivan. Right? From our history report. This must have been his sword."

"That makes sense," Cleo said. She quickly pulled *Bale's*

Tales from her backpack, rested it on the boulder, and flipped to the right page. The boys gathered around her as she held the lantern over the open journal. "This drawing here," Cleo continued, pointing to the drawing of the tree with the sword leaning against it, "and this one," she flipped through the book again and pointed to the drawing of the arca, "show the same thing."

Ollie said, "It's a sword leaning against the tree."

"But does *Bale's Tales* say anything about a sword in a boulder?" Ronan asked, scratching his nose with his upper lip.

"And where's the Stone?" Luke asked.

"Maybe it's inside the rock?" Andy proposed, "Like how the Athlia stone was inside the arca."

"How can we open a boulder?" Ronan asked.

Holding the lantern up high with her right hand, Cleo's eye caught a faint blue spark that shot out of the hilt.

"Did you see that?" Luke asked, taking a step closer.

"Yes!" Cleo said, her eyes large.

"What? What did you see?" Ollie asked.

Cleo examined the black pommel at the top of the hilt that was shaped like a bird's head and put her fingers between the rapier guard.

"Luke, can I see your Stone of Destiny?" Cleo asked. Her hands were starting to tremble.

Luke took the Athlia stone out of his jacket pocket and handed it over. She passed the lantern to Nia, then took Luke's Stone of Destiny and brought it closer to the hilt. Her five friends watched silently. Ollie focused his flashlight on the hilt.

She felt a slight pull, originating from the center of the

intricately patterned bronze hilt and drawing the stone in her hand closer. *It's magnetic!* Mechanically she returned the Athlia Stone to Luke while keeping her eyes on the hilt. She examined it again, moving even closer. Nia lowered her arm. The dim lantern light bathed the sword in a soft orange hue. In the centre of the hilt was a small, jagged-cut black stone, shaped like a diamond. The closer Cleo got to the sword, the more light she blocked, but she didn't need the light.

She ran the tips of her fingers between the rapier guard and the hilt, stopping where she thought she had seen the spark. Cleo gently pushed on the hilt. Pushing again, harder this time, she felt a piece of it shift slightly.

"What're you doing, Cleo?" asked Ollie.

"I can't see!" Ronan said, growing impatient.

"Hurry up, Cleo," Andy encouraged.

Nia adjusted the lantern. Luke squished in next to Cleo trying to get a better look.

"It's moving. I wonder," Cleo glanced at Luke. "Can you try, Luke?"

He hopped around to the other side of the boulder. Leaning in awkwardly, he pushed gently at the place Cleo had indicated on the hilt.

"I can't feel anything moving," Luke said. Part of his face was hidden behind the hilt.

"Wait," he said, pressing again. As he pushed, Cleo felt a piece of the sword moving against her finger.

The piece felt like it was welded tight into the design, yet it wiggled as both Cleo and Luke worked on it. The rest of the Order watched on in serious silence.

With a final push from Luke, a piece of the hilt came out and Cleo caught it as it slid between the hilt and rapier guard. In her hands, she held a jagged-cut diamond-shaped stone, black with blue veins running through it.

60

After they had compared the diamond-shaped stone to the Athlia Stone, they all knew what they had. "I can't believe it!" Luke said as Ronan handed the Stone to Cleo, suggesting she keep it in her backpack. "We have the third Stone of Destiny!" They all let out shouts of joy, and Nia placed the lantern on the egg-shaped boulder to give Cleo a hug.

They'd done it. The Order had worked together and now they had three Stones of Destiny and *Bale's Tales*. They had the full set! Cleo zoomed ahead in her mind to the opening of the museum display in Brillianton, Grandma CeeCee and her mom by her side, and the Order being honoured for their discovery. She tucked Bale's journal back into her pack, placed the new-found Stone next to Bale's Stone, and gave the bag a hug.

Just then a mysterious low rumble rippled like thunder through the cave. Searching for its source, Ollie was whipping his flashlight around, when the sound stopped abruptly.

"What's going on?" Andy's voice squeaked as he spoke. Cleo was surprised.

Andy's never afraid.

"Doesn't sound good," Luke commented from behind Cleo's left shoulder.

They all stood stock still, waiting for the next rumble. The moment stretched on.

"It's too quiet," Ronan commented. Ollie shot the light at Ronan. Ronan squinted into it, his shadow on the cavern wall behind him, "Hey, cut that out!"

Another loud rumble made Ollie's eyes go so wide Cleo thought they might fly out of his head. The flashlight, held by his shaking hands, created a strobe-like effect that reflected off the blade of the sword. He whispered loudly, "It's the curse."

A cracking noise echoed from high above them, quick bursts of sound at first, then a long RRRRRIIIIIIPPPPPPP as the ceiling of the cave split open. Sand and small rocks started falling. One rock knocked the lantern off the boulder, smashing the lantern into the ground.

"Duck!" Andy shouted. Then a terrible hailstorm of debris started pelting them. Everyone was yelling as they covered their heads. Cleo sprang back just in time, pulling Luke and Nia with her as a huge chunk of the cavern ceiling suddenly dropped, smashing down on the boulder, crushing the sword. Rocks of every size were still pelting down from the ceiling when the ground started to shake and form cracks. Just a few inches wide at first, the cracks grew in length and combined into a web of fissures that spread like a ripple from the boulder through the cavern.

"Run!" Cleo yelled.

They didn't get far. Above the tranquil pond, a chunk of the cavern ceiling crashed down, pushed the water out of the pond, and created a mini tidal wave.

"We have to get out of here!" Luke hollered, protecting his head from the falling rubble.

Water started to percolate upwards through the web of fissures in the cavern floor. As the cave shook in anger, the stream quickly transformed from a trickle to a roar, gushing in and creating an underground river. Cleo and Luke collected Ollie, Nia, and Andy who were crouched under an outcropping. "Where's Ronan?" Andy asked.

"I'm right here," Ronan replied, joining them. He had his hand on his forehead, covering a small cut and a goose egg. The cavern seemed to be disintegrating around them. They had to shout over the sound of crashing rocks and rushing water that was already at Cleo's knees.

"Which way?" Luke yelled.

"This way!" Andy said and led them away from the crashing ceilings, searching the space with the flashlight. The Order of Ravens moved sluggishly, following the current, dodging falling rocks that splashed into the water. Andy and Luke lead the way, Nia followed next to Cleo, and Ollie and Ronan moved right behind them.

The ceiling was now only sparsely dotted with glow-worms. The walls and ceiling were still shaking, dropping debris, rocks, and dust.

"The water keeps rising!" Cleo yelled through chattering teeth as she covered her head.

The temperature in their underground landscape had dropped, and the water was frigid.

"Where's the exit?" Ronan yelled.

"I don't know!" Andy yelled back.

"It has to be straight ahead," Nia offered. "The water is

flowing that way."

Shivering, Cleo noticed the falling debris was easing up. *At least that's something.*

Just when Cleo thought she could finally take a deep breath, they heard another strange sound. The flashlight beam zipped in circles ahead of the group, but the dark cave seemed to swallow the light.

Boom Boom BOOM!

They stopped. It didn't take long to see the complete picture. The exit ahead of them was collapsing. Boulder-sized rocks piled on top of one another in the water, creating a wall that completely blocked their path and dammed the flowing underground river.

"Turn back," Luke commanded, his words snapping Cleo out of her paralyzed state.

"Follow me!" Ronan yelled, pointing behind them and leading the way. Moving as fast as they could in water that now reached their waistlines, they went back the way they had come.

BOOM! BOOM!

With whiplash movement, Ronan pushed the Order members backwards to keep them all from being pummeled to death by large slabs of rock that suddenly plummeted into the water. They were trapped between two walls of fallen rocks and the water was still rising.

"What do we do?" Ollie asked. The ceiling had stopped shaking but the water had risen above their waists. Andy and Nia made their way to the closest barricade. Together he and Nia dove under the water.

"That one's blocked," Andy said, when they emerged a little later. They made their way to the second barricade and checked it out. Nia came up sputtering and began to cry, "We can't get through."

They were trapped.

Cleo hooked her arm with Nia's and glanced at her friends, her heart breaking. Dirt streamed down their dust-covered, bruised, and scratched faces, and everyone was shivering. Darkness seemed to envelope them even though Ollie had raised his arm to keep the flashlight out of the water.

"You guys wanted the Stones, you messed with that sword!" Ollie accused. "Now, look! This IS the CURSE!"

"Ollie, please STOP!" Cleo begged.

When Luke looked at her, Cleo knew that he was thinking the same thing as her.

We're going to die.

They all huddled together.

Nia wiped her eyes and in a shaky voice said, "At least we found the three Stones of Destiny when no one else could."

Solemnly, Luke put the Athlia stone in Cleo's palm. She looked at the blue veins in the black stone. Her teeth chattered from the cold and terror of their impending doom.

From Cleo's backpack, Nia fished out the stones they had found in *Bale's Tales* and the sword and laid them gently in Cleo's other hand.

They stood in a circle admiring the Stones in Cleo's hands. All three stones matched. All black, all with rough-cut edges and tiny blue veins.

"We did it," Luke said, his voice breaking.

Andy put his hands under Cleo's, and Ronan put his under Andy's. The others joined, standing in a circle with their stacked hands supporting the Stones of Destiny.

"Order of Ravens, together we stand," Andy said.

CLICK CLICK CLICK!

Suddenly, the Stones snapped together. One on top of the other. They fit like a three-layered sandwich in Cleo's palms. The rectangle was the bottom layer, the diamond-shaped stone fit lengthwise on top of it, and the oval-shaped stone braced the center of the diamond, almost like it was pinning the three stones together.

Cleo nodded in amazement and shivered.

"We d-d-d-did it," Luke said, his teeth chattering from the frigid cold.

Cleo thought of CeeCee and her mom, how proud they would've been. And how they would never know.

"And now we d-d-d-die," Andy said, interrupting the silence.

"And d-d-d-disappear like B-B-B-Billy," Ronan said.

"And the d-d-d-dark knight C-C-C-Caelen," Nia added.

Ollie yelled, "I t-t-t-told you g-g-g-guys—"

"The CURSE!" they all cried in unison.

A flash of blue light filled the cave.

61

Luke

Luke was standing outside the castle. He squinted his eyes into the bright sun, high in the sky. He felt the warmth of the spring day.

What happened? Where is everyone?

He checked the pocket where he always kept the Athlia stone. It wasn't there. He checked his other pocket. It was empty, and his inhaler was gone too. He moved quickly toward the courtyard. For some reason, Castle Chronos had a horse in the courtyard, and a horse-drawn carriage. He looked down to dodge horse manure as he walked in his sneakers. Gross! A handful of boys talked nearby. They wore the strangest clothes and leather boots instead of sneakers. Three men headed towards the main castle doors. Luke thought he might recognize his own professors, but he didn't. The men wore top hats and jackets with long coat tails. One had a pocket watch dangling from the wide belt on his waist. Luke was very confused.

Is this a vision—like when I saw the ghost lady or the blacksmith?

He was relieved to find Nia and Andy at the raven statue, just as Ollie and Ronan came running towards them. Luke tapped his chest with his fist as he inhaled, willing more air to come in.

"We thought we lost you guys," Ronan said.

"What IN THE WORLD is going on?" Cleo asked, running towards them.

Nia shrieked, hugged her, and brought everyone into a group hug.

"I can't believe we're still alive," Andy said, his voice squeaking a bit as he took in a deep breath, pushing back his hair.

"All our clothes are dry, too!" Ollie noticed.

"But how? After all that water in the cave?" Luke gasped for air, tapping hard on his chest.

"What's going on?" Ronan asked. "Everything is so weird."

"How did we get back to the castle?" Ollie asked. "And why is Chronos Castle under construction?"

They all looked at the castle, it seemed like the top half was missing and there was scaffolding around the exterior. "Where are our dorm rooms? Ronan asked looking at the building and counting.

"There's no eighth floor."

"Never mind that. Those kids are looking at us funny," Andy said. "We're not funny— they are!"

"Why?" Luke asked, wheezing. He really needed his inhaler. He blinked and looked at his friends still in their feverish conversation. He turned his attention to his watch. Its face was clouded over. It was so wet in the cave, water must have gotten in for sure.

What's happening?

He closed his eyes for a moment and then opened them, looking across the courtyard. A bunch of boys around their age were pushing and pulling at each other.

One of the boys yelled, "Bale, I'm going to get you!"

Bale?!

Luke froze in shock.

"Stop it Desseron!" shouted a small boy, who must have been Bale, as he ran zig-zagging his way through the grounds to get away.

Luke's mind raced. "The Stones?" he said as he tapped on his chest again, willing for air.

"I only have Bale's Stone—the rectangular one!" Cleo said. Her voice breaking, "The other two are lost!"

Luke was crestfallen.

"No, they're not. I have the one from the sword," Andy added, opening his hand, showing the diamond-shaped stone they had found in the sword belonging to the knight Godfriddis.

"What about Athlia's stone?" Luke whispered.

"It has to be here somewhere!" Nia said. They started frantically searching the ground around them.

"Got it!" Ronan said, holding the black oval stone with blue streaks.

But how is that possible? Cleo held all three Stones in the cave. Luke started to cough uncontrollably as he gasped for air.

"Luke, are you okay?" asked Ollie.

Andy, Ronan, and Cleo stood side by side, putting their Stones together in Cleo's hand.

CLICK CLICK CLICK!

The Stones stacked together like a sandwich, just as they had in the cave. A blue light flashed all around them. Instantly, Luke felt the world warp and go dark.

62

Luke

Luke was very groggy. Something was covering his mouth and nose. His eyelids were so heavy, he could hardly open them. As he moved his hand to remove whatever was on his face, his arm felt like it weighed a thousand pounds. Through his eyelashes he could only make out the silhouette of a woman with a long braid falling over her shoulder.

"It's an oxygen mask, Luke," he heard her kind voice say. "Just leave it." He felt a touch on his arm as she covered him with a blanket.

As he slowly came to, his eyelids too heavy to open, he could hear two people speaking in a hushed manner. He recognized the deep serious tone of Professor Morlia's voice. "The measurements were holding steady. We haven't seen a geomagnetic storm of this magnitude for centuries."

"I know, Professor, we were completely taken by surprise." It was Director LeCrucia. "The tornado was powerful but thankfully short-lived." There was a pause. Luke forced his eyelids to open. "But the damage from the explosion at the Eldritch Pitch is a real tragedy," Director LeCrucia said.

"Yes," agreed Professor Morlia. "The students will be very disappointed, especially two weeks before the Games are supposed to start."

"Once the fire is out, we will need to assess the subterranean damage," Director LeCrucia said. "In the meantime, it's far more important that everyone is alright."

Luke pushed himself up onto his elbow and noticed he was in an ambulance, lying on a gurney.

Professor Morlia saw he was awake. "Hey there, Luke. Welcome back."

"What happened?" he said with a muffled voice, forgetting he was wearing an oxygen mask.

"Our best assumption is that you and your friends were close enough to the pitch when the lightning struck the pitch and the field exploded. It's a miracle you weren't injured. You gave us quite a scare," Director LeCrucia said, "Thanks to Stephanie and Daisy, we found you. We're so grateful you are all alright."

Luke slowly remembered the events as they had unfolded. The strange storm … the forest … crossing a river … a stone hut … glowing fungus … a cave … the blue flash … And then … Luke couldn't explain any of the rest, so he didn't say anything at all.

"But you're safe now," continued Director LeCrucia. "Nurse Kelly will take care of you. Professor Morlia and I need to check on the rest of the chaos." The director lifted up the hood of her raincoat and hopped down from the back of the ambulance.

"Just get some rest here for a bit," professor Morlia said kindly.

Through the ambulance doors Luke noticed, as they

walked away, that it was pouring rain. Thunder boomed and lightning flashed in the distance.

Luke lay back down on the gurney and squeezed his eyes shut, trying to make some sense of it all. *Do I have a concussion?*

"I'm just going to check your oxygen levels," Nurse Kelly said as she placed a digital monitor on his finger. "Look at that! Back to normal," she said after a moment. "I will take off the mask now. And here's a new inhaler for you."

Luke accepted the medicine and tucked it in his pocket. Floating through his mind was a foggy recollection of the Order at the raven statue and the Stones clicking together. He checked his other pocket. He didn't have any of the Stones.

Adio poked his head into the ambulance. "Luke! Everything okay?" he asked.

Luke nodded. "Adio, where are my friends?" he asked, sitting upright.

"They're safe and sound. Search and rescue turned them up. When you're ready, they're waiting for you on the bench under the tarp shelter over by the police barrier."

Luke remembered that at some point he had promised the Order that when they got back to the castle, he would report that Recleren had attacked him.

"Adio, I need to tell—"

"Luke!" said Ollie as he poked his head in the ambulance door. "Thank goodness you're alright! He's alright, right, Nurse Kelly?"

"Yep. He'll just need to take it easy for a couple days," she said.

"Ollie, I just need to—"

"Can he go then?" Ollie asked interrupting Luke.

Luke looked at Ollie sideways.

Nurse Kelly handed Luke a blanket, "Cover up with this to keep warm. Chef François is serving sandwiches under the tarp. It is lunchtime after all!"

"Come on then! Everyone's waiting for you!" Ollie said.

Adio gave him a high five. Luke left the ambulance and joined Ollie outside. Luke was a little unsteady at first but managed to find his footing. The rain was falling in sheets, lightning was moving towards the forest. He pulled the blanket up over his head, and tried to get his bearings. He saw the rappelling wall.

"You're being weird, Ollie. What's going on?" Luke asked, as they hurried past two ambulances. Fire trucks and police cars were scattered from the outskirts of the manicured school grounds all the way down the valley towards the flaming Eldritch Pitch. Officers in uniform were patrolling the grounds. A couple police dogs on leashes were sniffing the area around the castle. Luke spotted several officers walking with Detective Anders and Professor Morlia. They all went under the police tape and disappeared down the hill. Chronos Academy staff, who were standing guard at the barrier, stopped any students who thought they might cross.

Ollie steered Luke past several tall orange safety pylons, towards the tarp shelter that had been set up on the sports courts. The other members of the Order were a sorry sight, sitting on a bench under the tarp, wrapped in their blankets.

"Did you tell them about Recleren and the attack?" Andy asked, not even saying hello.

"No, Ollie stopped me before I could," Luke replied defensively. Ronan gestured a wave at Luke but didn't say anything. He looked very pale.

"Good," Cleo said. She held a bucket on her lap and looked like she might vomit.

"What? Why?" Luke asked incredulously.

Cleo took a few quick breaths and then clung to the bucket, unable to speak.

"There's so many police officers here, there's no way Recleren would stick around," Nia replied, handing a juice box to Ronan.

Andy added, "If he's here they'll catch him."

Ronan slurped his juice loudly.

"I guess that makes sense," Luke said.

Andy interrupted, "Besides who cares? We have other problems!"

Nia replied in a hushed tone, "Everyone here thinks we were at the pitch when the lightning struck and the field exploded."

"We were," Luke said, but suddenly he wasn't sure. "Right?"

"We were," Ollie said. "But look—"

Ronan flapped his hand in the air and interjected, "The storm is still happening. Look at that lightning!" Luke could hear the thunder rolling. In the distance he saw the glow of the flaming Eldritch Pitch. The fire was clearly not under control, even with all the rain.

"But the tornado is gone," Nia added.

Cleo set the bucket on the ground. She seemed better. "Luke, when we left the hut, the storm and the rain were done, remember? And it was way after lunch."

Luke remembered eating a snack from Cleo's bag in the hut.

That was hours ago!

"But, Luke, at this exact moment," Ollie stomped his foot, "It IS lunchtime."

"But we did that stuff, right? The forest, the hut, the tree, the cave, and—" Luke's brain was still foggy as he searched for the words. "The weird castle? All that?"

"Yes!" Andy said. "The weird Chronos Castle. We know what you mean!"

Luke still felt like he might be going crazy. "So what happened to us?" he asked. "How did we get here?"

"We've been talking about that, too," Ollie said and then stopped speaking when Stephanie and Daisy, with their ponytails high on their heads, appeared next to Cleo.

Stephanie had the look of a puma ready to pounce. She looked right at Cleo and said, "Detective Anders just asked me what happened at the pitch. I told him when I left, you were there and the pitch was fine. It's your fault that it got wrecked."

Luke held his breath waiting for the response.

Nia scoffed, "Get real, Stephanie."

"No, she's right," Cleo said seriously. "I have the power to create a giant storm and blow up a field." She smiled at Luke and then started laughing.

When the four other Order members started laughing, Luke was completely confused, but he had never seen Stephanie turn so red.

"Come on, Daisy," Stephanie said and grabbed Daisy's arm. But Daisy shook herself loose from Stephanie's grasp. Daisy's ponytail fell out and her wet red hair tumbled around her shoulders. Stephanie seemed momentarily flustered, then flared her nostrils, and left abruptly to join Hayden and Lauren who were huddled not too far away.

Daisy was wringing her hands. "I'm glad you're all alive," she said sincerely. "Cleo, Nia, I'll see you back at our room later." She spun on her heel and ran toward the castle.

Luke suddenly remembered, "Do you guys have the Stones?"

"I have the rectangular one from *Bale's Tales*," Cleo nodded.

"I have the diamond one from the sword," Andy said, jiggling his arm under his blanket.

Nia opened her hand showing the oval Athlia Stone, offering it to Luke. He gladly accepted it.

"We can't let them touch," Ollie reminded them all. "Those Stones are cursed."

"What?" Luke asked.

"It's not a curse. When the stones touch, they click together, and then we travel," Cleo said succinctly.

Nia piped up, "We travel somewhere—"

"Not somewhere," Andy said. "Some TIME."

"We don't want the click click click," Ronan agreed. Colour was slowly coming back to his face.

"What?" Luke asked, trying to follow what they were getting at.

"From the cave we went back in time, and then forward again," Cleo summarized for him.

Nia added, "But wound up here at lunchtime."

"Just after the pitch exploded. It's weird," Ronan managed to say. He nestled further into his blanket, slurping a second grape juice box.

"Yeah. The weirdest," added Andy from his blanket cocoon.

"The Stones—" Cleo started.

"The cursed Stones!" said Ollie.

Cleo paused and lowered her voice, "The Stones are time

travelling stones."

Everything they were saying was starting to seep in. "How?" Luke asked.

Ronan piped up, "It's the click click click—"

"When the three Stones come together," Andy added.

"Like magnets," Nia said.

"But HOW?" Luke asked.

No one knew, so no one said anything.

Finally, Nia spoke. "Does *Bale's Tales* say anything about how the Stones work?" Cleo removed *Bale's Tales* from her puke-green backpack, while Nia kept a look out for the governor and any other adults. Cleo quickly flipped through the book. She stopped suddenly at one page. Her mouth dropped open and her eyes grew wide. "This is so freaky! I've never seen this before." She read out aloud:

I saw the strangest children today. All oddly dressed. One girl had very curly hair and was carrying the ugliest green bag on her back. One of the boys had yellow and black streaked hair! Desseron must be playing tricks on me again because after he knocked my book from my hands, the strange children disappeared. I did not find them anywhere.

"Streaked hair?!" Ronan said. "That sounds like me."

Baffled, Andy shook his head and said, "It *is* you! And Cleo."

"It's all of us!" Cleo exclaimed.

"They saw us," Nia said incredulously.

"I saw him," Luke said. "Billy Bale. Desseron and another kid were chasing him."

Cleo responded, "Desseron bullied Bale in the 1800s! It's in this journal, and now he's written about us."

"We're in *Bale's Tales!*" said Ronan shaking his head in disbelief.

Ollie spoke, "What if we had gotten stuck in the 1800s?! We never want to go through that again!"

"Oh poop. This is heavy," Nia added.

When Luke saw people jumping out of the way for a pair of men he said, "There's the governor!"

Cleo quickly returned the book to her backpack. They all watched the governor striding across the grounds, supporting a dizzy Mr. Ringwald. The raven master was pressing a large white gauze on his forehead. There was quiet under the tarp for several minutes. They didn't know what to do next.

Andy spoke up, "You girls should see your hair." He managed a smirk as he brought his arms out of the blanket and raised his hands up and out, extending the periphery of his hairline.

"You should see yours," Nia piped back grinning.

The group exchanged smiles.

"So what do we do now?" Luke asked solemnly.

"Well," Andy said, returning his arms under his blanket. "We already have a plan."

"We do?" Luke asked.

"Yep, and it's a doozy," he answered.

For the first time in ages, Luke burst out laughing. The Order all joined in.

63

Luke

It was late in the evening when the campus and surrounding area were given the all-clear. Director LeCrucia had insisted the Order make phone calls to their families. The group had dinner in Viking Hall and then finally headed to their dormitories.

In their dorm room, Luke, Ollie, Andy, and Ronan again compared the Stone recovered from Goffridis's sword to the arca's Stone. Cleo had kept the Bale Stone with her since it seemed the safest to keep the stones apart. Beside him, Ollie spoke. "The legend says the Stones are powerful. Powerful." Luke wondered if that was a kind of code for time travel, which was *powerful.* Luke looked back at the two Stones in Ronan's hand, Andy turning one of them over. Different shapes, but both with jagged edges and the exact same colour, black with blue streaks.

Luke glanced out of their window. The storm had completely cleared up and the aurora lights were lighting up the night sky. He spied Professor Morlia and Professor Torres quickly hauling a bunch of magnetometer boxes and equipment. The responsibility of the Order having all three Stones weighed on him. Now they'd need to decide what to do with them. Luke anticipated trouble. Cleo wanted to turn everything over to her mom's museum and he was sure that Nia would agree. It truly was the find of a millennium. But nothing had changed for him; he still planned to sell the Stones. Definitely separately, because together the Stones were too powerful and dangerous. Luke was sure Andy and Ronan would agree with him.

But what about Ollie? Luke wasn't sure. They could talk about it in the morning.

The four boys got ready for bed and climbed into their bunks. Luke would sleep with the Athlia Stone under his pillow. Andy put the Goffridis Stone under his mattress.

As Ollie drifted off to sleep, Luke heard him say, "I hope we're all pure of heart. I don't want the Order to be cursed." Luke recognized the quote from *Knights of Darkness*.

Luke woke up almost every hour to check that the Stone was still under his pillow and that everyone was alright. Eventually his dreams brought him to a familiar place.

Hiking in the woods with his dad, heading towards the campsite. His dad's voice, "Come on, Luke. Just a bit further, you can make it! When we get there, we'll build a campfire." Seated by the fire, his dad wrapping his arm over Luke's shoulder. "I love you, son."

Smelling his dad's musky aftershave.

"I love you too, Dad." Luke said.

"I know you do. I will always be with you," his dad replied.

Holding on tightly to his dad, Luke drew in his breath sharply and woke up, clinging to his wet pillow. He couldn't stop crying.

64

Luke

BANG BANG!

"QUACK!"

Luke woke up with a start and rubbed the crustiness from his eyes. He felt like he had barely slept.

Andy scrambled to open the door.

"Up and at 'em, lads!" Adio cried as he entered their bunk room with Ducky in his arms and Sir Lancelot by his side.

"Knock knock," said the robot.

"Who's there?" Andy said, yawning.

"Imma."

"Imma who?" Andy said, rubbing his eyes.

"Imma getting older waiting for you to open up."

Andy laughed and tapped Sir Lancelot on the head. The robot spun around and left.

"How are you boys doing?" Adio asked, grabbing a seat at the desk, draping his long arms over the back of the chair. "Yesterday was a pretty crazy day."

Adio doesn't know half of it!

"We're okay, I think," Andy responded for them all. "It

was a crazy day, and no Pandia Games—that sucks!

"Yup, it sure does," Adio agreed.

Ducky was quacking to get attention from Ronan who was still lying in bed. Ollie pulled the cover over his head.

"I have assignments for you, boys," Adio said.

Luke jumped down from his bunk.

Assignments? We're supposed to meet the girls at Bastion Tower this morning! We have lots to do!

"Okay," Andy shot Luke a furtive look.

"Ronan, a bit unusual this morning, but Director LeCrucia has many meetings scheduled at the House of Keys in Glimmerton. So you'll be taking care of Ducky until I get a few things in order."

Ronan groaned as he swung out of his bed and gave Ducky a quick pet on the head.

"Atta boy!" Adio continued, "And sorry Andy, I have a bit of bad news. Nothing totally disastrous, but Joe broke his leg during his own impromptu early-morning dryland practice. Nurse Kelly has asked that you join him. He's in her office."

"Oh, okay," Andy said. He put on a shirt. "Is he alright?"

"Yep. He's alright, but he's feeling a bit anxious and he asked for you."

"Okay," Andy said.

"Ollie, that brings me to you." Adio grinned and threw a few pillows at Ollie's head, still under the covers of his bunk. "The ravens have been acting out. Probably still rattled by yesterday's storm. Mr. Ringwald needs assistance and he told me you offered to help in the past. Are you good to go to the aviary?"

Ollie stuck his head out of the covers, sat up, and looked at Luke, panic stricken. He looked back at Adio and nodded.

"Wonderful!" Adio said.

"Uh, anything for me, Adio?" Luke asked.

"No, dude, Nurse Kelly wants you to take it easy today."

Adio made for the doorway. He smiled at the boys and closed the door behind him.

65

Cleo

Cleo was speed walking through Knight Hall, heading for the castle door. She shot a side glance at the swordless knight with the axe in the air. She wondered if this was Goffridis's armour, since his sword, now pulverized, had been hidden in the cave.

"Wow, Cleo, are you ever in a hurry!" Barbara came up beside her, carrying a stack of books. "I called you a few times but you didn't hear me." She tossed her purple braid over her shoulder.

Normally, Cleo would've been ecstatic to run into Barbara. But at this exact moment, trying to get to Bastion Tower, she was a little panicked. She tried her best to look relaxed and calm.

"I still can't get the events of yesterday out of my mind! But I remind myself that you are safe and sound," Barbara said, looking at her intently. "I know you spoke with your mother. I did too, and I promised to keep an eye on you."

Cleo nodded, thinking about the quick phone call yesterday and how relieved her mom had been that she was alright.

Barbara continued, "Anyhow, I'm so glad to run into you. A package was dropped off at my desk for you this morning. I want you to try to guess who brought it."

Now's not the time for a guessing game. "Umm …" Cleo said, trying to think as hard as she could. She was so flustered she couldn't think of a single name.

"Goofy girl! I'll give you a hint: he's a long-time bibliophile."

That didn't help Cleo much. Any book lover could be at the library.

Barbara smiled and shifted her stack of books. "He's got a white cat."

Cleo had no idea who Barbara was talking about. She was so distracted by the urgency of getting to Bastion Tower that she couldn't even imagine who would've sent her mail besides CeeCee, never mind dropping something off at the academy. When she shook her head and said she had to meet some friends, Barbara insisted that she first come with her to the library. She knew Barbara wouldn't give in. Cleo acquiesced and offered to carry a few of the books.

Under the library's glass dome, Cleo stacked the books she was carrying on the counter. The scowling face of the governor popped up from behind the stack and he straightened up to his full height. She jumped.

"Oh, Governor Grossvenor! Are you okay?" Barbara asked, surprised.

"Of course I am! Don't be ridiculous, Ms. Barakos!" He adjusted his white silk scarf to make each side hang down at equal length and passed his hand over his hair to smooth it.

"Well, it's just highly unusual for you to be behind the

checkout counter," Barbara commented.

"If you were doing your job properly, I wouldn't have to be back here," the governor replied.

Adjusting her backpack, Cleo felt sick to her stomach. All this time it was Cleo who had *Bale's Tales*, and the governor was being so mean to Barbara.

The governor was vigorously shuffling some papers and books around on the desk, as though he would find *Bale's Tales* right there. He held up a manila envelope. "What is this?" He read the cursive writing on the front. "'*For Cleopatra.*' Who's that? Oh, and look at this, a *Magic Awaits* stamp in the corner. Good grief."

The governor handed Barbara the envelope.

Barbara patted the column of books before her. "Oh, Hubert donated several items from his store to our library."

"Is the manuscript among them?" asked the governor, eyeing the stack greedily.

"Sadly, no. But I will keep up the search as I'm sure your priorities are dealing with the canceled Pandia Games."

"I'll decide my priorities! And I still have a few minutes before I depart," the Governor said. He traced his finger down the spines of each of the books that Cleo and Barbara had set on the counter.

Cleo was on pins and needles while she and Barbara waited for the governor to examine the books. *Why did Mr. Harbinger leave me an envelope?*

The governor seemed to be moving in slow motion as he carefully pulled an old brown leather-bound book from the middle of the stack. He examined the spine and opened the cover. He quickly slammed it shut. "This isn't it!"

"I know, it's very frustrating," Barbara said in a soothing librarian tone.

Since Cleo was planning to convince the Order to give her mom *Bale's Tales* and the Stones anyway, she wondered if she should say something to the governor. No, she couldn't do that. Even if it would help Barbara, she had taken an oath to the Order. There was something else. Since they had time travelled to the 1800s, a description of Cleo and her friends had been added to *Bale's Tales*. Cleo had been trying to figure out what that meant for her decision to hand in the journal. It was all getting complicated really fast.

Barbara slid behind the desk and began typing at the computer. "Mr. Harbinger thinks that perhaps the book you're seeking is no longer available, Governor. He suspects it may have been shredded a long time ago."

The governor's face contorted with rage.

"But! Because I am extra thorough," Barbara said, "I'm going to search the database one more time."

"You've already done that. Nevertheless, get back to me ASAP with what you find." The governor pinched lint from his dark suit and left.

"Cleo!" Barbara said and handed her the manila envelope with a smile and a wink. "Go ahead and open the envelope. Mr. Harbinger insisted that you get that letter today. And I promised him I would get it to you. I always keep my promises."

Cleo ripped the sealed envelope with her finger. In Hubert Harbinger's shaky cursive handwriting she read, "*Remember, Cleo, no one must know about the journal. There are forces at work that even I don't understand. Guard the book well.*"

"Well, what does it say?" Barbara asked.

Cleo's mind was racing. "Oh—he just wanted to see how I was liking the book I got at Magic Awaits earlier in the year," she lied, feeling a little guilty. Now she was even more desperate to get to Bastion Tower. "Barbara, I'm sorry, but I have to go."

"Sure, that's fine! I'm still feeling a little fluttery just thinking about what happened to you yesterday. I want you to come by and see me soon."

"I will. I promise!" Cleo practically sprinted out of the library.

66

Luke

Luke found the school eerily quiet. It was Saturday, which meant no classes. But there was no staff walking around, no Adio, no Sir Lancelot roaming the halls, even Ducky and Ronan were nowhere to be seen. Students were either in the Saloon or Viking Hall, talking quietly. Exhausted from the previous day's adventure, Luke found himself moving very slowly. He realized how truly hungry he was, and decided to have two plates of breakfast. Working his way through his meal, he noticed that the hourglass counting down to the Pandia Games had already been removed from the small stage.

After breakfast he made his way out of the castle to Bastion Tower. The grounds seemed weirdly calm after all the commotion yesterday afternoon. You couldn't tell from the cheerful sun and warm breeze today, he thought, that the same skies had been so terrifyingly electric and deadly the day before. Making his way through the shrubs, he pulled out the key and unlocked the bronze outer door. He went up the many steps to the top and waited for the girls.

It wasn't long before he heard footsteps nearing the doorway and was surprised to see Ollie.

"Wow, that was fast," Luke said, and rose from his chair.

"I didn't have much to do in the aviary." Ollie said. He grinned and made his way to unstack a chair when a man appeared at the doorway.

"Mr. Ringwald?!" said Ollie in shock, his voice pitching slightly.

With threatening strides, the man quickly crossed the tower room to Luke and Ollie. Narrowing his eyes, Mr. Ringwald barked, "You two get over there by that pillar!"

Ollie moved quickly and pressed up against the wooden column, tightly clenching the straps of his backpack. Luke joined Ollie, all the while his mind racing. *What's happening?*

Mr. Ringwald cocked his head, watching the two boys. His cold gaze sent shivers up Luke's spine. "Hiding something, Mr. Guilty Face?" Mr. Ringwald asked.

Luke's stomach plunged as if he was on a rollercoaster. He shook his head slowly from side to side, keeping his eyes on the raven master.

Mr. Ringwald slowly walked over to Luke and Ollie. "I'm talking about the cursed Stones of Destiny," he said, his voice like gravel. Both boys shrank back against the column.

Mr. Ringwald grabbed Luke by the collar and shook him.

Ollie's voice wavered as he spoke. "We don't know what you're talking about."

"Is that so?" the man said. He let go of Luke's collar. "Well then." His moustache twitched, and his eyes were large, full of zigzagging red veins. He looked like he hadn't slept in weeks. Luke could smell his nasty coffee breath and see the hairs inside his nose. The gauze on his wound fell over his eyes and he tore it off, exposing the gash on his forehead.

Abruptly, Mr. Ringwald slid over to Ollie and grabbed him by the throat with one hand. Luke quickly sucked in his breath. Ollie gurgled and his two hands slid over the man's lower arm, pulling on it.

Ollie choked out a whisper, "He's crazy from the curse."

Mr. Ringwald's eyes locked on Luke and his grip on Ollie's throat tightened. "I know the Stone is in your pocket, mister. Don't make me drag your friend across the floor before you give it to me."

Ollie's hands flailed at his attacker.

The truth was Luke had two Stones. The Athlia Stone in one pocket and the diamond-shaped Stone from the sword in the other.

Terrified for Ollie's life, Luke dug into his pocket and gripped the diamond Stone so tightly his knuckles hurt.

"No," Ollie wheezed.

Luke felt his eyes well up. He wouldn't trade their lives for the Stones, no matter the cost.

He held his arm straight out, palm up, the Stone sitting on it. Mr. Ringwald snatched the diamond-shaped Stone, scratching Luke as he did. Ollie slumped to the floor, gasping for breath and holding his throat while Luke stood close to him protectively.

Mr. Ringwald examined the Stone of Destiny, his eyes burning, his moustache twitching over a ferocious grin. "Finally. I have a Stone. All my life I knew the stories in the legend were true. After so long and all my searching, narrow escapes from death, the curse, all those who doubted me ever since I was a boy, the fishermen, the pirates, Anders. All the pain, those pesky black devils, and the torture dealing with those birds, this school, I'll show them."

"You're not a raven master at all, are you?" Luke asked. He pressed one hand flat against the column behind him, his knees buckling, his other hand grasping Ollie's arm.

Mr. Ringwald grinned again, holding the Stone up to the light from the window. He then barked a laugh, still gazing at the Stone.

"You're Richard Recleren!" Cleo's shocked voice came from the tower room door.

67

Cleo

"That's right. I'm Richard Recleren. Your friends here were just about to tell me the whereabouts of the rest of the Stones. Why don't you join them?" Recleren gestured for her to move over towards Ollie and Luke.

Cleo cautiously made her way over to the column and Ollie grabbed her hand.

"We don't know anything about these Stones," she said, her voice shaking. The dangerous criminal that had attacked Luke was there, right in front of them.

Recleren snarled, shaking the Stone in the air. "Really? What is this then? The whole time that little red box was in the aviary, nothing but bad luck befell me. Until the red box was moved from where I'd left it on top of the magazines."

"The arca," Luke choked out. Cleo saw that Recleren wasn't holding the Stone from the arca but rather the diamond-shaped Stone from Goffridis's sword.

"Ah yes, the arca. I smashed it but found nothing inside. It took me a while, but then I realized one of these cursed Stones had been in that tiny red box of trouble. I remembered

I had taken the arca from you, Mr. Guilty Face, at the STEM event. I knew it was you that had taken the Stone." Recleren took a moment to set his dark burning eyes on each of them. "Which of you has another Stone of Destiny?" He barked a laugh again. "Just kidding. Mr. Guilty Face, I know you have it. You'll find it in your other pocket."

Luke looked horrified.

"Oh, don't look so surprised, kid. I know all the tricks of a thirteen-year-old boy. I was one once, too." Recleren crooned, "Give it to me now."

Luke had tears in his eyes when he looked at Cleo and Ollie. Cleo silently nodded. Luke pulled out the Athlia Stone and reluctantly handed it to Recleren.

Cleo could have cried, too. She and Ollie stared at Recleren, gripping each other's hands. Cleo was terrified that Recleren would read her mind. If Recleren got all three Stones right now, who knew where—or when!—they could all wind up?

A tapping at the window drew the criminal's attention from the two Stones in his hand. Munnin. Recleren moved towards the window, gesturing wildly and shouting "Be gone, you black devil!"

"You were never so mean when you were Mr. Ringwald!" Ollie said in a confused and mortified voice.

"He's a master of disguise. That's what Captain Jumbo said," Cleo replied, her body shaking slightly.

"That's right, a *fake* raven master," Recleren barked. "LeCrucia was always too close, checking up on me all the time, so concerned about those birds. I wasn't about to be found out by her. So I started stealing again. As things disappeared on campus, it got her off my tail. It worked for a while."

The raven tapped at the window again. Recleren banged on the high window, "Go! Just go!"

In the seconds that Recleren's back was to the doorway, Cleo was surprised to see Ronan poke his head around the corner of the chamber entrance. He made a "sh" sign with his finger across his mouth. Ronan flashed Cleo the slingshot in his hand. He disappeared back into the stairwell.

As soon as the raven flew off, Recleren returned to the three students. "Where's the third Stone?" he asked, ferociously.

Cleo was petrified but knew there had to be a way out of this. While Recleren may know all the tricks of a thirteen-year-old boy, he didn't know anything about the tricks of this thirteen-year-old girl. Not only was Ronan there to help, Cleo knew that Nia was also hiding in the stairwell. Cleo and Nia had come up the tower stairs together. As the two girls had approached the tower room, they'd heard Mr. Ringwald's voice and his threats. They had both listened at the doorway, motioning silently to each other as they concocted a plan. When Cleo had stepped forward to say "Richard Recleren," Nia had stayed hidden from view with Cleo's backpack. The rectangular *Bale's Tales* Stone was still safe in the pack.

Ollie interjected, fuming. "It was you, wasn't it? Who trapped us below the tree! You tried to kill us!" he accused, pointing a finger.

Recleren answered, "I saw you headed to the pitch yesterday morning. I followed, keeping my distance. Then that godforsaken storm hit. I ran to the forest for cover and waited it out. When the storm let up, I saw you lot in the forest and followed you, waiting for just the right time." His eyes glazed over with a crazed intensity as he continued his confession. "But then you kids disappeared into that tree. I didn't know if it was evil magic or good magic, but I knew Mr. Guilty Face had the Stone from the arca. So I entered the tiny hollow, I tripped on something, smashed my head, and the trap door banged shut."

He touched the wound on his forehead. "Once I got the trap door opened again, I followed you in the underground cave. I kept my distance and heard your cries and poor me's. I had just barely wiggled out of that tiny shaft when the cave started to shake. I was blinded by a flash of blue light. The next thing I knew I saw you lot stepping on horse manure at the raven statue in the olden days!"

Cleo couldn't believe her ears. Recleren had been sucked into their time travel escapade!

The criminal went on, "Then my brain flipped again and I'm here. I know I traveled through time. And there's only one way that could happen. You have all three Stones of Destiny."

"When Detective Anders hears about all of this, you're going to be in big trouble!" Cleo shot at him.

Recleren glanced at her and then lunged at Luke, and grabbed the boy's collar. "And just who would the good Detective hear it from?" he laughed. He shook Luke hard. "It won't be you lot."

There was no mistaking the threat. *Recleren is going to kill us!*

"Anders!" Recleren scoffed. "Anders won't get me! No. I will have those Stones, and then I will be free from this curse, my debts, this island, and Anders forever. Give." He tightened his hold on Luke's collar and jerked the boy forward with each word that followed— "Me. The. Last. Stone!"

Cleo's brain had been spinning from the moment

she'd walked into the tower room. But slowly her fear was morphing from a frozen state to hyper focussed. The solution became crystal clear. The whole Order of Ravens was in danger: her only friends, their oath, their shared purpose, and everything they'd been through, good and bad. Cleo felt a surge of bravery as a part of her woke up, a part of her that she never knew existed. They had one shot, one shot to live and get through this.

I need to get him to Traitors' Gate.

"It's in a hiding place in the stairwell!" she blurted out.

Recleren cocked his head and half smiled at her. "Show me." He shoved a breathless Luke to the floor and growled at the boys, "You two stay right where you are."

As Cleo went through the doorway, Recleren was right behind her. She hoped her plan would work. She descended the twisting staircase, Recleren following closely as she slowly went down, down, down.

"Where is it?" he shouted angrily. "You better not be playing games!"

Ronan poked his head low around the curved inner wall of the staircase below them. Quick as a whip, he cocked his slingshot and released it. Cleo ducked just in time. The rock hit Recleren's injured forehead and he screamed, dropping the two Stones like hot potatoes, to clutch at his head. Ronan sprinted up the steps between them. Ronan shoved Recleren against the outer wall while Nia, nimble and swift, grabbed the Stones and ran down the spiralling stairs yelling, "Run!"

68

Luke

When they heard Recleren's scream, Luke and Ollie scrambled down the spiral stairs of the tower, their steps echoing as they tried to catch up to their friends.

Luke peered over the railing into the center shaft of the staircase. Recleren was hot on Cleo's heels. Nia and Ronan's heads bobbed further down the staircase in front of the pack. Scrambling down behind them, Luke watched in horror as Recleren grabbed Cleo, and struggling against each other, they went tumbling down the stairs.

Luke screamed, "Cleo!"

Recleren was cursing as Cleo fought against him while they continued to tumble down.

As Luke and Ollie rounded another curve, they found Cleo was immobile, sprawled on the steps three stairs down from Recleren who was wobbling to a standing position. "Get up, Cleo!" Luke called to her. She did not respond.

Recleren turned his crazed eyes towards Luke and struggled to right himself, his lip and forehead bleeding. "Where is the third Stone?!" Further down the steps, Ronan fired shots at Recleren.

Realizing instantly where they were, Luke moved up several steps in Ollie's direction with determination. "Right through here," he said. Recleren followed him as close as his shadow. Luke jammed his shoulder hard against the outer wall of the stairwell. With a crack and then a grinding noise, a square opening appeared.

Luke saw the whites of Recleren's greedy eyes as he lunged for Luke. Recleren had a vice grip on Luke's arm and grunted as he tried to yank Luke into the opening. Terrified, Luke struggled with all his might to keep himself out of Traitors' Gate.

Roaring, Ollie and Ronan rushed at them and pushed Recleren into the open cavity. Luke desperately wrestled to release his arm. Nia grabbed the back of his shirt to keep Luke from being dragged into the deathly steep tunnel.

"Nooooo!!!" They heard Recleren call just as the floor beneath him gave way and the door slammed shut.

"Dun-dun-dun—" Ronan began.

"DUN!!" Nia, Ollie, and Luke chimed in.

Ronan grinned as he holstered his slingshot in his back pocket, then swiped one hand against the other, job done.

"Something's wrong with Cleo," Ollie said as he crouched to grab Cleo's arms. Cleo lay now on her side, her entire body crammed on one step. They sat on the steps, watching Cleo nervously. After a few moments, her eyes fluttered open and she said she ached everywhere. Nia helped Cleo sit up.

"How many fingers?" Ronan demanded standing over her.

Cleo looked woozy, but she answered correctly, "Three."

Luke was so relieved that she seemed okay. With her

arms slumped over their shoulders, Luke on one side of her and Nia on the other, they helped Cleo back up the tower stairs to the grand chamber.

69

Cleo wasn't sure how long she'd been sleeping. Lying still, she opened her eyes. She felt bruised and sore. Her body ached all over, and her head thumped. Faint light flickered from the sconces and she realized she was in Bastion Tower. It had turned into a dark and dreary night. There was a sweater under her head, and another covering her.

Andy burst through the tower room door. He shook off his raincoat, saying, "Guys! You'll never guess what happened!" He grabbed a chair and turned it backwards to sit on.

Cleo sat up a tad, but all eyes were on Andy.

"I just came from Nurse Kelly's because of Joe. While I was there she got a call from the police. Captain Jumbo got Recleren! He was fishing and spotted a guy swimming in the ocean. When he helped him onto the boat, he recognized him and tackled him!"

"And now Detective Anders is down at the Glimmerton dock and Richard Recleren is in handcuffs. They called Nurse Kelly because Recleren seems to have some kind of amnesia. He can't remember anything!" Andy showed them the book he had in his hands. "And I finally got this from Barbara. It's only the end of the school year but still. It's the *Knights of Darkness Early Days* book. What happened to you?" he asked, suddenly noticing Cleo.

The others yelped with happiness when they noticed she was awake. They helped her into a chair as they all spoke at once. Cleo tried to focus her mind on what they were saying.

"We didn't take you to see the nurse," Luke started to explain,

"'Cause you had woken up a few times and talked," Nia added,

"You seemed okay," Ollie nodded, "with a few bruises."

"Just needed some rest," Ronan finished.

"How long was I out for?" Cleo asked, slightly concerned.

"A while actually," Luke answered and gave her a pained smile.

"Just take it easy, okay?" Nia suggested as she sat next to her.

Then the Order of Ravens explained everything to Andy, right up to how they helped Recleren find his way to Captain Jumbo.

Andy shook his head in disbelief. "And you're telling me Ringwald is Recleren, Recleren is Ringwald? That's so crazy! I can't believe I missed the whole thing!"

Cleo rubbed her head and noticed her fogginess had dissipated. She cleared her throat and said, "We need to decide what to do with the Stones, and *Bale's Tales*. I thought we should give them to my mom's museum. But ..." She pulled out Mr. Harbinger's note from her backpack and passed it to Nia to read it aloud.

"Well," Andy said, "since we don't have to worry about

Recleren looking for the Stones anymore, and he can't remember anything anyway, maybe we should wait a few days to figure it out? I mean, no one's been able to find the Stones in, like, hundreds of years. A few more days won't matter."

"And no one knows we have the Stones," Nia reviewed. "What about Mr. Harbinger? He knows we have the journal."

"I wondered about that, too," Cleo said. "But when I first met him at Magic Awaits and asked him what the Stones looked like, he said he didn't know. I don't think he knows that there was a Stone *in* the book. But he does know the book is important." She added, "He did tell me not to tell anyone."

"And his note says there are forces at work," Ollie said. "The curse!"

"The governor is still looking for *Bale's Tales*," Cleo added with grave concern. "Maybe he wants the Stones?"

Nia bit her upper lip. "Let's hide everything here in the tower. We shouldn't be carrying the Stones, or *Bale's Tales*."

Cleo turned slowly to Luke. "Luke, what do you think? What do you want to do?"

They all stopped and looked at Luke. Luke gave a weak nod, "I'm not sure."

In the end, they all agreed to hide two of the Stones of Destiny in different cabinets. Luke would return the Athlia Stone to the cavity under the fireplace brick where he'd first discovered the arca. "The ghost lady will protect it," Ollie said as he helped Luke replace all the bricks they had removed from the fireplace in the attic.

Cleo chose the crate that held the framed photos and paintings and put *Bale's Tales* inside it.

After wrapping the final Stone in paper and shutting it in the bottom drawer of a cabinet by the wall, Andy stood abruptly. "OK, we hid the Stones. Great. We hid *Bale's Tales*. Great. Luke has weird visions or whatever. Great. Let's go. I'm starving." He made his way to the door. "Spending the day with Joe was exhausting."

Their giddy laughter echoed through the stairwell as they started down the spiral tower stairs.

Despite the life-threatening events, Cleo felt pretty happy as they stepped into the night air. The Order of Ravens had found the Stones and protected them from falling into the hands of a criminal. They were seekers and protectors of treasure.

And they were all okay.

70

Cleo

All Chronos Academy students were gathered at Viking Hall for dinner on June 1st when the Pandia Games were supposed to have taken place. Because the Games were cancelled, many professors were using the opportunity to give extra assignments. Cleo found that to be more than acceptable—more opportunities to learn—but some of the other students did not.

"I have to get this zoology stuff," Andy whined. "I got an FM on my last exam, but I've been given a second chance. Maybe you can help me, Cleo?"

"FM?" Cleo asked.

"That's not even a grade," Nia snickered next to her.

"Yes it is," Andy insisted. "It means failed miserably. The rest of you are doing great. Even Ronan did better than me. He got a TA."

"Totally acceptable," Ollie said with a smirk. Cleo smiled.

"I still can't believe Richard Recleren was here at Chronos Academy, all this time," Luke said, looking up from reading the *Gazette*. "Director LeCrucia says they are in shock, and—" Luke began to read the paper verbatim: "'*We have never had such a breach before. We will be looking into how this occurred. We are conducting a close investigation with Detective Anders of the Glimmerton police.*'"

"What about the curse?" Ollie asked, chewing on his fingernail.

"There's no curse, Ollie. We just had some bad luck," Cleo said reassuringly.

"Right. So what? Cleo, did we have any good luck?" Ollie asked.

"We're alive," Andy said.

"And it's good luck that Recleren has amnesia," Ronan said.

Ollie scoffed.

"Well, at least we can figure out this Stone of Destiny mystery in peace," Nia added.

Director LeCrucia stepped up to the podium on the little wooden stage at one end of Viking Hall. "Good evening, students," she said. "I have two important announcements. First, regarding the Pandia Games. After much deliberation and consideration, the Games will take place next year at Chronos Academy."

The crowd cheered.

"Yes, very exciting," the director agreed. "The support of the governor was key to this decision. The Eldritch Pitch will be redone and in better shape than ever. Now, before we think of next year, let's give thanks to Coach Typhoon for all his hard work *this* year on the Games."

The crowd went wild as Coach Typhoon came striding up the center aisle. With three large steps, he got onto the stage and pumped his fists in the air with excitement. The students began to chant, "Coach Typhoon, Coach Typhoon."

"Well, I'm glad the pitch is getting fixed," Andy said, raising his voice and leaning over the table as he applauded. "I plan to make the team next year. Coach Typhoon will never know what hit him."

"Me too!" Nia yelled. "Look out, Andy, competition." She gently punched him in the shoulder.

"Me too," Ronan grinned and punched Andy just a little bit harder on his other shoulder.

"Whatever," Andy said. He smiled and rolled his eyes.

"And me," Luke called from across the table.

Still clapping, Ollie and Cleo looked at each other and shrugged their shoulders.

They all started laughing.

Coach Typhoon finally stepped back down and took his place at the table between Professor Morlia and Professor Gregor. The crowd quieted again as Director LeCrucia raised her hand at the podium and asked for everyone's attention.

"Now for the second announcement. We have just informed your parents that, in light of everything that happened in the past week, we at Chronos Academy want you to have a longer summer holiday. Exams are cancelled, and school will be ending two weeks early."

Along with the rest of the students in Viking Hall, Cleo and her friends erupted with joy.

71
Luke

The evening before going home, there was an atmosphere of celebration. The air was warm, the night was clear, and the sky was filled with blue and green aurora.

Luke placed his finger into the dial of the red rotary phone and called his mom.

She answered on the second ring.

"Luke, sweetheart, I'm just packing. I have an early flight out tomorrow. I can't wait to see you! You must be so excited to be coming home," she said.

"Sort of," Luke replied.

His mom paused. "You wouldn't, by any chance, like it at Chronos Academy?" she said playfully.

"Maybe. I made some friends," Luke said smiling.

"And obviously had some adventures." He could hear happiness and apprehension in his mom's voice.

"Kind of," Luke said, not wanting to say much more. After all, he'd made an oath to the Order of Ravens.

"So, I take it you want to return in September?" his mother asked.

"For sure!" Luke answered quickly.

His mom chuckled. "Done. And I'm happy for you. I can't wait to see you. Love you."

"Love you too, Mom," Luke said.

As he stepped out of the phone booth, he noticed the rest of the place was empty except for Cleo finishing a call two booths over. He waited for her.

She looked cheery as she left the booth, and she joyfully relayed her news. "My grandma CeeCee, who is so awesome, is picking me up tomorrow, and my mom is coming with her! And my mom and I talked. I mean, really talked," she said, wiping her eyes and sighing.

Luke wondered what that was about. "Do you think you'll *ever* tell your mom about the Stones of Destiny?" He held his breath as he waited for her response.

"I always thought I would, and share with Grandma CeeCee, too. But I took an oath to the Order of Ravens," Cleo grinned. "I'm not going to tell them." She paused and touched the goose egg on her head. It had faded since her fall with Recleren down the tower steps. "Besides, things are complicated."

Luke was relieved. He smiled broadly. "I've thought about it lots, too. I don't want to sell the Stones anymore."

"Really?" Cleo asked.

"Yeah." Luke was silent and serious for a minute before continuing. "My dad is gone. I know he is. I can feel it now. I had a dream about him and ... and he said goodbye." Luke hadn't dreamt of his dad since then. He used his sleeves to wipe away tears.

"I'm sorry, Luke," Cleo whispered.

Even though the dreams had been painful, they had been

the only place Luke had seen his dad since he disappeared. But lately Luke had been thinking there might be another way.

"Maybe I can use the Stones somehow to see my dad again—" Luke began.

Cleo interrupted, "You mean time travel? Luke, we don't even know how the Stones work. Even if we did, it's too dangerous."

Luke dropped his gaze. Cleo was right, the Stones were complicated. He shook the idea from his head, for now.

"Come on," Cleo said encouragingly. "The Order's waiting for us."

72

THE STRANGER

It was 3:30 in the morning in the tiny town of Painswick, England. In a nearly empty dingy pub, two men sat on opposite sides of a square wooden table near the fireplace. A lamp on the wall next to the hearth cast a soft glow. A half full beer glass sat in front of each man, a newspaper folded to the side. Small streams of light emerged from the dying fire as the logs blackened and became less radiant. One man's face was mostly hidden in shadow by his deep hood.

Seated across from him, the governor of Pandia sipped his pint as he watched the man closely. The man had stubble on his chin and had been speaking with measured calm words, revealing glimpses of yellowed teeth. He sat rigidly with his hands placed on his lap. The governor knew the man was holding back his rage.

Through clenched teeth, the man said, "Recleren was incompetent. He couldn't even make sure that Corax disappeared forever. As we speak, that overhyped bird nanny is making his way back to Chronos Academy." He held up the copy of the *Glimmerton Gazette*. "This implication that

Recleren was after the Stones of Destiny will make LeCrucia suspect there is more going on." The shadowy figure tossed the newspaper back onto the table.

The governor said haughtily, "You misjudged Recleren when you brought him into this. He was not the best man for the job of unearthing the Stones."

"Silence!" the man commanded, pounding the table with his fist. The glasses rattled.

With his eyes downcast, the governor said quietly, "Like the others before her, LeCrucia has failed in her experiments to extract Lambros, or to create it. So the only Lambros element that exists on this planet, is still within the Stones of Destiny. And with the geomagnetic storm, LeCrucia missed an opportunity to study the X points." The governor looked up, "I can assure you, they are far behind your understanding." He paused, then added, trying to sound excited, "I must say though, when she discovered that Ringwald was Recleren, LeCrucia became rather frayed."

Silent rage filled the space between the two men.

The governor looked down at his pint on the table and twisted the glass. He smoothed his silk scarf, then gently cleared his throat apologetically. "Recleren's implication in a search for the Stones of Destiny is merely the hearsay of that ridiculous fisherman. With Recleren out of the picture and unable to corroborate the story because of his amnesia, the fisherman has no influence on the investigation."

The other man slowly pulled his fist from the tabletop, relaxing his hand back into his lap.

The governor handed over a small piece of aged red metal to the man. "I found *this* in the Raven Tower at Chronos Academy," he said.

The other man stared at the piece of metal, barely an expression crossing his face, as he leaned forward. He nudged his hood back, exposing his long white nose and sunken cheekbones. The skin on the left side of his face was scarred and smooth where, like a tattoo, long-healed burns marked his face. The rims of his eyes were red as he examined the piece of metal. "So after all these centuries, we have found the arca!" The corners of his mouth lifted ever so slightly, though when he spoke, his quiet voice was menacing. "Where is the Stone that lay within it?" he asked accusingly.

The man gave the governor no chance to respond. "It is plain to see you do not have it," the man said. "I want to know who has the arca's Stone and what else they know! You will not fail me. If you do, your privilege and power—everything you cherish, governor—will be gone. And so will you."

The governor smoothed his silk scarf. "I will not fail you, Caelen. You have my word."

ACKNOWLEDGEMENTS

We embarked on this journey five years ago! It's been quite the ride creating this world and living in it for so long. And it was so much fun! We look forward to the next chapter in our creative journey together.

T.E.: Thank you to my two wonderful children who read the book in its many stages of development and provided valuable input including, the hook for Chapter 1 and saving one of our characters from death (I can't say who). I am truly grateful to my husband for his unwavering support throughout this journey and for his insightful feedback on this book. A special thank you to my sister who provided thoughtful guidance and comments after reading our story multiple times. And thank you to my parents - for always being there for me.

It is not lost on me that my writing adventure began with my first trilogy series, *Scout & Jet*. Thank you to my readers for your support and enthusiasm. It means a lot to me!

D.E.: I am ever so grateful for the ongoing love and support of my husband and children who answered the command-question cycle "Listen to this sentence. How does this sound?" followed by, "What about this?" and then "Okay, what about this?" more times than they probably ever thought they would. Over the five years that have gone into the making of this book, there were many days when we lived in parallel universes. They went to school, and did homework, and lived normal lives in the present, while I roamed the halls of Chronos Castle, or spent the day waiting for a ghost in a castle attic, or on the side of a cliff—in my mind and on my computer screen. I may have been holed-up in our basement for the weekend doing a super-session of revisions, or on an all-day call with my writing partner while at the lake. This project has been with us to a lot of places. Even more than our fish Patrick.

We want to thank our early readers who slogged through one heck of a mess - some of them more than once: Kiki, our kids, Mike, Joanna, Alex, Birgit, and Kara (Jayna & Calla). And of course, thank you to our editors, Lynn Slobogian and Merel Elsinga, who helped us transform our story and helped us refine it when we could no longer see where changes were needed.

And thank you to all the amazing kids we know who have inspired us to want to tell this story. Go forth to adventure!

About the authors

Theophany Eystathioy has had a diverse career as a scientist, author, educator, and speaker while raising two wonderful kids. She has a PhD (Cellular and Molecular Biology), served as an adjunct professor at the University of Calgary, and worked in the field of intellectual property. She is also the author of the *Scout* & *Jet* series, short chapter books for young readers. As a guest speaker, she enjoys sharing the world of science and the art of writing with students. When she is not teaching, writing, or dreaming up stories, she enjoys reading, art, a great cup of coffee, and spending time with her husband and two children. Dr. Eystathioy lives in Calgary, Canada.

For more information check out littlephds.com. To reach the author, contact SecretsofChronos@gmail.com

About the authors

Dee-Ann Evans has an MSc in Medical Physics from the University of Texas. She worked as a clinical scientist for ten years and has presented her clinical and research work internationally. Now she spreads science by writing books and through her work with students as a science presenter, science fair coach and judge, and as a member of the board at the STEM Innovation Academy. She lives with her family in Calgary, Canada, and spends her summers with her kids and husband at the lake. In her spare time she works as a project manager in cancer care.

To reach the author, contact SecretsofChronos@gmail.com